The
Elm Park
Time Travelers

Todd Daley

Todd dafey 200 @ comcast.net

(Verona, NJ)

authorHOUSE®

AuthorHouse™
1663 Liberty Drive
Bloomington, IN 47403
www.authorhouse.com
Phone: 833-262-8899

Published by AuthorHouse   04/04/2024

ISBN: 979-8-8230-2427-3 (sc)
ISBN: 979-8-8230-2426-6 (e)

Library of Congress Control Number: 2024906250

Print information available on the last page.

CONTENTS

Chapter 1   A Sad Farewell 1

Chapter 2   Norton Heads North 5

Chapter 3   A Beached Barge in the Kill van Kull 8

Chapter 4   Cleaning Up the Merry-Go-Round 13

Chapter 5   Hal's Notebooks 17

Chapter 6   Miscellaneous Topics 22

Chapter 7   20th Century Issues 29

Chapter 8   Backyard Basketball Game 36

Chapter 9   Baseball Stars of Yesteryear 44

Chapter 10   Target Practice in the Woods 51

Chapter 11   Norton Stays at the Flats 58

Chapter 12   Roasting a Gator and Star Gazing 64

Chapter 13   A Holdup Thwarted 76

Chapter 14   The Moulin Rouge 85

Chapter 15   The Crystal-Ball Gazer 94

Chapter 16   Putting Magnets on the Merry-Go-Round 102

Chapter 17   Getting Bats from Scott's Mountain 111

Chapter 18   Dr. Emil Gets an Intern 122

Chapter 19   Blocking Trupp with Sand 130

Chapter 20   Showdown on the Bridge 138

Chapter 21   Dispute over Pussyfoot 146

Chapter 22   Alfred Sees His Ancestors 152

Chapter 23   Freddy Takes a Time Trip 154

Chapter 24   Mildred Takes a Time Trip 157

Chapter 25   Searching for Brad Owen 160

Chapter 26   The Trial of Brad Owen 167

Chapter 27   A Bad Storm Brewing 174

Chapter 28   Nancy Takes a Time Trip 178

Chapter 29   A New Plan for Trupp and Company 181

Chapter 30   Norton is Taken 188

Chapter 31   Two Immigrants Arrive in Elm Park 194

Chapter 32   Ambush on Morningstar Road 200

Chapter 33   Charlie Takes a Time Trip..208
Chapter 34   Billy Takes a Time Trip..213
Chapter 35   Blanche Takes a Time Trip..216
Chapter 36   The Rev Takes a Time Trip 223
Chapter 37   An Ordinary Merry-Go-Round.................................232

About The Author 234

"Three o'clock is always too late or too
early for anything you want to do."
Jean-Paul Sartre

CHAPTER 1

A SAD FAREWELL

TOM HALEY HAD RECEIVED A BRIEF LETTER FROM CONNIE MULLIN, HIS elementary school sweetheart in Bloomington. His sister, Cara, had gone down there to visit their foster family and had bumped into Connie. Tom was working in the A & P before starting C C N Y in the fall. City College was tuition-free but there were expenses like books, bus, ferry, and train fare. And now that he was eighteen, he could stop in at Kaffman's and have a beer or two. Since Tom neither drove nor had a car, he took a bus to the South Jersey town, where Connie picked him up, He scarcely recognized the pretty sandy-haired country gal – a shimmering and voluptuous young woman in full bloom. She drove big 1950s Buick sedan. They went to a diner where they each ordered a club sandwich that Tom hardly ate.

"Come. I know a place where we can have some alone time," Connie said, grabbing his hand as they walked to the parking lot.

"Nice car. I like the color."

"Me too. People say red cars get in more accidents. I don't see what the color has to do with it," she replied.

"Because folks who drive red cars are likely reckless drivers."

"Don't worry. I'm a good driver," Connie said – gunning the big car as they left onto Delsea Drive, Bloomington's main thoroughfare.

"Ride 'em cowgirl," Tom said nervously

"Reach under the seat. There's some whiskey take a swig. It 'ill help you unwind."

Tom did as he was told. After a few sips he did feel calmer. He sensed that he would remember this day for the rest of his life. They drove out of town – reaching a remote dirt road enclosed by evergreen trees and dense foliage on both sides.

"Welcome to lover's lane. You probably have a place like it on Staten Island."

"Yeah. South Avenue on the West Shore."

"Ah hah! So, you.ve been around the track a few times," she replied with a knowing smile.

"Actually, there was a little cemetery across from the P S 21 schoolyard that was favored by teenagers. I guess every locale has secluded places where young lovers can escape to," Tom said in a near whisper.

"What was her name?"

"Joanie."

"Why aren't you with her now?"

"Her family moved to Indiana."

"Sorry. It must have broken your heart."

"It did. Life throws a curveball from time to time."

"It sounds more like a bean ball. Have another sip."

Tom took a big gup of from the whiskey bottle.

"I said a sip. This is not beer we're drinking."

Connie drove the big Buick down a bumpy dirt road with woods on one side and a corn field on the other side. The trees and the tall corn stalks afforded them solitude with a pleasant background of chirping crickets – interrupted by a critter rustling in the weeds and a bird fluttering above them. There was no breeze and it was a warm, muggy night.

"Are there any wild bears around here?" Tom asked – peering out the windows.

"Hunters have killed some. The rest have been captured and brought to Pennsylvania. Aside from nasty racoons and sly foxes your safe from predators in this neck of the woods."

She turned on the radio from which Elvis Presley's voice emanated:

"Wise men say
Only fools rush in
Take my hand
Take my whole life too
For I can't help
Falling in love with you"

The song brought tears to Tom's eyes – triggering feelings of loss and loneliness he had felt as a child upon learning that he and Cara would be leaving the Smiths to live in New York with his biological mom.

"Wow! You're an emotional guy," Connie observed. She stared at him for a few seconds and then took a sip of the whiskey.

"It just all the changes that are going on – graduating high school. Soon, I'll be in college."

"You'll do fine. Don't think about it too much."

Smiling at him, Connie unbuttoned her blouse, "I hope you don't mind, but I'm hot."

She was bursting through her bra. Tom stared at her. "The term cornfed describes you to a T, Connie."

"Around here, we do eat a lot of corn."

"Do people still grow turkeys in Bloomington?"

"They're more into chickens and pigs. The Smiths, the folks you lived with, were the only ones who had turkeys."

"You're sweating. Let me help you with that shirt,"

They began kissing, hugging, and petting. Before long, they were naked from the waist down. Connie slid the passenger seat back, deftly slid off her own trousers, and helped Tom remove his jeans. By this time, Tom was hyperventilating.

"O K, Tom. Breathe slowly and take a sip of the whiskey. I don't want you to have a heart attack."

"I need to use something," he said – taking out his wallet.

"No need. I'm on the pill," Connie said with a straight face that made Tom wonder, but he wanted so much to believe her that he quickly closed his wallet.

Gently pushing Tom down on the reclined seat – they hardly began kissing, when she mounted him and he entered her. Sighing and groaning she began moving up and down slowly.

"Are you good?" she asked.

Tom closed his eyes and smiled.

"I'll take that as a yes," she murmured, as she continued to move up and down.

Within minutes, Connie hummed the Elvis Presley song which turned into a soft moaning of the song's melody. Tom, overwrought and stressed did not come – despite a formidable erection. As she continued to hum, Tom listened to the young woman's humming was in a dreamlike spell of enchantment. It was truly magical. Determined to get this young man – so familiar and so strange – to come that she kept on moving back and forth and squeezing him for some time.

Finally, Tom raised his hand. "I'm kinda sore can we stop awhile?"

3

"O K. Let's take a break. Rome wasn't built in one day." She took a hankie from her pocketbook an began dabbing his sweaty face.

"You're sure that you've been taking the pill?"

"Stop fretting. It's all good," she replied with a breathy smile. She wiped her breasts and pressed down on the skinny young man.

Before long they were at it again with renewed energy and fervor. Tom remembered their grade school romance. Her wonderful smile which captivated him as a youngster could lite up a room. He was a ten-year old boy in love for the first time. Magically, that special feeling returned. Tom gasped and he came – the fluid gushing and gushing. Moaning, she hugged Tom so hard he was breathless.

"Oh my God. You're like a river – Tom's River."

They kissed and hugged. Tom closed his eyes for a few minutes. Connie rested on top of him. Checking her watch, she got dressed. "You better put some clothes on before we leave these woods. The folks in Bloomington are funny about naked men."

Tom dressed hurriedly. Suddenly. he realized that he would never see Connie again. He felt sad and regretful. He'd remember these moments for the rest of his life with profound melancholy.

"Will I see you again?"

"Let's not think about that. You'll be going to college in the fall. You got your whole life ahead of you. And I've made promises that can't be broken."

Tom began to weep quietly.

"Please don't do that. You're not the only one hurting."

"Can I write to you?"

"Hold off awhile. I'll figure something out. Let's get you back to the bus station."

In town as the Greyhound bus pulled up, they kissed and embraced feverishly. When the door opened, Connie pushed Tom away and he nearly stumbled climbing the steps of the rumbling, fume-ridden bus. Clamoring to a seat with his suitcase, he waved at Connie who stared at him through tear-filled eyes.

CHAPTER 2

NORTON HEADS NORTH

CONNIE MCCOMBS WIPED THE BAR WITH A DAMP CLOTH IN THE DIMLY lit bar. Ralph's had only a few customers – regulars from the town. Like most of South Jersey, Bloomington was losing people. The family farms of a generation ago had been taken over by corporate farmers. Her older son, Norton helped out most nights. But he was bored – unlike Bobby who loved working in the bar and growing corn, wheat and other vegetables in their ten-acre farm. It was clear that Norton was a city guy, while Bobby was a small-town boy from the get go. Folks had made remarks about how different the two brothers were with regard to inclinations and appearance.

Norton had dark hair and brown eyes, while Bobby was a sandy haired and blue-eyed – like his mom. Both brothers were tall and athletic – enjoying sports, particularly baseball and basketball. In high school, Bobby was a catcher, while Norton pitched. Unfortunately, a shoulder injury stymied Norton's pitching ability, so he played first base. While bad knees forced Bobby to the outfield. In semipro baseball, neither brother could hit a curveball or had the bat quickness to keep up with a fastball. Hence, the game had outgrown them. Bobby, was an extrovert who enjoyed farm work, taking care of pigs and chickens, as well as the quaintness of small-town life.

Norton, an introvert, disliked the drudgery and tedium which was the farmer's lot. Though, he was a bit more mechanical than his brother when it came to fixing fam machinery. Norton preferred visiting the Bloomington public library to tending a vegetable patch and growing corn. The sound of a rooster crowing, the first thing in the morning, did not appeal to him as it did to his brother. He always had a desire to visit New York. Norton had once read a passage by Washington Irving referring to New York City in its early days as "Gotham" – because of the wild goats that roamed the city – chomping on its abundant crab grass, clover, dandelions, chickweed, honeysuckle, and gingko trees. Gingko trees had been around for 250 million years – well before dinosaurs walked on the Earth.

Norton had a keen interest in the sciences and time itself. When he was a kid, he used to play with horseshoe magnets – determining which metals and rocks were attracted by magnets. He discovered that rocks containing iron, could pick up iron nails like a magnet. Other metal, like copper, tin, and aluminum were not affected by magnets. Norton also discovered that hematite, an iron ore with a reddish-brown color, was not magnetic. But magnetite, a shiny black iron ore was definitely magnetic. Reading a science book he borrowed from the library, Norton learned that the Earth's magnetic field induced magnetism in magnetite. Once, he put his horseshoe magnet and the magnetite next to his watch for a week to see if magnetism affected time. His watched appeared to be running slow by a few minutes, but he wasn't sure. It was an old Timex watch.

Norton was intrigued by the concept of entropy as it related to the passage of time. The fact that time only flows forward could be explained by the pieces of a jigsaw puzzle. There was only one ordered arrangement of the puzzle that made the picture. No matter how many times you shake the box – the pieces will not form the picture, but inevitably wind up in a disordered arrangement. The fact that all energy transformations wind up as random heat energy seemed to be a result of time's forward direction. Yet, Norton was not totally convinced. Perhaps, time could be reversed under the influence of powerful gravitational, electric, or magnetic fields.

The night Norton packed his suitcase, Connie told him the truth about his biological dad: A man named Tom Haley who was a high school science teacher on Staten Island. She handed Norton a piece of paper with his father's address: 269 Pulaski Avenue, plus a letter – explaining Norton's origins. Facts he had been apprised of a few months before his departure. Hugging her melancholy son, Connie's eyes filled with tears.

"You're breaking my heart, but I understand this place is not for you. If you don't write to me every week, I'll drive up there myself and drag you back to Bloomington by your hair And, get a haircut. We may be farmers, but we're not hillbillies. And tell Tom I said – hi."

Holding back his own tears, Norton said, "I love you And I love dad. What are you going to say to dad?"

"Just that you're a city boy. And you going to New York to seek your fortune."

"Sounds pretty good to me. I promise I'll write to you every week. And I'll make you proud of me." With another kiss and a long hug, Norton left the house.

CHAPTER 3

A BEACHED BARGE IN THE KILL VAN KULL

ELM PARK, STATEN ISLAND

BUFFETED BY A CHILLY APRIL WIND, TWO MEN, ONE ELDERLY AND THE OTHER young, trudged along the Mariners Harbor waterfront peering at a barge beached onto the bottle-strewn sand. Derelict ships, ramshackle warehouses, and broken docks were as common as squawking seagulls on the Kill van Kull – not far from the looming Bayonne Bridge. Surprisingly, the water appeared cleaner than Freddy had remembered from the past.

"Like, is that a merry-go-round or am I seeing things?" Hank inquired of the older man, who smiled widely and rubbed his hands.

"It ain't a roller coaster. That's for sure," Freddy von Voglio said – smiling and rubbing his hands.

"Not in good shape. Merry-go-rounds supposed to be like colorful and bright. It looks muddy. There's a large animal cage next to it," Hank responded.

"This must have been some kind of a circus. Can't tell what color it used to be. It's covered with seaweed and crap from the Kull. There's probably graffiti and cuss words underneath. Kids put graffiti on stuff," Freddy related with his mirthless grin.

"Like, you might let kids do what they want – etcetera. Not gonna stop them," Hank said walking into the muddy water until it reached his ankles.

Hank, a telegraph operator in Port Richmond, was a terse talker. Nancy once called him a talking telegram.

"I got an idea. Get a flatbed truck from Manny and haul it back to Elm Park," Freddy said – rubbing his hands.

"Like, Manny's gone. That guy Greg runs the shop now."

8

"Don't matter. He owes me a favor for chasing those kids trying to break into his garage."

Within an hour Greg used a chain to drag the merry-go-round from the barge onto his flatbed. Though in need of a paint job, the amusement ride wasn't in bad shape. Slowly, with Freddy and Hank onboard, Greg drove slowly along the Terrace and turned on the gently sloping of Morningstar Road towards Elm Park. The flatbed truck turned on Kalver Place, past the old meat-packing plant and then onto Pulaski Avenue.

"We're heading for Eggert's Field. Drive onto to the field – right there," Freddy yelled – pointing to the right.

The field had a small vegetable and flower garden – bordered by weeds, cattails. daisies, morning glories, and other wild flowers nearly in full bloom. To the rear were grapevines, a strawberry patch, and gingko trees starting to grow leaves as the sun got hotter – in anticipation of another long, hot, humid summer.

"Like, what about the vegetable patch?" Hank asked nervously.

"There's plenty of room. The flowers are expendable – just watch out for the carrots and beans, and the potatoes," Freddy said with a wry smile.

He seemed to enjoy the truck trampling the flowers put in by the women of the neighborhood. "And if you mess with my corn and my watermelons, I'll punch in the schnoz," Freddy said with another wry smile.

"Avoid the veggies and save our schnoz – etcetera. Hank relayed to Greg who nodded. He knew that Freddy's bark was worse than his bite.

As Freddy's roommate, Hank knew that Freddy's wry smile was often not a smile. It was often a warning – don't tread on me or my garden.

Under Freddy and Hank's direction the flatbed truck rolled onto the edge of the field – about fifty feet from the three-unit condo opposite Nancy's house. Slowly, Greg raised the flatbed so the merry-go-round slid to the ground twenty feet from the sidewalk. Freddy walked around the merry-go-round, rubbed his hands, smiled widely, and gave a thumbs up to Greg.

"Like, its perfect. All we got to do is get it to run," Hank said – looking doubtfully at Freddy.

"Too bad Sam's not around. He knew his way around motors." Turning to Greg, how about you?"

Greg opened the door of a metal case. "It's a gasoline engine. Probably needs a tune-up, oil change, and some gasoline."

Looking at Hank, "I'll pay you fifty bucks," Freddy offered with a quick smile.

"I'll do it for a hundred," Greg replied – examining the engine. "The thing needs ball bearings and a new gasoline tank. It's supposed to have eight horses I see there's a missing horse. Got to cover that hole with floor boards and install wooden stool where the horse was."

"Seventy-five – not a penny more," Freddy countered – to which Greg agreed.

"What about the lights?" Freddy asked – noticing lights embedded in the merry-go-round's ceiling.

"There's no electricity, Freddy. Or haven't you noticed?" Nancy remarked with a straight face. She was a slender woman in her mid-thirties who was pretty – not in a decorative way, but in a functional way.

"We may be getting electricity soon," Hank said.

"Like, don't hold your breath Hank," Nancy said – imitating the latter's overuse of the word like.

"Everybody in Elm Park is a comedian," Freddy said to Greg –smiling at the slender woman. "By the way, there was an animal cage next to the merry-go-round. It must have been part of a circus."

Nodding, she wondered if the world would ever have fun stuff like circuses and zoos again.

"I'll make sure the horses are bolted to the floor and get new straps so nobody gets hurt," Greg answered – inspecting the horses.

"Like, the horses won't go up and down?" Hank asked.

"If I can get the thing to go round and round – it'll be a miracle," Greg replied.

At that point Nancy Perez, a slender woman in her mid-thirties, emerged from the house with a bucket of soapy water and a wet cloth. Carefully, she removed the grime from the number 269 which had been there since Hal's dad, Tom Haley, screwed them into the panel between the two front doors in the late 1950s. With so much change, Nancy tried to connect with the past. The awful randomness of life was frightening. It seemed that whenever you walked out the front door, you took your life in your hands. But Nancy was no wilting lily: there's nothing stronger than a broken woman who has rebuilt herself. Shakespeare said that flowers are slow, while weeds make haste. Nancy was a realist – who never swooned and never pretended. Wearing her lustrous black hair in a pony tail, she spent little time in front of a mirror Nancy had flawless light-brown skin and rough-hewn beauty that was pure, austere, and somber.

Nancy had lost Hal two years ago in an ambush on Pulaski Avenue perpetrated by thugs who had been terrorizing the North Shore. Hal was struck by a bullet that pierced his stomach and lodged in his spine. Dr. Zatlas could do little for Hal but ease his pain with a sedative. A deadly accurate shooter, Nancy killed one of them and wounded the other in the ensuing shootout. She was about to kill the second thug, but allowed a python to finish him off slowly and painfully. Hence, Hal the gifted teacher and lifelong keeper of notebooks, was gone from her life. She treasured his notebooks not only for their content, but because reading them was like having a conversation with him.

Ironically, a year and a half later, Sam Worthington suffered a similar fate at the hands of another thug, who demanded money. Sam, with his usual street bravado, told the guy to screw himself. The thug shot him in the heart pointblank – killing the burly black man instantly. Then, the coldblooded killer jumped into his car, stepped on the gas and smashed his car into a telephone pole. The car burst into flames – incinerating himself before Nancy arrived to pump two bullets into his charred body. One might view the assailant's awful death as poetic justice. Nevertheless, her beloved Sam – loyal, brave, and resourceful – was dead. The kind, brave black man had patrolled the neighborhood – keeping everyone safe in the absence of police. By his very presence, Sam lifted the spirit of the Elm Park neighborhood. And a neighborhood with its residents, animals, trees, and houses is a very heavy thing to lift.

Hence, in a span of eighteen months, the slender Hispanic woman had lost two wonderful men in a manner that was remindful of the old wild west. Though not particularly religious, Nancy found an old copper cross in her jewelry box. Placing the cross on a gold-plated chain, she wore the cross from that day onward. One day, the chain broke, so she attached the cross to a string. Someday, she'd get a new chain. There was a Bobby Darin song Hal used to like, which echoed in her mind.

"Somewhere beyond the sea,
Somewhere waiting for me
My lover stands on golden sands
And watches the ships that go sailing
I know beyond a doubt
My heart will lead me there soon"

Nancy recalled seeing the movie "Chinatown" with Hal on TV. – starring Jack Nicholson and Faye Dunaway. It was about a wealthy businessman willing to commit crimes and kill people in order to gain control of the land rights for the lakes and rivers that supply water for the city of Los Angelos. At one point, the Nicholson asks the businessman how much land, how many houses, how many millions do you need? When is enough ever enough? After the Covid-20 pandemic killed millions of people – decimating the infrastructure in city after city, state after state, and country after country – factories had closed, millionaires saw their fortunes evaporate and their mansions crumble from neglect.

CHAPTER 4

CLEANING UP THE MERRY-GO-ROUND

LOST IN THOSE MELANCHOLY THOUGHTS, NANCY FELT TORTE, HER tortoiseshell cat, rubbing against her leg. Grateful for the big cat's company, she rubbed the cat's head as he purred loudly. Glancing across the street, she was put her somber thoughts out of her mind. Hal had once said that words were pictures of our thoughts. She was amused to see Freddy, Hank, and another man tinkering with a merry-go-round. Crossing the street with the bucket, she called out "I got divvies on the first ride."

Smiling widely and rubbing his hands, Freddy replied: "You bet. Maybe you can give us a hand cleaning it up."

"That's what the bucket's for Mr. von Voglio," she replied – crossing the street.

"Merry-go-round needs fixing, Work before play – etcetera," Hank added tersely.

"But all work and no play makes Hank a dull boy" Nancy replied – causing the awkward telegraph operator to blush.

Within minutes, she was hard at work herself – scrubbing the horses, while Hank swept the wooden floor of the merry-go-round. There was something to be said for hard work in keeping one's demons and bad memories at bay.

But they weren't at work very long when another interloper came upon them. It was the eccentric man, Billy Bumps, babbling to himself. "Now, what are those people doing with a dumb merry-go-round?"

"Hello, Billy. Want to pitch in? I'll get another cloth and you can wipe down the horses."

"No. I'm tired and my back is sore."

"So, Blanche gave you a workout last night?" Freddy called out – rubbing his hands and elbowing Hank.

"Listen to him," Billy said to his invisible partner. "But, we wouldn't mind having a ride on it."

"Remember the story of the little red hen? No help, no rides for you or your friend," Freddy replied.

"Hank, take a break. Give Billy the broom."

Billy reluctantly swept the floor of the merry-go-round, while Hank sat down on the curb. Soon they were joined by Alfred Banks, the black kid who lived upstairs from Nancy. An avid coin collector, he crawled around – searching the merry-go-round for coins.

"What's the kid doing – looking for gold?" Billy asked his unseen companion.

"I'm a numismatist. There might be some valuable coins here."

"I'll help. Four eyes better than two," Hank said, joining the youngster on the wooden floor.

Between two buckled floor boards, Alfred saw something metallic reflecting the sunlight. With nimble fingers, he slid out an old nickel. "Wow! It's a 1928 buffalo nickel."

"Very impressive kid," Freddy said – smiling widely and rubbing his hands briskly.

"They're worth ten bucks. Wait 'til I tell my mom," Alfred exclaimed as he dashed across the street

"Boy looks in boards. Finds buffalo coin," Hank said – looking towards from Freddy to Billy.

"But, I saw it first," Billy protested.

"Let the kid keep it. Blanche 'ill grab it from you as soon as you walk into your house," Freddy said with a grim smile.

Billy shrugged and went back to sweeping out the merry-go-round. Searching her cellar, Nancy found a gallon of red paint and some paint brushes. Freddy pried it open, stirred it, and began painting the floor and inside walls with the paint. He was joined by Hank and even Nancy, who liked to paint. Billy sat down on Nancy's porch and watched the others paint.

"Hey Billy, you know who I saw the other day?" Freddy called over.

The latter shrugged his shoulders, but looked worried.

"Granny Schmidt. She was looking for Dooley's liquor store. I told her it closed long time ago. But Kaffman's will sell her a pint of the hard stuff," Freddy replied with a wide smile.

"Granny Schmidt? She must be close to a hundred years old," Nancy remarked.

"If Granny's back in town, it means Doris is back too," Billy said to his partner.

Billy and Doris had been an item until the sensual red-haired Blanche Boulette came along. Back in the late 1960s, Blanche had been a go-go girl at South Shore bar called the Pigsty. She danced on a platform behind the bar – earning a small fee plus tips. But it was a rough place, with fight breaking out frequently and complaints called in by neighbors. Finally, a local councilman prevailed upon the city to close the bar down. Moving on, Blanche took some night courses in typing, bookkeeping, and steno. Pretty, congenial, and resourceful, Blanche soon landed a secretarial job in Manhattan which paid better than her go-go dancing gig.

"What are you worried about? Blanche can handle her. Now that would be a catfight I wouldn't mind seeing," Freddy commented – rubbing his hands.

"Didn't Hardy's coffee shop take over where Dooley's used to be?" Billy asked after conferring with his invisible sidekick.

"Yeah. Folks are into coffee and buns instead of booze. Which is a good thing."

"Blanche doesn't let us drink. She thinks it makes us stupid," Billy said – referring to his alter ego.

"That's a good thing, Billy Boy. Booze only makes you stupid," Freddy commented.

"She doesn't even let me save stuff – calling me disposophobic."

"What's that?" Freddy asked with a wry smile.

"It's a person who can't throw anything away," Nancy answered.

"Not too shabby," Freddy responded.

"It's one of the words Hal taught me," Nancys replied – putting down her paint brush.

There was an awkward silence as Freddy, Billy, and Hank looked at their feet.

Nancy recalled Hal mentioning the quote that there were no atheists in foxholes by Kurt Vonnegut, one of his favorite authors. Vonnegut explained that that this was not an argument against atheism, but against foxholes.

Growing tired of painting and the gossip, Nancy said "I need a break. I'm going back to the house for a while." After a while, the others put down their paint brushes – admiring the freshly painted merry-go-round.

There was a rustling in the underbrush a hundred feet or so beyond the small vegetable patch. Freddy, followed by Billy, pocked around among the tall grasses. Suddenly a ten-foot long kingsnake wrapped itself around Freddy and then entwined Billy and began squeezing the two me. Billy shrieked as Freddy jabbed the reptile repeatedly with his knife, which did not stop it from tightening its hold on the two men. Nancy had just opened her front door when she heard the commotion across the street. Pulling her 22-revolver gun from pants pocket, she dashed across the street and fired twice – putting two bullets into the snake's large spoon-shaped head. The constrictions ceased and the white-striped and brown reptile oozed blood. Shaken, Freddy and Billy extricated themselves from big snake.

"Nancy's a good shot," Billy said to Freddy –ignoring his invisible sidekick.

"The best around," Freddy said with a wry smile.

And then in a break from his usual aloof behavior, Freddy gave Nancy a hug and Billy did likewise.

"She saved our lives," the latter said quietly to his unseen sidekick

Holding a box of Cracker Jacks, Billy offered some to Nancy and Freddy. The latter took some, but the slender woman abstained.

"Wow, displays of affection and generosity from our senior citizens. Or you going to roast the snake, for dinner?" the slender woman asked half-seriously.

"What was the prize?" Freddy asked.

"Cracker Jacks don't have prizes anymore."

"Now that's a shame," Freddy replied with a wry smile.

"Am I gonna roast the snake? Nope," he replied – taking the bloody snake and tossing it into the iron barrel, adding some gasoline, and igniting the creature.

Suddenly tired from her ordeal with the snake and the aimless talk, Nancy said goodbye and left the two men, who were unshaken by the encounter with the big kingsnake. But she realized that the attack of the kingsnake was the latest animal invader onto the Staten Island from the South – alligators, iguanas, llamas, and coyotes. These creatures were grim reminders of global warming – a phenomenon created by mankind's callous disregard of Mother Nature.

CHAPTER 5

HAL'S NOTEBOOKS

She picked up one of Hal's notebooks that discussed some effects of global warming – such as the melting of the polar ice caps, which could raise ocean levels by 230 feet. Coastal cities would be inundated. In fact, New York City was building walls of concrete around the island of Manhattan to prevent flooding from rising levels of New York Bay. Bu extension, Richmond Terrace could also be flooded by the Kill van Kull as wound its way from Mariners Harbor to St. George. On the South Shore of the Island, the beaches and boardwalks would also be flooded by the rising waters of New York Bay.

Nancy put down that notebook and rested on the couch in the middle room, but could not fall asleep. Restless, she grabbed another notebook. This one had statements by philosophers and memorable lines from well-known novels.

"Call me Ishmael." – Moby Dick by Herman Melville

"The unexamined life is not worth living." — Socrates

"Man is the measure of all things, of things that are, and of things that are not." – Protagorus

"Everything existing in the universe is the fruit of chance and necessity." – Democritus

"Experience is the teacher of all things." – Julius Caesar

"Be tolerant of others and strict with yourself." – Marcus Aurelius

"A prophet is not without honor, except in his own country, among his own relatives, and in his own home." – Jesus Christ

"Even a fool is considered wise if he keeps silent, and discerning if he holds his tongue." – Proverbs 17:28.

"Common sense is not so common." — Voltaire

"The simplest explanation of a phenomenon is the best." – William of Occam

"The smallest sparrow could not fall from the sky without God knowing it." – St. Thomas Aquinas

"Ife inflammate omnia: Go set the world on fire." – St. Ignatius of Loyola

"All the world's a stage and all the men and women merely players." – William Shakespeare

"I think, therefore I exist. And if I cease to think, there would be no evidence of my existence." – Rene Descartes

"I live my life as I deem appropriate and fitting. I offer no apologies and no explanations." – Aaron Burr

"The most important factor in survival is neither intelligence nor strength but adaptability." – Charles Darwin

"Live your life as though your every act were to become a universal law." – Immanuel Kant

"The tyrant dies and his rule is over, the martyr dies and his rule begins." – Soren Kierkegaard

"Metaphysics is the finding of bad reasons for what we believe upon instinct." – F. H. Bradley

"Government is an institution that holds a monopoly on the legitimate use of violence." – Max Weber

"From each according to his abilities, to each according to his needs." – Karl Marx

"There are no facts, only interpretations." – Friedrich Nietzsche

"Diligence is the mother of good fortune." – Miguel de Cervantes

"Eternal vigilance is the price of liberty," – Thomas Jefferson

"When you can do the common things of life in an uncommon way, you will command the attention of others." – George Washington Carver

"Humanity is like an ocean. If a few drops of the ocean are dirty, the ocean does not become dirty." – Mahatma Gandhi

"There are causes worth dying for, but none worth killing for." – Albert Camus

"Ethics is knowing the difference between what you have a right to do and what is the right thing to do." – Potter Stewart

"The function of the artist is to make people like life better than before." – Kurt Vonnegut

"Before I build a wall I'll ask to know what I was walling in or walling out.'" – Robert Frost

"For every wicked action, there's a stronger action of redemption." – Jeanine Cummins

"The ability to keep your mouth shut is usually a sign of intelligence." – Holly Goldberg Sloan

"We can discover the meaning of life though suffering and sacrifice." – Victor Frankl (holocaust survivor)

"Success in life is largely a matter of luck. It has little to do with merit." – Karl Popper

"Dost thou love Life? Then do not squander Time, for that's the stuff Life is made of." – Benjamin Franklin

"The time traveler (for so it will be convenient to speak of him) was expounding a recondite matter to us." – The Time Machine by H. G. Wells

"Time is not a line but a dimension, like the dimensions of space." – Cat's Eye by Margaret Atwood

"Dew evaporates. And all our world is dew, so dear, so fresh, so fleeting." – Hedy Lamarr

"Time is nature's way to keep everything from happening all at once." – John Wheeler

"It's never too late or too soon. It's always the right time." – Mitch Albom

"I have measured out my life with coffee spoons" – T. S. Eliot

"Cynics know the price of everything and the value of nothing." – Oscar Wilde

"It was a queer, salty summer, the summer they executed the Rosenbergs and I didn't know what I was doing in New York." – The Bell Jar by Sylvia Path

"A Saturday afternoon in November was approaching the time of twilight and the vast track of unenclosed wild known as Egdon Heath embrowned itself in moment by moment." – The Return of the Native by Thomas Hardy

"Three hundred and forty-eight years, six months, and nineteen days ago today, the Parisians awoke to the sound of the bells in the triple circuit of the city, the university, and the town ringing a full peal." – The Hunchback of Notre Dame by Victor Hugo

"An ordinary young man was on his way from his hometown of Hamburg to Davos- Platz in the canton of Graubunden." – The Magic Mountain by Thomas Mann

"It was the best of times, it was the worst of times, it was the age of wisdom, it was the age of foolishness, it was the season of light, it was the season of darkness, it was the spring of hope, it was the winter of despair, we were all going direct to heaven, we all going direct the other way." – A Tale of Two Cities by Charles Dickens

"A destiny that leads the English to the Dutch is strange enough, but one that leads from Epsom into Pennsylvania, and thence into the hills that shut in Altamont and the soft stone smile of an angel, is touched by that dark miracle of chance." – Look Homeward Angel by Thomas Wolfe

"He was an old man who fished alone in a skiff in the Guld Stream and he had gone eighty-four days without taking a fish." – The Old Man and the Sea by Ernest Hemingway

"In my younger and more vulnerable years my father gave me some advice that I've been turning over in my head ever since. Whenever you feel like criticizing anyone, just remember that all the people in this world haven't had the advantages that you've had." – The Great Gatsby by F. Scott Fitzgerald

"The busy and credulous play of children is a preparation for life, while the rule-ridden and time-killing play of adults is a preparation for death." – The Job by Sinclair Lewis

"If any document was due for destruction, one had only to find the nearest memory hole and drop it in. Whereupon it would be whirled away on a current of warm air to an enormous furnace." – 1984 by George Orwell

"We live in a world in which the irrational has become the basis of consensus." – V by Thomas Pynchon.

"Let's talk sense to the American people. Let's tell them the truth, that there are no gains without pains, and no easy decisions." – Adlai Stevenson

"We do not remember days, we remember events." – James Joyce

"If we didn't make mistakes, we'd never learn anything." – Thomas Edison

"Life is not what you accomplish as much as what you overcome." – Robin Roberts

"Nice guys finish last. What are we out at the park for except to win? – Leo Durocher

"Let me make one thing perfectly clear." – Richard Nixon

"A calm and modest life is the best path for happiness. One's happiness should not be rooted in worldly success." – Albert Einstein

"Stay calm under pressure, think long term, spend time at the beach, and come out of your shell" – Sea Turtle

"Anything that can go wrong will go wrong, and at the worst possible time." – Murphy's Law

"A good teacher is like a candle – It consumes itself to light the way for others."—Mustafa Kemal Ataturk

A listing of sports fanatics: gym rat, pool rat, tennis rack, football freak, and baseball brat, stickball stud, and soccer mom.

There was a quote by Bertrand Russell that captured Hal's attitude toward learning: "All acquisition of knowledge is an enlargement of the self, but this enlargement is best attained when it is not directly sought."

And there was a citation from St. Paul – 1 Corinthians 13: "Love bears all things, believes all things, hopes all things, endures all things. So faith, hope, and love abide these three – but the greatest of these is love."

There was an interesting entry on the Roman historian, Plutarch, who wrestled with the chicken-egg controversy in terms of which came first. He said that the chicken came first because the protein found in egg shells can only be produced by hens. Plutarch had been dealing with the question of whether the world had an origin. An empiricist, Plutarch said that time was the wisest curriculum for such questions. With regard to the matter-reason dichotomy, he took the Greek point of view that reason ought to prevail. In addition, Plutarch pointed to the imbalance between rich and poor as the oldest and most fatal ailment of the world's republics.

There was material on Charles Dowd, who created the four U S time zones – Eastern, Central, Mountain, and Pacific in 1870. Dowd had to overcome opposition by state and local officials. This was done because of the need for railroads to set up time schedules for the entire country. At the time, there were 500 railroad companies in the U S A. On November 18, 1887, clocks at the Western Union Telegraph System were stopped and restarted at specific locations in each of the four time zones. Tragically, Dowd was killed by a southbound train at a railroad crossing.in Sarasota Springs in November 1904. A spherical sundial honoring Charles Dowd still exists in Sarasota Springs, New York State.

CHAPTER 6

MISCELLANEOUS TOPICS

IN ANOTHER SECTION OF THE NOTEBOOK, HAL HAD INFORMATION ON Mercury, the smallest planet of the solar system with a diameter of 3,030 miles – less than half the Earth's. Mercury was first viewed by the Sumerians in 2,000 B C and Galileo got a better look at the planet through his reflecting telescope in 1631. Mercury, the closest planet to the sun, orbits around the sun every 88 days at an average speed of 105,947 mi/hr. In contrast, the Earth orbits around the sun at roughly 66,616 mi/hr, nearby Mars orbits the sun at 53,979 mi/hr, giant Jupiter orbits the sun at 29,236 mi/hr. and distant Pluto orbits the sun at only 10,623 mi/hr. Consequently, the greater the distance of a planet from the sun, the slower its orbital velocity. This is because the sun's gravity grows weaker with greater distances.

Further on, there was material on Mars, referred to as the red planet. Galileo first observed Mars in the telescope he invented back in 1609. Mars' red color is due to the layer of iron oxide (rust) covering its surface. Stephen Hawking once said that if mankind continues to overpopulate and pollute the Earth, we'll be forced to move to Mars. It has a thin atmosphere of carbon dioxide – whipped up by strong winds and dust storms. Mars has weaker gravity than the Earth – actually 38% of the Earth's gravity. While the Earth's escape velocity is 25,000 mi/hr, Mars' escape velocity is just 11,2000 mi/hr. Pockmarked with many craters, Mars has one huge mountain – 13.6 miles high. In contrast, the tallest mountain on Earth, Mount Everest, is 5.5 miles high. It has two small moons – Phobos and Deimos. Mars has a diameter of 4,220 miles – about half the Earth's diameter. There may be life on Mars in form of microbes – viruses and bacteria. There also may have been liquid water on Mars in the distant past.

The Martian polar ice caps are believed to be composed of frozen water and carbon dioxide. Mars is considerably colder than the Earth, but in the summer it gets as warm as 70^0 Fahrenheit at the equator. The Martian day is about the same length as an Earth-day, but the Martian year is nearly twice as long as an Earth year. The Martian northern hemisphere is unmagnetized, but the southern hemisphere has a fairly strong magnetic field. In contrast, the Earth has a magnetic north and a magnetic south pole. The biggest crater on Mars is called Huygens Crater, which has a diameter of 292 miles in diameter. The second biggest crater is Schiaparelli's Crater, with a diameter of 275 miles. The many craters on Mars were created by meteors crashing to the Martian surface.

Another entry talked about water, which is found everywhere in the solar system. It's a common substance in comets and asteroids. Water is found in craters on Mercury, on the ice caps of Mars, on Saturn's moon Enceladus, and on the dwarf planet of Ceres in the asteroid belt between Mars and Jupiter. Ceres, the biggest asteroid, has a diameter of 588 miles and an average temperature of -100^0 F. It was first observed by Giuseppe Piazzi in 1801. The surface of Ceres is heavily cratered with a mixture of water ice and carbonate minerals.

Enceladus, first observed by Galileo, is pocketed with many impact craters and over a hundred geysers – shooting out water, gases, and solid material. It's very small with a diameter of 310 miles and extremely cold. The most interesting fact about Enceladus is the existence of a salty ocean under its icy surface. Organic compounds exist there – ammonia, methane, alcohol, and the constituents of amino acids – the building blocks of life. Hence, there may be life in the form of microbes on this tiny moon of Saturn. Jupiter's moon, Europa, also has liquid water beneath its frozen surface. In addition, this moon has a very thin atmosphere consisting of oxygen and traces of water vapor. There also may be simple organisms existing below Europa's icy surface – in its ocean. Like Enceladus, Europa is extremely cold with temperatures as low as -260^0 F. Its diameter of 1,940 miles is slightly smaller than that of the Earth's moon.

Hal had a brief entry on soil, which he defined as a mixture of fine rock, dirt, clay, water, bacteria, fungus, oxygen, and nitrogen. For acidic soil, one should add lime and for alkaline soil, sulfur must be added. The North Atlantic Coastal Plain has soil good for growing corn, wheat, vegetables, flowers, and trees – including white oak, red oak, black oat, dogwood, pine, hickory, and holly. Glaciers from the last Ice Age transported rocks, gravel, sand, silt, and clay. The fertile soil was sorted and layered by glacial melt, rivers, and streams – creating downer soil –ideal for growing a wide variety of crops. The glacial deposits led to New Jersey's moniker – "the Garden State" and the transported sand, silt, and clay also benefited the soil of nearby Staten Island, which was likely joined to New Jersey in the past.

There was an entry on the Coriolis Effect, which is created by the Earth's rotation. The effect was first proposed by French mathematician, Gustave Coriolis in 1835. Contrary to popular notion, the fact that water flows down drains in clockwise direction is due to the position of faucet and shape of the sink. Winds, birds, and airplanes are directly affected by the effect – deflected to right in Northern Hemisphere and to the left in the Southern Hemisphere. Migratory birds automatically adjust for the Coriolis effect. The effect causes hurricanes to rotate counterclockwise in Northern Hemisphere and rotate clockwise in Southern Hemisphere. In the eastern half of the U S A, prevailing winds travel west to east – carrying rain and snow storms with them.

Hal also had material on cave men or Neanderthals, who lived between 40,000 and 400,000 years ago in Europe and Asia. The Neanderthals built fires to protect their caves from predators and to cook food. Their diet consisted of meat and vegetables – including spices. The reasons for their extinction were small population size, inbreeding, and competition with Homo Sapiens or modern man. The latter emerged from Africa about 300,000 years ago. Early mankind started out as hunter-gatherers—moving from place to place. With the development of agriculture about 13,000 years ago, human beings built villages and cities. Civilizations grew – marked by social classes, division of labor, language, laws, and culture. The ancient Greeks had a two-fold purpose – the search for knowledge and the desire for virtue. Unfortunately, these noble goals have never been attained for the bulk of mankind to this very day.

There was an entry on evangelicals – 82 million of them or 30% of the country's population before the Covid-20 pandemic. Self-described as "born again" Christians, the beliefs of evangelicals are rooted in the Bibe. They believe in the resurrection of Jesus Christ, the forgiveness of sins, and a new life into which they will be born. There was also the story of the two sisters, Mary and Martha. The latter complained to Jesus because Mary was washing Jesus's feet, instead of helping her with the housework. Jesus defended Mary – saying that there would always be chores to do, but he, himself, would not be around much longer. The moral of the story was to place priorities on the essential things in life.

There was some historical material that related to the current issue of abortion. Hal asserted that the right to abortion originated with the 9th amendment of the Constitution – the right to privacy. The framers – James Madison, Alexander Hamilton, George Washington, Benjamin Franklin,

Roger Sherman, George Mason, William Patterson, William Livingston, and Charles Pinckney, among others – believed that people had the right to make decisions affecting their lives – free from government control. George Washington, a deist, once said that the country was not founded on the Christian religion: "American should have a foundation free of the influence of clergy." Thomas Jefferson concurred: "Christianity neither is, nor ever was a part of the common law." After the Constitution was adopted in 1787, Benjamin Frankin was queried. "Well Doctor, what have we got – a republic or a monarchy?" His response: "A republic, if you can keep it."

The issue of abortion had become so highly politicized that rational debate was nearly impossible. Abortion had been performed by midwives in ancient Greece by using the herb – birthwort. An ingredient from the juniper plant, sarin, had been used in the Middle Ages to induce abortion. However, sarin is quite toxic. In his writings, Ben Franklin recommended a wild herb –"stinking goosefoot" – to ease childbirth and to induce abortions.

Curiously, many of the states which had outlawed abortion were the same states still permitting capital punishment. The 8th amendment, which prohibited cruel and unusual punishment, did not disallow capital punishment – the harshest penalty that could be imposed on an individual. In A Tale of Two Cities, Charles Dickens described the notorious Madame Defarge knitting sweaters on a rocking chair next to the guillotine. Unaffected by the sight of a victim's head being chopped off and rolling into a special basket. She was particularly merciless towards those nobles she believed had mistreated her family. This occurred during the bloody French Revolution, which eventually lead to the ascent of Napolean as emperor. France, a civilized country, did not give up the guillotine (the French Razor) as a method of execution until 1977.

There was material about a popular T V during the 1950s, called "I Led 3 Lives" about the complicated life of Herbert Philbrick. Philbrick was an advertising executive, a member of the Communist Party, and an FBI informant. During World War II, Russia was an ally of America, fighting Nazi Germany who had invaded the large continental country. But with the advent of the Cold War, everything changed as the Communist Party adopted a hardline Marxist-Leninist tone. Philbrick began reporting on meetings with the Communists to the FBI – for which he was paid a salary, plus expenses. The TV show was based on Philbrick's book of the same title. The show reflected the somber mood of the 1950s, continually reverting to images of Philbrick trudging through the streets of Boston lugging his heavy briefcase wherever he went in the gritty New England city.

There was a curious entry about the number zero, which came from India. They used the symbol 0 to represent the numeral around the 5th century A D. In Babylon, 5th century scribes used spaces to denote the absence of a number. The mathematician, Fibonacci, brought the Arabic numerals back to Italy from his travels through North Africa. The Fibonacci sequence was given: 1, 1, 2, 3, 5, 8, 13, 21, 34, 55, 89, 144, ... Hal went on to list the occurrences of this sequence in nature: petal arrangements, tree branches, pinecones, sea shells, tree trunk spirals, and even spiral galaxies. It appears that nature itself has an affinity for Fibonacci spirals, Hal concluded.

In another of Hal's notebooks there was material on Stonehedge, the ancient array of tall stones where Thomas Hardy's Tess of the DUrbervilles met her tragic death. Stonehedge was constructed in England around 2500 B C, from huge stones weighing 25 tons each and standing thirteen feet high. The stones are aligned so the sun's rays pass through them on summer solstice. Whether the builders of Stonehedge were Saxons, Celts, Danes, Romans, or Phoenicians have not been determined. It may have been built as a pagan religious site, as a place of healing, or for astronomical observations. Hal also had an entry on a modern-day Stonehedge called Manhattan-Hedge. On the island of Manhattan, the buildings along 14th, 34th, 42nd, and 57th Streets are aligned so the sun's rays pass all the way through from the Hudson River to the East River on the first day of summer. This phenomenon has no particular religious or philosophical meaning other the builders were adhering to Manhattan's rectilinear grid.

There was a section on the annual migration of birds from the north to warmer climes. Many birds have a built-in navigation system – an internal compass that utilizes the Earth's magnetic field to navigate over long distances. But experience and landmarks aid the bird's migratory journey. There are neural connections between the bird's eyes this internal compass. Hence, the bird might actually be able to see the Earth's magnetic field. Examples of American migratory birds are: sparrows, robins, blue jays, orioles, ducks, geese, falcons, cranes, and snowy owls. During the past fifty years, approximately three billion birds have been lost in the U S A and Canada. In the northeast alone, this loss from the effects of global warming and increased urbanization, amounts to 1/3 of all birds. Specifically, this scary phenomenon can be attributed to o loss of bird habitat- fewer grasslands and forests. The population of red wolves has declined to near extinction due to excessive hunting and habitat destruction. The rain forests of Central America are vanishing due to cattle grazing, and the growing of coffee, bananas, maize, and sugar cane. Only water fowl—ducks, geese, and the common loons seem to be flourishing.

Hal also compiled material on the monarch butterfly, which migrates from Canada and northern U S A to southwestern Mexico. The journey takes longer than the individual lifespan of the butterfly – taking four generations of the monarch to make trip. The lifecycle of a monarch butterfly has four stages – egg, larva (which grows into caterpillar), pupa, and adult butterfly. In the caterpillar stage, they feed on milkweed plants. However, milkweed plants are being killed by fungi which cause leaf spot and root rot. Once in Mexico, the butterflies cluster together in fir trees. The branches of these trees protect from extreme weather conditions. Butterflies feed on nectar from milkweed, goldenrod, and white, purple, and pink phlox. Butterflies can see colors and ultraviolet light. The ability to remember colors of flowers and associate them with sugary foods is essential to the survival of butterflies.

There was also an entry about the ubiquitous white butterfly, or cabbage butterfly, which is smaller than the monarch butterfly. The cabbage butterfly can be found in gardens, weedy areas, plus suburbs and cities. The female white butterfly has two black spots on its wing, while there's a single black spot on the male's wing. The white butterfly is a symbol of rebirth and good luck. White butterflies are often confused with moths which are fat and fluffy. In contrast, white butterflies are slender with long thin antennae. Along with bees, wasps, and bats – butterflies cross-pollinate flowers, vegetables, herbs, and fruit, which is critical to plants. Like birds and bees, butterflies have been threatened by the use of pesticides and the loss of their habitat. The entry ended with a quote by Charles Dickens: "I only ask to be free. The butterflies are free."

Nancy never failed to stop and peer at butterflies when she was in the backyard or walking in Eggert's Field. The reason: Hal once told her that he'd come back to her in the form of a monarch butterfly. He was obviously joking but she took him seriously. To realize the miracle of reincarnation as a delicate, ephemeral insect like a butterfly was ridiculous, but the sight of one of those fluttering creatures – made her heart skip a beat. And she ran over to it – calling out – "Is that you Hal?" – even in the presence of other people. Like birds, butterflies fly thousands of miles – crossing international boundaries with the freedom often denied people.

There was an entry on the hermit crab, a crustacean adapted to occupy empty mollusk shells to protect their fragile exoskeleton. The mollusk shells produced by snails, mussels, and slugs are not being replenished – leaving the hermit crab virtually defenseless. Hence, hermit crabs now occupy plastic cups, tin cans, and other discarded containers for protection. Mollusk shells are mostly composed of calcium carbonate. And there appears to be insufficient calcium carbonate in seawater due to acidification of the world's oceans. This acidification is a result of increased carbon dioxide absorption associated with the burning of fossil fuels.

There was also material on the Sahara Desert, the largest subtropical desert in the world – encompassing 3.5 million square miles. The Sahara Desert has grown by 10% over the last century. And it is increasing by 2,934 square miles each year. North African countries, like Tunisia, Algeria, Sudan, and Ethiopia, have been planting palm trees to slow down the advance of the Sahara Desert. Trees prevent soil erosion, slow down desert winds, put nutrients back into the ground, and help the soil to retain moisture. The project was being financed by the World Bank.

Hal had material on explorers, starting with Hernando de Soto, who explored Florida, Georgia. Alabama, and discovered the Mississippi River. In 1542. Then, de Soto ventured into South America – conquering the natives. The Incas had a developed agriculture, irrigation, and a network of roads tunnels, and bridges. They also kept historical and government records, collected taxes, and distributed food. Another explorer was Giovanni de Verrazzano, who in 1524 was the first to sail into New York Harbor, up the Hudson River, and along the Atlantic Coast past Rhode Island – all the way up to Newfoundland. Next, came Henry Hudson, the English explorer – sailing from Holland on a tiny ship, the Half-Moon, into New York Harbor and sailing up the Hudson River in 1609. Hal made a reference to the fact that the Hudson River was named after its discoverer, Henry Hudson, but the Mississippi River was not named the De Soto River. However, the De Soto – a midsized car –was named in honor of the Spanish explorer. De Soto was manufactured by the Chrysler Corporation from 1928 to 1961, but the car lost market share to Oldsmobile and Buick and was discontinued.

An explanation was presented on how the White House acquired its white color. Originally, the President's house was a red brick structure, but it was partially burned down and scorched by British soldiers in 1814. As a result, lime-based whitewash was applied to the building, and then it was repainted in with white lead paint in 1818. Another version stated that the White House had a porous sandstone coating which absorbed water and froze during the winter. The lime-based whitewash prevented the condensation-and-refreezing process from occurring, until white lead paint was applied to the White House in 1818.

CHAPTER 7

20ᵀᴴ CENTURY ISSUES

A DESCRIPTION OF BUREAUCRACY WAS PRESENTED BY THE GERMAN sociologist Max Weber in the early 20th century. Weber described bureaucracies as highly structured, formal, and impersonal organizations. He said they were the most efficient organizations because of division of labor, strict rules, and formal procedures. However, bureaucracies tend to impede innovation, creativity and the sharing of ideas. And the bureaucratic structure discourages interpersonal relationships – resulting in feelings of detachment and alienation. Communication in bureaucracies is largely from the top level down to the lower levels where the real work of the organization is done.

There was a brief sketch of Alfred Delp, a German Jesuit priest, who was a leader of the German resistance to the Nazis. He was falsely implicated in the plot to overthrow Adolf Hitler. The Nazis arrested and executed him in 1945. His body was cremated and his ashes disposed of in an unknown location near Berlin. He said, "My chains are without any meaning, because God found me worthy of the chains of love." He asserted that every human being is entitled to living space, daily bread, and protection of the law – as a common birthright." Delp also said "All of life is Advent." Advent is the season of preparation for Christ's nativity and his expected return in the Second Coming.

There was a section on Pablo Picasso's painting Guernica, which depicts the bombing of a Spanish market by German and Italian airplanes during the Spanish Civil War. The mural-sized painting, done in blue, black, and white, shows a gored bull, a horse, a dead baby, a screaming woman, and flames. In 1937, Picasso was questioned about this antiwar painting by a Gestapo officer: "Did you do this?" Picaso responded, "No, you did." Though neutral during the second world war, Spain sent 50,000 volunteers to fight with the Germans on the western front of the Soviet Union. Spanish dictator, Francisco Franco ruled Spain with an iron grip from 1937 until his death in 1975. Under his rule, there were an estimated 26,000 political prisoners. During the Cold War,

Franco permitted the U S A to build air and naval bases in Spain. After his death, Spain returned to democratic rule.

In addition, there was material on the Quakers which have sects in America, Europe, Asia, and Africa. Richard Nixon, our 37th President, was born into a poor Quaker family in California. Historically, Quakers were opposed to slavery, military service, and violence in general. William Penn, a Quaker who founded the colony of Pennsylvania, did own several slaves – despite slavery's unpopularity in Pennsylvania. Quakers emphasize Bible readings so each person can see 'the light within." However, Quakers did oppose Charles Darwin's Theory of Evolution when it was first conceived in 1859. Though a Quaker, Nixon used the giant B-52s to carpet bomb North Vietnam, especially Hanoi, and neighboring Cambodia in 1968-69. Nixon's key advisor on Vietnam was Henry Kissinger, who urged the bombing campaign. Eventually, Kissinger negotiated with North Vietnam's Le Duc Tho to end the war. Both Kissinger and Tho were awarded the Nobel Peace Prize for their efforts. However, the latter refused to accept the award – saying that the U S was the aggressor in the 17-year long war.

Approximately 250,000 tons of explosives were dropped on North Vietnam by Nixon – compared to 180,000 tons dropped on Japan during World War II. Another 2,756,940 tons of bombs were dropped on neighboring Cambodia. Going back to 1965 when Lyndon Johnson escalated the war, the total amount of rockets, missiles, and bombs dropped on North Vietnam exceeded one million tons. More than 20,000 people have been killed by mines and unexploded bombs and another 65,000 injured since 1979. Kids would find cluster munitions – playing catch with them – until they blow up. During the nineteen-year-long war (November 1955 to April 1975), there were 2,000,000 civilian deaths, 1,100,000 North Vietnamese soldiers and Viet Cong deaths, 5,000 South Korean soldier deaths, and 58,300 American soldier deaths. An outcome of this tragic war was the realization that overwhelming military might does not guarantee victory in third-world countries.

Jimmy Carter, our 39th President, ended the state of war between Egypt and Israel in the Camp David Accords in 1978. Israel returned the Sinai Peninsula to Egypt and the two countries have lived in peace ever since. President Carter also negotiated the Salt II nuclear arms treaty with Russia – limiting nuclear weapons and establishing nuclear parity between the two nations. The agreement established methods of verifying compliance. Despite his foreign policy success, the Carter Administration was damaged by the Iranian hostage crisis, when U S embassy staff was seized by Iranian students.

Carter was also plagued by inflation, high interest rates, and high oil prices. Carter's push for energy conservation and alternative energy sources like sun, wind, and nuclear – was largely ignored.

After he was defeated by ex-movie star Ronald Reagan, Jimmy Carter started Habitat for Humanity, which built thousands of homes for poor people across America. The program requires recipients of these houses to participate in rehabilitating their new homes. Carter, himself, contributed to the sweat equity to refurbish these buildings. Carter has also worked to push democracy and observe free elections throughout the world – especially in 3rd-world countries. The Carter Center joined the battle to eliminate Guinea worm disease in the 1980s, when there were 3.5 million cases in Chad, Ethiopia, and South Sudan. It is extremely painful. The adult worm, one meter long, emerges from the skin forming a blister. The illness is spread in contaminated drinking water. People were taught to filter their water and cook food – especially fish and frogs well. Thanks to the Carter Center, UNCEF, and the World Health Organization, Guinea worm disease joins small pox and polio (with some exceptions) as eliminated diseases.

There was a brief entry on the bubonic plague, which swept through Europe during the 14th century. This disease killed fifty million people – nearly half the population. It was spread by rats and the fleas that lived with rats and even mice. Symptoms included fever, chills, malaise, muscle cramps, and seizures. In extreme cases, gangrene of the extremities can result. Control of the local rat population in urban areas was crucial in preventing outbreaks of the disease. Today, antibiotics are used to treat bubonic plague.

In still another notebook, there was an entry about a lake in Ontario, Canada (Crawford Lake) where traces of radioactive plutonium have been found on the lake's bottom. The testing of nuclear weapons has been conducted by nine countries – the USA, Russia, China, England, France, India, Pakistan, Israel, and North Korea beginning in the 1940s. The first atomic bomb was detonated July 16, 1945 in the New Mexico desert 120 miles south of Sante Fe. The last nuclear bomb test conducted in continental U S A was done at the Nevada nuclear test site in 1992 in an underground cavity. Before that, atmospheric testing had been carried out until 1963, when a Russian-American treaty (negotiated by Kennedy and Khrushchev) stopped all such nuclear testing above ground. The U S A tested its hydrogen bomb developed in 1952, on Eniwetok Atoll in the Pacific Ocean. The H-bomb had the power of 10.4 megatons of TNT – vaporizing the island it was set off on and leaving a mushroom cloud that stretched 60 miles across and 120,000 feet high. Hal had said that the cosmic ray burst from outer space which disabled the world's stockpile of nuclear weapons, along with nuclear weapons, was an act of God. Perhaps, it was God's way of ameliorating the worldwide devastation from the Covid-20 pandemic which decimated so many people.

In weird juxtaposition, Hal had material on the three basic subatomic particles – electrons, protons, and neutrons. Electrons have a negative charge, protons, a positive charge, and neutrons, as the name implies are neutral. IIn the Bohr model of the atom, protons and neutrons exist in the nucleus, while electrons orbit the outside the nucleus in shells. When outside the nucleus, neutrons will last about fifteen minutes before disintegrating into a proton, electron and antineutrino. Neutrons are key to nuclear fission – splitting Uranium-235 to release huge amounts of energy in the atomic bomb.

Albert Einstein predicted that both matter and antimatter would respond in the same way to gravity. This assertion was verified many years later by experiments. According to the Big Bang Theory, equal amounts of matter and antimatter were created at the beginning of the universe. This was approximately 13.7 billion years ago. However, there appears to be very little antimatter around on the earth – almost none. Theoretically, when matter collides with antimatter – there's an explosion and annihilation results. For example, if an electron collides with a positron, they're annihilated and a high-energy photon is released.

There was also information on a recently discovered subatomic particle, called the tetra quark, which is composed of two quarks and two antiquarks. Quarks, the fundamental building blocks of matter, have electric charge, mass, spin, and color. Like electrons, protons, and neutrons, these elusive particles are affected by nuclear, gravitational, and electromagnetic forces. The name "quark" comes from two lines in the obscure James Joyce novel – Finnegans Wake – "Three quarks for Muster Mark. Since he has not got much of a bark."

In addition, there was material on the 18th century chemist, Antoine Lavoisier, who explained combustion as the combination of an element with oxygen from the atmosphere. He demonstrated the law of conservation of matter in chemical reactions – sometimes called Lavoisier's Law. Lavoisier also developed the modern nomenclature for chemical compounds. A substance's name should reflect its chemical composition. For example, rust is called iron oxide, salt is called sodium chloride, and limestone is referred to as calcium carbonate. Prior to Lavoisier, scientists erroneously referred to the four basic substances as earth, air, fire, and water. During the French Revolution, Lavoisier was falsely accused of tampering with the tobacco he sold. A judge refused the great chemist's appeals for mercy and he was sent to the guillotine. "The Republic needs neither scholars nor chemists."

Material on the French mathematician, Pierre-Simon LaPlace, followed the entry of Lavoisier. Applying Newton's law of gravity, LaPlace stated that a planet's orbital eccentricity and angular velocity were invariable. A determinist, LaPlace stated that if you know the precise location and momentum of every atom in the universe, you can determine their past and future positions for any given time – using Newton's laws of classical mechanics. The notion of entropy in modern-day theories of thermodynamics refutes LaPlace's assertions. When a gas does work by pushing a piston, it does cool down. But the overall entropy or disorder of the system increases over time — since the end-product mechanical work is random heat energy.

There was also an entry on alloys which are mixtures of metals – which are stronger and more resistant to corrosion than their constituent metals. Steel is an alloy of Iron with trace amounts of carbon and manganese. Alnico is an alloy of iron, aluminum, nickel, and cobalt. Alnico is ferromagnetic – from which the strongest magnets are made. Nichrome is an alloy of nickel, chromium, and iron. It has a high melting point and is used in heating coils. Brass is a shiny alloy of copper and zinc. Much harder than aluminum, brass is used to make bullets. Bronze was the first alloy developed by the ancient Greeks and Romans. Bronze, an alloy of copper and tin, was used in sculpture and to make swords and shields. Its earliest use was in western Eurasia in 3500 B C and in China around 2000 B C.

There was some material on the heavy metal lead – Latin name plumbum and chemical symbol Pb. Plumber is the name given to a person who works with lead pipes. Lead was used extensively by the ancient Romans in water pipes and for pots, bowls, and dishes. Lead may have been one of the causes of the decline of Roman civilization. Lead poisoning causes vomiting, irritability, loss of appetite, and cognitive impairment. In the 18th century, Benjamin Franklin warned that tainted liquor from lead-lined still heads caused ill effects on drinkers. In modern times, lead was a gasoline additive because it reduced engine knock and improved efficiency. Also, lead was added to paint to improve its color and durability, to reduce its drying time, and to make it more moisture resistant. Then, in 1978, lead was banned from household paints – interior and exterior. However, lead is still used in paints applied to bridges.

Another heavy element is mercury, the only metal which is liquid at room temperature. Because it expands uniformly with higher temperatures, mercury was once extensively used in thermometers. Because of the dangers associated with mercury, reddish alcohol is often used in thermometers. Dentists use silver amalgam – made from mercury, silver, tin, zinc, and copper – for tooth fillings. Hydrargyrum is the Latin name for mercury and its chemical symbol is Hg. In the 17th and 18th century, people who made hats used mercury in the process. Mercury, in the form of mercury nitrate, enables the fur fibers to mat together – producing higher quality felt. And hatters often worked in poorly ventilated rooms – inhaling mercury vapors for hours. Unfortunately, mercury has deleterious effects on the brain – causing tremors, slurred speech, and sometimes hallucinations. Hence, the term "as mad as a hatter" was common at that time.

There was also a brief entry on the light metal, Lithium, used in the rechargeable batteries found in cell phones, hybrid cars, and electric bikes. It has also been used to treat those with bipolar disorder and manic depressives. Lithium toxicity can cause confusion, shaking, and nausea and even result in kidney damage. Lithium is a soft, flammable, and highly reactive element. In the U S A. Lithium has been mined in Neveda, California, and North Carolina. Lithium is also found in Canada – Quebec and Manitoba. In addition, this valuable metal has been found in the Australia and in the salt flats of Bolivia, Chile, and Argentina.

In addition, Hal had an entry on Paul Robeson, singer, actor, professional football player, lawyer, and black activist. Robeson once said that "artists are the gatekeepers of truth. We are civilization's radical voice." His father, William, was born into slavery – escaping from the plantation in his teens. Robeson was once grilled by J Edgar Hoover, head of the FBI, because he had praised Russia. "In Russia, I felt for the first time like a full human being. No color prejudice like in Mississippi or Washington." When Robeson couldn't find a hotel room in his hometown, Princeton, he stayed at Albert Einstein's house. In a speech at Lincoln University, a historically black university, Einstein called "racism a disease of white people."

Joined by her big tortoiseshell cat, Torte, Nancy soon fell asleep – thinking about those wonderful books most of which sat on the bookshelf in the front room. H. G. Wells' book on time travel impressed her. It would be wonderful if you had the ability to travel through time. I could see my parents and the friends I went to school with – along with Hal and Sam. Just to be able to live again in the pre-covid world with its ordinary concerns would wonderful. Nancy had a strange dream. She was riding on a merry-go-round as a little girl while her mom watched her nearby. Suddenly she was flying through the air – seeing New York City far below. Then she was crossing the ocean – flying over the continents – Europe, Asia, and Africa, and back to North America again. In a panic, she was looking for Staten Island but couldn't find it.

Nancy woke up, fed Torte, the big male cat and then checked on Boxie, the hand-sized green-and-yellow box turtle. She had made Hal set Snappy free in the early spring because the feisty turtle was getting bigger and his snapping jaws stronger. Unlike the placid Boxie, Snappy bit anything placed near his beak – celery stalks, carrot sticks, pieces of wood, and fingers. Even Torte, the formidable rat killer, had stayed away from angry turtle. It reminded her of something Sam used to say: "I don't go looking for trouble, it usually finds me."

CHAPTER 8

BACKYARD BASKETBALL GAME

NANCY OPENED THE SCREEN DOOR TO THE BACKYARD STOOP. AS THE wooden screen door closed, the sound of it slamming shut reminded her of her childhood in the flats.

She sat on the back stoop, accompanied by Torte and Boxie, warmed by the morning sun's rays. Bored she grabbed a basketball from the sunporch and took some shots at the basket in the backyard. Hal had attached the rim to a three-by-four-foot wooden backboard with four bolts and then the board to the old garage with several five-inch nails. After all those HORSE and one-on-one games, with the basketball bouncing hard off the basket, both rim and backboard were as sturdy as they had been when Hal erected them four years ago.

Before long, her next-door neighbor – Mildred Aimsley called out from her second-floor window, "Nancy, may I join you in some healthy exercise?"

"Sure. Come on down."

Soon the prim woman was shooting baskets – imitating Nancys two-hand set shots – though with less accuracy than her deadly accurate neighbor. Nancy showed Mildred how to dribble the basketball on the crab grass, which was very sparse on the segment of the yard closest to the basket. The opposite side of the backyard had a rickety picket fence and an ancient pear tree which still bore pears.

Nancy and Mildred played a raucous game of HORSE, which Nancy made close by deliberately missing a layup. Mildred's common law husband, Reverend Staller stuck his head out of the same window, "May I join you ladies?"

"Sure, Rev. The more, the merrier."

Within a few minutes Stan Staller, clad in old baggy jeans, a stained gray sweat shirt, and black high-top sneakers joined the two women in the back yard. No athlete, Staller's dribbling was worse than Mildred's and his shots were wide of the mark. But he seemed to enjoy a rare moment of play.

"The good Lord, in his unbounded wisdom gave me little skill in games involving spheres – baseball, stickball, soccer, and basketball."

"Would that you spent more time in schoolyards and less time perusing the Bible, Stanley," Mildred declared with a slight smile.

"Ah, the Rev's not too bad. He just needs some practice," Nancy piped in.

Stan gave her a quick smile and took a shot from the side, which was an air ball.

"I'd say the Rev needs a lot of practice," Freddy von Vogilo called out, as he entered the backyard. Though well into his seventies, Freddy had the joie de vivre of a man half his age.

Stan smiled and passed the ball to Freddy. "Indeed I do."

Freddy took one of his line drive jump shots that hit the backboard and went straight up about four feet came down into Nancy's hands. She faked a shot and passed to Freddy, who bobbled it and then drove hard to the basket. The shot caromed off the wooden backboard and bounced high in the air – getting stuck in the old pear tree on the opposite side of the yard. The big mulberry tree adjacent to the garage wall was probably older than the pear tree. Likely, it was planted when the flat-roofed yellow stucco house was built at the start of the 20th century

Reverend Staller went over and shook the tree – dislodging the basketball and three overripe pears that had remained on the tree over the winter. Looking at Nancy, "Would you like one?"

Nancy shook her head but Freddy took one and bit into it. The Reverend placed the other two on the crab grass near the pear tree and joined the others taking shots at the sturdy basket.

Mildred went over to Freddy, "May I have a bite?"

"Sure. I'd never turn down a pretty girl," he said – offering Mildred a bite with his usual wide smile.

"Freddy, would that you show me how to take a two-handed set shot," the prim woman asked.

"Sure. What did you say your name is?"

"Mildred Aimsley and my partner is Stanley Staller. Have you met Stan?" she asked nodding towards the former soapbox preacher.

"Do I know the Rev? I found him by the railroad tracks," Freddy responded – rubbing his hands and smiling widely.

"That's true. You and Hal saved my life. Thanks be to God," the self-styled man of God exclaimed.

At the mention of Hal, Nancy's eyes filled with tears. Mildred gave her a hug. "Do you want to go for a walk?"

"No, it's alright," she replied – wiping her eyes and smiling briefly.

At that moment, Alfred came down and ran onto the grass. "Can I take a shot?"

Freddy passed the ball to the youngster who took a one-handed set shot from the foul line and swished it. "Not bad, maybe you should give the Rev lessons."

Alfred, took Reverend Staller aside and showed him how to hold the ball. "Before you shoot, eyeball the basket for a couple of seconds and then let go."

"The kids got good eyes. He can spot a coin in a floorboard or among weeds from fifty feet," Freddy declared with a wry smile.

Alfred, Freddy, and the Reverend took shots at the hoop, while Nancy and Mildred sat down on the back steps watching the men play and talking quietly. Nancy seemed to appeal to the prim middle-aged woman's maternal instincts. She took one of Hal's notebooks to look over while the men played basketball.

"I like to read Hal's notebooks. He had them organized according to subject matter – science, philosophy, history, literature. Reading them is an education in itself."

Opening up a notebook, she read aloud. "Plato's metaphysics: dual nature of reality – the world of objects and the world of ideas. Objects, which are imperfect and changeable, are the source of opinions. Ideas, which are perfect and eternal, are the source of knowledge. Plato asserted that ultimate reality was the world of ideas. And wisdom was the pure knowledge of ideas. In a similar vein, Kierkegaard said that power lies not in authoritarian control, but in the enduring legacy of one's ideas and values."

"Here's an entry about another Greek philosopher, Xenophanes, who made fun of the gods on Mt. Olympus because they behaved and looked like ordinary people. If horses, or oxen, or lions had hands, they would draw gods that looked like horses, oxen, or lions. In other words, gods always have the same bodies as the beings that worship them."

"There's material on a philosopher named Friedrich Nietzsche, who Hal said was a favorite of the Nazis. Yet, Nietzsche said German nationalism was petty, narrow, and warlike. He said there was no such thing as absolute truth. Nietzsche challenged objective knowledge and Kant's idea of the categorical imperative – a moral principle applicable to all people across all cultures. When it came to love and friendship, Nietzsche was not a fan. He said love is blind and friendship closes its eyes."

"Science is about finding better approximations rather than finding absolute truth. Nietzsche said that man is relentlessly destructive of nature. Must have been an ecologist. He contradicts himself: everything matters and nothing is important. With regard to the future, Nietzsche said the future lasts forever and future generations would understand him better than his peers. Here's something: The earth is like the breast of a woman – useful as well as pleasing. Nietzsche also said God is dead and modern man is his murderer. Not exactly the life of a party."

"I think I've heard enough about Mister Nietzsche," Mildred responded.

"Me too."

"Here's an entry on a guy named Soren Kierkegaard who says you need a leap of faith to believe in God, which is not provable by observation or reason. He also said that existence can only be viewed and understood subjectively.

"Try to tell Stan that leap-of-faith stuff and you'll get an argument. I mean there are certain paradoxes in Christianity which defy logic," the prim woman responded.

"Hal states that cause-and-effect laws require a leap of faith. Like Newton's third law – action and reaction. The air leaving the balloon is the action and the balloon darting about is the reaction."

Nancy continued to read. "If you drop two rocks from a roof, they'll hit the ground the same time. Proving that all objects have the same gravitational acceleration. It's called g and it equals thirty-two feet per second squared."

"Here's an entry about Saint Thomas Aquinas – a Dominican monk from the Middle Ages. Aquinas said free will is the basis of morality. Private property is O K, but everything must be shared. Aquinas also opposed levying interest. He said that the soul is present in every part of the body. Aquinas asserted that God knows both general and particular truths. If a sparrow falls from a tree, God would know about it."

Reading some more, she asked, "Do you know who Saint Rita was?"

No one responded, so Nancy continued. "Saint Rita is the patron saint of lost causes, including abuse, loneliness, parents, widows, and the sick. Saint Rita's parents married her off to a stranger at age twelve. He was cruel and abusive, but after many years of patience and prayer, her husband became kind to her. After the death of her husband and two sons, Saint Rita was accepted into a convent. She had several mystical experiences. While praying the stigmata of a single thorn appeared on her forehead."

"What are stigmata?" Mildred asked.

Looking through Hal's notebook, Nancy read from it. "Stigmata are marks on a person's body – often on the face – indicating God's grace."

"Theology is as complicated as science. I suppose that it's all for the good. Would that we never stop learning. But, Stan sometimes goes off the deep end."

"How's that?"

"He's into theosophy," the prim woman replied.

"What's that about?"

"It's an occult group. They believe in reincarnation."

"Reincarnation would only be good if you could remember the dumb things you did the first time around. Hal said that Pythagoras believed in reincarnation and if you were bad, you'd come back as a dog. Pythagoras was the right-triangle guy."

"I hated geometry. Would that we got a second chance in life. I don't think I'd choose a soapbox preacher the second time around," the prim woman said – trying not to smile.

"Let's get some coffee and donuts. They just reopened Hardy's. Remember Winnie Luco and Johnny O'Toole?"

"How could I forget those two ne'er-do-wells?"

"They gave up their burglar trade. They're respectable businessmen now."

The two women walked up Hooker Place towards Morningstar Road. And soon returned with a bagful of donuts and Styrofoam cups of coffee.

"I remember Hal talked about the guy who invented the machine that makes donuts. He changed the course of history as much as Henry Ford."

Perusing one of Hal's notebooks, Nancy searched for the man's name. "Here it is – Adolph Levitt. And the guy who invented blue jeans – Levi Strauss."

"I recall reading about Benjamin Franklin, who invented the potbelly stove, the lightning rod, and bifocal glasses. Would that someone could invent a machine that reverses time. That would be something," Mildred replied.

"Hal said that Franklin invented the long arm for grasping books from shelves."

"Didn't Benjamin Franklin start the first postal service in Philadelphia?"

"Yes, he did. Franklin was ahead of his time."

"'magine getting letters in the mail again? That would be a miracle. Indeed, to see Hal again. And Sam too – would be a real miracle," the prim woman said

"Miracles don't happen in this day and age," Nancy replied sadly.

There was a list of the worst educated states – Arizona, Louisiana, Nevada, New Mexico, Alabama, South Carolina, Oklahoma, Noth Carolina, Florida,

Tennessee, Mississippi. and Texas. Not surprisingly, the best educated states were mostly in the northeast – New York, New Jersey, and Massachusetts. Of course, Nancy understood that a person could be in a poor school and still learn a lot.

There was an entry on Albert Camus who had been linked with the French existentialist Jean-Paul Sartre, but Camus called himself an absurdist. Like Sartre, he believed in free will and taking responsibility for one's actions. Camus said a person wastes time searching for the true meaning of life. In a twist of Descartes' famous statement, Camus said: "I rebel, therefore I exist." He said that man lives in a perpetual state of conflict – searching for meaning in a silent, indifferent, and cold universe. With regard to nuclear weapons, Camus said "We have nothing to lose except everything." As a member of the French Resistance against the Nazis during World War ii, Camus developed his philosophy, which came to be known as absurdism. A realist, Albert Camus asserted that every political ideology is contrary to human nature.

There was material on Hedy Lamarr, which Nancy read out loud. "Hedy Lamarr was an Austrian-born movie star, of Jewish lineage, with a film career extending from the late 1930s through the 1950s. With Auschluss, the takeover of Austria by the Nazis, Hedy was forced to flee her native country –eventually migrating to America. The green-eyed, dark-haired beauty was chosen by Louis B. Mayer to star in "Algiers" – launching her into a movie career Working with a piano player, George Johann Antheil, Lamarr invented a radio-directed torpedo, which improved its accuracy. The torpedo's guidance system would shift its frequency to match that of the transmitter – a phenomenon called resonance. Thus, the receiver could pick up guidance information without enemy eavesdroppers interfering. Since pianos have 88 keys, the system utilized 88 different shifting frequencies until a match was obtained. The invention of Lamarr and Antheil aided the Allied effort during World War II. Today, this technology is used in cell phones, military radios, global positioning satellites, and the linking of desktop computers to corporate networks.

"I recall Hedy Lamarr. She had beauty and brains. Would that more of us had the opportunity to contribute to mankind. Sam's life, like Hall's, was snuffed out too early. He was just coming into his own. Would that the handgun had never been invented," the prim woman responded.

"Sam started reading some of Hal's books, as well as his notebooks. We used to read to each other. He said that we're never too old to learn something new. If Sam came across a word he didn't know – he'd look it up. There was a section in one of Hal's notebooks on unusual words. Let me find it. Here it is."

angst – a feeling anxiety or dread about the world.

buffoon – a ridiculous person but amusing person; a clown.

fetish – sexual fixation on objects or parts of the body.

sesquipedalian – anything very long: a word, a snake, a novel.

terebinth – tree of moderate size.

tourbillion – vortex or whirlwind.

pellucid – transmitting light, transparent.

chance-medley – accident or casualty.

bedlam – originally a hospital for the insane.

denouement – unraveling of a plot.

devolve – transfer power to a lower level.

déjà vu – a feeling of having seen something before.

shrew – a scolding woman; a small mouselike animal with long snout.

sepulcher – a place of burial or tomb; an altar.

poodle-faker – a ladies' man; a newly commissioned officer.

deism – God, the creator of the universe, does not intervene in human affairs.

nihilism – rejection of all religious and moral principles; belief that life is without knowledge, meaning, or morality.

serendipity – finding something good or useful by chance.

"Sam got a kick out of these unusual words. Like Hal, he liked to learn new things and he had a good sense of humor."

"It's good to talk about Hal and Sam – keeps them alive in our memory," Mildred replied.

Resuming her reading, Nancy saw an entry about the banker, J. P. Morgan, who was the head of U.S. Steel during the early 1900s. Morgan also helped to create General Electric at that time. During the Panic of 1907, Morgan called his fellow corporate heads to tell them to stop selling their stocks and to cease withdrawing their money from the banks, He also urged President Teddy Roosevelt to regulate the country's banks. As a result, Roosevelt created the Federal Reserve which regulates our banking system and manages monetary policy. To the present day, our bank deposits are guaranteed and kept safe in banks throughout the land.

The entry ends with a warning not to keep your dollars under the mattress—bed bugs chew dollar bills. Nonetheless Tom had withdrew ten thousand dollars in cash—hiding the bundle in floor boards under the refrigerator. He felt the world was headed for hard times when credit cards and checks would not be accepted. Currently, the banks paid less than one percent interest on savings – fulfilling the Jesuits' decree against the levying of interest on loans and savings. Following was a brief entry on the Jesuits. Whether the Jesuits themselves adhered to St. Ignatius of Loyola's urging for self-denial, nonviolence, and humility, was debatable Under Loyola, the Jesuits started out as a quasi-military group in Spain forcing non-Catholics, especially Jews, to convert through coercion. Their modus operandi was the ends justifies the means.

CHAPTER 9

BASEBALL STARS OF YESTERYEAR

THERE WAS AN ENTRY ABOUT HACK WISON, WHO WAS ONLY FIVE FEET SIX inches tall with an 18-inch neck, a large head, and short legs. In 1930, Wilson batted .356, hit 56 homeruns, and knocked in 191 runs. The latter (191 RBIs) is a record which will never be broken. Wilson was called the "sawed off Babe Ruth." In 1925, Hack Wilson hit the longest homerun ever at Ebbets Field and later hit a very long homerun at Wrigley Field – striking the centerfield scoreboard. In a twelve-year career, Wilson batted .307, with 1481 hits and 244 homeruns. In 1948, Wilson was discovered unconscious in his home after a fall. He developed pneumonia and died of internal hemorrhaging at the age of 48. Once the highest paid player in the National League, Hack Wilson died penniless. In contrast to Babe Ruth's funeral where thousands attended, there were only a few hundred at Wilson's funeral. No tombstone existed at his gravesite, until Chicago Cub players chipped in and bought one. A true baseball immortal, Hack Wilson once said: "Talent isn't enough. You need common sense and good advice."

There was material on Jim Eisenreich, who overcame agoraphobia – playing with the Twins, the Royals, the Phillies, the Marlins, and the Dodgers in a 15-year major league career. Eisenreich had 1,160 hits and maintained a career batting average of .290 with 52 homeruns. In 1996, Eisenreich had his best year – hitting .361 for the Phillies. Agoraphobia is the fear of particular places, such as the outdoors and crowded spaces. Often running in families, agoraphobia troubles women more often than men. Some people with agoraphobia cannot leave their homes or become anxious in crowds. It can be caused by traumatic childhood experiences or even by bullying. Agoraphobia can be treated through cognitive therapy in which the patient is gradually exposed to the feared situation.

There was another entry on the October 3rd, 1951 Giant-Dodger playoff game at the Polo Grounds in New York City for the National League pennant. The Dodgers Don Newcombe (20 – 9) went up against the Giants Larry

44

Jansen (23 – 11) in a low-scoring game. In the bottom of the 9th inning, Bobby Thomson came to bat with Don Muellar and Whitey Lockman on base. Dodger Manager Chuck Dressen decided to take Newcombe out of the game. There were two pitchers warming up in the bullpen – Clem Labine and Ralph Branca. The bullpen coach said Labine was bouncing his curveball into the dirt, so Dressen called on Branca to relieve starter Newcombe. Branca's second pitch to Thomson was a high fastball which Thomson pulled down the line – just clearing the short-left field fence 315 feet away. The Giants radio broadcaster Russ Hodges shouted: "The Giants win the pennant! The Giants win the pennant!"

Nancy recalled Hal talking about Bobby Thomson, a Curtis High School alumnus, visiting the St. George school when his dad, Tom Haley, taught in the 1970s. He was on hall duty – patrolling the main entrance – when Thomson walked up to the front door to take part in a reception for the school's alumni. Thomson mentioned the limestone gargoyles that marked the Curtis façade, which had given him pause when he had been a student there. The ex-New York Giant wore a nice beige suit, which contrasted with Tom's chalk-covered Sears suit. He asked Tom if he was the principal. Tom replied that he was just a teacher – physics and general science. Shaking Tom's hand, Bobby Thomson said, "Keep up the good work." Then, a student came up to them and escorted Thomson to the teacher's cafeteria, where the reception was being held. Purportedly, Bobby Thomson once said "the 1951 homerun against the Dodgers was the best thing that ever happened to me."

Sam also liked a story he read in Hal's notebook about a baseball player, named Russ Meyer – known as "the Mad Monk" – who was hot-tempered and combative. He been a pitcher for the Brooklyn Dodgers and the Philadelphia Phillies in the 1950s. Meyer was 17 – 8, 15 – 5, and 11 – 5 during his three best years with the Dodgers. He had a lifetime record of 94 wins and 73 losses, an ERA of 3.99, and 672 strikeouts in a 13-year career. While pitching for the Dodgers, Meyer was thrown out of a game by the umpire for arguing over a called pitch. Inside the dugout, he kept yelling at the umpire and even grabbed his crotch. This was caught by T V cameras – resulting in a flood of phone calls from viewers. As a result, the "Russ Meyer Rule" was adopted forbidding T V cameras from showing dugouts during baseball's Golden Era.

There was also an account on Dusty Rhodes, who was a slow runner, a poor fielder, and a big drinker. But in 1954, everything came together for Rhodes when he batted .341 with 15 homeruns and 50 RBIs – leading the New York Giants to the pennant. Manager Leo Durocher said Rhodes was the greatest pinch hitter he ever saw. Dusty Rhodes boasted that a night of heavy drinking had no effect on his hitting ability. This seemed to be true throughout his career and especially in 1954 at the Polo Grounds, where the right field fence was a mere 296 feet down the line – tailor -made for the left-handed pull hitter. In the World Series, Rhodes hit two homeruns and two triples – leading the Giants to a four-game sweep of the Cleveland Indians. Dusty Rhodes had picked cotton as a youngster and saw combat in the Pacific during the Second World War. Thus, the pressure of coming to bat in a clutch situation did not affect him. When Durocher was about to choose a pinch hitter, Dusty Rhodes already had the bat in his hands.

Another item was devoted to a muscular first baseman named Ted KLuszewski. Kluszewski was a slugger for the Cincinnati Reds during the 1950s with a lifetime batting average of .298 and 279 homeruns. In his eight best years, Kluszewski hit 25, 13, 16, 40, 49, 47, 35, and 15 homeruns in the friendly confines of Crosley Stadium, where center field was just 387 feet away. Kluszewski, who could hit a baseball five hundred feet, wore a sleeveless uniform – revealing his big biceps and shoulders. Opposing pitchers shuddered when the six-foot-two-inch, two-hundred-twenty-pound batter came to the plate. A back injury in 1957 curtailed his major league career, probably preventing Kluszewski from entering the Hall of Fame. Nonetheless, Ted Kluszewski was a formidable power hitter who seldom struck out. After retiring, Kluszewski became a batting coach for the Reds. Pete Rose said, "Klu was a nice man, a gentle man – a prince."

Then, there was an article about Dick Allen, who played for the Phillies and four other teams in a 15-year major league career – hitting 351 homeruns, 1,848 hits, and 1,119 RBIs. In his ten best years, Allen hit 29, 20, 40, 23, 33, 32, 34, 23, 37, and 32 homeruns. Allen was troubled by alcohol and racial issues during the late 1960s and early 1970s. He got along well with his teammates and helped future Hall of Famer Mike Schmidt with his hitting. Willie Mays said Dick Allen hit a ball harder than anyone he'd ever seen. In Connie Mack Stadium, Allen cleared the 65-foot left field grandstand and the 65-foot scoreboard in right field. In Detroit, he hit a ball that traveled an estimated 530 feet. Allen used a very heavy 40 ¾ ounce bat in era dominated by hard-throwing pitchers. He was subjected to catcalls, boos, and racial abuse by Philie fans. In fact, he sometimes wore a batting helmet while playing in the field because of bottles tossed at him. Unfortunately, Dick Allen missed election to the Hall of Fame by one vote.

Another story in Hal's notebook favored by Sam was about Preacher Roe. Like Russ Meyer, he was a 1950s Brooklyn Dodger. Not an overpowering pitcher, Roe developed a spitball to go along with his curveball and slider. The saliva on a baseball interacts with air currents to break erratically – making it hard to hit. Preacher Roe had good control over the spitter, which was not always the case. And he took a lot of time between pitches to annoy batters and keep them off balance. His best years were from 1948 to 1953 when he averaged 15 wins and 6 losses. Preacher Roe pretended to be a country bumpkin, but he was smart. Roe had attended Harding College in Arkansas before entering the major leagues. Preacher Roe had a lifetime record of 127 wins and 84 losses, an ERA of 3.43, and 956 strikeouts in a 11-year major league career. He was called "Preacher" because he liked a local minister who took him on horse-and-buggy rides as a youngster.

There was also material on hard-throwing pitcher, Jack Sanford, who played in the major leagues from 1956 to 1967 – mostly for the San Fransisco Giants. Over his 12-year career, Sandford compiled a 137 – 101 win-loss record with 1,182 strikeouts in 2,049 innings and an ERA of 3.69. Sanford's four best years were 1957, 1959, 1962, and 1963 during which he compiled win-loss records of 19 – 8, 15 – 12, 24 – 7, and 16 – 13. In 1957, Sanford struck out 188 batters – leading the league. In 1962, Jack Sanford won 16 straight games – one short of the major league record. Sanford had labored in the minor leagues for seven seasons before reaching the majors. He was hampered by a lack of control over his pitches and his temper. Coach Larry Jansen helped Sandford with those issues and also taught him to start batters off with a curveball or slider and then come in with his formidable fastball. From that point on, Jack Sandford became a star.

The split-fingered fastball was discussed in the same notebook. Because of its sudden drop as it approached the plate, the split-fingered pitch was often referred to as the dry spitball. With the so-called splitter, the baseball is not wedged as far down as with the forkball. Roger Craig, who pitched for the Dodger and the Mets, plus other teams, was a master of the split-fingered fastball. It is easier on the pitcher's arm than the curveball or slider. He used it to get the batter to hit a ground ball with runners on base – resulting in a double play. Roger Craig pitched twelve years in the majors – attaining a 74 – 98 win-loss record with an ERA of 3.83. After retiring, Craig became a pitching coach. Reds manager, Sparky Anderson, called Roger Craig a man of genius. "He's so optimistic, he could find some good in a tornado."

There was material about a hard-throwing relief pitcher, Ryne Duren, who pitched for the New York Yankees from 1958 to 1961. Duren wore thick glasses and had control problems with his 100 mph fastball. As part of his shtick, Duren first few pitches sailed over Yogi Berra's head while warming up. In a ten-year major league career, Ryne Duren struck out 630 batters in 589 innings with a 3.83 ERA. Duren also threw 38 wild pitches over the course of his major league career. Casey Stengel said if one of Duren's fastballs struck you in the head, "you'd be in the past tense." In 1983, Ryne Duren received the Yankee Family Award for overcoming alcoholism and for his services as an alcohol abuse educator.

There was also an entry about NBA great Wilt Chamberlain, who from 1959 to 1963 compiled per game averages of 37.6, 38.4, 50.4, and 44.8 – exceeding Michael Jordan and LeBron James in their best years. Chamberlain maintained 30.1 ppg and 23.9 rebounds over his 15-year NBA career. There was also material on Robin Roberts, Hall of Fame pitcher for the Phillies, who compiled a 286 – 245 won-loss record, with 2,357 strikeouts in 4,688 innings, and an ERA of 3.41 over a 19-year career. Roberts yielded 505 homeruns – second only to Jamie Moyer who gave up 522 homeruns in a 25-year career. Moyer at 49, was the oldest pitcher to win a game. Knuckleball pitchers Phil and Joe Niekro compiled 318 – 274 and 221 – 204 won – loss records respectively pitching over 24 and 22 seasons respectively.

Robin Roberts and Early Wynn had parallel careers as pitchers, though Roberts pitched in the National League, while Wynn pitched in the American League. Roberts won 286 games in a 19-year career, while Wynn won 300 games in a 23-year career. Roberts won at least 20 games six times, while Wynn was a 20-game winner five times. Roberts struck out 2,357 batters, while Wynn struck out 2,334 batters. However, Roberts was the better control pitcher walking 902 baters, while Wynn walked 1,775 batters. Also, Early Wynn was a more intimidating pitcher – regularly throwing at batters, which Robin Roberts seldom did. Hence, batters were more likely to dig in against Roberts, who gave up 505 homeruns, than with Wynn who yielded 338 homeruns. Once the two pitchers met at a bar. Wynn offered Roberts a cigarette, but Roberts turned him down. Then, Wynn offered to buy Roberts a drink. The Philly hurler again refused Wynn's offer. – saying he didn't drink. "No wonder you don't walk anybody."

There was a list of pitchers who had given up the most homeruns:

James Moyer – 522, Robin Roberts – 505, Fergie Jenkins – 484, Phil Niekro – 482, Don Sutton – 472, Frank Tanana – 448, Bartolo Colon – 439. Warren Spahn – 434, Burt Blyleven – 430, Tim Wakefield – 418, Steve Carlton – 414, Randy Johnson –411, David Wells – 407, Gaylord Perry – 399, Jim Kaat – 395, Tom Seaver – 380. It is noteworthy that Don Drysdale, who had a 209 -166 win-loss record and 2,486 strikeouts, only gave up 280 homeruns in a 14-year career. One reason was Drysdale's willingness to "brush back" hitters who crowded the plate.

In addition, there was a story about the boxer Ruben "Hurricane" Carter, who was a contender for the middleweight title in the 1960s. He had fought Emile Griffith, Harry Scott, Dick Tiger, Jimmy Ellis, and Joey Giardello. There had been a triple murder in a bar in Patterson, New Jersey and Carter, along with a friend John Artis, were picked up by the police. They were interrogated for 17 hours, released, and then re-arrested a few weeks later. Carter and Artis were convicted and given life sentences. A customer, who had been shot, said the shooters were black men. But neither Ruben Carter nor John Artis, had ever been identified as the shooters by witnesses and there was no forensic evidence. Also, the expended bullets did not match the guns allegedly used at the crime scene. In 1985, a federal appeals court set aside the convictions of Carter and Artis under a writ of habeas corpus. Thus, Ruben Carter was released after serving 19 years in prison. The judge said the prosecution had been predicated on racism rather than reason. After being set free, Hurricane Carter moved to Canada where he created an organization to help people unjustly accused of serious crimes.

"I can see why Sam would appreciate that story about the boxer wrongfully accused of a murder simply because he was black," Reverend Staller said.

"Sam was very brave. Would that there were more people in the world like Sam Worthington. A kind man, looking out for his neighbors and protecting us from the Brown Shirts," Mildred remarked.

"In many ways, Hal and Sam were remarkably similar."

"Had they known each other, they might have been good friends," Mildred remarked.

"Actually, they were acquainted. But Sam Worthington left the Island as a teenager and only returned after Hal had died."

Mildred was aware of the circumstances of both men's deaths. Shot down in the streets by thugs bent on revenge. Since the Covid-20 pandemic, the country, indeed the entire world, was under the throes of anarchy. In 2019, he last time data was compiled, gun violence was the third leading cause of death for young people between 20 and 24. And 18% of all deaths in the country was from gunfire. With the absence of police in post Covid-20 America and the widespread availability of firearms, gun deaths of people of all ages had continued to increase.

And with the closing of public libraries and the burning of books by the Brown Shirts, it was easier to get a gun than to obtain a book. Unfortunately, some of the notorious Brown Shirts were still around – even with the absence of their leader, Darren Trupp. Mr. Trupp had attempted a coup d'tat when his term as President was over. In a rare moment of righteous rage, the American people rose up and put the former real estate magnate on a jet plane bound his retreat on the island of Lau in the Fijis. The Fiji Islands are roughly a thousand miles southeast of New Zealand – once known as a good place to reside in case of a nuclear war.

CHAPTER 10

TARGET PRACTICE IN THE WOODS

"I HAVE AN IDEA. I'LL BE RIGHT BACK," NANCY SAID. SHE ENTERED THE house and returned with a handbag.

"I hope that your bag doesn't have what I think it is," Mildred said – looking at the slender woman's large handbag.

"It is, Mildred. Let's go for a walk."

Mildred shrugged her shoulders and followed Nancy. They crossed into Eggert's Field and walked towards Walker Street. Crossing they seldom trafficked road to the small woods behind the flats. The latter were ten attached brown stucco houses which had been erected in the early 20th century. There was a small wooded area with tall grasses, wild flowers, and a meandering stream passing through it. Nature had recaptured this area, which was once used as backyards for the resident of the flats.

With the raging Covid-20 epidemic of 2025-26, rents for the apartments had plummeted to the point they were rent-free. The Section 8 program, in which the federal government-subsidized low-cost apartments for the poor, no longer existed. The supply of housing had exceeded the demand throughout the country. Charge somebody for rent? You might as well charge them for the air they breathe or the water they drink. Even food prices plummeted for a while, but when food inventories declined, that was no longer the case. But with so many abandoned farms and idle land, enterprising folks were starting gardens in their backyards and on their apartment rooftops.

Reaching the small woods, Nancy and Mildred followed a narrow path which led to a clearing about six-foot wide and a hundred feet long. At one end of the path was a bullseye painted on four-foot high by three-foot wide plywood board nailed to a tree. The opposite end had a wider clearing from which the shooter would take aim at the bullseye.

Looking at the slight hollow at the back of the clearing, Mildred excitedly "That's an arroyo."

"A what?"

"It's a dry stream bed. There must have been a stream running through the woods," the prim woman explained.

"You're right. There was a stream back there when I was a kid. It dried up. If you walk through the woods towards Lake Avenue, you'll find a pond that's now like a swamp."

"Since it dried up, you can call it a metaphysical stream," Mildred quipped.

"O K. This is not a metaphysical gun. It's a real gun."

Nancy showed Mildred how to set her feet, hold the gun from her extended arm, at eye level, and aim the gun at the target.

"Hold the gun steady and aim for five or six seconds and then fire."

Mildred did as she was instructed, paused, and then fired. Her first two shots missed the tree but her next two struck the target.

"Excellent, Mildred. You're a natural."

"Your gun – it's rather heavy," the prim woman observed.

"Yeah. That's the thing that surprised me when my dad taught me how to shoot. Guns are heavy. But you get used to it. Do it again."

"I don't want to use up all your bullets. Would that we could dig the bullets out of the tree and reuse them," Mildred said, handing Nancy her gun back.

"Not to worry. They're 22-caliber bullets. Easy to get," Nancy replied reloading the revolver.

The strait-laced woman fired three times. Every bullet hit the target.

"Not too shabby. You're now my deputy," Nancy said, putting the gun in her handbag.

Mildred did something Nancy had never seen. She squealed in delight – giving Nancy a big hug. Crossing Walker Street, they stepped on some rocks in a small stream running through the woods. Suddenly, an alligator slithered towards them.

Quickly, Nancy pulled her gun out and shot the alligator twice – once in the snout and once between its eyes – killing the sizeable reptile instantly.

Mildred gasped as Nancy calmly put the gun back in her shoulder bag. "Wherever you go, carry your gun."

"Was that an alligator or crocodile?" the prim woman asked.

"It was a gator. They're new to this area – thanks to warmer winters. Alligators have a wider snout than crocs. They're brown or gray, while crocs are green."

They walked back to Pulaski Avenue. "I got something for you. Wait her."

Nancy ran into her house and returned with a shopping bag. It contained a 22-caliber revolver and a cloth bag of bullets.

"From now on, carry this gun in your pocketbook. Make sure it's loaded."

"Would that I never have to use it," Mildred said in a subdued voice.

"Would that you're never without it. Maybe we should give the Rev lessons in handling a gun."

"Does carrying a gun mean I'm a vigilante or just being vigilant?" the prim woman asked.

"Good question. Vigilance is just being watchful of possible danger, whereas a vigilante acts to protect his neighbors where there are no cops around to do it."

"I guess people have to learn to be kind to one another," the prim woman replied.

"Hal once said there should be a rule book for conduct – just like the rule book for baseball."

"Stanley would say there is such a book – the Bible. As far as teaching him how to use a gun, he doesn't like guns. Besides, Stanley's nearsighted." Mildred replied with a quick smile,

"He is? I've never seen him wearing glasses."

"Like many men of the pulpit, Stan is rather vain."

"Vanity of vanities, says the Preacher, vanity of vanities! All is vanity. A generation goes, and a generation comes, but the earth remains forever."

"Wow, Nancy I'm impressed."

"I guess I got more out of Sunday school than the nuns realized," Nancy replied, blushing. "Hal liked reading Ecclesiastes."

"Indeed, it's a world-weary view seldom found in the Bible," Mildred remarked.

"For everything there is a season, and a time for every matter under heaven; a time to be born, and a time to die; a time to kill and a time to heal; a time to weep, and a time to laugh, a time to mourn, and a time to dance," Nancy recited.

"Hal liked the story of the Prodigal Son, who returns to his father's house after many years with no contact. Nevertheless, this son is greeted with warmth and gifts, while the dutiful son who stayed to help his father is taken for granted. When the latter objects, the father says that your brother was lost and now he is found. I guess the message is one of redemption and forgiveness of sins."

"Redemption is good. We've certainly had our share of bad times. Would that happier times come our way," Mildred said – hugging the slender young woman.

At that moment, Quinn, the red-haired dwarf approached along with Bubba —walking on all fours. At a signal from the broad-shouldered dwarf, the black bear stood up and started walking on his hind legs. Bubba was a trained circus bear – obedient and docile. The twosome had an apartment in the flats where kids in the attached stucco houses scoured the woods for wild berries, grapes, scallions, and edible greens for Bubba. Children loved Bubba – spending time petting and talking to the bruin, who had a canine's need for human companionship. However, kids were afraid of Quinn, whose short red hair stood straight up when he was mad. When Quinn snapped his fingers, Bubba waved his arms and moved side to side in an awkward dance routine. Quinn took out a banjo and began strumming and singing.

"Baby, let me be your teddy bear
Put a chain around my neck
And lead me anywhere
Oh let me be – oh let him be
Your teddy bear
I just wanna be your teddy bear"

Nancy and Mildred applauded the impromptu song and dance routine. Nancy reached into her handbag and took out a plastic bag. She put some raisins in Bubba's big paw. aplastic bag, which the black bear ate carefully – not dropping a single raisin. Then, he bowed hi large head and clapped his paws.

"Thank you, Ma'am. Food ain't easy to come by. We're heading for the waterfront. Fishermen leave fish heads and half-eaten clam shells that Bubba can snack on Luckily, he's not a fussy eater. Are you Bubba?"

The big bear made a sound half-way between a groan and a grunt, which seemed to be an unenthusiastic affirmative.

At that point, a black car with tinted window pulled up. There were two men inside. The passenger side window was lowered and a heavyset man yelled to them, "We're from the city. Do you have a license for that bear? All animals – dogs, cats, bears – gotta have licenses."

"Says who?" Quinn asked – removing a small club from his backpack.

The husky man got out of the car and pulled out a gun. Instantly, Nancy drew her 22-pistol and shot the gun from the thug. The driver, who was totally bald, started to get out of the car when Bubba rushed over and roared. Thinking better about such a move, he remained sitting.

"Mildred could you kindly pick up the gun?" Nancy pointed her gun at the heavyset man.

"Now, get in the car. And don't show your face around here again!"

With a sheepish smile, the gangster did as he was told. And the car sped away.

"Do you think they'll be back?" Mildred asked.

"Your guess is as good as mine. In the meanwhile, make sure you carry your gun when you leave the house."

Turning to Quinn, "Do you want a gun?"

"I have one in my backpack. I use it as a last resort. Right Bubba? If that gun comes out, I shoot. And I shoot to kill," the red-haired dwarf replied grimly.

"Would that it never happens," the prim woman remarked.

"Would that we lived in a safer world – right Bubba?"

The bear moaned at the slim young woman who stroked him lovingly.

"See you around ladies and thanks for your help" Quinn said – leading the bear down Pulaski Avenue, in the direction of the abandoned railroad tracks at the end of the street.

Passing the apartment house, Quinn nodded at Freddy von Voglio. "Did I hear a gun go off a few minutes ago?" the latter inquired.

"You did. Some crook tried to pinch money from me and Nancy shot the gun out of his hand."

"Ain't none quicker than Annie Oakley," Freddy replied – smiling widely and rubbing his hands vigorously.

Quinn continued to the end of Pulaski Avenue with Bubba. He led the back bear down the steep incline to the rusty railroad tracks. There was a patch of purple elderberries, dandelions, sedge, and other grassy weeds that Bubba liked to eat. Quinn sat down on the tracks and watched his sidekick munch away. Getting sleepy, he used his knapsack as a pillow for his large head, and soon was fell asleep. The black bear nestled next to his master and was deep in slumberland.

The sound of Bubba moaning woke the dwarf up. It was the same two crooks trying to snatch the black bear. There was a rope around Bubba's neck like a noose, which had been pulled tight. One of the men had a gun aimed at the dwarf. It could have been a machine gun for all Quinn cared. Charging the husky man, Quinn bowled him over – knocking the gun lose. At that point, Bubba grabbed the rope tied around his neck, yanked it from his captor, and squeezed the accomplish in a bearhug. Within minutes, Quinn had both men, who were howling fearfully, tied together with the rope.

They walked up the incline to Pulaski Avenue, where the car was parked. With Bubba's help, the dwarf threw them in the trunk and drove the car down Morningstar Road – turning onto Richmond Terrace. The greenish-blue water of the Kill van Kull loomed to the right. Driving onto the debris-filled sand, Quinn headed slowly to where the water was about three-foot deep. With high tide, the car would be inundated and the men would be submerged. As they walked away, Bubba stopped in his tracks and started to moan. The smart circus bear realized the men would drown.

"Alright, you win." Quinn went back, opened the trunk, and loosened the ropes a bit. A few hard tugs and they'll be free. Are you happy now?" the carrot-toped dwarf asked – leaving the trunk open.

Bubba gave a squeal-like sound. But Quinn returned to the car, took a metal cup, filled it with seawater and poured it into the gas tank. The intelligent black bear seemed puzzled by what his master did.

"Cars don't run on seawater. You don't want them running us down in the street."

Bubba replied with moan that seemed to say, "Now I understand."

The odd twosome walked back up Morningstar Road and eventually turned onto Pulaski Avenue. Where Nancy was looking at the merry-go-round.

"We had a run in with those two creeps by the railroad tracks." The dwarf related.

"I hope you didn't kill them."

"No. We left them in the shallow water of the Kull. Bubba had me loosen their ropes and keep the trunk lid open."

"Bubba, you have a good heart," Nancy said, as she went over to the tender-hearted bruin and stroked his head and chest. The latter moaned happily – enjoying the slender woman's caresses.

"So, what's with the merry-go-round?" Quinn asked.

Bubba looked at it curiously – not sure what its purpose was.

"Are either one of you mechanical?" Nancy asked – looking from the dwarf to the bear.

"Very funny. We're in the entertainment business – not the repair business."

Seeming to understand Nancy's question, Bubba walked around the merry-go-round – scrutinizing the apparatus as if he to ascertain the cause of its malfunctioning.

"Just asking. Greg is trying to get parts it. Maybe, someone will pop up who's mechanical," the slender woman said.

At that moment, a tall dark-haired man in his mid-thirties appeared on Pulaski Avenue. Nancy studied his countenance. There was something eerily familiar about his face, his bearing, and even the awkward way he walked. At the same time, church bells from the big Pentecostal church in Mariners Harbor began to toll. Though not particularly religious, Nancy found the tolling comforting in a world where anarchy existed and mayhem broke out frequently. She had read somewhere that Pentecostals were into faith healing and speaking in tongues.

Hal had talked about Amon Dakota, the so-called Mariners Harbor Messiah, who had clairvoyance and healing powers. But there was no mention of Amon ever speaking in tongues. When Hal first met Amon, he was living in an old tugboat anchored in the Kill van Kull. He had rehabilitated a Victorian house in the Harbor as a shelter for alcoholics, drug addicts, and the homeless. But he was criticized by the local press as a do-gooder and trouble maker. Local people opposed his homeless shelter – setting a fire to the place. Then, Amon's efforts on behalf of the Island's down-and-outers were halted when he was killed in a drive-by shooting. After television reports about his community work, there was favorable mention of Amon Dakota's good work in a local newspaper – the Staten Island Advocate.

CHAPTER II

NORTON STAYS AT THE FLATS

FROM THE WAY THE SLENDER WOMAN SCRUTINIZED HIM, NORTON SENSED THIS woman knew him in a mysterious way. "I have a letter from my mom in Bloomington. I'm sort of connected to this place," he said looking around Pulaski Avenue.

Glancing at the letter, which was three pages long, Nancy had an inclination about its contents. "I'm not sure about letting you stay in my house. By the way, my name is Nancy Perez."

"What's your name?" Quinn asked abruptly.

"Norton McCombs. I'm from a farm in Bloomington, South Jersey."

"You look like a farmer or a hillbilly. One or the other. Right Bubba?"

The gentle black bear seemed confused, but moaned affirmatively.

"He looks harmless to me. Norton can stay with us until he gets settled," the red-haired-dwarf decided.

This seemed to please Bubba, who approached Norton tentatively. The latter patted and stroked the bear gently.

"Is he a circus bear?"

"Yes, he is. Bubba is the smartest circus bear ever. Take your bags. Come on with me."

"Wait!" Nancy called out – running into the house. She emerged with a shopping bag.

"Here's some sandwiches, some pears, and a bunch of grapes. Share it amongst yourselves. Make sure Bubba gets a pear and some grapes."

"Share and share alike. Thanks Annie Oakley," Quinn said, taking the food.

Norton followed Bubba and the red-haired dwarf as they walked towards the brown stucco flats. "What rent do they charge around here?"

"Rent? With so many people dying from the virus, there's lots of empty houses. Nobody charges rent," Quinn replied.

As they walked towards the flats, Norton was stunned to see an animal that looked like a llama. "Is that what I think it is?"

"It's a llama all right. It roams around the North Shore. Freddy wanted to kill it, but Nancy said she'd shoot him if laid one hand on it," Quinn replied.

"Where did it come from?"

"Probably escaped from the Staten Island Zoo, which no longer exists. Llamas can live off grass and weeds. And folks around here feed it veggies."

"I think they are related to camels. Except they don't have humps and they're good at climbing mountains," Norton related.

"Don't get him mad. He'll spit in your face. He did it to Freddy when he raised his knife like he was gonna slit the llama's throat."

"O K. I'll remember that," Norton replied – smiling about the knife-wielding octogenarian being spat upon by the llama.

The apartment shared by Quinn and Bubba was in a rough state. The front room where Bubba slept had a bare wooden floor, upon which straw was strewn. There was a small single bed with a soiled quilt and an old pillow where the dwarf slept. In the middle room there was an old couch with broken springs and frayed pillows. The apartment was dusty, dingy, poorly lit, and smelled like a barnyard.

"Pardon the odor. Bubba needs a bath."

The bear moaned his opposition.

"You're getting a bath. Like it or not," Quinn said firmly to the big bear.

"You'll sleep on the couch. Toss your bags over there."

Norton noticed a big cardboard box of mops, push brooms, rug sweepers, floor waxers, feather dusters, pot scrubber, brushes, powdered cleansers, plus containers of bleach and dish detergents. It was surprising, since the apartment needed a thorough cleaning.

Noticing Norton's amazement at the cleaning stuff, "I used to sell that stuff for Fuller Brush – until I noticed they were short changing me. So, I quit and kept their stuff. They came to my door to take it back. I signaled Bubba to go through his wild bear act and they backpedaled from my door. Right Bubba?"

Norton pointed to a small mop on a long pole. "What's that?"

"It's a fan duster. You can also dust ceiling fixtures. You may have noticed, I'm lacking in height."

"We have that in common," Quentin said with a smile.

"Lets eat," he said leading the young man and the bear into the kitchen. Norton was happy to observe that this room was brighter and cleaner than the rest of the apartment.

"Why did you call her Annie Oakley?" Norton asked, looking from Quinn to the bear – the latter of whom who seemed to shrugged his shoulders.

"She's the fastest and best shot on the North Shore. Nancy's a one-man – or shall I say – a one-woman police force."

Quinn set the table, while Norton took out the sandwiches, which were jelly and peanut butter, and fruit. He wasn't especially hungry but felt that he ought to have a sandwich. Quinn snapped his fingers, which was a signal for Bubba to sit on his chair – actually a sturdy bench. Quinn sliced the pear into pieces and cut up a carrot and celery stalk into segments – placing them on a metal tray, which served as the black bear's plate. Immediately, the bear began to gobble up the pear pieces

"Whoa! Where's your manners, Bubba? Slow down!"

Like a naughty child, the bruin stopped eating and gave his master an innocent look that said: "I haven't had a bite to eat all afternoon."

Norton was amazed at Bubba's obedience. "The bear listens to you better than most kids listen to their mom."

"I'm Bubba's mom, dad, and trainer – all rolled up into one person," the dwarf replied grimly.

"How did you acquire him?'

"I found him in the woods in North Jersey in Sussex County. Near the town of Andover – working in a sideshow with some snakes. One of them bit me. I was pissed off and went for a walk in the woods. I ran into this bear cub all alone – crying for its mamma bear. I thought I'd lead it back to the mother, when I stumbled upon the mamma bear and the guy who had shot it through the head. The son of a bitch was carving its heart and liver out with a knife. He turned and saw me and took a step towards me and the baby bear. I whipped out my knife, which was bigger than his. I told him the next step would be his last. He turned back to his butchering and I headed out of the woods with Bubba."

"How long ago was that?"

"About ten years. Bubba is a ten-year old. Just as ornery as any ten-year old."

"He's well-trained and seems to be as gentle as a pup."

"Bubba's smart. He's learns quick. We're a team – me and Bubba against the world," Quinn said, petting the black bear, who moaned in the way a cat purrs when it's content.

They finished breakfast and the red-haired dwarf led Bubba to the small woods behind the flats, where the bear did his business. Then, they walked down Pulaski Avenue where the merry-go-round stood on Eggert's Field – not far from the sidewalk.

Greg was hard at work – repairing the ancient merry-go-round. He had replaced the sparkplugs, tuned up the engine, installed a new gasoline tank, and installed a wooden stool in place of the missing horse. In addition, Greg patched up the floor with plywood. Nancy was there washing the horses and dusting the metal pipes upon which the horses were mounted. As Norton, Quinn, and the bear approached, Nancy stopped her cleaning and looked closely at Norton. Although nothing was said, it was clear to the latter that the slender woman had read Connie Mullin's letter.

"How's it going?" Norton asked.

"It's good. Some of the horses no longer bob up and down. Busted gears I can't find parts for," Greg replied.

"It's just as well. We don't want anyone being tossed from a horse. Do we Bubba?" Nancy remarked.

The bear moaned fearfully – keeping his distance from the merry-go-round,

"It's O K buddy. I'll put you on the stool and we'll go for a ride together."

The black bear stared at the contraption – keeping his distance. When the dwarf tried to get him to step up onto the platform, the bear moaned fearfully – refusing to step onto the carousel.

"Quinn, Bubba's scared out of his wits. Let the poor animal be," Nancy implored the stubborn red-haired dwarf. She glanced at Norton to see how he reacted.

Shrugging his shoulders, Quinn stepped into Eggert's Field where he searched unsuccessfully for some blue berries. Despite his size, Bubba was as timid as a kitten and not nearly as playful.

Nancy stopped her cleaning of the horses and ran inside her house. She returned shortly with a bowl of chopped pears – smothered in syrup.

"I made this dessert specially for you, Bubba," the slender woman said – holding it out for the bruin.

"You're gonna spoil him."

"We all need to be spoiled from time to time."

Nodding, the dwarf watched as his bear slurped up the chopped pears.

Soon, they were joined by Freddy von Voglio and Hank Anker. Freddy, entering his eighties, was the unofficial mayor of Elm Park. He was still a hard-throwing stickball champ and a formidable basketball player – known for his line-drive jump shots and break drives to the basket. Hank worked as a telegraph operator in Port Richmond. He had a terse manner of speaking – seldom using adjectives and adverbs. When he was at a loss for words, Hank used etcetera.

With the unreliability of both electric and telephone lines, the telegraph was the preferred method of communication. Basic services, such as electricity, gas, and telephone had still not been restored on the Island, in the city, and in most parts of the country. Before the Covid-20 pandemic, America had been the world's leader in oil production – followed by Russia, Saudi Arabia, Canada, Iraq, China, United Arab Emirates, Brazil, Kuwait, and Iran. However, it was also the biggest consumer of petroleum products. But solar flares, earthquakes, and the worldwide Covid-20 pandemic had severed oil pipelines and destroyed industrial and governmental infrastructure. Though the world was awash in petroleum, there was little demand for it by the pandemic survivors. An oil company executive suggested mixing petroleum with chocolate syrup so folks could drink it. And allegedly there were scientists in the few surviving laboratories attempting to do exactly that.

Watching the bear and the others, Norton felt an instant liking for Nancy and for the residents of Elm Park. Unlike Bloomington, he quickly felt at home in this neighborhood of odd balls, where acceptance and tolerance went hand in hand. Norton scrambled onto the floor of the merry-go-round when he saw Greg fumbling with a wrench. He held the gasoline engine in place, while Greg bolted it to the floor. He also helped Greg adjust and oil the gears, replace the spark plugs and tune up the six-cylinder engine. Fortunately, the thick belts which actually turned the carousel, were in good shape – requiring only minor adjustments.

Just then, Elm Park's other senior citizen, Billy Bumps, walked along the street towards the group hovering around the merry-go-round.

"Here comes the looney bird to add his two cents," Freddy commented with a wry grin, as his fellow senior citizen approached them.

"Would you listen to that guy," Billy said to his invisible companion.

"You want a ride? It's a double fare for you and your friend," Freddy continued, rubbing his hands.

"That guy's a real comedian. Isn't he? The other day, we saw a big lizard in the woods behind the flats," Billy said to his unseen sidekick.

"It's called an iguana. I've seen him too, but iguanas don't taste so good. So, I let him be," Freddy replied with a grimace.

"Did you hear that?" Billy said to his sidekick. "Freddy will eat the ass of pig – but turns down a lizard,"

After conferring with his invisible comrade, Billy asked: "How about raccoons? There's lots of them messing around garbage cans."

"Nope. Coons are nasty critters and lots of them have rabies. I've seen them going about in bands of two or three. Not to be messed with," Freddy replied with a grimace.

Norton remembered reading that the Whig Party of the 1830s was labeled "the coon party" because of their sympathy to African Americans. How that word had become detached from the raccoon, a distant cousin of the weasel and the bear, was a profound mystery to Norton. Abraham Lincoln was a member of the Whig Party, before forming the Republican Party prior to the Civil War. Later on, the word "coon" was used as an ethnic slur against black people. It seemed that people were quick to dehumanize those they considered inferior. But that behavior was as old as civilization itself. The chatter around him drew Norton out of his thoughts. Observing the friendly banter between the two men, Norton smiled. It was another reason for the newcomer to like this bustling place.

CHAPTER 12

ROASTING A GATOR AND STAR GAZING

At that moment, a sizeable alligator appeared at the edge of the field heading towards the group. It was entangled in some chicken wire Freddy used to partition the garden. Despite cold winters, the presence of alligators and iguanas on Staten Island was a grim indicator of climate change. Freddy took his big hunting knife from its leather sheath and lunged towards the reptile – plunging the knife into the alligator's snout and locking its jaws closed.

"Wow! Did you see that? Nailed the gator quick as a wink," Billy said to his unseen sidekick.

"Is it a gator or a crocodile?" Norton asked.

"It's a gator. Has a wide snout and it's gray—while crocs are green and live in saltwater. You ain't gonna find crocs around here," Fredy replied – grinning and rubbing his hands.

"No crocodile tears hah? Not too shabby, Mister von Voglio," Nancy said – putting away her drawn gun.

"This place is the big leagues. Where I came from, folks don't move very fast. And they don't mess with alligators or iguanas," Norton observed.

"That's why they call it the Big Apple, if you're not quick – the bear eats you," Freddy replied. Then, eyeballing the black bear: "No offense, Bubba."

"Unlike you, Bubba's fussy. I'd take a bite out of you before Bubba would," Quinn said – showing his teeth with a grimace.

Ignoring the red-haired dwarf, Freddy began skinning and carving up the alligator. In a corner of Eggert's Field, was a makeshift oven fashioned from bricks with an iron grating. Near to the oven was a crude wooden table and two benches – built by Freddy at the start of the Covid –20 pandemic a few years back. With practiced efficiency, Freddy butchered the alligator – tossing away the head and the feet, but keeping the tail to be sliced and diced. He also kept the legs and the ribs. Soon, the septuagenarian had a roaring fire going – sizzling the alligator and sending out pleasant fumes.

"Come and get it!" Freddy called out.

He had a large brass bell which he rang – summoning the folks along Pulaski Avenue, as well as those living on Morningstar Road and nearby streets. Altogether, more than thirty-five people, including children, showed up to partake in "alligator-fest.

Soon the entire neighborhood was eating the roasted gator. Nancy and Lucille, Alfred's mom, contributed tomatoes, corn, homemade bread and apple juice to go along with the main dish. Most of the neighborhood joined in the impromptu feast. In a post pandemic world, few people stood on ceremony – responding to any opportunity to celebrate life. Among the participants was Kenny Worthington, a retired TA bus driver and his niece, Wilma, a pretty black teenager. Though Kenny raised her, Nancy recalled that Wilma was actually Sam Worthington's daughter. The twists and turns of fate were uncanny. And Elm Park was a tightknit community where lives were linked by friendship and or family. Acting on impulse, Nancy introduced Wilma to Alfred. It was clear that there was an immediate attraction between the two teenagers.

"Do you know how to play stoop ball?" Alfred asked Wilma, who shook her head.

Going to the sunporch, the youngster took out a Spalding and an old baseball glove. Positioning himself in the middle of the street, Alfred threw the Spalding against the front porch steps and caught the rebound.

"Freddy taught me. He said it helps you to throw and catch better, and it sharpens your reflexes."

After several tosses and catches, Alfred gave Wilma the glove and the Spalding. "Now you give it a try."

The cute teenager threw the ball too high so it bounced off the front door and returned slowly. Then, her next toss hit the edge of a concrete step and sailed over her head. After a few more tosses, she got the hang of it – throwing and catching the Spalding like a seasoned stoop ball veteran. Tiring, she sat down on the front step and talked quietly with Alfred – midst the chirping of crickets. Summer nights were meant for young lovers and for looking at the stars. There are an estimated 1,700 nearby stars in the sky in the Milky Way – for folks to gaze at. In addition, there are roughly 4,000 satellites – most of which are invisible to the naked eye.

Joining them on the front porch, Nancy thought of the night she had first met Hal at the high school dance. Since, they both lived on Pulaski Avenue, they were not strangers – but had never spoken. Walking her home, Hal pointed out the unusual configuration in the nighttime sky above the roof of the brown stucco flats. Five planets and the moon were lined up: Uranus, the moon, Neptune, Jupiter, Saturn, and Venus. Though it was clear night, it was hard to discern those six celestial bodies from the other stars in the sky. Hal said he'd get his telescope and ran back to his house – returning within a couple of minutes with a small handheld telescope. – dusting the lens with his handkerchief.

"Look eastward, towards Morningstar Road."

"Wow, you're right. They're all lined up. Very cool.," she replied – returning the telescope and giving her tall skinny date a big kiss and a hug.

"Wait. I'll be right back."

She returned with her name and phone number inscribed in a heart. "Call me!"

Hal walked and skipped back to his house a few blocks along Pulaski Avenue.

A dozen years later, Nancy joined Alfred and Wilma – thumbing through one of Hal's notebooks. She came to an entry on Valentine's Day and read it out loud. "Saint Valentine lived in the third century A D when the Roman Empire was collapsing. St. Valentine, a priest who ministered to persecuted Christians, was the patron saint of lovers, epileptics, and beekeepers. Maybe that's where the expression – the birds and the bees – came from. He was martyred by Emperor Claudius II for marrying couples to spare husbands from Rome's war with France and England. Valentine's Day is celebrated on February 12th in America and various dates in other countries — in honor of lovers everywhere."

"There's some stuff on Saint Francis of Assisi, who lived a life of poverty during the twelfth century in Italy. He preached to animals and took care of lepers. He believed that like people, animals possessed souls. Animals of all kinds – birds, snakes, rabbits, and wolves followed him in his wanderings through the countryside. After experiencing a vision, Saint Francis was left with stigmata on his body – the image of nails on his hands and feet, plus wounds in his side which seeped blood. Saint Francis is the patron saint of animals and the environment. Here's a quote: Ask the beasts and they will teach you the beauty of this earth."

Next, she happened upon a silly entry on judging things: "You can't judge a book by its cover; an egg by its shell; a car by its paint job; a forest by its trees; a house by its front porch; a baseball team by its uniform; a political party by its slogans; a college by its campus; a city by its skyscrapers; a church by its steeple; a woman by her figure – or can you?"

It was a pleasant night with a crescent moon that afforded a nice view of the stars sparkling in the sky. As people peered at the panoply above, Hank said he was going to get his telescope. Returning from the apartment house around the corner, Hank brought out his telescope, along with a pair of binoculars. Children and teenagers were given the first crack at the telescope and binoculars. Nancy ran into her house to retrieve one of Hal's notebooks devoted to the stars. Even with her sharp eyes, she had trouble reading Hal's notes.

Mildred also ran into her house – returning with a big flashlight. "Would that the batteries are still good," she said – handing the flashlight to Nancy.

"Give us a little prayer, Rev that the flashlight works," Freddy said – backing up the prim woman's request.

"Lord, give those old batteries a few more hours of life. That we may see the stars in the sky. The jewels of your creation," the Reverend Staller intoned – looking reverently at the sky above Pulaski Avenue.

Reading from Hal's notebook, Nancy recited. "The brightest star in the sky is Sirius – better known as the Dog Star," Nancy.

"Why is it called the dog star?" Alfred asked.

Checking Hal's notes, Nancy responded. "Because its part of Canis Major – the Great Dog Constellation. So named by the ancient Greeks since it marked the dog days of summer. Early July though the middle of August when the sun is sizzling."

"I'll take the dog days of summer before the icy days of winter anytime," Freddy said – rubbing his hands.

"Sirius is eight-point-six light years from the Earth."

Flipping to another section, Nancy read out loud. "There are four states of matter: solid, liquid, gas, and plasma."

"What's plasma?" Alfred asked.

"Let's see. Plasma is found in the stars. About 99% of all matter in the universe is in the plasma state. It's atoms with electrical charges – positive and negative. Then, there's dark matter, which we'll get to later," Nancy responded.

"The guy who invented the telescope was Galileo Galilei. He saw craters on the moon with it. He also dropped two rocks from the Leaning Tower and proved everything falls to the ground at the same speed," Alfred continued – impressing Wilma.

"If I'm not mistaken, the moon causes the tides," the Reverend stated.

"Isn't our moon the biggest in the solar system?" Alfred asked.

"Let's see," Nancy said – looking through the notebook. "No, our moon is the fifth largest – after Ganymede, Callisto, and Io which belong to Jupiter and Titan which belongs to Saturn. By the way, Jupiter has 95 moons, Saturn has 146 moons plus seven rings, and Uranus has 30 moons."

"I thought Saturn had three rings," Alfred replied.

"No, the Hubble telescope has observed seven rings around Saturn. And they found thirteen rings around Uranus, five rings around Neptune, and four rings around Jupiter. Saturn's rings are composed of ice, rock, and dirt. They're estimated to be one hundred million years old. The rings of Uranus, Neptune, and Jupiter likely have the same composition. By the way, Uranus and Neptune are gemstone factories that rain diamonds."

"That's where I'm headed – Uranus and Neptune," Freddy said with a rub of his hands.

"How old is the Earth?" Wilma asked.

Checking Hal's notes, Nancy answered. "About Four-point-six billion years old."

Picking up a stone, Wilma said, "It's amazing that a small stone could be that old."

"Getting back to Galileo, he dropped rocks of different weights from the Leaning Tower of Pisa over and over – observing they struck the ground simultaneously. So, he proved that all objects fall at same rate of speed due to gravity – neglecting the effect of air resistance. This happened sometime between 1589 and 1592."

"Isn't that called induction – the basis of all scientific laws?" Alfred asked.

Perusing Hal's notes, Nancy responded. "Yes. It says here that induction itself is a leap of faith that cause and effect are forever linked. And there is a law that says you can't measure the position and velocity of an electron accurately."

"That's Heisenberg's Uncertainty Principle which applies to atoms and subatomic particles," Alfred commented.

"Wow! You're an amazing kid," Freddy exclaimed – smiling widely and rubbing his hands vigorously.

Reading on, Nancy stated: "Einstein didn't like the quantum theory which described an atom's position in terms of probability. He said that God does not play dice with the universe. But in Galileo's time, things were more certain."

"Wasn't Galileo persecuted by the Catholic Church for his discoveries?" Mildred asked.

"Hal mentioned that Galileo was reprimanded and forced to recant his scientific findings by the Church. Four hundred years later, Pope John

Paul II apologized for persecuting Galileo, but the charge of heresy was not overturned."

"Why is the moon reddish during a lunar eclipse?" Nancy asked – enjoying her role as teacher.

"I know," Norton said – raising his hand like a third-grader. "The atmosphere scatters the blue-violet wavelengths allowing the red-orange wavelengths to come through."

"What do wavelengths got to do with it?" Nancy asked.

"Because the color of light depends on its wavelength," Norton responded.

Alfred raised his hand. "I know a way to remember the planets in order: My very excellent mother just served us nachos aplenty. Mercury, Venus Earth, Mars Jupiter, Saturn, Uranus, Neptune, and Pluto."

"Wow! You're an expert on the planets," Norton replied.

"Actually, Pluto is a dwarf plant. Its diameter about 1,470 miles, about one-sixth of the Earth's," Alfred said – checking his own notebook on the planets.

"And here's another thing. The sun reverses its magnetic poles every eleven years. And its radiation affects the planets. The clouds of Neptune have vanished. And it's three billion miles from the sun."

"That's amazing, Alfred. I've always been interested in magnets. Did you know that a compass is a tiny magnet?"

He showed the boy his compass.

"Yeah. And it points towards the Earth's north pole."

"Sometimes when people get excited or argue, my compass goes a little haywire," the boy remarked.

Nancy looked from Norton to Alfred with a nod of approval and proceeded.

"Ganymede, the biggest moon in the solar system, has a very thin atmosphere containing oxygen. It also has an ocean of water beneath its crust. But it's very cold, with temperatures reaching two hundred ninety seven degrees below zero."

"Do any of the planets have magnetic fields?" Norton asked.

Nancy shuffled Hal's notes until she found an answer. "Besides Earth, Mars, Jupiter, and Saturn have strong magnetic fields. And Mercury, the closest planet to the sun, has a weak magnetic field."

"I'm very interested in magnets and magnetic fields. Einstein said gravity and motion can affect time. Maybe magnetic fields can also affect time," Norton related.

"How did Einstein know so much?" Alfred asked.

"He said that he stayed with a problem longer than most people. I guess you can call it curiosity," Norton answered.

"What are you gonna do? Build a time machine?" Freddy asked.

Norton shrugged his shoulders.

"I'm intrigued. Two heads are better than one and three heads are better than two. Maybe Freddy and me can help with your time machine," Nancy responded.

"I'd like to help too," Alfred chimed in.

"Sure. It will be a joint effort," Norton replied – giving high-fives to everyone.

"Hal talked about a time warp – a break in the space-time continuum. He said that clocks started ticking with the big bang that created the universe," Nancy related.

"Look, I'm no scientist. But this stuff about time warps makes as much sense as a clock running backwards," Freddy remarked — smiling and rubbing his hands.

Checking Hal's notes again, Nancy read out loud. "According to Einstein, common sense has to do with everyday experience, but that has no bearing on the way the universe works," Nancy replied.

There was a high-pitched sound emanating from the merry-go-round – like a baby animal. Though spooked, the slender woman ignored it. And the others didn't seem to hear the peculiar sound.

Returning to Hal's notes, Nancy read on. "Galileo Galilei was the world's first great scientist. He studied the pendulum, the basis of early clocks – proving that its period of oscillation depends only on its length. He and a Dutch scientist named Huygens invented the telescope at about the same time. And as I said before, Galileo measured the acceleration of gravity when he dropped those rocks off the Leaning Tower of Pizza. Isaac Newton credited Galileo for his own discoveries in physics – asserting that he his first law of motion was derived from Galileo's concept of inertia."

"Who was this Huygens fellow?" Norton asked.

Nancy turned the page. "Christian Huygens invented the pendulum clock and formulated the wave theory of light, which contrasted with Newton's corpuscular theory of light. Huygens said that wave fronts are composed of circular waves all lined up moving in the same direction."

"Would that waves were easier to grasp. My head is aching," Mildred complained.

"Mine too," Wilma agreed.

"I think I can explain how waves move through a medium. If you throw a rock in a pond, circular waves will move out from the point where the rock hit the water – in bigger and bigger circles," Norton

"Now that makes sense – even to a dummy like me," Freddy said with a rub of his hands and a quick smile.

"You're not a dummy. And neither are we," Billy chimed in – turning to his ever- present sidekick.

"Isaac Newton demonstrated that sunlight can be broken up into the rainbow colors with a triangle-shaped glass – called a prism," Nancy continued.

Conferring with his unseen partner, Billy recited: "ROYGBIV – red, orange, yellow, green, blue, indigo, violet."

"Everybody wait up. I got something to show you," Alfred yelled – running into his house, which was upstairs from where Nancy lived.

He returned with an apparatus consisting of five steel balls suspended from strings of the same length. "It's called Newton's Toy."

He demonstrated how it worked. "If you pull one ball back, it collides with the others and one ball rebounds out. If you pull two balls back, then two balls rebound out from the rest," Alfred explained, as he pulled one, two, or three balls and released them.

"What does Newton's Toy show?" Mildred asked.

"It's like a mirror. If you lift one ball and let it hit the others – one ball will bounce out. If you lift two balls, then two balls will bounce out, Alfred replied.

"It remembers how many balls are lifted. Keeps the same number each time," Freddy said – patting the pockets of his baggy pants.

Conferring with his invisible partner, Billy called out: "Conservation of Energy."

"From my high school days, I recall Kepler's laws of planetary motion. The first law says the planes orbit around the sun not in a circle, but in an ellipse. The second law says the planets move faster when close to the sun and slower when farther away. The third law says the planets closest to the sun have shorter year than those farthest away."

"Would that you talk more about the planets and less about God in your sermons," Mildred suggested.

Getting back to Hal's notes, Nancy continued to read. "The motion of a planet around the sun is called the two-body problem – in which the sun's gravity acts upon the planet. The same principle can be applied to all central force fields – gravitational, electric, or magnetic fields – acting on a single body. The paths of such a single body can be predicted accurately. On the other hand, three-body problems are nonlinear and much more difficult to solve. In the universe, there are many binary star systems, but few trinary star systems."

"It's interesting. Hal rejected the notion of parallel universe. The idea of another version of himself existing in a parallel universe living a different life was absurd. Hal sighted Occam's Razor that it's foolish to do with more what can be done with less. So, there was only one big bang."

"What that Occam's Razor stuff mean?" Billy asked his invisible sidekick.

"If you hear hoofbeats – think horses, not zebras," Nancy responded with a straight face.

Getting back to Hal's notes, Nancy read some more. "The earliest clocks were sun dials, which indicated time from the angle of the sun's rays. There were also sand-filled hour glass, pendulum clocks, and wind-up watches to measure time. The most accurate clocks are atomic clocks. One such clock consists of a hundred thousand strontium atoms that move along a narrow laser beam. Strontium is a soft white-yellowish metal with an atomic number of 38. The device which must be kept at a temperature close to absolute zero. But the strontium atomic clock is extremely accurate – losing or gaining a second in fifteen billion years. In the 1950s, when the U S A and Russia were testing atomic bombs in the atmosphere, there were high levels of radioactive strontium-90 in milk.

"Why does time go slow when you're bored and fast when you're having fun?" Mildred inquired.

"That's probably a subjective phenomenon," the Rev replied

"But, that doesn't mean it's not real. I think time is more subjective than any other dimension," the prim woman responded.

Norton took all this in with amazement. He was astonished by Nancy's lecture and the others' interest in science. It appeared that the doings of his new neighbors were impressive. There were also elements of farce, fiasco, and humor — underlying the seriousness of it all. Yet there was an effort to bring joy to a world filled with deprivation, disease, and death. Everybody did what they could to overcome the bad things occurring in the pandemic. Esprit de corps and a sense of humor were survival skills. One by one, the children, then the teenagers, and finally the adults peered through the telescope or the binoculars, or both if they chose.

Nancy remembered a field trip to the Hayden Planetarium in New York City a long time ago. Sadly, she realized that many of the children and teenagers had never been to a planetarium or even a museum. She had gone there with her high school science class – accompanied by her teachers and a few parents. It was a magical trip that was one of the high points in her young life. Summoning her courage, the slender woman began reading:

"What you see when you look at the stars is the Milky Way, our own galaxy, which has a hundred billion stars. The Milky Way is like a giant plate one hundred thousand light-years in diameter. And most of those stars have planets orbiting around them."

"How many planets where aliens live?" Hank asked.

Looking through Hal's notes, Nancy responded. "There are probably three hundred million planets in the Milky Way which are habitable."

"So how come we never see purple aliens – except in movies?" Freddy asked.

"They're afraid of us. Countries going to war." Billy replied. And after conferring with his invisible partner, "Plus, violence and crime in the streets."

"You got a point there, Billy Boy," Freddy said to his eccentric neighbor.

Wilma called out, "What's a light-year?"

"It's the distance light travels in one year – about six trillion miles," Alfred responded.

"Alfred's right. The distances between stars are so great they use light-years instead of miles," Norton blurted out.

"What are stars made of?" Billy Bumps asked.

Checking Hal's notes, Nancy answered. "Mostly hydrogen and helium, with trace amounts of carbon, oxygen, sulfur, magnesium, iron, nickel, and every other element found on earth."

Returning to Hal's notes, Nancy continued: "Stars begin as a stellar nebula, a big cloud of gas. Gravity contracts the cloud and hydrogen is fused into helium – forming a yellow star — like our sun. Over billions of years, the star becomes a red giant, next a white dwarf, then a neutron star, and finally ends up as a black hole."

"Black holes have strong gravitational field. Nothing can escape a black hole -it draws in other stars, planets, and comets," Alfred chimed in.

"My Uncle Kenny showed me a falling star last month. It was cool," Wilma said.

"It was a meteor. A piece of debris from a comet. Stars can't fall from the sky," Alfred said in a didactic tone.

"Meteors can also come from asteroids breaking up as they enter the Earth's atmosphere," Norton commented.

Getting tired of reading, Nancy handed the notebook over to Norton, who proceeded to read. "Approximately 85% of all matter in the universe is dark matter and about 68% of all energy in the universe is dark energy. Dark matter neither absorbs nor reflects electromagnetic waves. So, it's undetectable.

"I know what EM waves are – radio waves, infrared rays, light, ultraviolet light, gamma rays and x-rays. They all travel at the speed of light," Alfred called out.

Norton continued, "The energy of an EM photon depends on its frequency."

"I know the equation," Alfred said – writing on his notebook and showing it tom everyone: $E = h \times f$

"Wait a minute. How do they know dark matter exists?" Freddy asked.

Searching though Hal's notes, Norton read out loud. "Astronomers predicted the existence of dark matter from the motion of galaxies. Dark matter prevents the galaxies from collapsing inward. Matter cannot always be observed directly, but we can infer its existence from the way it affects nearby matter. And dark energy counteracts gravity – otherwise the entire universe would collapse into a giant ball."

"That's how the universe began. A giant ball of matter exploded. According to the Big Bang Theory," Alfred explained.

"Which was about thirteen point eight billion years ago. Hal once said that in outer space, there's plenty of time and space out there," Nancy interjected.

"Excuse us, but we think you forgot something," Billy said – conferring with his invisible partner. "Where does God fit into this picture?"

"God said – let there be a big bang. And all the stuff that makes the stars went kaboom!" Freddy replied – rubbing his hands and smiling widely.

Reading some more, Norton stated: "Lord Kelvin predicted the existence od dark matter back in 1884. Kelvin's known for the concept of absolute zero, when all molecular motion ceases. He also formulated the three laws of thermodynamics –the most important of which is the second law. It states that when a system does work, there's an increase in entropy or disorder."

"That's wrong. When Blanche does work to clean up the house, all the dirt and disorder is gone," Billy remarked, after conferring with his invisible sidekick

Changing the subject, Nancy started to read Hal's notes on comets. "Comets are made up of rock, dust, ice with a long tail of gas. When they get near the sun, the tail heats up and glows,"

"Halley's Comet returns to the Earth every seventy-five years. The next time we see it will be in two thousand sixty-one," Alfred stated.

"I guess we won't see it," Billy said to his partner.

"Your twin will see it, but not you Billy," Freddy said – smiling widely and rubbing his hands.

"You're no spring chicken yourself. We might surprise you."

"With that woman of yours, you better stay young and spry," Freddy snapped – referring to the femme fatale, Blanche Boulette, who was reportedly as lusty as an alley cat in heat.

"I noticed you limping when you walked down the street, Billy."

"It's just my back. We were weeding my garden," the eccentric man replied.

"I guess when you get tired servicing Blanche – your partner takes over," Freddy replied – enjoying Billy's discomfort.

"Guys, put a lid on it. There are children here," Nancy said.

CHAPTER 13

A HOLDUP THWARTED

GETTING BACK TO HAL'S NOTES, NANCY RESUMED READING. "ENCKE'S Comet wss discovered by Pierre Mechain in 1786. But the comet's orbit wasn't computed until 1819 by Johan Franz Enke – for whom the comet is named. It has low luminosity and is best viewed with a telescope. With a core diameter of just three miles, Enke's Comet is a small comet. It has an elliptical orbit that passes close to Mercury at perihelion and near Jupiter at aphelion. The comet passed close to Earth in July 1997 and will not pass close again until June 2177. Like many comets, Enke's Comet causes meteor showers."

There was a brief entry on the discovery of quartz on an exoplanet, which Nancy read aloud. "This exoplanet is seven times bigger than Jupiter and it's 1,300 light-years from Earth in interstellar space. Quartz, is made from silicon dioxide, the second most abundant mineral on the earth – behind feldspar. Quartz is used to make glass, watches, sand paper, and foundry sand – whatever that is. Silicon dioxide is what you find at the beach – sand. Imagine finding a planet that had summer weather all year long and was one big beach?"

Then, she read aloud material on Voyager I. "Back in 1977, Voyager I was launched from Florida by a Titan-Centaur rocket. Currently, the space probe is about 13.8 billion miles from the sun – in interstellar space. Still, there's enough sunlight to read a book out there. The space probe is powered by plutonium oxide thermoelectric generators. Radio signals from Voyager I take twenty-two hours to reach the Earth. The space probe made flybys of Jupiter, Saturn, and Saturn's biggest moon, Titan. Voyager I has instruments to measure gravitational fields, magnetic fields, and electromagnetic waves. It can also measure the atmosphere and temperature of Jupiter and Saturn, and analyze Saturn's rings. Titan has a thick atmosphere of nitrogen, hydrogen, and methane. Titan has methane clouds, plus rain, rivers, and seas of hydrocarbons like methane and ethane. It's extremely cold – with temps of nearly three hundred degrees below zero. In addition, Voyager I has instruments that measure cosmic rays – high-energy particles from the sun, the stars, and distant galaxies that move at nearly the speed of light. Voyager I is a twelve-foot diameter bowl." Tiring, Nancy put Hal's notebook down.

Looking towards Eggert's Field, they noticed a couple of bats darting about in the sky – eating mosquitoes.

"Bats are one animal I try to stay away from. They carry rabies," Alfred said.

"Something else Hal talked about," Nancy said – resuming her reading. "Bats are mammals which eat as many as three thousand insects every night – mosquitoes, wasps, flies, beetles, crickets, grasshoppers, spiders, and roaches. Bats pollinate bananas, cacao, mangos, figs, dates, and peaches. Less than one percent of all bats carry rabies. You're more likely to get rabies from skunks, racoon, foxes, and coyotes. Did you her that Freddy?"

"Back before this covid stuff, I got rabies shots. So, I'm good," Freddy replied with his usual wide smile.

"What's cacao?" Alfred asked.

"That's the cocoa bean, where chocolate comes from," Nancy replied, thumbing through Hal's notebook. "It grows on a big thirty-foot-tall tree in Mexico and in South America – the Amazon River basin."

"Too bad there aren't cocoa bean trees around here," Alfred said.

Suddenly, there was a large bat flying over Eggert's Field. Freddy started to reach into his pocket of his baggy pants for his 22-caliber pistol, but Nancy grabbed his arm. "Freddy, leave it alone. It's one of those megabats that eat fruit."

"How do you know? Maybe it has rabies."

"No. Hal talked about them. Unlike other bats, megabats don't navigate by means of echolocation. They eat fruit and don't get rabies. Skunks, raccoons, and foxes are more likely to have rabies."

"Alright. It ain't often you see in these parts." Freddy said – admiring the big bat along with the others.

But the presence of the big bat was another sign of global warming The megabat originated in Asia and then spread to Africa. It likely hitched a ride on a ship to the South America, where it gradually migrated to places like Florida and parts north. Hal once said, if you wait long enough – every creature on earth will come to Staten Island. It got darker and things quieted down after Nancy closed her notebook.

The kids got tired of looking through the telescope and headed home. Hank returned the telescope and binoculars to his apartment around the corner. Mildred, Stan, and Norton helped Freddy clean up the grill and dispose of the paper plates and food scraps in a big iron barrel near the trees on the Walker Street side of Eggert's Field. From time to time, Freddy threw some gasoline in the barrel to start a roaring fire. Any food left in the barrel would attract racoons, rats, and other vermin.

Though fearful, Bubba was fascinated by the fire. The red-haired dwarf didn't want the bear to get too close to the flames. "O K, Bubba, lets go for a walk in the woods."

Turning to Norton, "I left the door open. Come around when you're done cleaning up."

Norton nodded, as he stared at the flames beginning to shoot out of the barrel. Looking at the merry-go-round, which was still being worked on, he noticed a baseball wedged under one of the horses. There was also a Spalding in the mouth of one of the horses, He pocketed the baseball and the Spalding. All he needed was a catcher and he could loosen up his arm.

Seeing the tall thirtyish man grab the baseball, Freddy smiles widely. "Remind me tomorrow to get my catcher's mitt. You can pitch to me."

"Sounds good. I guess you don't want to leave any food around," the young man responded.

"Theres enough two-legged vermin around here without attracting the furry our-legged variety," Freddy said to bystanders captivated by the eight-foot-high flames leaping out of the iron barrel.

When the work was done, Nancy motioned to Norton to join her on her front steps. "Did you have a nice time?"

"I did. The food was great and the folks around here are very nice." Norton replied.

"Yeah. It's an interesting mix. Young and old, rude and polite, serious and funny, quarrelsome and cooperative. We got all kinds in Elm Park."

"Have you lived here a long time?" he asked – looking up and down the block.

"Grew up in the flats. This is my world. Welcome to my world."

Suddenly, beat-up yellow car stopped in front of the house. "Who called a cab at this hour?" Nancy exclaimed.

Two men got out of the car aiming guns at them. Nancy recognized them as the two bumblers, who had tried to extort money out of Quinn – claiming Bubba was an unlicensed animal. One of them, husky and menacing, seemed to be calling the shots. The driver, totally bald, appeared to be a reluctant participant in the heist.

Nancy, caught off guard was slow to pull her 22-caliber revolver and one of thugs shot the gun out of her hand. Norton reached into his pocket and threw the Spalding at the man with the menacing bearing, who ducked and smiled. But then Norton threw the baseball harder – catching him in the gut and knocking the wind out of him. Mildred, aiming from her front porch, fired her gun – hitting the other culprit in the thigh. He squealed like a pig and fell on the pavement. By this time, Nancy picked up her gun and aimed it at the thug who was gasping for breath from Norton's hard-thrown baseball.

Together, Norton, Nancy and the Reverend Staller deposited both men in the car, which was an ancient yellow cab. Nancy wanted to shoot out one of its tires. But Norton said it would better to allow them to drive away. Nancy nodded and put her gun away. Mildred collected their guns. "Would that you hooligans never show your faces around here!"

"That's right. We don't tolerate hooligans, hoodlums, or desperados" Nancy yelled – trying to keep a straight face.

"Would thou wert clean enough to spit upon!" Norton exclaimed.

Nancy and Mildred looked at the tall newcomer with amazement. "That's a line from Shakespeare."

"You're as bad as Hal. Using a literary reference to lighten the moment."

"Stan does the same thing – except it's a reference from the Bible," Mildred.

The ex-soapbox preacher recited solemnly – "Matthew 19 – Jesus said unto him: If thou will be perfect, go and sell what thou hast and give it to the poor."

Norton followed with a quote from Karl Marx – "From each according to their ability, to each according to his needs. When you think of it – possessions can be a burden – because everyone wants to steal your stuff."

Nancy and Mildred looked at each other knowingly and at their menfolk with tolerance. "Would that our thoughts were happier," said the prim woman.

"I have a poem by John Dryden about a happy man," Norton said – removing a piece of paper from his wallet.

> "Happy the man and happy he alone,
> He who can call today his own;
> He who, secure within, can say
> Tomorrow do thy worst, for I have lived today,
> But what has been, has been, and I have had my hour."

"Well, I guess that's better. But you know what really bugs me?" The slender woman asked.

79

"Would that you spare us your pet peeves," the prim woman said – fearing that Nancy would blurt out an obscenity.

"When people say – you see what I'm saying. It should be – you hear what I'm saying."

"How about – you feel what I'm saying?" Norton interjected.

Nancy responded by punching Norton in the shoulder – harder than she intended.

Playing along – Norton acted as if the slender woman had injured his shoulder.

"Oh sorry. Sometimes I don't know my own strength."

"I'll be right back."

While she was gone, Mildred turned to the tall congenial man. "I think she likes you."

"Well, she has a funny way of showing it."

"Would that you'll survive."

Nancy returned with some muscle rub which she applied generously to his supposedly damaged shoulder.

Then there was a clanging sound of a large bell coming from a panel truck with a sign painted on each side: Shelly the Sharpener. The driver, a middle-aged woman, pulled a string connected to the bell – ringing it repeatedly. Instantly, folks ran out of their houses with knives, scissors, straight-edged razors, hedge clippers, sickles, grass whips, garden spades, and lawn mower to be sharpened.

The muscular woman worked diligently – sharpening everyone's implements. She took time to ask her customers about their health and the doings of the neighborhood.

"When they told me the Truppers had been routed from the Island, I knew it was you guys – especially that woman," she exclaimed – pointing to Nancy, who smiled modestly.

Freddy helped Shelly – holding the implement in place while she turned the sharpening grinder manually. "Let me know when you get tired. I'll take over," he said with a rub of his hands and a quick smile.

"Freddy, you should know by now. I never get tired. Remember the time I beat you at arm wrestling?"

"I had a bad day," the senior citizen explained to Shelly and the others.

"You want a rematch?"

"Not today, Shelly. I gotta get back in shape."

The sturdy woman smiled. "Any more blades?"

"Wait, I almost forgot." Freddy pulled out his long hunting knife.

"You're lucky I'm not squeamish," she said – wiping off some dried blood with an old cloth and applying his hunting knife to the grinder.

As evening approached, a dwarf, pulling a suitcase on wheels, appeared in Eggert's Field, but he was not accompanied by Bubba. There was a red fox walking by his side.

"Is that Quinn?" Norton asked.

"No, Quinn went back to the flats with Bubba after having some of the barbecued alligator this afternoon. He' a dead-ringer for Quinn – except he's got brown hair."

As the dwarf walked across the field – reaching the sidewalk. Nancy waved to him. "Welcome to the neighborhood."

The dwarf, who was about the same size as Quinn nodded and crossed the street with the fox, who behaved like an ordinary canine – sitting on his haunches and looking from his master to Nancy and Norton for cues.

"Howdy, my name is Quentin and this here is Foxy. Stand up Foxy and dance."

The red fox stood on his hind legs walked a few steps and turned in a circle. Quentin immediately rewarded the fox with a few scraps of met from a paper bag.

"Wow! He's as smart as Bubba."

"Smarter. There ain't nothing smarter than a fox. So, where's my sweet brother hanging out these days?" Quentin responded.

"He's got a place in the flats," Norton responded – pointing towards the attached brown stucco houses.

"I want you to meet Mildred and Reverend Staller. The Rev gives us spiritual support and Mildred provides us with protection," Nancy remarked.

"Protection?"

"She quick and deadly with a gun – like me."

Quentin looked from Mildred to Nancy with a slight smile. "I feel safer already. Females are stronger than males. Right Foxy?"

"Are you hungry?" Nancy asked.

"When you have a fox, you never go hungry – provided you don't mind eating squirrels, rats, mice, and moles. He caught a rabbit this morning. I roasted Br'er Rabbit and we shared it. I ate the carcass and Foxy had the legs. Nice and juicy. Right Foxy?"

"Would that you spare us the gruesome details," Mildred commented.

Quentin smiled. "Sorry. My brother always said I was uncouth."

"Would that your brother was as friendly as you," the prim woman said.

"We're fraternal twins – no more alike than any two brothers. I'm two inches taller than Quinn which pisses him off. Do you want the cotton tail? It'll give you good luck," Quentin replied – offering the rabbit's tail, which was singed.

Mildred declined, but Norton said he'd take it. Nancy gave him a questioning look.

"A rabbit's tail brings good luck."

"You told me you were into science as a kid. Collecting minerals and doing stuff with magnets with magnets," the slim woman remarked.

Nancy remembered Hal composing a list of items bringing bad and good luck. Signs of bad luck were an owl flying overhead, a rooster crowing in the afternoon, two bats flying together, and a raven sitting on electric wires. There were more signs of good luck: a double rainbow, acorns on your windows sill, a turtle in your backyard, a jar of pennies, a rabbit's foot and a horseshoe.

"It can't hurt. Like your wearing that cross on your neck."

"I was gonna let you sleep on the sunporch. Show Quentin where Quinn lives and don't come back tonight," Nancy said – waving goodbye and walking up her front steps. Then she told Norton to wait up, went inside, and returned with a few cans of soup from her kitchen cupboard.

"What happened?" the dwarf asked.

"Sometimes I don't know when to keep my big mouth shut," Norton replied – petting the red fox.

They walked towards the flats where Quinn and Bubba were sitting on his stoop. "Well looked what the cat dragged in! Bubba, say hello to my long-lost brother."

Not sure of what was expected of him, the black bear looked from one brother to the other. Then, he moaned softly

"It looks like you and the vulpes need a place to stay," Quinn said, eying the suitcase. It was clear that the red-haired dwarf was a reluctant host.

"Just for the night. I'm in a pickle."

"Let's see how Bubba and the fox get along."

The fox approached the black bear wagging his bushy tail and cautiously sniffing the big animal, who responded by timidly petting the fox. Unlike the brothers, the animals appeared to accept each other.

"Would that people were as friendly as their four-legged pets," Norton remarked – imitating Mildred Aimsley.

"Unlike the two-legged, four-legged critters aren't looking to take advantage of their siblings," Quinn replied grimly.

"That's fine. Me and Foxy can sleep in the woods behind the flats," Quentin said.

"No. Bubba doesn't mind. Come in. I'll rustle up some grub. You too, Norton. The more the merrier. Right Bubba?"

The black bear moaned affirmatively and the three men walked upstairs, where the irascible red-haired dwarf lived with his mild-mannered bear. Norton brought the canned goods given to him by Nancy – vowing to keep his thoughts about other people's accoutrements to himself.

The three men had a modest supper of homemade pea soup and bread, while the bear, sitting on his sturdy bench, had his usual fare of chopped veggies, sprinkled with mint leaves, blue berries, wild grapes, and a pear from the old tree in Nancy's backyard. Quentin opened up a can of dogfood from his stash, which the fox ate slowly – as befitting the vulpine family.

"See how the fox eats – Bubba? Watch him and learn some manners."

Watching the red fox, the black bear moaned apologetically.

"Ah, he's a good boy," Quentin said – stroking the bear gently.

The two brothers talked of their experiences in circuses and sideshows – giving impromptu shows to earn their keep. Both had traveled as far west as Ohio and up and down the east coast from Maine to Florida.

"There were places that weren't welcoming, so me and Foxy would grab our stuff and vamoose."

"Me too. But if they got nasty with Bubba, I'd respond in kind. You'd be surprised how flashing a big hunting knife cools hotheads down real quick," Quinn said with a grimace.

It was clear that Quinn was the alpha twin, while Quentin was more congenial brother. Yet, Quinn seemed happy to see his brother. "I hope you stick around for a while. We got a lot of catching up to do."

"Sure. The traveling life has given me plenty of adventures, but I get weary of all the coming and going. Some folks welcome you, while others tell you to keep moving," Quentin related – petting the red fox, who was as gentle as the black bear.

"Yup. When folks don't want me around, I leave. But, if they try to push me around, the knife comes out. And if that don't work, I signal Bubba to go into his angry bear act. People back off when Bubba gets aroused."

The two brothers continued to share "war stories" from their itinerant life. Norton listened as they swapped adventures – enjoying their comradery – until he fell asleep on the old couch.

"I don't know about you, but me and Bubba are ready to hit the hay," Quinn said – speaking truly because the straw-covered front room served as the bedroom for himself and the black bear. In a corner was Quinn's bed – literally a child's bed. He went into a closet and took out a spare mattress and blanket that fit the child's bed – carrying it into the middle room.

"You can sleep in the middle room with Foxy – across from Norton," he said to his brother.

"That's perfect. Me and Foxy are grateful for your hospitality," Quentin replied.

"I'm gonna do a show with Bubba at the Moulin Rouge, a rundown nightclub, on Forest Avenue. They're always looking for local talent. Come with me tomorrow. We'll show them what the Miller brothers can do."

CHAPTER 14

THE MOULIN ROUGE

AFTER NORTON TOLD NANCY ABOUT THE PLANNED SHOW AT THE LOCAL nightclub, she was excited to go with him to see Quinn and Quentin perform their acts. She invited Mildred and Reverend Staller to come along with the group. Thanks to Greg's careful maintenance, Nancy's old blue Dodge ran well. Greg had taken over Manny's auto repair shop on Morningstar Road, upon the latter's retirement.

Despite the size of the big six-passenger sedan, Nancy would have to make two trips to the Moulin Rouge, which was a couple of miles away. Since they were performing, she transported Quinn and Bubba and Quentin and Foxy first to the Moulin Rouge. Coming back, she drove Mildred, the Reverend, Norton, and Freddy there. Everybody was dressed up for the occasion: Freddy sported chinos with a bright red collared shirt, Mildred wore a flowery dress, the Rev wore a blue suit with the ministerial white collar, and Norton had on clean blue jeans with a a white collared shirt and a yellow polka-dot tie And Nancy wore a summery pink dress cut just above the knees – revealing her pretty legs and dimpled knees.

They were greeted by Doxie – a hulking androgynous bouncer, with long blonde hair and a deep voice. Freddy, who had seen her in action, bade the big woman a friendly hello, and a wide smile. Over the years, Doxie had expanded her role somewhat, she told some jokes to warm up the audience. She told a couple of jokes in rapid-fire manner.

"A date is a job interview that last all night long. I myself have never been hired. A good place to meet men is at the cleaners. They usually have jobs and bathe. I don't like online dating. I prefer to meet someone through alcohol and poor judgement."

"Doxie, slow down a bit," Freddy called out.

"O K. That's what I love about this job – the remarks from the peanut gallery," Doxie bantered.

"Love your job, but don't expect it to love you back," Freddy called out.

Complying, the big woman proceeded at a slower pace. "What does the sign of an out-of-business brothel say? Beat it. We're closed. Why does it take 100 million sperms to fertilize one egg? Because they won't stop to ask for directions. What's the difference between a genealogist and a gynecologist? A genealogist looks up the family tree and a gynecologist looks up the family bush."

There was some scattered laughter – as if people had forgotten how to relax and laugh at jokes.

Encouraged, Doxie plunged forward. "What does the receptionist at a sperm bank say as clients leave? Thanks for coming. The other day I saw someone fishing in the murky water of the Kill van Kull. He must have been an expert fisherman – a master baiter. A horse walks into a bar and the bartender says why the long face. A hippo walks into a bar and the bartender says take two seats. A job application asked me for three references. I wrote Wikipedia, Google, and the Oxford Dictionary."

This time, there was more laughter. As Nancy returned to the night club. Looking around the place after missing most of Doxie's monologue, Nancy was surprised to see the place was jammed with customers. Apparently, in the post-pandemic world, there was a hunger for escape into the realm of fun and fantasy.

Doxie launched into another joke. "A ventriloquist is telling a dumb blonde joke through his dummy, when a platinum blonde jumps to her feet. What gives you the right to stereotype blondes that way? What does hair color have to do with a person's intelligence? Flustered, the ventriloquist apologizes. The blonde says, you keep out of this. I'm talking to that little jerk on your knee!"

Finishing her routine, Doxie delivered a one-liner. "Anybody who sees a psychiatrist ought to have his head examined."

The joke made Nancy wonder what became of psychiatrists in the post Covid-20 world. And where were dentists and doctors? She wondered if Dr. Emil still lived in the small house in the grassy field under the Bayonne Bridge. Hal had set him up there – wresting him from the Truppers – to administer to the local people. The slender woman was blessed with a strong constitution and good teeth, so she was lucky in that regard. Her mind wandered. Things that folks did in the past for fun – like going to the movies or go to the Staten Island Mall – no longer existed.

Turning to Freddy, she asked "Remember the Saint George theater on Hyatt Street? What happened to it?"

"They renovated the place from top to bottom. They do plays, concerts, puppet shows, magicians, and stuff about voodoo. and astrology," he replied smiling and rubbing his hands.

"Would that folks didn't go for voodoo. It's utter nonsense," Mildred replied.

"Maybe, but people act loony during a full moon," Freddy remarked.

"Voodoo's real. I've seen people taken over by spirits," Quinn interjected.

"What about the Ritz Theater in Port Richmond? Are they into voodoo also?' the slender woman asked.

"The Ritz is a showroom for flooring and tile. It's owned by the Porko family." Quinn said grimly.

"That's a peculiar name," Norton declared.

"Not if you saw them. They all look like Porky the pig," Quinn answered.

Bubba moaned humorously, as if he understood his master's joke.

"Too bad they don't show movies on the Island. Folks need laughs and entertainment," Quentin chimed in.

"There used to be a couple of movie houses open in New Dorp and mid-island," Nancy said, though she doubted they were still showing movies.

The group was given a large table by two young men, the Grey brothers, who knew Nancy, Freddy, and Quinn. Albert and Allen Grey lived on the second floor at the far end of the flats. Everyone ordered beer except Nancy, who asked for club soda. Quinn and Quentin downed their drinks quickly and bid the others goodbye. At a signal from the manager, a tall androgynous woman named Doxie, they headed for the room behind the small stage with Bubba and Foxy.

"What does Moulin Rouge mean?" Norton asked.

"Its French for red mill," Mildred replied.

"Are you French? Norton asked.

"Would that I were. I guess you could say I'm generic American," the prim woman replied.

"Technically, you're Anglo Saxon," the Reverend stated didactically.

"That's bull shit – pardon my French – we're all American. Black, white, yellow, brown, red, or green," Freddy said with a wry smile and quick rub of his hands.

"The problem today, Mister von Voglio is bad manners. But I do appreciate your sentiments. Americans are too color conscious," the prim woman responded.

At that moment, Billy and Blanche walked into the nightclub and Nancy jumped up – giving Blanche a hug and Billy a peck on his cheek.

"How did you know we were here?" Nancy asked – making room for the odd couple – the earthy Blanche, who oozed sensuality, and the eccentric Billy talking to his unseen comrade.

"We heard it through the grapevine that Quinn and Bubba were doing a show here. I figured the Pulaski gang would come to see their act."

"Whenever Bubba performs, it's great. He's the smartest bear in the world. And we're gonna see Quentin and Foxy's routine, which is supposed to be super," Nancy said to the older woman.

Though in her mid -sixties, Blanche Boulette looked dazzling in a tight, low-cut turquoise dress, which displayed her womanly assets. Before meeting the Billy Bumps, Blanche was involved with Jake, the turtle man who was an aficionado of turtles. A Bradford guard working at the Con Ed power plant in Travis, Jake roamed the swampy fields of the power plant – searching for turtles. He collected harmless box turtles as well as their feisty cousins – snapping turtles. He once took a coyote pup, but it was too wild even for Jake, so he returned it to its den. Jake's final moments on earth were spent in the arms of Blanche, Elm Park's red-haired femme fatale. She let it be known that she helped Jake make that fearsome life-death transition in ecstasy. Blanche Boulette was the stuff of urban legends.

Just then Albert and Allen Gray walked over to the table. Albert leaned over and whispered to Nancy, "There's some men in the parking lot who look like trouble."

"Thanks for the heads up," the slender woman replied – checking her gun, which was in her handbag.

Looking across the dimly lit nightclub, Nancy noticed the two men who had twice attempted to commit larceny against her neighbors. The heavyset thug with the menacing look stared at Nancy angrily while his baldheaded companion whispered something to him. The former shrugged his shoulders and looked away – listening to his wiser companion. It reminded Nancy of what Hal had once said about criminals: The most common elements in the universe are hydrogen and stupidity. But Hal also said that people can learn from their mistakes.

"Would that you not stare out those bumblers," Mildred said in an undertone.

"If you forgive other people when they sin against you, your heavenly father will also forgive you," Reverend Staller intoned.

"Yeah. Let bygones begone," Freddy agreed with an unhappy smile.

"I think they're conmen," Billy said to his invisible partner.

"Billy, forget those men Get Doxie's attention and order some champagne for us. In fact, get drinks for everyone – our treat."

"On my tab? She wants us to buy the drinks," he complained to his comrade.

"Yes. You can afford it. Billy is one of those people who cries all the way to the bank," Blanche said, winking at Nancy and Mildred.

"Oh my God. Would you listen to her." But the eccentric side talker, who knew how to stretch a dollar, reluctantly ordered drinks for everyone.

"How did you two start dating?" Nancy asked.

"Well, despite his invisible friend – I liked him. So, I said when can I come over and sit on you and your friend's faces?"

"That 'ill do it every time," Nancy responded.

"Shortly, Doxie – aided by Albert and Allen – brought everyone their drinks. The menfolk, including the Reverend, had beer, while Nancy and Mildred drank ginger ale. Blanche, the bohemian, had white wine.

"Thanks, Billy. I'll get the next round," Norton aid – sipping his beer,

Raising his glass, the Reverend proposed a toast. "Let us drink to the health and well-being of everyone at the table – especially the ladies – Mildred, Nancy, and Blanche.

"Yeah, especially Blanche – the party animal."

Then, Quinn and Bubba, joined by Quentin and Foxy ran onto the small stage and began their act. As Quinn strung his banjo and began singing, he was joined by his twin brother. The black bear waved his arms and did an awkward two-step, while the fox, standing on his hind legs, danced in a circle and howled in rough harmony with the two brothers.

> "As I came trotting over the hill
> I spied a fox and he be sleeping
> A cute little fox and he be hiding
> Hiding from the hare, the badger, and the bear
> Tweet tweet went the birds in the greenwood trees.

At that point, three masked men walked into the nightclub with guns drawn and announced a holdup. Doxie threw a chair at one of the thieves and Billy threw his beer at another. Albert and Allen grabbed a big pot of hot water – attempting to douse the intruders, but missed – making the floor slippery. As Nancy drew her 22-caliber pistol, one of the thugs aimed at her but was tackled by the heavyset man who had tried to shake them down a few weeks earlier. His bald-headed comrade jumped into the fray – tussling with the thug who was nearly blinded by Billy's errant toss of his beer. Everybody was slipping and sliding on the wet floor – the expression "thick as thieves" came to mind. The third masked aimed his gun at Doxie only to have it shot from his hand by Nancy. Norton grabbed his gun as it slid along the floor. Within minutes, the three bandits were disarmed, subdued, and tied up. Taking out his compass, he noticed it pointed south – instead of north.

With the pandemic, the decline population, and the absence of most government services, calling the police was out of the question. Using Nancy's roomy Dodge and Blanche's compact Ford, the three culprits were driven over the Bayonne Bridge to that blue-collar New Jersey town which was now mostly inhabited by unemployed factory workers, lost souls, and ne'er-do-wells. Nancy recalled Hal taking about Chuck Wepner – "The Bayonne Bleeder" – who fought Muhammad Ali in 1975 – lasting 15 rounds and actually knocking Ali down with a blow to the midsection in the 9th round. Like much of the metropolitan area, Bayonne was only a shell of its former vibrant self. If you remove the people from a city or town. it's just a ghost town – remindful of the old wild west. It wasn't just Bayonne. Cities on the east coast from Boston to New York to Atlanta, but cities throughout the country – Detroit, Columbus, Dallas, Indianapolis, Denver, Phoenix, Los Angeles and San Francisco – had lost millions of people.

Returning to the Island, they drove back to the Moulin Rouge where everyone helped to clean up the small nightclub. After sweeping up the broken glass, washing the tables, and mopping the floors, Doxie served drinks free of charge, while Quinn and Quentin renewed their song and dance routine – though Bubba set on the sidelines upset by the gunplay that had occurred earlier. Foxy did his howling and dancing and dancing routine and then joined the black bear – sitting on the floor next to the gentle bruin.

Getting ready to leave, Nancy conferred with Doxie. "I have an extra gun. Come to my house on Pulaski Avenue and I teach you to shoot."

The big androgynous woman hesitated momentarily and then nodded. "The cops ain't around. I guess we gotta be our own cops."

As promised, Doxie showed bright and early at Nancy's door. Norton, sleeping by himself in the sunporch, heard the big woman knocking on the door. "Nancy should be out soon, I heard her stirring about in the house."

Nancy emerged with two cups of coffee – one for Doxie and the other for herself. In response to a questioning look from Norton, she exclaimed: "Go inside and get your own coffee. I'm not your slave."

The two women sat on the steps – sipping coffee. "I have an extra twenty-two, which I'm giving you plus bullets. I'll show you how to aim and shoot."

After finishing her coffee, Nancy went inside and came out with her handbag and a 22-caliber pistol – plus a small box of bullets. We'll load the gun when we get to the clearing. A gun is worthless unless you know how to use it."

Doxie examined the pistol like it was a strange animal ready to bite her. She put the gun and bullets carefully into a canvas bag she had brought for the occasion.

"Let's start before people are up and about. They walked down Pulaski Avenue past the flats, the ten attached brown stucco houses built during the early 20th century. Leading the way, Nancy trekked into the small woods directly behind the flats. As she hoped, no one was around. There was a small clearing – about a hundred feet long – at the end of which was a target painted on a rectangular wooden board nailed to a tree. The board was roughly the size of a basketball backboard. Nancy and Doxie stood at the other end of the clearing and peered at the target.

"Wait a minute. Let me get my glasses," the androgenous woman said reaching into her pants pocket and putting on wireframe glasses.

"You must be nearsighted."

"Yes, I am. But I hate wearing them. They make me look like Grandma Moses"

"Grandma Moses started painting pictures when she was seventy-seven and painted for the next twenty-three years. Her paintings are in galleries all over the country."

"How do you know all that?" Doxie, asked getting

"Hal had material about her in one of his notebooks."

"He put stuff like that in his notebooks?" the big woman inquired

"Yup. Reading them was like an education-in-itself."

Nancy showed Doxie how to load the gun and hold it steady, arm extended at shoulder height. "Now eyeball the target for a couple of second and then pull the trigger. The big woman fired off a shot which struck the tree about three feet above the wooden board.

"Not bad. Try it again."

Doxie fired a second time and struck the board itself six inches about the painted target.

"Do it again."

Doxie's third shot landed in the target's outer circle. The fourth and fifth shots hit the near the center of the target.

"Not too shabby."

Doxie's sixth shot struck the inner circle of the target.

"You're a natural."

Doxie started to reload her gun.

"No. That's enough. Until I get more bullets from Stan the Bakery Man, we don't want to waste them."

"Shit! That was fun," the big woman said smiling.

As the women started heading back they were astounded by the sight of an animal that was definitely not of local origin. It was a long-snouted aardvark, an anteater from sub-Saharan Africa. The nocturnal yellowish-gray animal was actually related to the elephant. In addition to its piglike snout, the anteater had rabbit-like ears and was as big as a well-fed pig. How the exotic creature came to the small woods was anybody's guess. As with the alligators, pythons, coyotes, wolves, and the tapir – the unexpected presence of the ant-and-termite-eating aardvark was another curious reminder of climate change.

Pulling her gun and then putting t it away, Nancy exclaimed. "Now I've seen everything. An aardvark on Staten Island."

"Aren't you afraid it will attack?" Doxie said – moving behind the slender woman.

"We're a bit too much for it to chew on. Aardvarks are anteaters – not meat eaters."

Doxie smiled and Nancy shook her head. "Never a dull moment in Elm Park."

As the two women walked along a path that led them out of the small woods to the backyards of the flats – going around until they were on Pulaski Avenue. Then, they walked up Walker Street and turned onto Morningstar Road and approached Mislicki's Bakery. Years ago, Harry the Horse had erected that sign – an Elm Park landmark. Stan Mislicki, was a man who wore many hats – baker, lawyer, suppler of guns and ammo, plus miscellaneous merchandise, and local historian. The bakery had a storeroom where merchandise was available for free – shoes, boots, coats, scarves, hats, clothes, and blankets, plus housewares like pots, pans, and dishes. Stan had taken over the role of gun supplier after Gerald Hopkins and his assistant, Mason, were transferred to Manhattan where they ran the resistance for the entire metro area. The devastating Covid-20 pandemic had driven the Truppers to the countryside, where critters such as alligators, snakes, coyotes, wolves, raccoons, and tapirs kept them busy – along with the not-so-passive resistance of local people.

Hopkins had come up with the idea of flying an airplane over a Trupper rally in St. George – zapping them with a nonlethal laser. Many of the followers of Darren Trupp wore brown shirts and trousers – a uniform chosen in total ignorant of history. Nancy and Sam liked the plan – readily agreeing to carry it out. Chester Worthington, Sam's 21-year old cousin was a skillful pilot willing to fly his Cessna Skyhawk over the Truppers, while Nancy and Sam zapped them with their laser. Once the plane was directly above the Truppers, the icy-hot laser beams were aimed at the charismatic Darren Trupp and his lieutenants – singing the coiffed hair on their heads. No one enjoys having their heads sizzled from above. The ensuing disorderly rout of the Brown Shirts, led by their peerless leader, erased his political charisma and weakened the bond with his followers. The news of the rout spread like wildfire. Within a matter of days, Damon Trupp's hold over the common man had evaporated.

Terms like the common man or the man on the street are hard to define, since everyone thinks of themselves as above average. Statistically, regression towards the mean implies that a person with a high-test score will regress downwards to a lower score the next time. While a person with a low-test score will progress upwards to a higher score the next time. In other words, both high and low achievers, given enough time, will move towards the population mean. The very term average reminded Nancy of the song Everyday People: "The butcher, the banker, the drummer and then. Makes no difference what group I'm in. I am everyday people, yeah, yeah."

CHAPTER 15

THE CRYSTAL-BALL GAZER

NANCY AND DOXIE ENTERED THE BAKERY WHERE STAN WAS HELPING HIS sisters Anna and Donna with the baking. A familiar face, Wilma, was waiting on customers behind the counter. Smiling at them, Wilma asked, "Do you know what a baker's dozen is?"

"A dozen means twelve whether you're a baker, a butcher, or a candlestick maker," Nancy replied.

"Nope. A baker's dozen is thirteen. You always give the customer an extra donut for free."

"In that case we should order a baker's dozen of donuts," Nancy replied.

"When I was a kid, my mom took me to a place in the city - Horn and Hardart's. They had soup, sandwiches, and deserts like pie or pudding in coin-operated windows. Everything was priced a quarter or less." Doxie related.

"The automat. I remember folks talking about that place. Their motto was you could dine on a dime. We'll never see prices like that again."

To lift the slender woman's mood, Doxie insisted on buying the donuts –jelly, cream, and chocolate before conducting business with Stan. After choosing the donuts, she also bought some chocolate chip and oatmeal cookies, Wilma rang them up on an ancient cash register. Then, Nancy said the magic word –"gator-skater" – causing Stan to removed his white apron, went outside and up the staircase leading to his office.

The office had two big windows, a big desk cover with legal forms, documents, and folders, plus several file cabinets. It was in need of a good dusting and a thorough vacuuming. On the wall behind Stan's desk was his law degree– earned at Brooklyn Law School. In the corner was a big stack of the local newspaper – the Staten Island Advocate. Stan went to steel file cabinet, unlocked it and took out a 22-caliber revolver and a small box of bullets.

"Here you go Doxie. One of these days, I'll take in the show at the Moulin Rouge."

"You're a worse packrat than I am," Nancy remarked – looking at the pile of newspapers.

"Yeah. I used to follow the doings of the Elm Park kids – Tom and Hal, Joey Caprino, Mike Palermo, Buddy Porchinski, and the others in the little leagues. Kids nowadays don't seem to play ball."

"There's no little leagues for them to play in. Harry the Horse's not around anymore, so there's no stickball on the street," Nancy replied – thinking about Hal's love of fastpitch stickball.

"Harry was a kid at heart and the best carpenter in Elm Park," the middle-aged lawyer said – looking out the window towards the entrance of the Bayonne Bridge, which was nearly traffic free – despite the midday hour.

"Who was that fellow they called the turtle man? He used to go to the Moulin Rouge with that redhead, Blanche" Doxie inquired.

"That was Jake. He collected turtles – including snapping turtles. When he died, Hal took a box turtle, which I still have. Fortunately, Boxie gets along with my cat, Torte."

"Didn't Jake work at the Con Ed plant?" Stan asked.

"Yeah. Hal moonlighted there – helping him catch the turtles. Once they caught a big mean snapper put him in a cage. One of the bosses from the plant got wind of it. So, they had to let it go."

"That must have been fun," Stan said – smiling.

"Hal said releasing a snapper is almost as hard as catching it. Snapping turtles don't like being messed with at all."

They heard someone moving around in the next office.

"That's Lora. Let me introduce you to her," Stan said – knocking on the door before entering.

"I was wondering when you'd come in," a pretty long-haired woman in her early thirties, called out.

Lora was working on a copper bracelet. The small room was lined with shelves –laden with copper trinkets of every description – earrings, bracelets, anklets, necklaces, brooches, hearts, badges, platters, and plaques. In addition to her metallurgy. Lora had a growing reputation as a clairvoyant. In troubled times, people wanted to know what would befall them. To her credit, the long-haired woman urged clients to take her crystal-ball predictions with a grain of salt.

Stan introduced the young woman to Nancy and Doxie. "I know who you are. Your husband, was Mr. Haley, my science teacher at Curtis High School," she responded.

Hal had told Nancy about Lora Langley, a legend at Curtis. She used to walk down the long hallways of the St. George school – jingle-jangling her copper bracelets, anklets and necklace merrily Lora firmly believed that the copper trinkets enhanced her health, lifted her mood, and warded off evil spirits. Hal sort of agreed – reminding everyone that the roof of Curtis High School and the Statue of Liberty were made of copper – eroded by moisture into a greenish compound called verdigris.

Recalling that Hal had been killed on the street by thugs a few years back, Lora gave Nancy a hug. "I'm so sorry about what happened to Mr. Haley. He was a great teacher – setting off matchhead rockets and blowing up stuff in the classroom."

Nancy nodded. She almost mentioned that she had also lost another special person, Sam. Instead, she simply paused, closed her eyes, and took a deep breath. The death of a loved one never stops hurting. In her case, it had happened twice.

"Come back in a few days. I'll have something for you," the pretty brunette said.

As they walked down the stairs, Stan asked: "What do you think of Lora?"

"She's a lovely young woman," Doxie replied.

"We're getting married in the summer. I guess you could call it a May-December romance," the middle-aged lawyer said, somewhat embarrassed.

"Love has nothing to do with age. Just hold on to each other," Nancy said quietly.

Out in the street she continued the conversation in a whisper, "And pray that they're not taken away by trigger happy thugs."

"What did you say?" Doxie asked.

"Nothing. I was just thinking out loud."

A few days later, Nancy walked up the staircase next to Mislicki's Baker—entering Lora's workroom. Expecting Nancy, she smiled and her got up from her workbench and went to a shelf, where she took down a copper-chain necklace with two heart-shaped pendants hanging from it. One was inscribed with the name "Hal" and the other said "Sam."

"How did you know about Sam?" Nancy asked – choking back tears. She removed her cross from its string and placed it in between the two copper pendants.

"Everybody in Elm Park knew Sam. He was Elm Park's guardian," the long-haired young woman replied. She put the copper necklace around Nancy's neck, stood back, and pointed to a mirror for the slender woman to see herself.

"Wow! It's gorgeous. Where did you learn how to make copper jewelry?"

"My mom made costume jewelry. Gold and silver were too expensive, so she worked with copper. She believed that copper protects you from germs – you know viruses. I've never come down with Covid-19 or Covid-20. So, there you are."

"How does it do that?" Nancy asked—noticing a crystal ball on one of the shelves.

"I'm not sure. Copper releases copper ions on its surface that can kill microbes. Mr. Haley used to talk about ions – they're atoms with electric charges."

At the mention of Hal, Nancy gasped.

"Oh, I'm sorry. But sometimes I feel his presence." She went to a shelf and took down the big crystal ball.

"Do you want to look at it with me?"

Nancy shivered, but she nodded.

"There are three images that you see in a crystal ball – fire, bubbles, and clouds. Fire represents danger. Bubbles indicates new people in your life. And clouds mean peace and happiness. Give me the name of a person in your life."

Nancy blurted out Hal. The crystal ball became cloudy. "It appears that Hal is in a better place and he's happy."

When Nancy said Sam's name, the crystal again became cloudy. "Sam's also in a good place and he's happy."

"How about Darren Trupp?"

Lora peered into the crystal ball, which darkened at first and then glowed with flames.

"Mister Trupp is dangerous!"

Nancy recalled Hal saying Trupp's popularity illustrated the difference between humans and animals. Animals would ever allow the dumbest one lead the pack.

"But Darren Trupp is on an island in the Pacific Ocean," Nancy said – talking directly to the crystal ball.

"Let's hope he stays there. But I'm not so sure about that. Trupp wants to return to the States. Anyway, I see a stranger who walks with a limp," Lora said – shaking her head.

"Norton? But he doesn't have a limp," Nancy responded, somewhat puzzled.

This time, the crustal ball filled with bubbles – followed by clouds.

"The new guy in the neighborhood is a good thing. And a strange-looking animal and a big bat flying around that field, I see another field with lots of bats," Lora said – starting to put the crystal ball back away.

"Wait. I see other things here, but it's blurry. It looks like a merry-go-round and a big clock. You're on the merry-go-round with the stranger. And then you're on the merry-go-round alone. The clock hands are moving backwards and then forwards. And there's a bunch of magnets. It's kind of weird. Now the picture is fading," the pretty clairvoyant said – putting the crystal ball back on the shelf.

"Norton is very interested in magnets. Why, I'm not quite sure. Anyway, I guess we're done," Nancy said – standing up and giving Lora a hug.

"Yeah. I'm exhausted. Crytal ball gazing kind of wears you out." But then the ball glowed with a faint orange color, "Hold up – that's unusual – I don't see colors very often," the long-haired woman said.

"Kind of weird, but thanks. I appreciate everything you've done for me," Nancy said – opening her purse.

"Don't be silly. You're the heart and soul of Elm Park. Just stay safe and be happy," Lora said – giving Nancy a parting hug.

The next day, Nancy saw Norton walking around Eggert's Field near Walker Street, where a stream ran through a wooded area. They happened upon some eggs that weren't the eggs of a duck.

"Freddy just shot an alligator. He's cutting it up and roasting it."

"No thanks," the slender woman replied.

"I'd like to move the eggs to the small woods behind the flats, where they'd be safe. By the way that's a nice necklace," the tall man said.

Nancy nodded, but didn't go into any explanations. "Good idea – let's move them. Knowing Freddy, he'll come back tomorrow and fry those eggs for breakfast."

Nancy went home and returned with a shoe box. They trudged to the small woods and carefully put the hard-shelled alligator eggs in the box.

"I know where to bring them. They walked to the end of Pulaski Avenue, past a broken fence and down a shallow gorge. It was overrun with tall grasses, bushes, gingko trees, and even some wild flowers intruding on the railroad tracks – defunct for more than 75 years. Way back in the 1940s, the Staten Island Railroad had a branch that ran along the North Shore. Nancy and Norton placed the alligator eggs in a small hollow in the dense foliage.

"What if a raccoon or possum eats them?" Norton asked.

"That's Mother Nature, which is God's will. But Davy Crockett will never starve," Nancy replied with a quick smile.

"You mean Freddy?"

"Who else. I've seen him eat gators, snakes, frogs, rats, and fried grasshoppers. The guy has no boundaries when it comes to food."

As they headed back up the incline, they heard rustling in the grass. A tiny orange-striped kitten was following them.

Nancy went "Psst."

But the cat was leery. Norton reached into his pocket, took out tinfoil with cheddar cheese and tossed the feral kitten a few pieces. It gobbled up the cheese. "That's one hungry pussy," he quipped – to which Nancy snorted.

Norton tossed so more cheese, which the cat quickly ate and then walked around Norton's and then Nancy's ankles – rubbing against them and meowing.

"It looks like you made a new friend. See if you can pick it up. I'd say it's about six weeks old."

Norton picked up the kitten and they walked up the hill onto Pulaski Avenue. "It's a male. I think we should call him Tiger."

"Then Tiger it is. But you're responsible for feeding him and taking care of his cat box. In the sunporch – where you're staying tonight," she replied, which made Norton smile.

Passing Kenny Worthington's house, Nancy said they should ask him if the kitten was his.

Kenny indicated the kitten was not his cat. "Nope, it's one of those feral cats by the railroad tracks. If I wasn't allergic, I'd take one of them in."

"Uncle Kenny's allergic to everything," Wilma said angrily.

"As long as I'm not allergic to teenagers, you're O K," the retired bus driver replied.

"Whatever."

"Listen. You can come over and visit with Tiger whenever you want. And see Torte, my big tortoiseshell cat, also," Nancy offered.

This seemed to please the cute teenager, so they left with Wilma somewhat consoled.

There was a ramshackle house next door where a tall elderly man stood in the doorway, who was vaguely familiar to Nancy. He waved to Nancy who stopped to talk to him.

"How are you, Charlie?"

"No complaints."

"How are you doing with food?"

"Not bad. I grow a lot of my own eats. And I trap raccoons, squirrels, foxes, and other critters from the woods."

She introduced Norton to the man. "This is Charley Krepinski, retired detective. One of the best baseball players in Elm Park," Nancy related.

"I was a southpaw. Played pitched semipro baseball – going up against Joey Caprino, the knuckleball guy. Then, I hurt my shoulder and my pitching days were over."

"The same thing happened to me. I guess there's only so many fastballs you can throw – without something tearing," Norton replied.

"Hal used to talk about Charlie's great arm and strong hands. He once hit a Spalding beyond the little graveyard across from P S 21."

"I was stupid. Should have developed a curveball. But, with all the crap going on around here – it doesn't matter."

"Charlie, stop by my house and I'll give you some can goods."

Charlie thanked the slender woman and shook Norton's hand – leaving the latter wringing his hand. She had heard that Charlie was not one of those detectives who believed everyone was guilty – just because the cops said so.

"Sorry. That's the one thing I never lost – a strong grip."

Walking back along Pulaski Avenue, they noticed an animal rooting about in Eggert's Field near the clump of trees bordering on Walker Street. It seemed that the vacant lots and fields of the area were slowly being taken over by strange flora and fauna.

"Is that a wolf?" Nancy asked – checking her shoulder bag for her gun

Norton, focusing on the kitten, wasn't sure, but quickened his steps back towards her house. Pausing momentarily, he scrutinized the animal, which was gray with a white underbelly. It made strange yip and yap sounds. "That's a coyote. There were lots of them in South Jersey. They eat rabbits and deer, and will attack dogs. Usually they hunt in packs, but that guy looks like a lone wolf."

"You mean lone coyote," Nancy replied. A deadly accurate shooter, she wasn't that concerned about the animal.

"Even when raised as a pup, coyotes are hard to domesticate. They're less trustworthy than dogs."

"Hal worked with a Bradford guard at the Con Ed plant, Jake, who was into exotic pets – snakes, turtles, and coyotes. He kept a big snapping turtle in a wire cage in the guardhouse. One of the Bradford bigshots got wind of it and made Jake release it back into the swamps. Then, he tried to domesticate a coyote pup, but it was too wild. So, he had to return it to its den near the plant.," she related.

"Coyotes are great tunnel builders. Coyote dens can be connected to tunnels forty or fifty feet long. They can have from two to six pups in a litter. Coyotes are aggressive and territorial, and often have rabies – so I wouldn't advise having a coyote as a pet."

"I didn't know you were an expert on coyotes. You have a Ph.D.in coyotes. No, I 'll stick to cats for pets. I'm not crazy about dogs – no fan of walking dogs especially in the winter."

"Me too. I'm a cat person."

"As was Hal," Nancy replied – looking at him with a smile.

Later, Norton was sent into Nancy's dungeon-like cellar to retrieve a cat box, which he filled with litter. She also gave him two plastic bowls – one for wet cat food and one for water.

"When Tiger's six weeks old, you can supplement his diet with dry cat food."

"So, a three-week old kitten is like an infant?"

"Tiger won't be a teenager until he's six months."

Nancy went inside and returned shortly with a photo of her as a little girl – holding a cat."

Norton studied the photo of Nancy in pigtails with a cat cradled in her arms. "You were a very pretty girl – still are."

The slender woman was about to punch him in the shoulder, but blushed instead. "Typical guy – throwing complements around like tossing rocks into the ocean."

"There was a quote by John Updike – ever heard of him?"

"Sure. Me and Hal read Rabbit Redux together. I think it was set in the 1960s."

"Anyway, Updike said a photograph offers us a glimpse of the abyss of time." Norton recited.

"Sometimes I feel that time is an abyss. A deep bottomless pit that sooner or later we'll fall into and never be seen again," she replied grimly.

CHAPTER 16

PUTTING MAGNETS ON THE MERRY-GO-ROUND

ALFRED KNOCKED ON NANCY'S DOOR, "I FOUND A BUNCH OF HORSESHOE magnets in a box behind that closed deli on Morningstar Road."

"Karisi's. It's been closed for years. I want to put them in the merry-go-round. Can Norton help me?"

Nancy knocked on the door to the sunporch. "Alfred wants you to help him place some magnets in the merry-go-round."

"Sure, I'll be right out."

He emerged from the sunporch, carrying his sneakers which he quickly put on and laced up. Within minutes, Alfred and Norton distributed the horseshoe magnets along the floor of the merry-go-round – with Nancy supervising their placement. She believed that the magnets should be evenly distributed around the circular floor of the carnival ride. Norton and Alfred concurred. With the job done, they happily retired to their respective apartments in the flat-roofed yellow stucco house.

Before going into the house, Nancy looked at the merry-go-round across the street. It appeared to be glowing – though the lights were not working.

"Norton, come outside for a second and look at the merry-go-round," she called out, which the latter did.

"Now that's weird. The whirligig has a life of its own," he said – blinking and starring.

"It's weird. The magnets have something to do with it," the slender woman replied.

"I've always felt that magnets have power beyond their connection to electricity. I think magnets have an effect on time.—like gravity. Einstein predicted that a strong gravitational field can slow down time. How to demonstrate the effect of magnetic fields on time is the big question."

"Maybe you're on to something. But don't let it go to your head," Nancy responded with a smile and light rap to his shoulder.

On a mild April morning, Norton was awakened in his sunporch bedroom by the thudding sound of a rubber ball bouncing off the front porch steps of a neighbor's house. A heavyset man, not much younger than Freddy von Voglio, was throwing a Spalding against the steps and catching the carom. It was Joey Caprino, former semipro pitcher and retired stockbroker playing stoop ball. As a youngster, Joey had spent hours throwing and catching high bouncing Spalding, which helped to sharpen his reflexes. Never a hard thrower, Joey developed a knuckleball and pitched in a semipro league on weekends. During the week, he worked on Wall Street as a stockbroker, until the Covid-20 pandemic caused the stock market to crash. Like many former Elm Park residents, Joey had recently returned to his hometown – living humbly and prudently – recalling the halcyon days of his boyhood.

Norton was awakened by the sound of a baseball pounding into someone's catcher's mitt. Peeking through the sunporch blinds, Norton saw a husky man in his early forties wing up and throw a pitch at Freddy von Voglio – dressed in catcher's gear mask, chest protector – crouching and extending an old catcher's mitt. A pitch thrown by the burly pitcher seemed to flutter a bit. Though Freddy got his mitt on it, the baseball bounced off his chest protector.

"Make a fist before you throw that damned knuckleball," Freddy yelled.

Granny Schmidt, who had been watching the game of catch from her bedroom window, called out. "What's matter, you baldheaded bastard? Don't you know how to catch the ball?"

Freddy, who despite his age, had most of his salt-and-pepper colored hair—except for a bald spot at the top of his head – yelled back. "I have more hair than you Granny and I'm sober."

Granny responded by tossing an empty beer can out her window, which Freddy caught. "Why didn't you throw me a can that has some beer in it?"

"Buy your own beer, cheap skate," she called out before giving him the finger and slamming the window shut.

Norton enjoyed the exchange between Elm Park's oldest residents, which had more humor than rancor. Another plus for Elm Park in his opinion.

Norton, watched as Joey threw a variety of fast balls, curves and his dancing knuckleball. After twenty minutes are so Freddy, no youngster began to tire.

"Norton have you after caught a knuckleball?"

"I've pitched and even caught in a pinch. I'll give it a shot," Norton said.

After donning the chest pads and mask, Norton crouched in readiness as Joey wound up and delivered. Norton was somewhat more agile than Freddy, who was no youngster – managing to hold on to Joey Caprino's fluttering knuckleball. The game of pitch and catch went on for another twenty minutes with no mishaps. At last, Joey held up his hand, this is the last knuckler which Norton caught cleanly.

"You know a curve bends because of Bernoulli's Principle – the spinning makes the air move faster and drops the air pressure. So, the baseball moves left for counterclockwise spin – the curveball. And it moves right for clockwise spin – the screwball. The faster the spin, the greater the movement or break."

"I guess if I pitched on the moon, where there's no air – I wouldn't have a curveball. That's why I never pitched on the moon," Joey remarked.

At this point, Nancy emerged from the house – calling out: "Is Norton any good?"

"Not too shabby for a South Jersey guy," Joey yelled back. "He explained how a curveball works. But I throw the knuckleball. It's easier on your arm – no strain on your elbow" Joey called back.

"I'm glad he's useful for something," she replied in a deadpan manner.

"She's one tough lady," Freddy said – smiling widely and rubbing his hands vigorously.

"Bernoulli's Principle is the reason airplanes fly. The air moves faster over top of wing than the bottom," Norton explained.

"I'm afraid to ask why," Freddy said with a wry smile.

"Because the top of the wing is curved – makes the air move faster. The difference in air pressure above and below the wing creates lift."

"That's why I never liked to fly. Suppose you wake up one day and the laws of science don't work anymore?" Freddy replied – smiling and rubbing his hands.

Opening her window again, Granny Schmidt yelled, "The young guy's better and smarter than you, Baldy." The dowager yelled slammed her window shut for the second time. Norton sensed that their exchanges were enjoyable to both participants – allowing them to vent pent up frustrations that life piles unto folks in all walks of life.

Just then, Lora walked down Pulaski Avenue and stopped at Nancy's house and knocked on her door. Nancy, who had just walked down her long hallway, hastened back to the front door.

Happy to see the pretty long-haired woman again so soon, Nancy embraced her. "I was thinking about you. I had a dream you brought me something."

"Indeed, I've brought you this big magnet. You mentioned that Norton is doing something with magnets. I found it behind the bakery hidden in some tall weeds. Something drew me towards it."

Nancy invited Lora in for coffee and toast, which Lora accepted. Lora regaled Nancy with her experiences at Curtis High School – walking through its long dark hallways.

"They were kind of scary, so I'd shake my copper bracelets and anklets, and hold my copper necklace to give me courage. Something I've done in my life whenever I was nervous or scared."

"Hal always spoke fondly of the girl with jingling copper bracelets."

"He was a great teacher. The kids, myself included, would get into hassles. But he always found a way to keep the pot from boiling over."

"I wish he was here."

"He is sitting in that chair right across from," Lora replied – pointing to the empty chair by the kitchen window.

As Nancy looked at the chair, the curtains moved slightly – though the window was closed. "Hal, I miss you so much."

"I see his eyes fill with tears. But now he's fading. Apparitions are very fleeting."

Neither woman spoke and both had lost interest in their coffee and toast.

"Let's go outside and see what the neighbors are up to," Nancy said – to which Lora readily agreed. Nancy never ventured outside without her 22-caliber pistol safely stored in her shoulder bag.

They crossed the street, where Norton, Freddy, and Joey were engaged in a three-way catch. Lora brought the big horseshoe magnet, which she placed on the floor of the merry-go-round. There was a momentary humming sound, which gave pause to both women, but they shrugged and said nothing. Then, they took a walk through Eggert's Field – looking at Freddy's vegetable garden and the wild flowers. The megabat appeared in the sky and swooped a few feet above them – causing the two women to duck. But then, the big bat flew above the tree tops making several passes – before landing in a tree on the edge of the field.

Walking towards Wolstein's factory, which had been closed for decades, they crossed Granite Avenue. Back in the 1950s, Wolstein's made Bosco chocolate syrup, Yoo-Hoo chocolate flavored drink, Mars bars, plus food additives. The two women were surprised to notice that the chain-link fence had been repaired and there was a new gate at the factory's entrance. Once a symbol of the country's industrial demise, the factory had been idle for years.

With the huge demographic decline brought on by the Covid-20 pandemic, America's industrial base had collapsed. For the most part, the U S A produced nothing in the way of food or factory goods. In effect, people were living off past savings – in terms of canned food and manufactured products. But now the humming of machinery could be heard. And there was a newly painted sign which said: Wolstein's Fish Company. Taking advantage of clean estuaries, fisherman were again taking fish from New York Bay and the Kill van Kull: Striped Bass, Flounder, Perch, Bluefish, Bowfin and Walleye The adjacent parking was filled with cars, panel trucks, a trailer truck and a TA bus.

"I told you things were getting better," Lora said.

"You're definitely a soothsayer. But I don't know if I'd eat fish from the Kull."

"Stan told me that factories were beginning to open up and the Con Ed power plant would be online soon," Lora replied.

"I guess a smart person like Stan beats a crystal ball any day of the week," Nancy said with a smile.

"Hey, most of the time I'm on target with my predictions. But, not all the time."

As they walked back across Eggert's Field, the two women were confronted by a strange looking creature that looked like a cross between a pig and a rhino. It was a large animal with a snout and protruding teeth.

"What is it?" Lora asked.

"I think it's a tapir. Hal told me about them. Like gators, pythons, kingsnakes, iguanas, coyotes, llamas, and megabats – it's not native to the Island," Nancy said in an undertone, as she took her gun out of her shoulder bag and aimed.

The animal sensed danger – pausing for a moment before charging the slender woman. Firing twice, Nancy put two bullets into the tapir's head. The big animal took another few steps, squealed, and then dropped right in front of her.

"Wow! You must have ice water in your veins." Lora exclaimed.

"Hold on to me. I'm about to pass out," Nancy said – leaning on the long-haired woman. Reaching Pulaski Avenue and crossing the street, Lora supported Nancy until they reached the front porch of her house where the latter plopped down. Norton emerged from the house and quickly returned with a glass of water, which Nancy sipped and gradually regained her equilibrium.

"What happened?" he asked.

"She just shot and killed a tapir. It was very scary."

"Don't walk into that field without a gun. This area's like the Amazon jungle."

"I always carry a baseball and some rocks in my pocket," Norton replied confidently.

"Now you listen to me. Bring the twenty-two I gave you."

Norton nodded. Sitting down next to the slender woman, he gave her a hug. They sat holding each other for a while – each lost in their own thoughts. Usually upbeat and self-confident, Nancy had a feeling of angst about the fierce creatures invading Elm Park.

"I feel like we're living in the tropics– not Staten Island."

Norton was perusing Hal's notebook. He came across an entry that interested him and read aloud. "Compsognathus was a fierce meat-eating dinosaur about the size of a chicken, with sharp teeth and claws. Compsognathus ate vertebrates like possums, tree shrews, and rodents. A biped, it could run at speeds up to forty miles per hour. Compsognathus lived about a hundred million years ago – near the end of the Jurassic Period, when the Earth had a tropical climate and the polar icecaps had melted.

"Imagine running into a Compsognathus?" Nancy asked.

"No thanks. So, how's the little red hen doing?" he responded.

"I should check on her – see if there're any eggs."

They walked down the alleyway to the backyard henhouse. Sure enough, there were three eggs, which Nancy carefully gathered and brought into the kitchen.

"Hal wanted to buy Little Red from Rudy, but Rudy refused to accept any money. In fact, he threw in a bag of feed for her. In the winter, I bring her in the house."

"Torte and Little Red gat along and the same better be true for Tiger or he'll get the heave-ho. Along with you," she asserted – trying not to smile.

"Did Rudy sell you the gun?"

"No, that was Connor, the mason. He had this panel truck which said Connor Concrete Corps. My mom, Rosa, Hal, Freddy, and Harry the Horse worked with Connor on fixup jobs all over the Island. Connor sold me the twenty-two pistol with a box of bullets for fifty bucks – after some hard haggling," Nancy replied – shaking her head.

"What happened to Connor?"

"Like Rudy, he moved to Florida, which from what I hear – is no picnic."

"So, you're a confirmed Staten Islander?"

"It's as good a place as any. Like hanging out with you – it's better to stay with the SOB you know than the SOB you don't know," she replied – suppressing a smile.

"I'll take that as a complement," Norton replied.

"My friend, Lora, brought a big horseshoe over and we placed it on the floor of the merry-go-round. Have you thought about your experiments with the merry-go-round?"

"She brought another magnet over?" He paused for a moment – pondering." I think the arrangement of the magnets is key to the success of the time experiments."

"Everything in life is a matter of arrangement," Nancy responded.

"James Joyce once said that places remember events."

"Of course. These houses hold the memories of Pulaski Avenue. The question is how to get them to reveal their secrets," she replied.

"What's the expression – if these walls could talk? How about chattering trees and babbling brooks?"

As they looked towards Eggert's Field, they saw a tall furry creature moving about just beyond Freddy's vegetable garden. Norton squinted to get a better look. "Is that bigfoot or sasquatch?"

"Yeah sure. We're in the Himalayan Mountains. It' just Freddy goofing around." She withdrew her gun and fired well over the head of the incognito monster."

Freddy responded by tearing of his headpiece. "It's me guys. Hold your fire – Annie Oakley."

"If I had fired my gun, you'd be a dead sasquatch," Nancy called out.

Freddy, held up a well-worn boot, "Does this look like a big foot?"

"No. It looks like its time for you to get new boots. Ask Stan. He's got tons of contraband in a storeroom behind the bakery."

"Stan the Man?"

"Stan Mislicki, the lawyer and supplier of all kinds of stuff," Lora chimed in proudly.

The following day bright and early, Nancy knocked on Norton's door on the screen porch: "We're going to the shooting gallery for a practice session. Bring your gun."

The so-called shooting gallery was a one hundred-foot long and six-foot wide clearing in the little woods behind the flats. There was a bullseye painted on a three-by-four- foot plywood board nailed to a tree at one end of the clearing.

Wasting no time, Nancy took out her 22-caliber pistol and fired three shots – all striking the target near the center of the bullseye. Stepping back, she motioned to Norton to do likewise. The tall ex-farmer fired – missing the tree entirely. The second shot struck the tree a few feet above the target. Firing a third time, the bullet landed on the outer ring of the painted bullseye – four or five inches from its center. On the fourth shot, the Norton the bullet struck the target close to the center. Norton raised his arm to fire again, but Nancy grabbed his arm.

"That's enough. I don't want you wasting bullets. You have a good eye."

"I pitched semipro baseball in South Jersey. Had to go to the outfield because of a shoulder injury, but I always had good control."

Walking back, they crossed Walker Street traversing through the small woods, until they came to the small stream on the edge of Eggert's Field. They were astonished to see three flamingos wading in the stream – feeding on the algae and insects, and whatever nutrients existed in the stream. The long-legged water fowl had bright orange-pink feathers on their wings and white feathers below. Balancing on one leg, the flamingos stopped feeding momentarily to look at the two women, but then resumed nibbling from the stream bottom. The flamingos became alert – looking towards Eggert's Field where Freddy was approaching with his gun out.

"Oh no you don't, Freddy. I'll shoot that gun right out of your hands," Nancy said, with her gun already out of her shoulder bag and aimed at the octogenarian.

"Ah! I heard flamingos are good eating," Freddy protested.

"And you'd be good eating for the gators after I shoot you," the slender woman snapped, as Norton stifled a laugh.

Putting his gun away, Freddy grumbled and walked back towards Eggert's Field in the direction of Pulaski Avenue. Nancy and Norton watched the Flamingos, who had somehow wandered a thousand miles from their home in the South. Perhaps these beautiful birds saw the Island as a sanctuary. Hal once told her that flamingos breed best when there's a bunch of them around. So, zookeepers put mirrors around the pond to make it look like they were part of a big flock. But she'd have to keep a close watch on the trigger-happy octogenarian. Watching the three-acre field, she saw Freddy aiming his gun at a wild turkey that was flying above his corn stalks.

As Freddy was about to pull the trigger, Nancy shouted, "Have mercy!"

It was enough to distract Freddy. The turkey eluded the bullet and flew across Eggert's Field towards Granite Avenue. Sensing danger, the bird continued flying above Wolstein's factory – heading west towards Mariners Harbor.

"Looks like you'll be eating gators, snakes, and snails tonight Freddy" the slender woman called out.

"Maybe I'll snatch one of your hens in your backyard," Freddy snapped.

"Maybe, someone will put some buckshot in your backside," Nancy replied.

"That's the trouble with this place – all chiefs and no Indians."

"I'm not a chief – I'm just an Indian," she called out.

"So, you're a squaw?"

"That's an insult. I'm a nari."

"A what?"

"A nari, a thalli, a mahila. All of them polite Indian names for a squaw," she replied.

"I like nari," Norton suggested.

"Me too. Nari means maiden – as in maiden maverick," Nancy responded.

"Then, Nari it is," Freddy exclaimed – smiling widely and rubbing his hands. He started to walk down the street towards his apartment on Hooker Place.

"Hold up. Just call me Nancy," the slender woman called out.

Freddy nodded. "I'd never remember Nari anyway.

With the matter of a nickname unresolved, Nancy and Norton sat on the stoop feeling the gentle rays of the April sun. Their brief respite was interrupted by the sight of a young black man bouncing along towards them.

"Hi! You're Chester, as I recall," the slender woman called out.

"Like yeah. I got a weird request from the farmers on the South Shore. They like grow stuff. Corn, wheat, tomatoes, lettuce, onions, carrots, peppers, and melons. They also got apple and pear trees, and grape and blueberry bushes."

"So, you want us to weed their gardens?" Nancy asked.

"I pulled weeds and watered crops as kid," Norton chimed in.

"No, we need bats to pollinate the crops. The fruit trees, melons, and veggies ain't doing so well" Chester replied.

"I thought bees and butterflies did that," Nancy said.

"Like, have you seen many bees and butterflies around?" Chester answered – looking from Nancy to Norton.

CHAPTER 17

GETTING BATS FROM SCOTT'S MOUNTAIN

"I HAVEN'T SEEN ANY BATS FLYING AROUND HERE. YOU'LL PROBABLY NEED lots of those ugly critters," Nancy replied.

"So, there's this bat cave in Scott's Mountain, in western New Jersey. Where a guy, Bob, catches the bats and puts them in cages. Like, they call him Bob the Batboy," Chester related.

"Bob the Baboy hah? Sounds like one of Freddy's friends. What about rabies? Bats are known to have rabies," Nancy inquired.

"Like, these bats are clean. Rabies is very rare in bats. Raccoons, coyotes, foxes, skunks, cats, and dogs are more likely to have rabies."

"You're sure about that?"

"Like yes. There's a place in New Jersey where I can refuel the Cessna – Sky Manor Airport in Pittstown. It's about halfway between the Island and Scott's Mountain."

Turning to Norton, she said: "What do you think. Does Chester have it all figured out?"

"Sounds pretty good to me. I'm game," he replied.

"Here's my plan. I don't think we should risk flying the Cessna all the way to Scott's Mountain in western Jersey. We'll need a bunch of cars and a panel truck to transport the bats in their boxes to the Island. We'll take the Goethals Bridge to Jersey and drive out to Scott's Mountain get the bats, which better be in locked cages. If one of those rat-faced creatures gets loose in my car, I'll jump out – even if I'm going sixty."

"Chester, how many bats are we talking about?" Norton asked.

"Bob has forty bats – two each in a cage."

"Hoe big are the cages?" Norton asked.

"Like, a bird cage. Bigger – maybe a parrot cage."

111

"So, that's twenty cages. How much is he charging?" Nancy asked.

Fifteen bucks per bat – for a total of six hundred dollars," Chester responded.

"Forget it. Nobody has that kind of money," the slender woman replied

"Like, the bats will remain in the area – reproducing and nesting in trees, shacks, and attics. Bob would probably do it for twelve bucks each," Chester countered.

"We'll do it for ten bucks per bat – a total of four hundred dollars not a penny more," Nancy said firmly.

"I think Bob would settle for that," Chester replied. It was clear he had little talent for haggling over prices.

"You're authorized to set the price on his behalf?" she asked.

"Like, yeah. Me and Bob go back a long time. He grew up on the Island – the South Shore."

"He doesn't mind slumming with us North Shore folks?" Nancy said – trying to keep a straight face.

"Like, if you get along with bats, you can get along with anyone – even you guys," Chester replied with a smirk.

"Everyone is a comedian nowadays," Nancy replied.

"I got my sense of humor from my dad. He drove a TA bus for forty years," Chester responded – referring to Kenny Worthington.

"OK. I'll talk to Freddy, Hank, Joey, Mildred, the Rev, Stan and the others Then, I'll get back to you tomorrow."

Later, Nancy and Norton bumped into Freddy, who was far from enthusiastic about the bat scheme. "I remember him—Bob Bernardo. He was a J D – broke into houses and stole cars. Made Winnie Luco and Johnny O'Toole look like altar boys."

"We'll check out the bats before I hand over the four hundred bucks. If there's any funny business, I'll make Bob the Batboy tap dance back into his bat cave," the slender woman vowed.

"Just shoot him in the nuts. That's a lot of money for flying rats," Freddy remarked with a wry smile.

Nancy was able collect the money in varying amounts from the good people of Elm Park – including fifty bucks kicked in by Norton and herself to come up with the four-hundred-dollar fee for the bats. The next step was the logistics of transporting the bats from Scott's Mountain in western New Jersey. After much haggling, they recruited four vehicles – Nancy's old Dodge, Freddy's Ford clunker, Joey's big Buick sedan, and Greg's panel truck. It was decided that each car take three of the cages, placed in the backseat, while Greg's truck transport the remaining eleven cages of the rat-like creatures back to the Island.

Three days later, at six AM in the caravan of three cars and a truck headed for New Jersey – crossing the blue-green Kill van Kull on the poorly maintained Goethals Bridge. Freddy, nervous about driving over a hundred miles, opted to go with Nancy in her Dodge and let Norton drive his big Buick with Chester. Crossing the old bridge, like the other three bridges linking Staten Island with New Jersey and the Verrazzano Bridge linking the Island to Brooklyn was no longer painted or maintained. The ideas was cross at your own risk which people did when obliged to travel off the Island. With the country's (and the world's) population roughly a quarter of pre-Covid-20 levels, traffic congestion was a thing of the past. Happily, bridge and tunnel tolls were also a thing off the past.

The caravan, lead by Nancy, headed west along various routes – winding up on Route 80 which dissected New Jersey. Once known as the "Garden State" – New Jersey had attracted industry due to lower taxes and lax air quality standards in the past half-century. New Jesey had been a bedroom community as a result of affordable housing and proximity to New York City. But the Covid-20 pandemic changed everything – fewer people, closed stores, and shuttered factories. As with New York and other states, government at all levels had disappeared.

The only good news was the world was no longer threatened by nuclear war. There had been a powerful cosmic-ray burst from outer space, which disabled the world's nuclear weapons. The source of this extraordinary cosmic-ray burst was a distant supernova in the Pinwheel Galaxy – approximately 21 million light-years away. This fortuitous event was attributed to divine intervention. At least that was the prevailing belief of Nancy, Hal, Sam, Freddy, Mildred, and especially Rev Staller along with the good people of Elm Park. After two hours of tedious driving through traffic-free highways and roads, the three-car and one-truck caravan arrived at Scott's Mountain in the northwestern part of New Jersey.

Bob Bernardo and another man in overalls were standing in a lot overgrown with weeds and brambles. In the background loomed the tree-covered Scott's Mountain. Barely discernable was the cave in which the bats lived and flourished. Next to the Bob and his coworker were presumably the twenty cages with the paired bats inside. In addition, there was an extra cage with a white duck quacking unhappily inside it.

Nancy, Freddy, Norton, Chester, Joey, and Greg disembarked from their vehicles – walking about and shaking the stiffness from their limbs and the achiness from their backs. Bob Bernardo stepped up – shaking hands and introducing his companion Brewer, who like Bob, was clad in dusty overalls. There were inquiries about the long trip and the usual preliminary joking and backslapping prior to the exchange of the bats and the agreed-upon sum of $400 that Nancy had bargained with Chester.

"Like, Nancy and I did some haggling and arrived at a sum of four hundred dollars for the twenty bats," Chester said, with some hesitation.

"What? I told you that I wanted six hundred bucks for the bats," Bob replied heatedly.

"Now listen, Batboy. We bargained in good faith with your guy, Chester, and that's the price we arrived at," Freddy responded heatedly.

"Wait a minute," Nancy interjected – counting and inspecting the cages carefully. "One of the cages has only a single bat and there's an eleventh cage with a duck inside it."

"Well, one of the bats good loose and flew away. So, we threw in an egg-laying duck," Brewer said in gravelly voice – speaking for the first time.

"You're sure it lays eggs?" Nancy asked – eyeballing the latter closely.

"Yup. Duck eggs are bigger and better for you than chicken eggs," Brewer replied – keeping his eyes riveted on the slender woman.

It was clear to Bob and Brewer that Nancy was the leader of the Staten Islanders.

"Everybody O K with the Duck?" she replied – checking with the group, who nodded.

"We call her Daffy," Bob said.

"How old is Daffy? We don't want no old ducks," Freddy asked with a wry smile.

"She's about a year old. Ducks live to about ten years if you take good care of them," Brewer responded.

"Nice doing business with you," Nancy said – shaking hands.

"You know what? We'll throw in some moonshine," Brewer said – walking to a small shed and returning with a half-gallon of homemade whiskey.

Nancy was about to decline, but Freddy grabbed the bottle and thanked the bat-keeper who moonlighted as a moonshine maker. With great care, Bob and Brewer used copper wire to makes sure the doors to the bat cages would not open. There were two bats in each of the twenty cages for a total of forty bats. Each of the three cars would transport three bat cages – placed in the backseat respectively. The remaining eleven bat cages were put in the back of Greg' panel truck. Daffy, the egg-laying duck, was held by Freddy with its legs tied together. As with the initial trip, Freddy sat next to Nancy in her big Blue Dodge for the return trip.

As Nancy crossed the Goethals Bridge looming over the shimmering blue-green water of the Kill van Kull, Daffy eluded Feddy's grip and starting flying around Nancy's roomy Dodge – causing her to swerve almost into a siderail of the bridge. Then, the

The rambunctious duck landed on his Freddy's mostly bald pate – sitting their content. "As long as Daffy doesn't lay an egg, I'm O K," Feddy said – holding his head still with a grim smile.

This respite lasted a few minutes and then the duck flew down and landed on the octogenarian's lap, where it sat quietly. Soon, the rhythmical motion of the car lulled the small white duck into an uneasy nap. Freddy too, joined Daffy in the land of Morpheus. Nancy always reserved a big part of her heart for animals. Her menagerie now included the big male cat, Torte, the orange-striped kitten, Tiger, Boxie, the green-and-yellow box turtle, plus Little Red, the egg-laying hen in the backyard wooden henhouse. Hopefully, Daffy the white duck, who appeared pretty big, would get along with Little Red Hen. For the most part, animals got along well with each other and with humans – despite mankind's intruding on their habitat since the dawn of civilization. With the dramatic drop in world population, there was a chance for animals to flourish once more. Like viruses and bacteria, people had a strong proclivity to multiply rapidly – to the detriment of other species.

The plan was to immediately drop the bats directly off at the South Shore farm, which was located in Annadale. The caravan of Nancy's old Dodge, Freddy's Ford clunker, Joey's Buick sedan, and Greg's panel truck kept within sight of each other. From the Goethals Bridge, they drove along the nearly empty Staten Island Expressway taking bumpy roads like Huguenot Avenue, Drumgoole Boulevard, and Amboy Road – reaching Annadale, which was largely a ghost town. Finally, they came upon to a big white clapboard house and a freshly painted red barn and silo, with a big sign proclaiming: "Annadale Community Farm"

Nancy got out of the car, while Freddy tied Daffy's feet together and secured them to the front seat head rest with the same string. The farm proprietors, Jim and Joe Smith were there to greet them at the end of a long dirt road that led to the edge of the vast cultivated field.

The two brothers, clad in overall, appeared to be identical twins. After introducing themselves to Nancy and Freddy as Joe and Jim Smith, Freddy grinned and rubbed his hands. "Do you guys still make those cough drops?"

They both laughed and Joe responded. "Nope. There's a lot of Smiths around. We're ain't related to the cough drop guys."

"I sure wish we were. I'd of given up the farming life a long time ago," Jim chimed in.

Taking command, Nancy introduced the other members of her group: Joey, Chester, and Greg.

"Wow. This is a pretty big operation. Like one of those collective farms," Norton said – taking in the chicken coop, the turkey cage, the pigpen, the barn, the cows grazing in a fenced-in corral.

"I hate that term – collective farm. Sounds like Russia or China. This here is a community farm. Nobody is forced to work – strictly voluntary. Altogether, it's about two hundred fifty acres." Jim replied.

Norton nodded and looked to Nancy to make her pitch.

"So what do you have growing here?" Nancy inquired – focusing on the vast cultivated fields.

"We got corn, wheat, melons, potatoes, green beans, lettuce, tomatoes, peppers, onions, radish, cucumbers, squash. You name it," Joe answered.

"Looks like apple and pear trees yonder," Greg remarked.

"Yup. Plus, blueberry bushes and grape vines," Jim said – pointing towards said bushes and vines.

"Do you make your own wine?" Joey asked.

"I'm glad you asked. Cause I'm gonna give you folks a couple half-gallon jugs to take back home," he replied – leaving and returning shortly with two jugs.

Getting down to business, Nancy spoke up. "We have eighteen cages of bats for you.—total of thirty-six bats. I'm keeping 2 cages for myself three bats. One bat flew the coop. So, they gave us a duck which we're also keeping."

"Well, the problem is – we don't have much money to pay you. Until the crops are harvested," Joe said.

"This will be a barter deal – six bushels of produce for the 36 bats. And throw in two turkeys in November and two more in December," Nancy said boldly.

The two Smith brothers looked at each other for a few seconds, shrugged their shoulders, and then Jim responded. "Sounds fair enough, It's a deal."

"Do we need to sign a contract?" Jim asked.

Nancy took out two pieces of paper from her shoulder bag and briefly wrote out the term on both papers: thirty-six bats for six bushels of produce and four turkeys. Then, she, Freddy, Joey, Norton, and Greg signed both copies – along with the Smith Brothers. Returning to the vehicles, Nancy, Freddy, Norton, Joey, and Greg took out the bat cages. When it came to releasing the 18 cages of bats, the Smith brother took charge because the cages had to be placed at various locales of the farm.

The Elm Park group sat on some benches under a small clump of trees and watched the brothers, along with two teenagers – Dan and Don – carry the bat cages to distant locales on the vast farm. Once released the bats flew about in circles as if confused – eventually nesting in trees that marked the boundaries of the smaller plots from which formed the big community farm was formed.

"And if we have a surplus that nobody wants – it's yours," Jim replied.

Hands were shaken all around. Joe smith ran back to the house and returned with still another jug of wine with glasses. "Let' toast to the deal."

Everybody had some wine except Nancy. In addition, she insisted the other drivers – Norton, Joey, and Greg have just a small glass each. Freddy took a second glass – smiling widely and rubbing his hands vigorously. A small box of veggies that were sufficiently ripe to eat was placed in Nancy's big Dodge – along with the two bat cages and the squawking duck, Daffy. Then, the Elm Park group said their goodbyes, entered their vehicles, and started on their homeward journey. The three-car and one truck caravan headed north on the rut-filled roads of the South Shore: Amboy Road, Drumgoole Boulevard, and Huguenot Avenue – before reaching the mostly traffic-free unlit Staten Island Expressway. As with the trip to the Annadale Farm, the return trip was uneventful. Freddy, sitting in Nancy's Dodge with Daffy on his lap, was lulled to sleep by the car's motion and the two glasses of home-brewed wine.

Arriving on Pulaski Avenue, Freddy carried Daffy to Nancy's backyard. "Let's see if Daffy gets along with Little Red."

As Nancy and watched, Freddy placed the white duck into the six-foot long by four-foot wide wooden henhouse. The red hen, who was about half the size of the white duck, went up to the latter and pecked it—letting Daffy know she was the boss. The white duck quacked and settled in a corner – as if the henhouse had been her abode for years.

"Looks like the two birds are gonna get along fine," Freddy remarked – smiling and rubbing his hands.

Viewing the event from her second-floor window, Mildred exclaimed, "Would that people accepted each other as readily as our feathered friends."

"Animals follow Jesus's dictum of love thy neighbor far better than human beings," Rev Staller called out from the same window.

Then, Nancy removed the two cages from the backseat of her car – giving one cage to Freddy and taking the other. They walked across the street as everyone watched, looked at each other and paused. The large bat appeared and circled Eggert's Field – as if it sensed that something was about to happen.

"O K, Freddy. Release your bat," she exclaimed.

The cages were opened and the three small bats flew above the field – joining the megabat as they circled the field – as if inspecting the vegetables and flowers from above. The bats even flew close to the merry-go-round – giving the old whirligig an aerial inspection. Then the four bats flew around a big mulberry tree on the field's edge and landed there for resting and perhaps getting acquainted.

"See that old hut on the other side of the field? I betcha they wind up hanging out there," Freddy said.

"Fine. As long as those scary critters don't hang out on my roof," Nancy said – eyeballing the hut which wasn't far from Granite Avenue.

The wooden hut had broken windows and a missing door – making accessible to the bats, as well as field mice, squirrels, possums, and possibly raccoons. Sure enough, the three small bats landed on the shed's roof while the megabat hovered above them. Shaking her head, she sighed deeply, which Freddy noticed.

"You O K?"

"I'm fine."

But her eyes welled with tears. Freddy gave her an awkward hug and Norton came over – ready to do the same, but hesitated when the slender woman shook her head. Nancy was trying to remember a word that Hal had used for her sad mood – angst. It was a vague feeling of discomfort with one's existence. Hal once mentioned a favorite philosopher – Soren Kierkegaard, who was an existentialist.

Finding material on him in one of Hal's notebook, Nancy proceeded to read out loud: "Kierkegaard said all we can experience is the moment – the existential present. He described consciousness as a succession of moments which are temporary, precarious, and risky." Which did not make much sense. to Nancy, but she read on. "Kierkegaard said that truth is not objective, but subjective. He asserted that truth is subjectivity and subjectivity is truth. He also said that humans do not think out their choices in life, they live them. Which makes sense."

Nancy handed the notebook to Norton who looked through it briefly and then put it down. Freddy crossed the street and started weeding his vegetable garden which was beginning to sprout. Just then, a burly man, coming from Granite Avenue, walked through Eggert's Field. His face was bizarrely painted like a circus clown.

"Sir, you're trampling on my veggies. Could you walk along the path?" Freddy called out.

The stranger deliberately stepped on some sprouting carrots. Freddy responded by pulling out his big hinting knife. "Step on my veggies one more time and it'ill be your last – clown face."

The heavyset stranger pulled out a knife and lunged towards Freddy who jumped back with surprising quickness. Getting ready to lunge at Freddy again, he grinned like an evil circus clown, as he pointed his knife at Freddy's face. "You're pretty quick for an old guy."

With lightning speed, Nancy stood up, pulled her 22-caliber pistol from her shoulder bag and fired. Hitting the stranger's knife-holding wrist – causing him to drop the knife, which Freddy grabbed.

"Shit! I'm bleeding," he yelped.

By that time, Mildred and the Rev came running out to the street. Fortunately, it was a superficial wound. Soon he was bandaged by the prim woman, who packed him a sandwich in a plastic bag along with a couple of peaches. The Rev gave the man, whose name was Roy, some loose change along with priestly advice to stay on the straight and narrow path of life. Then, the man, grumbling and bemoaning his fate, was sent on his way. Nancy had an uneasy feeling that they had not seen the last of Roy, the ill-tempered clown.

Left alone, the bats did their work of pollinating the crops, flowers, bushes, and fruit trees of Elm Park. More and more veggies sprouted in Freddy's patch with each passing day. Despite the terrible effects of the Covid-20 pandemic on the world, Mother Nature still did her work the sunlight grew plants and warmed the planet – enabling animals and people to live on the earth. The Earth – our tiny outpost in the solar system – surrounding by millions and millions of miles of empty space. This miracle of life, granted by God, unfortunately had been treated with disdain by mankind since the dawn of civilization. For mankind, the pinnacle of evolution, had a definite proclivity to murder, exploit, subjugate, and wage war on fellow human beings from the dawn of civilization.

A few days later, Nancy and Norton were sitting on the front steps, enjoying the mild April sun. Freddy was working in his vegetable garden when a dog-like animal appeared at the far edge of Eggert's Field. The sweet odor of honeysuckle permeated the morning air – a welcome sign of spring.

"That's a coyote," Norton shouted – starting to reach for his gun.

Lightning fast, Nancy pulled her gun from her shoulder bag and crossed the street.

"Freddy, stay where you are. I got this."

Freddy, aware of the slender woman's speed and deadly accuracy, crouched down.

Nancy waited until the coyote, who was the size of a big dog, intruded onto Freddy's plot about sixty feet away. She fired twice – striking the coyote in the head both times – killing it instantly.

"Looks like we're gonna be eating barbecued coyote tonight," Freddy exclaimed – smiling and rubbing his hands with glee.

"No thanks. I'll stick to hot dogs and bean," Nancy replied – returning the 22-pistol to her shoulder bag.

"Coyotes aren't bad. They taste a bit like duck with a hint of pork," Norton said.

"So if you crossed a duck with a pig, you'd get a coyote."

"That's impossible. I'm not even sure you can cross a coyote with a dog," Norton replied.

"Let me ask Freddy." She called over to the octogenarian, "Can you cross a coyote with a dog?"

"It's been done. They've crossed coyotes with Shepherds, Huskies, and Labs. You get a dog that's feral – can't be trusted," Freddy said with a wry grin.

"Yup, the crosses are called coydogs. Coyotes can be nocturnal or diurnal – depending on circumstances. But, you're more likely to see them at night – when people aren't around."

"I forgot that you have a Ph.D. in coyotes," Nancy said with a smirk.

Norton bowed down to her "If you bow any lower, you'll never get up. I'm not the queen of England."

"No, you're just the fastest gun on the Island, which holds more sway in this neck of the woods," Freddy interjected.

Just then, Nancy and Freddy was approached by Lucille Banks. She was concerned about her teenaged son, Alfred. "He has too much time on his hands."

"Can you send him to school?" Norton asked.

A few years earlier, Hal had been running a school of sorts for the youngsters of the neighborhood. With his untimely death, his so-called "unstructured school" closed its doors forever. It has been said that death transforms a person to an idea. This was particularly true for Hal Haley. There were no public libraries operating anywhere on either the North or South Shore, Hence, the Island became an educational desert.

"The closest school is a private academy on the south shore. There's no bus service to get him there. I couldn't afford the annual tuition of five hundred dollars anyway. And Alfred's been spending a lot time with Wilma, Kenny Worthington's niece."

"I catch your drift. Teenagers with too much time will start playing doctor," Freddy said – shoving his hands into his baggy pants.

"I have an idea. Dr. Emil can take Alfred under his wing as an apprentice," Nancy suggested.

"Does he still live alone in that house under the Bayonne Bridge?" Freddy asked.

"For the most part," the slender woman replied – trying not to smile.

"I heard a certain lady makes house calls on him," Freddy said – smiling widely and rubbing his hands vigorously.

"Men are worse gossips than women." Turning to Mrs. Banks, "Would you approve of Alfred working under Doctor Emil as an apprentice? He could use the help and we'd have someone to take over his practice eventually."

"Sounds good to me. My son's bright and energetic. But he needs a purpose and a path in life."

"Then, let's do it. We'll send him to Dr. Emil tomorrow," Nancy replied.

"I'll have him ready bright and early," Mrs Banks replied.

CHAPTER 18

DR. EMIL GETS AN INTERN

DR. EMIL HAD BEEN WRESTED FROM THE TRUPPERS A FEW YEARS AGO AND brought to the cottage in the grassy field. He was provided with bandages, over-the-counter and prescription drugs, and an oxygen pump, and an EKG monitor. As with the rest of the Island, electricity was undependable – off more often than on. Like everyone else, Dr. Emil functioned in a 19th century world. A copy of the Hippocratic Oath was posted on his wall. The middle-aged physician was told to administer to any person or animal who was brought to his door. From time to time, the good doctor was checked upon by Nancy, Freddy, and others from Elm Park. They brought him food and baked goods, plus beverages – including whiskey.

Elm Park's femme fatale, Blanche Boulette, occasionally took leave of Billy Bumps to go to the good doctor for a checkup. Rumors were that the physical exam Dr. Emil's concluded with a roll in the hay Thus, the middle-aged doctor seemed to enjoy his medical practice – tending to sick and ailing of the area. Dr. Emil also took care of pets – including feral cats and dogs. He drew the line with snapping turtles, snakes, and alligators. He also avoided raccoons, skunks, foxes, coyotes, and any animal that appeared to be rabid. However, there were signs that Dr. Emil was beginning to slow down. He complained of long hours and fatigue. More than once, the general practitioner requested an assistant to lighten his load. As the only doctor in the vicinity, he regularly worked six days. Sundays, he'd leave his cottage early and head for Richmond Terrace to walk along Kill van Kull – heading east or west – depending on his mood.

On this particular Sunday morning, Dr. Emil had just stepped of his small house – stopping briefly to feed the friendly light-brown rats a cup of Cheerios. Though not yet eight o'clock, the sun's rays were already heating the air as another warm April day was in the offing. Walking along the winding path on the grassy field, Nancy, Freddy, and Alfred approached the doctor. He recognized Nancy and Freddy, but was surprised to see the black teenager accompanying them, who was vaguely familiar.

"Hey, Doctor Emil. How are you this morning?' Nancy called out.

"We got some help for you. This whipper-snapper is Alfred," Freddy said – turning to the youngster, "Say hello to Doc Emil."

Suddenly becoming shy, Alfred mumbled "Hi."

"He's black," the physician responded – looking from Nancy to Freddy in confusion. It was apparent that despite his busy practice and Blanche's conjugal visits, the last few years of isolation were not beneficial to the man's social skills.

"I'm brown," Nancy replied curtly.

"And I'm old. So what?" Freddy responded with a wry grin and a quick rub off his hands.

"Is he smart?" Dr, Emil asked bluntly.

"Sure is. He one of those coin collectors. What 's the word?"

"I'm a numismatist. I found a 1928 buffalo nickel in the merry-go-round awhile back," Alfred related.

"I have a 1996 Roosevelt P dime. I'll get it." He went inside his cottage and returned with the dime – handing it to the boy.

"Wow! Thanks. The P dime is worth ten bucks," Alfred replied – examining the coin carefully.

Not one to mince words, Nancy got right to the point. "We want you to train Alfred to be a doctor."

"He needs to go to medical school like I did," the physician who was in his fifties responded.

"Have you noticed there ain't no schools, or colleges or med school open anymore?" Freddy said with an unhappy grin.

"O K. But what is the boy's background?"

"I was in Hal's home school, with Wilma, Ron Luco, Johnny O'Toole, and a bunch of other kids from the neighborhood.," Alfred replied.

"Hal said he was by far the brightest of the bunch," Nancy said – nodding her head towards the black teenager.

"So, what did you study?" Dr. Emil asked with some irritation.

"We covered algebra, history, English, and science – including chemistry and physics."

"How about anatomy, physiology and diseases?" the doctor inquired.

"We didn't get to that. Hal said he didn't know much biology," Alfred said – looking at Nancy.

"My husband had just gotten a biology textbook – when he was gunned down on Pulaski Avenue." Turning to the youngster, "I'll gave you the book. Have you been reding it?"

"I'll start reading it tonight," Alfred replied sheepishly.

"I recall the incident. It was terrible. Hal rescued me from the Brown shirts. Though I didn't appreciate it at the time." Turning to Alfred, "He seems to be bright enough."

"He's a sharp cookie and a good kid," Freddy interjected.

Looking at the posted copy of the Hippocratic Oath on his wall, "First, do no harm. Second, respect the hard-won knowledge of the physicians I follow. Third, medicine is an art as well as a science – requires warmth, sympathy, and understanding. Fourth, an ounce of prevention is worth a pound of cure, Fifth, treat the patient – not the disease. Finally, respect the patient's privacy."

Alfred took out a piece of paper and copied the Hippocratic Oath. "I'll memorize it."

"Excellent, it's settled. What time do you want Alfred to report to you each day?" Nancy asked.

"Most days, I'm open for business eight AM," Dr. Emil replied.

"He'll be at your door at eight o'clock tomorrow morning," she replied.

"Set your alarm clock for seven my boy. Your future starts tomorrow," Freddy pronounced – smiling and rubbing his hands

"I'm gonna be a doctor's assistant. Whoopi!"

Bright and early the next morning, Alfred knocked on Dr. Emil's door. There was no response. After some more knocking, the fourteen-year-old boy sat down on the stoop of the small house and waited. A light brown rat approached him slowly as if waiting to be fed. Alfred reached into his pocket and broke off a small piece of carrot, which the rat took gingerly in its front paws and nibbled on it gingerly. The boy broke off a bigger piece and offered it to the rat who again nibbled on it in the same careful manner.

"You're a polite guy – ain't you?"

Just then, the door opened and Dr. Emil emerged – sitting down next to the teenager.

"That's Ratty. He joins me for breakfast every morning," the doctor said – giving the friendly rat a piece of celery.

Alfred detected the odor of alcohol on the physician's breath, but said nothing. They sat quietly enjoying the quiet of the early April morning. Soon, a young woman approached with two children, a boy and a girl, in tow. They were about to start school on the South Shore and needed vaccinations.

Lecturing Alfred and the mom, Dr. Emil said, "Kids entering school need three vaccinations: MMVR, rubella and polio. So, I'm giving them all three."

He prepared the required three vaccinations and then stopped. "Actually, my assistant will do it. I'm a little shaky this morning – nerves. The first shot is MMVR is for measles, mumps, varicella, and rubella."

"What's varicella?"

"It's chickenpox."

"And rubella?"

"It's German measles."

Dr. Emil handed the first needle to Alfred, who injected the older child, a boy, calmly as if he had been administering shots for years. Receiving the second needle, Alfred inoculated the younger child, a girl, who whimpered but calmed down when Alfred gave her and the brother lollipops. Proceeding with more confidence, Alfrred administered the next three vaccinations to each child – hepatitis, PCV, and finally polio.

"What's hepatitis?" Alfred aske, after he administered the final three needles.

"It's inflammation of the liver, in which makes your skin and the whites of your eyes yellowish. If unchecked, it can lead to cirrhosis of the liver –as can heavy drinking. Don't ever drink."

"What's polio?"

"Polio is a crippling disease. Many people became crippled and even died from it until Jonas Salk came along in the 1950s with his vaccine. The Salk vaccine was composed of killed polio virus. Once injected, the dead virus stimulates the body's immune system to manufacture antibodies which fight the polio virus."

"So, what do I owe you, doctor?"

"Looking from the mom to Alfred, Dr. Emil shrugged. "Five bucks, if you have it."

"That's very fair," she responded – handing the middle-aged physician a ten-dollar bill.

As the woman got ready to leave with her children, she paused. "You'll make a good doctor young man. The world needs you so much."

A few days later, Freddy was working in his vegetable garden, while Norton poked around near the stream near Walker Street. Nancy sat on the front porch with Alfred who talked about his job assisting Dr. Emil.

"Is he still drinking?" the slender woman asked – keeping her eye on Norton tramping around the under the trees at the edge of Eggert's Field.

"Yeah. But, he's not getting as drunk."

"Why's that?"

Hesitating momentarily, the boy blurted "I dilute the alcohol he drinks – adding water from time to time."

"And he doesn't notice it?"

"No. He just reaches for the bottle out of habit. Like, when things are slow and no patients are around."

"That's funny. But it makes sense. Just about everything we do is a habit," Nancy said eyeballing Norton.

"I guess you're saying a person should develop good habits. Instead of bad habits."

"I hope he's got his gun. That place is teeming with nasty critters – gators, snakes, coyotes, raccoons, tapirs. It's a jungle" he commented with an unhappy grin.

At that moment. Norton gave a yelp. Instantly, Nancy and Alfred dashed across the street and into the field. A small alligator had gotten hold of Norton's sneaker and wasn't letting go. Within seconds Nancy was at the stream's edge. She took out her gun and fired twice – putting two bullets into the alligator's head. The alligator's jaws released Norton's right foot, but it had bitten through the canvas shoe and blood was seeping out. Alfred removed Norton's sneaker and sock. He was horrified to see the last two toes were severed. Gasping, Nancy steeled herself, took out her hanky and put the toes in the cloth. Alfred used his handkerchief and to wrap Norton' foot, which was bleeding profusely. Freddy and Alfred helped Norton into the backseat of Nancy's big Dodge. As she accelerated down Pulaski Ave onto Hooker Place, she yelled at Norton: "Where was your gun?"

"I left it in the sunporch. I'm not crazy about carrying it around with me."

"You're an idiot."

"Nancy, get 'im to the doctor first. You can kick him in the ass later," Freddy barked.

The Dodge turned onto Morningstar Road and headed towards the looming Bayonne Bridge – turning onto the grassy field where Dr. Emil's cottage was situated at the end of a long winding pathway. Driving along the rough pathway, Nancy pulled up within ten feet of Dr. Emil's doorway. As if aware of the emergency, the superannuated physician ran outside with a blanket and spread it out on the grass. Nancy, Freddy, and Alfred helped Norton out of the car and laid him on the blanket.

"What happened? Did you have a knife fight in a phonebooth?" the middle-aged doctor asked – looking at Norton's bloody foot.

"He was bitten by a gator," Freddy replied.

"Take deep breaths and look up at the sky. Count backwards from a hundred by threes – to get your mind off the pain," Nancy said.

Though in pain, Norton was quiet – trying to breathe and count backwards as instructed.

"I have an idea," Freddy said – handing Norton a wooden stick. "Bite the bullet, as they say."

Norton bit down on the stick and it appeared to help a little.

Fortunately, Dr. Emil had alcohol, iodine and plenty of bandages. He carefully cleaned Norton's foot with the alcohol. Then, Alfred emerged from the cottage's frig with ice to slow down the bleeding. The electricity had been on the past few days, a bit of luck on an unlucky day. Nancy held up her bloody hanky with the severed toes.

Shaking his head, the physician said, "There no way I can sew them back on."

"Toss them. Over there in the high grass," Norton said.

"Out of sight, out of mind," Freddy said – tossing the severed toes across the field with a quick grin and a brisk rub of his hands.

Nancy shuddered – recalling Thomas Aquinas's assertion that the soul is present in every part of a person's body.

Alfred rushed over to the octogenarian and wiped his hands with an alcohol-soaked rag.

"Thanks, kid. My hands have been bloody and pissy before. I draw the line at dog shit. Ain't nothing worse than doggie doo."

"I can give you some rubbing alcohol to take home as a germicide. I don't have much to spare. So, this powder here – ground up turmeric – can kill germs. I'll give you some more bandages and a bottle of aspirin."

"Thanks, doctor. It was my fault."

"Accidents happen. Who's looking after you?"

"It was no accident. It was a hungry gator," Freddy said

"I'll keep an eye on him. He's got as much common sense as a ten-year old," Nancy replied.

"Come back in a couple of days. The biggest concern is the foot getting infected," Dr. Emil declared.

With Freddy, Alfred, and Nancy supporting him, Norton hobbled back to Nancy's Dodge.

Turning back to Alfred, Nancy smiled. "You're going to be a good doctor."

Back at the house, the threesome helped Norton up the front steps and the latter started to go into the sunporch.

"No. You're coming into the main part of the house, but if there's any funny business—I'll shoot off two toes on your left foot."

"Just shoot him in the nuts and he'll become a soprano," Freddy said – slapping Norton on the back.

"You mean Norton will sing like a girl?" Alfred asked – not quite catching Freddy's drift.

"He'll be singing like a canary when I get through with him," Nancy rejoined.

Fortunately, the upbeat Norton was a fast healer – despite the missing piggie toes. He was soon hobbling around the house, and along the alleyway between the front and back stoops. with the aid of a cane. Amazed at his fact recovery, Nancy was easy on the ex-farmer from South Jersey, and did not berate Norton for his lack of good sense. Their survival depended on quick thinking, good judgment cooperation, and courage. With the intrusion of strange critters like tapirs, alligators, pythons, anteaters, coyotes, foxes, plus the usual raccoons, possums and squirrels — Nancy sensed there been a sea change in the flora and fauna. Whether brought on by the unusually warm weather, the decline in human population or reduced car traffic, — the animal kingdom was taking back its habitat. Then, a sleek black sedan with tinted windows pulled up and a husky man, who looked familiar, got out – interrupting the slender woman's musings. It was a familiar face – attempting a smile to mask his obvious concerns.

Nodding and taking her hand, Mason delivered his message. "If you're not busy, Mr. Hopkins needs to see you as soon possible.

"Sure, I'll be right back."

She went inside the house, grabbed her shoulder bag, and checked her gun – making sure it was loaded. She gave Norton a quick hug. "I've got to see someone important. I think he's got a job for me."

Norton made a move to get his gun and leave with her.

"No, your job is to keep an eye on things around here. But, don't go looking for trouble. And take care of that foot."

Nancy hurried out of the house and jumped into Mason's car. "Where's Hopkins staying?"

"He's not far away," Mason replied – turning on Walker Street and driving past Morningstar Road up the hill to P S 21 – a school attended by Nancy many years ago. Disembarking from the sedan, they entered the schoolyard, where Hal and Freddy and Nancy, herself, had played fastpitch stickball, as well as basketball on the nine-foot-high baskets. The rectangular strike box was plainly visible on the big concrete wall. It was a one-size-fits-all strike box, regardless of the batter's height. Whenever the lithe woman came to bat, she felt at a disadvantage. However, Nancy's sharp eyes and quick reflexes which made her a deadly accurate shooter, also made her a skilled hitter. She never swung at a bad pitch and she usually made contact with the fast-moving Spalding. For a minute, the slender woman stood still and looked at the schoolyard wistfully – hoping that somehow Hal or Sam would appear.

Mason seemed to understand. "I know how you feel kid. I've lost loved ones in this war."

There were two boys, not more than ten or eleven, playing catch with an old, taped-up baseball on the grassy part of the schoolyard. Their gloves were oversized and shabby, but they had the rudiments of throwing and catching. There was hope for the world –kids still played baseball. They walked into the old elementary school, where Nancy had gone as a youngster. It seemed like it was a lifetime ago, but it couldn't have been much more than twenty years ago. Hal once told her that the average person has one billon thoughts in a lifetime. The hallways appeared as narrow and dark as they were when she was a ten-year old fifth grader. There were classrooms on either side of the hallway and a lighted office at the end – there destination.

CHAPTER 19

BLOCKING TRUPP WITH SAND

"I went here as a student. My favorite teacher was Miss Adams. I had her in the first and second grades," Nancy replied as they entered Gerald Hopkins' office.

Overhearing their conversation, Gerlad Hopkins commented. "The most important stuff you learn in life is in elementary school."

"I learned how to read and write, to count, add and subtract, my times tables. and how to get along with the other kids," Nancy said – approaching Hopkins and shaking his hand.

Hopkins showed all the signs of stress that his high-pressure job had placed on him. over the years. His face was lined, there were few red hairs left on his head. He wore baggy trousers held up by a tightened belt, and a loose suit jacket which indicated a significant weight loss.

"Here we go again. Thanks to your efforts in Saint George, the Darren Trupp rally had been disrupted and scattered to the four winds Who was the young fellow flying the plane?" Hopkins asked.

"That was Chester Worthington. He still has a hangar in New Dorp where he flies and maintains a bunch of Cessnas."

"Very good. This assignment will not call for an airplane. It appears that Mister Trupp is back in the States and wants to regain his stronghold in New York. Our spies tell us he's decided to set up headquarters in Bayonne, which is currently a ghost town. The oil tanks – except for a few tanks recently bought by a Staten Island company – are either empty or leaking oil."

"What company?" Nancy asked.

"Riche Fuel."

"I know them. They have a coal yard on Winant Street in Mariners Harbor. I guess they're back in business."

"Anyway, Trupp has not forgotten the rout and wants to enact revenge on the folks of Staten Island."

"Why the Bayonne Bridge? The other bridges are chained off with guards – paid by us. He'd never get through unless he had tanks, which he doesn't. The Verrazzano-Narrows Bridge has chains plus our armed guards at both entrances. Besides, its main span is nearly a mile long. It wouldn't be smart for the Truppers to get trapped on it with nowhere to go except into the unfriendly waters of New York Bay."

"I catch your drift. But, why not chain off the Bayonne Bridge also?"

"It's an issue of manpower. No offense, but who can you depend on besides yourself, Freddy, and the mechanic, Greg? I understand the newcomer, Norton, lost some toes to an alligator."

"That was Norton. He's an accident waiting to happen," Nancy replied with a half-smile.

"There's an older gentleman who talks to himself. His girlfriend, Blanche Boulette, is more capable. By the way, how is she doing?"

"That's Billy Bumps. Blanche is fine. But she has her hands full keeping Billy from harm. He's worse than Norton."

"Then, there's Joey, the knuckleball pitcher, and the telegram operator, Hank, the dwarf with the trained bear and his brother dwarf with a fox," Mason interjected.

"The auto mechanic Greg has his hands full keeping the clunkers of Elm Park running. The telegraph operator, Hank, is like Norton and Billy – not dependable in a pinch. As for the dwarfs – I'm not sure about Quentin, but Quinn is fearless and smart."

"Anway, there's a lack of manpower. That's why Mister Trupp and his Brown Shirts chose the Bayonne Bridge – as well as his wish to capture the woman who broke up his rally a few years back."

"So, if you put chains across the bridge, Trupp would choose another route."

"The Bridge has very light traffic. Most days only a few cars cross it per hour – mostly from Bayonne to the Island," Mason related.

"I have no idea why anyone would ever want to visit Bayonne – unless they're in the gasoline-and-oil business," Nancy said, with a hint of a smile.

"You're a typical Staten Islander – loyal to your quaint borough," Hopkins replied.

"So, what's the plan? Are we gonna zap the Truppers like the last time.?"

"Not this time. The Truppers have high-powered machine guns that could rip Mister Worthington's Cessa apart – killing you and your comrades. Not to mention the young Worthington himself, a trained pilot."

"We simply want to block Mister Trupp' path. And do it as he's crossing the Bayonne Bridge, which is about one-mile-long bridge. We've obtained four dump trucks, which are being filled with sand from a construction site on the Island – not far from New Dorp. You, Freddy, Joey and the mechanic Greg will be in each truck along with a driver already selected by my assistant, Mason. Originally, Norton was to be in one of the four trucks, but he was scratched after his run-in with the alligator. We spoke to your neighbor, Joey, who agreed to participate," Hopkins related.

"Can't the Truppers just drive over the roadway divider and continue heading to the Island?"

"No, it can't be done. The four-foot high concrete dividers cannot be breached without the vehicle getting stuck or overturned," Mason commented.

"How wide is the roadway itself?" Nancy asked.

"The bridge roadway for both directions amounts to eighty-four feet – including the six-foot wide center divider. That leaves a total of seventy-eight feet or thirty-nine feet of roadway in each direction. And as I said, the central concrete dividers cannot be crossed. With the ten-foot high sand piles, the only option is a U-turn back to New Jersey.

"It looks like a pretty good trap. What's that saying about a mousetrap?" Nancy asked.

"Build a better mousetrap and the world will beat a path to your doorstep," Mason answered like a pedagogue.

Nancy noticed that Mason never smiled. Not that Hopkins was a happy-go-lucky guy.

"It's more like a sand trap – forcing Mister Trupp and his associates to turn their vehicles around and head back to Bayonne," Mason explained.

"And that's when we plug them with our twenty-twos."

"No, you're going to shoot out their tires. Don't aim for the windows –they're bulletproof anyway. But, they may be open. I don't want anybody killed. We don't want to make enemies. We want to win over friends," Hopkins said firmly.

"So, when do we drive the sand trucks onto the bridge?"

Hopkins nodded to Mason and he explained.

"They're assembling a group of ten to twelve combatants in three cars near Kennedy Boulevard in Bayonne. Our intelligence says the Truppers will be moving in two days—Friday, May first. We want the four sand trucks at the entrance of the bridge tomorrow six A M sharp."

"The dump trucks should be moved from New Dorp to around here. Maybe drive them onto the P S 21 schoolyard and place two armed guards there to watch them," Nancy suggested.

"I have a guard in New Dorp, but two would be better. Your idea is a good one – we'll move the trucks here."

He said a few words to Mason who left the room briefly.

"Let's have some refreshments," Hopkins said – ringing a buzzer in his office.

Soon, Stan and Lora walked into the room carrying a pot of hot tea and a platter of biscuits, cookies, donuts, and a bowl of fruit salad.

"I'm sure you know Stan Mislicki, Elm Park's distinguished attorney and supplier of guns and bullets. Lora is our local crystal-ball reader and soothsayer. I don't make a move without consulting Lora Langley."

"So, how do you feel about the showdown on the bridge?" Nancy asked.

"Stop by the bakery later and we'll talk," Lora said in an undertone.

After barely sampling the fare offered, Nancy took a big paper bag filled with cookies, donuts, and biscuits for her neighbors on the street. While, Mason carried the canvas bag of guns and bullets – escorting her back to his black sedan and driving her back to Pulaski Avenue. Norton sat on the front porch with the big tortoiseshell cat, Torte, and the feisty orange-striped kitten, Tiger. She told Norton about the plan without going into too much detail.

"I want to help out. You know I'm almost as handy with a gun as you are."

"There'll be other times in the future. You need to heal and guard the house while I'm gone. Keep your gun with you all the time," she responded – giving him a donut.

Nodding, the ex-farmer munched on a donut and checked his gun. He sat glumly on the front steps, while Nancy distributed the goodies up and down Pulaski Avenue. Returning to the house, she told Norton, she was going to meet with Lora. Norton, in a better mood, was still accompanied by Torte and Tiger, as well as Boxie, the unflappable green-and-yellow box turtle.

"You O K?"

"I'm better. A man who masters patience, masters everything else in life."

"Who said that?"

"A patient person."

"Maybe it was a person with two missing toes. You can sleep in the main part of the house tonight. On the living room couch – don't get any ideas. Since Torte is cool with the kitten, you can bring Tiger with you. We'll use a kitchen chair to elevate your right leg. But if you bleed on my sheets. I'll shoot two toes from your left foot."

Smiling, Norton nodded. "I'll be hanging out with you guys tonight," he said to the menagerie sharing the porch with him.

Soon, Nancy was sitting in Lora Langley's office – more like a workroom – on the second floor of Mislicki's Bakery. Her office was directly across from Stan's bustling law office. Lora had placed the large crystal ball on her partially-cleared work table and had pulled down the shades. It was a bright sunny day in late April. Lora took out a silk cloth and wiped the crystal ball briefly.

"You didn't do that the last time," Nancy remarked.

"I'm acting on a hunch. Much of soothsaying is improvisation," the long-haired woman replied.

"O K."

"Get to the Bayonne Bridge early Friday morning. The Truppers will be ahead of schedule. I see three shiny black cars with tinted windshield and windows – all bulletproof. Armed men inside with Mister Trupp himself in the last car. One of them will toss a hand grenade. There's something preventing them from moving forward – looks like sand."

Then, the crystal ball began to darken. "Sorry, that's all I got."

"You did great, Lora."

Momentarily, the crystal ball brightened. "There's a tall man who aims at the grenade thrower. Don't recognize him."

"That's Charlie Krepinski," Nancy responded.

"Say your prayers, Nancy."

"Can't hurt – as Hal used to say."

The two women hugged each other and Nancy rushed out of Lora's workroom—heading for the end Pulaski Avenue near the railroad tracks where Charlie Krepinski lived. As if expecting a visitor, the tall older man stepped off his front porch.

"I got a feeling you need me for a job."

"It's Friday, May first, the day after tomorrow. Be at my house five-thirty A M sharp," the slender woman replied.

"All be there with my twenty-two, which I got from Connor, the concrete guy – years ago."

"Sounds familiar. See you Friday."

Nancy hustled back to Pulaski Avenue – formulating plans in her head, She'd get up in the middle of the night before – to make sure the sand trucks were ready to roll Friday morning. Inside the yellow stucco house, Norton was in the kitchen preparing supper, with Torte and Tiger at his feet. He was cooking a big pot of soup with cut-up carrots, celery, onions, plus six chicken bouillon cubes – seasoned with salt, garlic, basil, turmeric, rosemary, and sage.

"Smells good. What are you making – a witch's brew?" she asked – pecking him on the cheek and stooping to pet the big tortoiseshell cat and the little orange kitten.

"It's chicken-veggie soup with six different spices."

"Hal once told me that Dutch farmers selectively bred carrots for their orange color to honor William, Prince of Orange. Prince William led the Dutch Protestant revolt – that ultimately resulted in the formation of an independent Dutch republic," Nancy related.

"You are aware that some carrots are white, yellow, and even purple? We used to grow them in South Jersey."

"Oh shut up! You're worse than Hal."

Nancy wiped the kitchen table – setting out utensils, bowls, plates, glasses, and bread.

They sat down to eat and Nancy spoke up. "It's all happening on Friday – six A M. There'll be four dump trucks filled with sand. Freddy, Joey, Greg, and myself will be in each truck along with the drivers – selected by Hopkins and his sidekick Mason, That man, Charlie Krepinski will be also be with me in my truck."

"So, you dump the sand – blocking the Trupp caravan. But what if they use a snowplow to move the pile of sand?"

"I seriously doubt the Truppers have planned for such a contingency. But if so, I'd have to shoot the snowplow driver," Nancy responded grimly.

"What if they bring a ramp and drive over the divide to get to the lanes going in opposite direction?"

"The lanes on the other side have been blocked off by chains at the bridge's exit and entrance," she replied calmy spooning the soup.

"Looks like you guys have thought of everything," Norton said, after a pause of a few minutes.

"We'll know for sure by midmorning on Friday. Now shut up and eat your soup. By the way – the soup's good," she replied with a hint of a smile.

Thursday, another mild day, passed uneventfully. Nancy jumped in her blue Dodge and checked to see if the sand trucks had been moved to the P S 21 schoolyard. As promised by Gerald Hopkins, the four trucks were sitting there near the concrete wall with its strike box. She could almost hear the fast-moving Spalding slamming against the big wall – remindful of the carefree days of her youth. Sitting on folding chairs, were the two security guards – as promised by Gerald Hopkins. Though satisfied, she'd check again in the middle of the night.

Returning to Pulaski Avenue, Nancy saw Freddy working in his vegetable garden, while Norton watched him. Smiling widely, the octogenarian waved her over to his side of the street.

"You ready for Friday?" Freddy asked – rubbing his hands briefly.

"I'm as ready as I'll ever be," Nancy replied quietly.

Freddy was stirring something he called Brunswick Stew which smelled good.

"What's in it Freddy?"

"Tomatoes, corn, beans, red pepper – among other things," Freddy replied – rubbing his hands.

"What other things?" the slender woman inquired.

"A couple of skinned squirrels."

"No thanks."

The others were more daring, each taking a bowl of the fragrant stew. Tasting it, they commended Freddy for his culinary expertise.

"You ought to start a restaurant – The Squirmy Squirrel," Norton snapped.

"How about calling it – Squirrels, Rabbits, Raccoons, and Other Varmints?" Nancy suggested.

"Did you know Friday is May Day?" Norton mentioned.

"Hal said that May Day had to do with worker's rights. You know – the eight-hour day, forty-hour workweek, and minimum wage."

"That was back in the day – before the pandemic. Now, anything goes," Freddy replied with a wry smile.

Suddenly, Charlie Krepinski was there – standing next to them with a smile and a nod to both to the group. Freddy offered him a bowl of his stew, which the elderly man gratefully accepted.

"I remember dancing around the May Pole with other girls –winding a ribbon around the pole and singing a song."

She began singing in her unique nasal offkey way:

"May is the month
Of sunshine and flowers
Birds in their nests
And one or two showers.
Games to play and kites to fly
Or just looking at the sky."

136

Mildred came out – carrying a big platter of potato chips, cookies, and sliced apples. She was followed by the Rev carrying a big pitcher of iced tea. Fortuitously, the on-again-off-again electricity had been working that day – a fortuitous sign. Freddy pulled up his wooden table to the middle of the road and dusted it off. Nancy ran into the house and returned with a table cloth, plastic utensils, paper plates and cups. As if they had received a magic signal, Greg and Joey joined the group. Then, a man, who was familiar, appeared at the edge of Eggert's Field.

"I know you are. You're clown face!" Freddy exclaimed.

"I'm one and the same. But, I heard rumors that you folks need some help. I'd be willing to lend a hand," he said – appealing directly to Nancy.

Nancy looked from Freddy to Mildred and Reverend Staller. "What do you think?"

"What's your name?" the Reverend asked.

"Roy. I'm asking for a second chance. I'm not a bad bloke."

"Would, that everyone got a second chance in life. Give the man a chance to redeem himself," Mildred said.

After scrutinizing the stranger briefly, Nancy shrugged her shoulders. "O K. Be here Friday morning at five-thirty sharp. Have some of Freddy's squirrel stew and get to know the folks."

As the neighbors snacked on the food and drink, Nancy briefed them on the plan for the Bayonne Bridge showdown with the Truppers. "You aim for the tires – not the windows or windshields. We don't want anybody getting hurt. The four sand trucks will drive to the middle of the bridge, turn around, dump their sand, and head back. Blocking the Trupp motorcade from going any further."

"What if the Truppers start shooting at us?" Freddy asked.

"That's what the sand is for. We use the sand hill as cover and aim for their tires."

The folks enjoyed the food – snacking and chatting in the mild April weather. Feeling sleepy, Nancy decided to take a nap on the couch in the middle room. Generally, the slender woman was not a napper. The rest of the day passed uneventfully and Elm Park seemed to hold its collective breath in anticipation of the following day's showdown with the Truppers. Ever vigilant, Nancy got up in the middle of the night to check on the sand trucks at P S 21. The two guards were on duty and nothing was amiss with the sand trucks.

CHAPTER 20

SHOWDOWN ON THE BRIDGE

FORTUITOUSLY, FRIDAY WAS ANOTHER MILD, RAIN-FREE DAY. WHATEVER one's plans, good weather makes everything easier and augurs success. At a quarter to six, Nancy was the first there with Charlie and Roy – checking off everyone's name on her list as they arrived at the P S 21 schoolyard. In truck #1 would be Nancy and Freddy, truck #2 was Greg and Charlie, truck #3 was Joey and Roy, and finally in truck #4 was Hank and Mason – filling in for the injured Norton. All the trucks had assigned drivers and had passenger compartments large enough to accommodate three people. Nancy went around – checking on each truck making sure the drivers knew their destination and exactly what they had to do. The plan was to dump the sand a hundred feet before the apex of the bridge roadway.

Everyone was equipped with a 22-calper pistol, with orders to shoot at tires only. "There'll be three black sedans. Don't aim at the windshields or windows – they are likely bullet-proof anyway. We don't want anyone hurt or killed. The sand will stop them so they'll have to turn around go back to New Jersey. The dividers are four feet high. So, the Truppers only have one way to go – back to where they came from."

Just before everyone started, the slender woman recalled a Native American saying she had heard from Hal. Turning to Freddy, she said quietly: "Today is a good day to die."

Looking at his hands and grimacing, "That's fine for an old timer like me – go out in a blaze of glory. But not for you, young lady – you're too valuable."

The four trucks slowed down at the entrance of the Bayonne Bridge and then rumbled on until they reached a point one hundred feet before the crest of the roadway. Each truck stopped, did a u-turn and dumped its sand onto the roadway, the passengers disembarked, and then the trucks were driven back off the bridge. When the last truck had dumped its load of sand, there was a huge pile of sand – ten-feet high and thirty five-feet in diameter – covering most of the roadway. The big sand hill could not be easily traversed by a bulldozer and certainly not by a jeep or a sedan. The group arrayed along the hill provided an additional impediment – to the advance of the Truppers. Spaced roughly four feet apart with guns drawn were: Nancy, Freddy, Greg, Charlie, Joey, Roy, Mason, and Hank. The latter, a reluctant gunman, hunkered down in the pile with just his gun protruding above the sand hill.

"Remember, aim for their tires. We don't want casualties. Ready, aim, fire," Nancy yelled – poking her head a few feet above the sand and firing at the Trupper cars.

A few of the Truppers got out of their cars and returned fire. The roaring sound of guns going off was tumultuous and bullets whizzing past them echoed in their ears. There was also impact sounds of bullets embedding in the sand, grazing car fenders and thudding into the tires of the Trupper cars, and ricocheting off the steel girders of the bridge. Cool and deadly accurate, Nancy shot the guns from the hands of two Truppers. She recalled a quote Hal had read to her from Gerorge Washington: "In the midst of battle, I heard the bullets whistle and believe me, there is something charming in the sound."

A Trupper got out of a car holding a grenade. As he pulled the pin and cocked his arm to toss it, Charlie stood up and shot him in the leg. The grenade rolled several feet and exploded – damaging and the side windows of the Trupper car. A Trupper fired at Charlie – grazing him in the left arm and causing him to tumble off the sand hill. Roy scrambled down the hill and with Greg's help carried the ex-private eye back to a truck. There was one Trupper car, a limo, that lagged behind the others. Scrutinizing the car, the sharp-eyed Nancy saw the blonde-haired Darren Trupp sitting in the back. When the shooting began, he was no longer visible. Apparently, he was crouched on the floor.

As time went on more and more of the Trupper cars were struck – tires deflated, windows broken, and windshields pockmarked with spider-web bullet impacts. The Truppers were returning fire only sporadically. A Trupper driver doubled over from a bullet to the gut. He was carried back to his car. This seemed to take the fight out of them. In response to a signal, the Truppers retreated to their cars, made screaming u-turns and drove back to Bayonne. The Elm Park crew cheered, trekked down the arching bridge roadway – reaching the Bayonne Bridge entrance.

Nancy jumped in the truck with Roy and Mason, plus the injured Charlie – driving him to Dr. Emils house under the Bayonne Bridge. Fortunately, it was a superficial wound – quickly patched up by the good doctor and Alfred, his assistant. Soon, they joined the others already celebrating on Morningstar Road.

They had walked along Morningstar Road, where Stan Mislicki and Lora, Mildred and the Rev, Billy and Blanche, Norton, and the Cessna pilot, Chester, plus Quinn and Bubba, as well as Quentin and Foxy were all there to welcome them. A table was set up in front of Mislicki's Bakery with cookies, cakes, chips. pretzels, apple juice, and even beer shipped from Brooklyn by Gerald Hopkins himself.

A confirmed teetotaler, Nancy indulged in a can of beer – sipping it slowly to celebrate the utter triumph over the Truppers. She heard a flutter of wings above and caught sight of a brown-speckled owl swooping above the bakery, which gave her pause. Hal had once said that the sight of an owl flying during daytime was a sign of bad luck. She looked at him in surprise. "Don't get me wrong. I'm not into superstition," he responded. Nevertheless, she would mention to Lora when they were alone.

"Would that you not look so melancholy. You did well – repelling the Truppers with no loss of life."

We just dropped off Charlie Krepinski at Doctor Emil's office. He's being patched by the doc and Alfred right now."

"As to loss of life. I'm not so sure about that. One Trupper was hit in the gut. They'll be back – for sure," the slender woman replied grimly,

"It has been said that those who live by the sword shall die by the sword," Reverend Staller intoned.

"Where is that from?" Nancy asked.

"It's from the book of Matthew – if my memory serves me correctly," the Rev replied.

"Would that you reframe from your biblical references," Mildred snapped, which made Nancy smile, as did the sight of Norton helping out with the refreshments.

"You did well, Annie," the latter called out.

"Would that you refrain from using that appellation," the prim woman responded.

"I like the feisty version of you," Nancy said – smiling some more.

"I guess I've become a bitch."

"Not you. You're the last person I'd use the B-word on," Freddy said – smiling widely and rubbing his hands with relish.

One morning, Freddy was working in his garden when he noticed a speckled brown and white owl flying overhead. Nancy, sitting on her front porch, noticed the bird also. It was the very same bird she had seen flying above Mislicki's Bakery the other day. Though not superstitious by nature, the sight of the nocturnal bird gave her pause.

"I heard a cat yowling a while ago. And I don't mean alley cat," Freddy called over.

"Maybe that owl is trying to tell us something."

"I got my gun ready to shoot whatever it is that's yowling and hissing," he replied.

At that point, Mildred came out and joined Nancy on the front porch. "Freddy, please refrain from gunplay at the drop of a hat."

"Fine. When a wildcat attacks you, I'll sit back and watch you fight 'em off."

"You're as useful as Stanley when there's danger about."

"Now you know ole Freddy would come to the rescue of a damsel is in danger," the octogenarian replied with a smile and a rub of his hands.

"Thank you, Mister von Voglio. It's good to know chivalry still exists."

"It ain't what you do. It's why you do it," Freddy replied with his usual wide grin.

Suddenly, a large spotted feline appeared by the trees near Walker Street. It had no tail and was larger than the feral cats that prowled the neighborhood. In its mouth was a rat thrashing its legs in its final death throes. It was a young bobcat – native to the Pine Barrens of South Jersey. Like deer, coyotes, foxes, wolves, and alligators, the sizeable feline had swam across the Kill van Kull. Nancy, herself, could tread water and was a competent swimmer. But she knew many people who could not swim. It was amazing, how animals, unlike people, were instinctive swimmers This greenish-blue body of water was scarcely more than a stone's throw in width at certain places. Hence, a variety of critters routinely swam across the Kull to the Island.

Nancy recalled Hal telling her that his dad, Tom Haley. had never learned to swim until he entered C C N Y. During the1960s, the college mandated four semesters of physical education – swimming, wrestling, track, and basketball. To pass the swimming course, the student had to swim one length of the Oympic-sized pool. It took him eight weeks to overcome his fear of the water, learn how to float, and finally, swim from one end of the pool to the other. In the wrestling course, the instructor pitted Tom against a student who outweighed by thirty pounds. They grappled, groped, and strained for several minutes until Tom managed to flip on top of his opponent. And then Tom's nose began bleeding on his worthy opponent. Mercifully, the instructor ended the match to the relief of both combatants.

Nancy's meandering thoughts were interrupted by the sight of the spotted bobcat about to eat the rat. It was totally repulsive to the slender woman. It reminded her of Hal saying that Mother Nature is cruel by design, while mankind is cruel by choice.

"Did you see it? I'm gonna capture that cat and tame it. Or my name's not Frederick von Voglio!" Freddy vowed.

Nancy smiled. "I have an idea. Remember you said there was an old cage on that beached barge where you found the merry-go-round? It must have been used to transport animals from Florida. Maybe you and Greg can retrieve it and put it in his panel truck."

"Sounds good – if that barge is still there. I'll run over to the apartment and get Greg and Hank. Maybe Norton is well enough to help." Freddy said – heading towards the apartment building on Hooker Place.

Once a plan is formulated, the good people of Elm Park didn't waste time implementing it. Freddy, Norton, Hank, and Greg lugged the cage to Greg's panel truck – driving it back to Elm Park. It was a sizeable cage – five-feet high, with a four-foot by six-foot floor. By early afternoon, the cage sat thirty feet from the merry-go-round on Eggert's Field. It had been hosed down and scrubbed cleaned, with a red-painted plywood roof – matching the recently red-painted merry-go-round. As if awaiting the refurbishing of its new home, the bobcat watched the proceedings from a tree branch on the Walker Street border of Eggert's Field.

"How you gonna get that bobcat into the cage? Attach a chicken leg to a string and lead it into your cage?" Norton asked.

"Like, lasso it with a rope and pull it into the cage," Hank suggested.

"Maybe you guys should be put in a cage. Greg, drive them over to Dr, Emil's house. Tell him to give Alfred three tranquilizer darts. And a dart gun."

"All you need is one dart. It's a small bobcat – probably less than a year old," Freddy complained.

"I read somewhere that Calvin Coolidge had a pet bobcat. Called it Smokey," Norton related.

"You're just like Hal. Coming up with weird trivia like that. You're gonna use a dart? With you Keystone Cops the dart will probably wind up in Billy's backside. So, you better have extras.," the slender woman replied with the hint of a smile.

Turning to his invisible sidekick, Billy said, "I don't want it in my backside –do you?"

Freddy, Hank, and Greg returned with three tranquilizer darts and an air rifle to fire them. "As Elm Park's best shot, we figured you should shoot at the bobcat," Freddy said – handing the air rifle to Nancy.

"Would that we all be so competent," Mildred concurred, as the Rev nodded in solemn agreement.

With everyone looking at her, Nancy reluctantly consented. She aimed and fired the air rifle at the bobcat – striking it in the chest and shoulder with two darts. Within a minute or so, the cat fell off the branch and was carried by Freddy and Greg to the red-roofed cage near the merry-go-round. A quick examination indicated that the spotted light-brown bobcat was a male. A bowl of water and a tin plate of browned chop meat had been placed in the cage. On the opposite side of the cage was a folded blanket for the bobcat to lay down on. While everyone watched and waited, the bobcat woke up, walked around the cage –sniffing, clawing at the wire enclosure, hissing, and yowling. It snarled at the people staring at it outside the cage – unhappy about its confinement. Then, as if suddenly aware of its hunger and thirst, the young cat drank the water and gobbled every bit of the chop meat on the plate. Satisfied, the bobcat settled on the blanket and was soon sound asleep.

"Why don't you leave that wildcat alone? I hope he bites you in the nuts," Granny Scmidt yelled from her second-floor window.

"How many shots of whiskey did you have today?"

"At least I can hold my liquor – you baldheaded bastard," the crone yelled back and then slammed her window shut.

"O K, the show's over. Let Pussyfoot go to sleep," Freddy said.

"That's what you're calling him?" Nancy asked.

"Yup. Pussyfoot," Freddy replied – smiling widely and rubbing his hands.

The next day Nancy and Norton sat on the front porch – watching Freddy open the bobcat's cage. In his hand was a turkey leg which he extended towards the cat. Suddenly the cat lashed out and slashed Freddy's hand with its claws. Freddy dropped the turkey leg in the cage and withdrew his hand, which was bleeding copiously. Within minutes, Nancy was cleaning the slashes and administering iodine with Norton's help.

"Pussyfoot's got a temper," Freddy said with an unhappy smile.

"Maybe it's a female," Norton suggested.

"No, females don't bite the hand that feeds them. Give Pussyfoot some time to know you."

"Fine," Freddy said.

He turned to his veggie patch – weeding and watering his plants, and doing his best to ignore the young feral bobcat. Loosening the soil around his onions and carrots, Freddy unearthed a large black rock. Curious to see if it was magnetic, he placed a nail on it. The nail remained attached to the rock. Evidently, it was the iron ore magnetite – commonly known as lodestone. He cleaned off the rock and placed it on the floor of the merry-go-round. There was a whirling sound and the lights of the whirligig fluttered briefly. The machine seemed to have a life of its own. When told about this, Lora peered at her crystal ball and came to the conclusion that the merry-go-round might be a time machine. She suggested to Nancy and Freddy that they ought to fix it up.

Shrugging his shoulders, Freddy noticed a side of the ride where the seats were missing. A person standing there when the whirligig was in motion would fly off it – possibly getting hurt. Though he never studied physics, the octogenarian knew about centrifugal force. It was just common sense. He recalled seeing some two-by-fours and plywood in the basement of the Hooker Place apartment where he lived. Recruiting Hank to help him, Freddy carted the lumber, plus some tools, to the merry-go-round. With the two-by-fours and the plywood, the two men constructed a four-foot high barrier along the outer perimeter of the merry-go-round to prevent people from falling off the ride as it rotated.

Acting under Lora's specifications they got some more wood and erected a free-standing five-foot wide by six-foot high plywood board on the south side of the merry-go-round. She requested it to be painted white.

Looking at the plywood board, Freddy turned to Hank. "There's a half gallon of white paint in that basement. Bring it over with a couple of brushes and some rags."

"Like, can I help paint it?" the telegraph operator asked.

"Sure, Painting's the fun part"

His easygoing apartment mate nodded and soon retuned with the paint. Before long they had painted the plywood board white on both sides, along with the supporting two-by-fours. Turning to Hank, "Not bad – right?"

Nancy watched the two men paint the merry-go-round. "It looks great guys. As soon as it dries, I want to take a ride on it."

She was also intrigued by Freddy's new pet, the bobcat. Torte, her big tortoiseshell cat, and Tiger, the orange-striped kitten, sat with her. Before she could restrain him, Torte ran across the street to scrutinize the young male bobcat. As soon as Torte approached the cage, Pussyfoot rushed towards him snarling and extending its paw through the narrow openings of the wire cage. Scared out of its wits, Torte turned around and dashed back to Nancy's front porch. Curious to see what the fuss was all about, Tiger ran across the street to meet the formidable bobcat. This time, Pussyfoot was more neighborly sniffing and meowing at the orange-striped kitten. Tiger went so far as to stick its tiny paw through an opening which the bobcat licked as if wishing to groom the kitten.

"Seems that Pussyfoot has a paternal side."

"Yeah. They're better than most men when it comes to that," Nancy replied, as they walked back to the porch with the bold kitten.

"Animals let you know right away if they like you or not," Norton responded.

Mildred, who had been watching the proceedings from her front window joined them. "Would that people were as accepting as animals."

Soon, Reverend Staller walked over. "Indeed, animals don't dilly-dally or shilly-shally."

"That's one way of putting it – Rev," Nancy replied with a smile.

CHAPTER 21

DISPUTE OVER PUSSYFOOT

THE NEXT DAY, FREDDY EXTENDED ANOTHER TURKEY LEG WITH THE SAME bandaged hand as the day before. This time, the bobcat took the offering in his mouth, retreated to a corner, and ate it – leaving the bone which he licked clean.

Suddenly, a red pickup truck pulled up and a middle-aged man got out. "That's my cat. It escaped from its pen in my backyard."

"Prove it. Come over here and take it out of the cage," Freddy called over to the stranger.

The man, who was heavyset and grimy, walked over to the tomcat's cage and whistled, the cat withdrew to a corner and growled.

"Pussyfoot doesn't like you," Freddy said.

"Bullshit. He likes me plenty," the man replied – putting on some thick leather gloves.

The stranger reached into the cage and tried to grab the bobcat with a gloved hand. Pussyfoot snarled, grabbed the glove in his mouth – taking it off his hand and shaking the glove like it was a rat.

"Freddy's right. The cat wants no part of you," Norton remarked.

Turning red with anger, the man stormed back into truck – emerging with a rifle. "That bobcat belongs to me and I'm taking it home."

"Put the gun away," Nancy said in low, calm voice.

"What are you gonna do, lady? Give me a spankin'?" He replied – pointing his rifle at the slender woman.

Within two seconds, Nancy pulled her gun from her handbag and shot the man's left hand which had been pointing the rifle at her. He dropped the rifle and grabbed his hand, which was bleeding copiously.

Norton ran over and picked up the rifle, while Mildred and the Rev ran inside – returning with iodine and bandages. The man, who refused to give his name, was patched up. "I want my rifle back!"

"Sure," Freddy said – taking the bullets from the cylinder and smashing the rifle against the Nancy's front concrete steps – breaking the wooden stock.

"Here's your rifle – what's left of it. Now get out of here before we shoot out your tires."

"I'll be back," he said in an undertone.

A few days later, Norton was astonished to see Freddy walking Pussyfoot on a leash along Pulaski Avenue. He called Nancy out to the front porch. "Come on out. You won't believe your eyes."

Joining him on the porch, she smiled. "I'm not surprised. Freddy has a way with people and with animals."

"How did you do it?" Nancy yelled over to the octogenarian.

"Patience and salami. Pussyfoot loves salami, He'll do anything for a piece of salami – including accepting a collar. Attaching a leash to his collar is no big deal."

"So, taking him for a walk was the easy part," Nancy said.

"Yup. What animal wants to be couped up in a cage all day long?"

"Freddy, you have the makings of a great teacher," Norton called out.

"I have the makings of a great man," Freddy replied – stooping to pet the bobcat.

"Would that you show some modesty. You're starting to sound like Stan," Mildred called out from her second-floor window.

"Whatever modest talents I possess exist by virtue of the grace of God," Stan declared from the adjoining window.

"I didn't know you were such a humble guy, Rev." Nancy responded – causing Mildred to laugh and Stan's face to redden.

"I haven't figured out whether Stan's egoistic or egotistic," the prim woman replied,

"Egoistic means self-centered, which I'm not. Egotistic means I tend to overvalue my abilities to which I plead guilty."

"Fair enough, Rev. It's called the sin of pride."

"But allow me to say this, young lady. I've never seen a person as cool under fire as you," the preacher said solemnly.

"It's pure reflex. If I were to think about it – I'd freeze up"

"Never overthink," Freddy called out – heading towards the flats with Pussyfoot in tow.

Freddy had stopped to talk with the brothers Quinn and Quentin who were sitting on their stoop with Bubba, the trained black bear, and Foxy, the trained red fox. The two animals had become the best of friends – getting along

147

better than their owners. The both brothers were adept with animals, their person-to-person skills were not quite as good. Easier going than his red-haired brother, Quentin made an extra effort to accommodate his fraternal twin brother. Thus, the brothers more or less got along – performing with their animals at the Moulin Rouge and other nightclubs and venues on the Island.

"Maybe you could train Pussyfoot and become part of our show," Quentin suggested.

"I don't know about that. It's bad enough splitting our fee two ways. If it was three ways, we'd starve."

"Nah. The bobcat's my pet. There's plenty enough food for the both of us. Besides, I'm not in the entertainment business," Freddy replied with a wry smile.

Just then, a red pickup truck stopped next to Freddy and the young bobcat. The same unkempt burley man who had confronted Freddy the previous week, pointed a gun at him. "I'm taking my bobcat back. You don't have that trigger-happy woman around to protect you."

Freddy smiled at the grimy man.

"What's so funny, old man?"

"Somebody's about to hug you," Freddy replied – looking behind his adversary.

Just then, Bubba picked up the man, while Foxy snapped at his feet. The gun bounced on the street and Freddy pocketed it.

"I'm keeping the gun. And if I see you again, I'll shoot you in the nuts. Now, get out of here."

Cursing under his breath, the slovenly man jumped into his pickup truck and drove away. The bobcat, who had been cowering as a result of his old mater's intrusion, calmed down as Freddy talked softly and petted the animal. He introduced the bobcat to Bubba and Foxy. After some coaxing on Freddy's part, Pussyfoot, Bubba, and Foxy were on amicable terms. As the prim woman had often said – animals were friendlier and more accepting than their two-legged counterparts.

As Freddy walked back from the flats along Pulaski Avenue, he noticed a yellow-greenish glow emanating from the merry-go-round. Alfred waved to him from one of the horses on the ride. He was holding a small horseshoe magnet, he just found in the lot behind Mislicki's Bakery.

"Start the merry-go-round. I want to go for a ride."

"Put the magnet down. I'll strap you in. Make sure you hold on tight with both hands," Freddy yelled back.

He started the gasoline engine which powered the merry-go-round and engaged the gears. It was the first time anyone had ridden on it. Freddy stood in the middle of the ride engaged the gears. Slowly the whirligig began to turn.

Alfred called out, "Make it go faster."

Freddy shook his head. There was a high-pitched humming sound from the ride that bothered the octogenarian. Just then, Nancy emerged from her house and looked across the street at the revolving merry-go-round. She also heard the humming sound, which was like an animal whining.

"Freddy, stop the merry-go-round. I don't like what I'm hearing. Maybe we should get Greg to take a look at it."

Alfred volunteered to hop on his bike and get Greg to check out the machine. Within a half hour, the auto mechanic was checking out the engine, which appeared to be O K. He oiled the gears and then engaged them. Slowly the merry-go-round turned This time, the whining sound was diminished. Though, a high-pitched sound, similar to the cry of a coyote pup emanating from the machine from time to time.

"Freddy, don't run it too fast. Til we iron out the kinks."

Freddy nodded. "This thing seems to have a mind of its own."

"If you were sitting on a barge floating around the Kill van Kull, you'd act ornery too," Greg responded.

Later, Nancy walked over to Lora's office above Mislicki's Bakery on Morningstar Road. The local crystal-ball gazer had a pretty good batting average as a soothsayer. Unlike quack fortune tellers, Lora's predictions were specific and often on target.

Lora was making a small copper four-leaf clover. "This is for you. It's a good luck talisman."

"I wanted to ask you something. That kid, Alfred, has been riding on the merry-go-round. Freddy runs the motor. He doesn't let him go him go to fast."

"That's a good idea. An ounce of caution is worth a pound of mishap," Lora replied.

Polishing the four-leaf clover with a cloth, the pretty long-haired woman handed it to Nancy. "I'd like you to wear it on your necklace. Remove the necklace and I'll attach it in between the Hal and Sam pendants."

Nancy handed the copper necklace to Lora who carefully hooked the four-leaf clover in between the two hearts memorializing Hal and Sam – the two men who had done so much for Elm Park during the Covid-20 pandemic.

"Getting back to that merry-go-round, let's take a look at my crystal ball."

Lora lifted the large glass ball from the shelf and placed it on her workbench. She wiped the crystal ball with a silk cloth.

"Why do you do that?"

"First of all, the ball gets dusty on the shell. Copper shavings and dust is in the air. Secondly, the silk induces an electric charge on the crystal ball – energizes it."

"Ask it if the merry-go-round has any kind of power."

Lora repeated the question to the crystal ball glowed with flames and then became cloudy. Next, a clock appeared with its hands moving forward and then backwards.

"It looks like an old merry-go-round. There are animals living in it – wolves or coyotes. I'm not sure. There's a bunch of magnets on the floor and a clock running backwards," Lora said –looking into the big crystal ball.

"Magnets create magnetic fields. A clock running backwards means time is being reversed," Nancy responded.

"Maybe the magnets can reverse time? Turning the merry-go-round into a time machine?"

"Magnets have magnetic fields – that's why they pick up iron nails. Hal said that there were three types of fields – gravitational fields, electric fields, and magnetic fields. He said the flow of time can be affected by these fields."

"Well, I'm not a physicist," the pretty soothsayer replied.

"Neither am I. Hal was teaching me the basics of science – biology, chemistry, physics, and astronomy. He talked about Newton's laws of motion and Galileo dropping rocks off that tower in Italy. And about centrifugal force which acts on an object following a circular path – like standing on a merry-go-round."

"I guess you can think of that merry-go-round as a science experiment. But the crystal ball is saying proceed at your own risk. By the way, were you ever a go-go dancer?" Lora asked.

"No. I think Blanche Boulette was years ago. But what would you do?"

"Once the beast is out of the cage, you can't put it back. But you're messing with time. A disruption of time is an anomaly. I forget the term for it."

"A time warp. Hal said time is the fourth dimension."

"A trip through time is not like a trip to New Jersey. By the way, is the Bayonne Bridge still blocked?" Lora asked.

"Last I heard it was. Maybe we should put Trupp back two hundred fifty years when the Indians ran the country.

"Be careful, Nancy. Time travel is uncharted territory."

"Looks like I'll really need that four-leaf clover."

"That's why I made it for you," the long-haired woman replied – hugging her friend.

CHAPTER 22

ALFRED SEES HIS ANCESTORS

The following day, Nancy and Norton were sitting on the front stoop watching Alfred who again climbed onto the horse he had ridden a few days earlier. He picked up a magnet sitting on the floor – holding it in his hand. Freddy started the merry-go-round – again keeping it at a modest speed.

"I'm watching a movie," the teenaged boy called out – pointing to the white plywood board in front of him.

Freddy peered at the screen from ground, but saw nothing. But the same high-pitched animal sound issued from the merry-go-round.

Alfred described what he was seeing on the plywood board. "It's like a movie screen. There's a bunch of men picking cotton from a big field. They're all black. There's one white guy on a horse – yelling and cursing. One of the pickers is yelling back at the boss. They get in a fight and the picker grabs the whip from the guy on the horse and uses it on him. Then, he jumps on his horse and rides away. Another white man is shooting at him, but his rifle jams. Frustrated, he throws it away."

"It must have been before the Civil War – around 1860. That's more than one hundred sixty years ago."

Alfred, who was adept with numbers, began figuring. "Assuming twenty-six years per generation – that would be six generations. So, the cotton picker must have been my great-great-great grandfather. Woe!"

The screen darkened and the boy dropped the magnet and ran back across the street. By this time Mrs Banks has come downstairs. Nancy and Norton are astounded by what had just occurred across the street as Alfred ran to her all excited.

"Mom, I saw my great-great-great grandfather in the screen on the merry-go-round. He was picking cotton and he ran away from his bosses. Our ancestor was a runaway slave before the Civil War."

"Alfred – are you telling stories again?"

"No, Mrs. Banks. Something unusual is going on in that merry-go-round," Norton replied.

"The merry-go-round is a kind of time machine," Nancy added.

"Alfred! Get off the merry-go-round right now," his mom demanded.

Freddy slowed the merry-go-round, the teenager dropped the magnet, jumped off the whirling platform, and walked over to the front porch. He appeared to be shaken by what he had seen.

"Who's next?" Freddy asked.

No one stepped forward.

"I want to give it a shot," Freddy said.

Norton crossed the street and started the merry-go-round. Looking towards Nancy, the latter signaled to run it slowly.

CHAPTER 23

FREDDY TAKES A TIME TRIP

FREDDY PICKED UP THE MAGNET THAT ALFRED HAD DROPPED AND STOOD IN front of the white wooden board. "Take me back sixty years, when I was a teenager."

The whirligig began to rotate – making the same high-pitched whining sound of a coyote pup. An image began to form on the white board. It was of a dark-haired teenager bouncing along Morningstar Road in faded blue jeans. Despite the huge chasm in years transcended, the teenager was none other than Freddy von Voglio. He smiled warmly at the pretty girl him in the opposite direction. It was Mandy Adams a comely teenager with in a pink polka dot dress with long curly hair bound by pink ribbons. Clearly, there was chemistry between the two adolescents.

Both youngsters were students at Port Richmond High School – carrying the "popular" label. Freddy was a hard-throwing pitcher, with a keen batting eye who batted leadoff on the baseball team. His accurate two-handed set shot and hard-driving layups earned a starting spot on the school's basketball team. An indifferent student, Freddy's best subjects were gym and wood shop – though he liked 20th century American history – especially Franklin Roosevelt. Freddy's dad never tired of talking about the accomplishments of FDR's New Deal. Mandy's popularity accrued to her good looks, nice clothes, and her bubbly personality. No scholar, Mandy did just enough to squeak by in her typing, bookkeeping, business math, and steno courses. A big talker in all her classes, Mandy benefitted from teacher leniency as a result of her good looks, her benign manner, and her mom's key role in the PTA.

One day in late spring, Freddy was walking Mandy home after a pizza party with beer at a teammate's house – celebrating a come-from-behind baseball win. They walked into the small cemetery and sat on a bench across from the P S 21 schoolyard. Mandy was in an amorous mood and Freddy sensed this was the moment they would consummate their young love. She had loosened her bra and Freddy had pulled down her lace panties. With quick handed dexterity, Freddy had sheathed himself with the necessary protection. Desire and instinct took command. Many mounted Freddy sitting on the bench and before long climax was achieved by the star-crossed teenagers.

However, there was a problem in their budding romance. Mandy's family looked down on Freddy's blue-collar inclinations. With her parent's encouragement, Mandy's older brother, a student at Wagner College, had begun to bring his college classmates over for Sunday dinner. Eli. a fair-haired well-spoken accounting major soon caught the eye of the young damsel. Though not gifted academically, Mandy realized there was an entirely different life beyond high school. Soon, Freddy got a "dear John" phone call from Mandy.

As the picture on the white wall faded, Freddy walked across the street – sitting on the porch steps next to Nancy and Norton. "It was about a girl went out with in high school – named Mandy. She broke it off. It blew my mind, but I told myself there are plenty of fish in the sea. But you know what? There was never another girl like Mandy. Folks said I smiled different and I started rubbing my hands the way I do. My mom said I was rubbing Mandy out of my life."

"I know how you feel. When Hal was killed on the street – the world stopped. But with everything going on with the Covid-20 pandemic, I had no time to mourn. When Sam was killed within six months, I felt hollowed out."

Freddy had been an anchor in her life since she a youngster. Nancy recalled being bullied in junior high school by a group of white girls. Her dad had flown the coop and her mom, Rosa, was very busy working as a Bradford guard the Con Ed plant. So, she went to Freddy, who brought her to his apartment basement. Using oversized boxing gloves, Freddy taught her how to punch, duck, and block punches. Over a period of six months, he thoroughly trained Nancy – punching a speedbag, shadow boxing, and sparing with her in a roped-in twelve-foot square ring. Fredy also had her do pushups and sit ups every day. At the end of her training, the slender twelve-year old could pack a punch and was stronger than most boys her age.

"Now when those girls start up with you, use the element of surprise. Punch the biggest one in the stomach and then punch her face. You won't have to do anything more, because the others will run away."

Freddy was exactly right. After Nancy double-punched the biggest of her tormentors, the others turned and ran away like rabbits fleeing a fox. Nancy was never bothered again in junior high or senior high. Her self-confidence improved and popularity grew with both girls and boys, and even her grades got a boost.

Mildred approached Nancy, Freddy, and Norton sitting on the front porch.

"You seem to be lost in thought," the prim woman remarked – staring at Nancy.

Nancy shook her head. "Just thinking about some stuff from the past."

"I'd like to try the merry-go-round next."

"Why not. Here's the magnet I used," Freddy responded – handing the prim woman his magnet.

"Don't forget – stand and look at the white board," Nancy called over to Mildred.

CHAPTER 24

MILDRED TAKES A TIME TRIP

AGAIN, FREDDY RAN THE MERRY-GO-ROUND SLOWLY AND THE SAME HIGH-pitched whining sound of a coyote pup. A picture emerged of a young woman, in her early twenties, walking with a coworker to the Staten Island Ferry in lower Manhattan. The woman was Mildred Aimsley. Her companion was Brad Owen, an accountant with whom she worked at a small Wall Street firm. As a bookkeeper working under Brad, Mildred felt obliged to be compliant towards him. He had talked her into going to a diner on Stuyvesant Place, near her tiny apartment in St. George. Brad had a club sandwich, while Mildred had a salad that she hardly touched.

"So, let's see your digs.

"I've barely furnished it. I haven't even gotten curtains yet," Mildred replied nervously.

"I have an eye for color. I can advise you on decorating without spending a fortune," Brad replied – deliberately bumping his knee against her leg.

"My landlady doesn't want us to have any visitors except family."

"Tell her I'm your cousin Brad from Jersey," he replied – rubbing his knee against Mildred's leg.

"Would that you refrain from touching my leg," Mildred said in an undertone.

"Would that you not talk like that. I never heard anyone start a sentence with would."

"My mother spoke that way. But people from the Commonwealth of Massachusetts spoke in a formal manner."

"Sounds snooty to me," Brad replied, barely stifling a belch.

Reluctantly, Mildred walked with Brad to her place, a 3rd-floor studio in an old Victorian building on Westervelt Avenue a block from the Richmond Terrace. As she had described, the apartment was bereft of furniture except for two folding chairs, a small table and a studio couch.

"It's simple and its wanting – but it's mine."

"It ain't bad," he replied – plopping down on her couch."

"Would that you not use ain't."

"Do you have anything to drink?" he asked – checking her kitchen cabinets.

"Water, cola, or tea."

"Or me," he chimed in – grabbing her roughly and depositing her onto the studio.

"Would that you not treat me with such familiarity, Brad."

"Stop playing hard to get," he responded kissing and groping the young woman.

In vain, Mildred attempted to free herself from Brad, who was a husky six-footer. She attempted to knee the ill-mannered, aggressive accountant. Rather than deterring him, this angered Brad and he tore off her clothes – ripping her white blouse and tossing her blue skirt to the floor. Then, he began kissing her feet – making the prim woman feel befuddled.

"Brad, please don't do this to me. I'm a virgin," she cried out in tears.

"Yeah sure. All of you say that," forcing himself upon the petite woman.

Mildred felt like she was going to feint. As he pounded her, she passed out. When she woke up, her rapist was gone from the apartment. Mildred, consumed by fear and shame, never returned to her job – not even to collect her paycheck. Eventually, it was mailed to her address on Westervelt Avenue. A good bookkeeper, Mildred found another job north of Wall Street, but she was tormented for years by what Brad had done to her.

As Mildred walked back to the front steps, Nancy could see that she was tormented by what she had seen in the white wall. Nancy told Norton to go inside the house for so she could talk to the prim woman. Briefly, Mildred told her about what she had gone through as a young woman at the hands of Brad Owen.

"Don't you think the bastard should pay for what he did to you?"

"That is up to God. It is written in Romans: Vengeance is mine, I will repay," Mildred responded.

"That's all well and good, but if Brad is still around –he needs to be punished."

Mildred's eyes filled with tears as she nodded.

"I know someone who could help us. He lives at the end of Pulaski Avenue—Charlie Krepinski. He was a private detective – one of those guys who tracks people down. Do you have a picture of him?"

"Yes, I do. I followed his Wall Street career for many years and I have newspaper clippings with his picture," the prim woman replied.

"So, you thought about revenge yourself."

"Whenever I brought it up to Stanley, he'd repeat the line from Romans that only God has can wreak vengeance on the offender."

"No, vengeance will be ours – you and me. Let's go for a walk," Nancy said quietly.

They walked north on Pulaski Avenue almost to the very end, where the defunct Staten Island Railroad tracks ran along a grassy gully beyond a rusty chain-link fence. Beyond Kenny Worthington's neat house was a small cottage in need of a paint job, where Charlie Krepinski lived. In the driveway was an old station wagon – a woody – that looked like it hadn't been driven in years. As with their previous encounter, Charlie seemed to anticipate Nancy's visit, because he stepped out of the front door as the two women approached his rickety front steps.

"How are you doing, Nancy? What sort of job this time?"

"More in your line of work. Locating a dude who needs to pay for his misdeeds," Nancy replied – nodding towards Mildred.

Overcoming her embarrassment, Mildred recounted her awful experience at the hands of Brad Owen, the accountant she had worked with in Wall Street as a young woman.

"The guy needs to pay for his crime. I'll find him. It may take some time and effort. But, I'm a good at what I do. If he's still alive – I'll find hi."

"Now, don't lay a hand on him. Just find him. We'll do the punishment," Nancy stipulated.

"What is your fee? I have two hundred dollars," Mildred offered.

"No Fee. Just expenses – gas, tolls, and eats. Fifty bucks would be fine. If doubt he's left the country," Charlie replied.

"That's fine. I don't expect you to trek over the four corners of the globe," the prim woman responded.

CHAPTER 25

SEARCHING FOR BRAD OWEN

"The Covid-20 virus hit the airlines hard – spreading like wildfire in airplanes – killing pilots, and flight attendants. Even airplane mechanics and flight controllers were affected. Nowadays, the only way you can travel to Europe is on a merchant ship – of which there are very few. If Brad is alive, he's in the good old USA," Charlie explained.

Mildred gave Charlie information, newspaper clippings, and an old picture she had managed to save of her old nemesis.

Charlie studied the picture. "Can't say I know the guy, but from his picture," he paused a few moments. "He looks like a prick. Pardon my French."

"Would, that your efforts match the vehemence of your language, Mr. Krepinski."

"Would that I find this guy. It's time he paid for his crime. And I'm sure – what's your name again?"

"Mildred Aimsley."

"I'm sure, Mildred, that you weren't the only woman he's pulled that crap with."

Mildred became emotional as her eyes filled with tears. "Would that we lived in a world where people behaved with kindness, respect, and compassion towards other human beings."

"Ma'am You're talking about Armageddon – when Jesus returns and everyone has to account for their crimes."

"My partner, Stanley, is a preacher. He says to sin is to miss the mark."

"It depends on how far you miss the mark. There's a big difference between cursing someone and putting a knife in his heart."

"Or shooting him in the arm versus shooting him the head," Nancy chimed in.

"That's right. I was grazed in my left arm in the tussle with the Truppers. Had the bullet hit in my head or chest – it would have been a different story."

"So, where you gonna be looking for Mister Owen?"

"The Island naturally –starting with the Saint George – near the Ferry. Then, New Dorp, South Beach, and Tottenville just to rule those areas out. My gut tells me he lives in the city – either the Island or Brooklyn – maybe Bay Ridge or Brooklyn Heights. Is the Verrazzano Bridge passable?"

"It is. Our people – that is Gerald Hopkins' organization – who control that bridge."

"That's good to know

"Do you have a car?" Nancy asked.

"Unfortunately, I don't. I was wondering if I could borrow your car," Charlie said – eyeing her big blue Dodge.

"I'll drive you around Staten Island. We'll worry about Brooklyn and Manhattan later. We'll start tomorrow. See you at six A M. Bring your gun," she added – heading for her house.

Norton looked at the slender woman. "Can I come with you guys?"

And Freddy gave her a look which asked the same question.

"No. And neither can you, Freddy. We don't want a posse that could attract attention."

Bright and early the next day, Nancy and Charlie were heading along Richmond Terrace in her old blue Dodge. The parked on Westervelt Avenue – stopping to look at the Victorian building where Midred had rented an apartment, not far from Richmond Terrace. Just for the sake of thoroughness, Nancy and Charlie entered the building, knocked on door, and showed Owen's picture – soliciting information on the Wall Street accountant. Not surprising, no one knew the man who had lived in St. George more than twenty years ago. Many of the apartments were unoccupied – not unexpected in light of the devastation of the Covid-20 pandemic. Like Elm Park and Mariners Harbor, the area had the hollowed out feeling of a ghost town.

Nancy and Charlie even walked up Stuyvesant Place to Curtis High School and questioned the neighbors in the vicinity of the stately school, which had achieved landmark status before the pandemic – due to its gothic architecture. More recently, the school had been converted into an urgent care center and a food kitchen. Sadly, Curtis's extensive grounds – once decorated with flowers, rose bushes, shrubs and trees – was overgrown with weeds, covered with leaves, and littered with newspapers, trash, bottles, and cans. Neglect and decline were the fate of schools, post offices, and government buildings – as well as private establishments throughout the land.

"I got a hunch, Brad's a small-town guy. Let's try the South Shore –starting with New Dorp. Like the rest of the Island, the town of New Dorp had been hit hard by the Covid-20 pandemic. Most of the stores, restaurants, and businesses were shuttered and there were few shoppers in the stores and few pedestrians around. Nancy and Charlie trekked along New Dorp Lane, which also had the look and feel of a ghost town. Stopping into the stores that were open, Nancy showed the locals the pictures of Bra Owen, but nobody knew him. Tired they walked back to Nancy's blue Dodge and leaned against the front hood,

There was a middle-aged couple leaving a deli. As a joke, Charlie yelled," Do any of you yokels know Brad Owen?"

They both turned and walked towards them. The woman spoke up. "This was a long time ago – like twenty years. Brad tried to get frisky with me. I told my brother who beat him up. Then, he pulled the same stuff with another girl. Word got out that a bunch of guys were after him, so he hightailed it out of town. Never saw the bastard again – pardon my French."

"Any idea where he may have gone?" Nancy asked.

"He's still pulling the same stuff?"

"No, this was something that happened years ago. But wrongdoing must be punished. No matter how long ago it happened," Charlie replied.

"Were you the victim?" the woman asked Nancy.

"No. I'm quick and accurate with a gun. Had he tried that on me, I would have shot him within two seconds," Nancy replied in a matter-of-fact manner.

"Good for you, Ma'am," the man replied.

"You know what? I remember some talk through the grapevine that Brad lived in Brooklyn Heights. He hung around the promenade overlooking the East River – looking for pickups. It was years ago. With the pandemic, he may not even be alive."

"Thank you very much. What's your name?"

"I'm Betty and this is my husband Bohdan."

"Good to meet you both. I'd advise you guys to get a gun. We're living in a jungle," Nancy replied, as the couple continued their walk along New Dorp Lane.

Driving back to Elm Park, Nancy turned to Charlie. "Do you want to drop the whole thing or keep looking for Mister Casanova?"

"I'm a private eye. It's all about the joy of the hunt."

"Hal told me about Casanova – a gambler and a seducer. In middle age, after a lifetime of sexual escapades, he found religion and renounced his evil ways. Casanova had gambling debts, so he fled to Prague, where he lived as a philosopher and a Christian."

"You think Brad has seen the light/ and has become a good Christian?" Charlie replied.

"We can drive over the Verrazzano-Narrows Bridge or take a ferry boat that leaves Rosebank once an hour. Gerald Hopkins says there are armed guards on the Verrazzano, but who wants to get stuck on a three-mile-long bridge?" Nancy responded.

"We'll take the ferry. Where does it go to?

"Fort Hamilton area. Then we can take third Avenue to Brooklyn Heights and look for our frisky friend," Nancy replied.

"Sounds good. We'll leave the Island early tomorrow."

"You're ready to call it a day? Where's the joy of the hunt?" the slender woman replied – repressing a smile.

Hey! I'm no spring chicken, but I'm a tough old bird."

"O K, Charlie. See you tomorrow, bright and early – tough old bird."

Before sunrise, Charlie was at Nancys door. Smiling, she brought him a Styrofoam cup of coffee and a donut.

"Thanks," the private eye said – slurping the coffee and biting the donut.

"Don't thank me, thank Norton. Have it in the car," she called out – giving Norton a hug and a kiss.

Hustling to her big blue Dodge, she checked her gun in her shoulder bag. Within a several minutes, they raced down Morningstar Road, turned onto Richmond Terrace, heading for St. George, continuing on to Bay Street, and finally reaching Rose Bank. Nancy parked the Dodge on a side street where the greenish-blue water of New York Bay was visible beyond the trees. They walked to a boat yard where rowboats, motor boats and fishing vessels were tied to a rickety wooden dock. An old fisherman, named Sonny, agreed to take them across to Fort Hamilton in his fishing vessel.

Nancy introduced Sonny to Charlie. "He's a retired detective."

"I know you. You helped me nab a guy on the run from the cops," Charlie said, as the two men shook hands.

"I remember. Always willing to help law enforcement."

"I need to grab a criminal in Brooklyn Heights. It may take me a few hours. And then bring him back with us," Nancy explained.

"I got a driver who'll do that. No questions asked. He's lives near the docks in Fort Hamilton. Here's his address."

Sonny gave Nancy a piece of paper. And then they headed for Sonny's motor boat. Soon they were skimming across the rough waves of New Yok Bay – heading for Brooklyn. Fortunately, it was a mild day with a calm breeze. Charlie was a little seasick from the small boat's ups and downs in the waves. Nancy, steel-nerved with the sea legs of a mariner, handled the boat's jostling quite well. They arrived at a wooden pier larger and in better shape than the rickety dock on the Staten Island side of the Narrows.

Nancy and Charlie got off the motor boat and walked along the long pier in the direction Sonny pointed them. The slender woman walked briskly, while the detective struggled to get his bearings – shaking off his wooziness. There was a short, stocky man standing next to an old Chevy sedan.

"Hey Mickey. Take these folks to the promenade in Brooklyn Heights and wait for them. They're gonna grab someone and bring him back."

"Sounds like fun. I'm in," Mickey called back.

Nancy and Charlie jumped in the car and said hello.

"You're Charlie. I've worked with you before," Mickey said – looking at the retired detective. Driving along

"Yeah. You helped me nab a few bail-jumpers back in the day."

"Remember the guy who slipped out of his cuffs and tried to open the back door?" Mickey asked.

"Like it was yesterday. You turned around and bopped him with a billy club," Charlie replied.

"I'm Mickey – pleased to meet you miss. Are you a gumshoe?"

"No. I'm just a concerned citizen bringing back a guy who needs to pay his dues," Nancy replied.

"You look like a tough cookie," Mickey replied – eyeing her in his rearview mirror.

"She's the best shot in Elm Park. A marksman without equal."

"Awesome. Much needed in this day-and-age – with no cops around" Mickey responded.

"The rich hire their own armed guards. And some of them rob the people they're supposed to be protecting," Charlie commented.

"I guess folks need to be self-reliant in this day and age," Nancy replied.

"You can say that again," Charlie murmured, more to himself than the others.

The day started out as cloudy and overcast, but soon the sun emerged through the clouds. Soon, the early morning chill had dissipated midst the sun's warming rays. They drove along mostly deserted side streets and then got onto the Brooklyn Queens Expressway – locally known as the Gowanus

Expressway. On this once-busy artery there was some traffic – occasional cars and trucks headed in both directions. After thirty minutes, they got off the expressway – arriving in Brooklyn Heights. Mickey parked the Chevy in a deserted street strewn with bottles, cans, newspapers, and torn garbage bags, There were a couple of homeless men sitting near a steel girder cooking their breakfast in an old barbecue pit.

In the post covid-20 world, food and shelter were not easy to come by. The precipitous drop in population worldwide did leave a large stock of empty apartments and houses – though many were in need of repair. Supermarkets were few and far between. Vital government services like police, fire, hospitals, schools, and the post office were almost nonexistent. Hence, crimes ranging from larceny to burglaries to muggings and even homicides, were rampant. Vigilante justice, with all is shortcomings, had replaced the local police in maintain law and order.

Charlie patted his gun – secure in its belted holster – and Nancy checked her 22-caliber pistol in her shoulder bag. What pleased the tall detective about the young woman was her matter-of-fact attitude in confronting the habitual offender. As a stalwart defender of the vulnerable, Nancy Perez had become an Elm Park legend. His old stickball buddy, Freddy von Voglio bragged about her coolness under fire – calling her Annie Oakley. He looked over at the young woman and she nodded to him. After walking a block or so, they mounted a litter-strewn staircase to the promenade.

There was only a handful of people strolling on the expansive open promenade, which was marked with benches, fountains, and decorative street lights. There was a man in a pushcart – selling coffee and donuts. What caught their attention was a woman struggling with a husky middle-aged man who smiled at her like she was a spoiled child.

"Come on, Mollie. Sit down on the bench with me. I'll buy you a coffee and donut.

We'll chat and enjoy the sun," he said – putting his arm over the woman's shoulder.

"No! Get away from me. You're a groper."

"Molly, don't be that way. I promise I'll be the perfect gentleman," he replied in soothing tone.

"If you don't leave me alone, I'll scream."

Looking around, the man replied. "There's no cops around. Just folks minding their own business."

Unwilling to wait another second, Nancy strode over to the couple. "Take your hands off her, Brad."

"Mind your own business! How do you know my name?" Brad replied.

"We're bringing you in for sexual assault," Charlie said – pulling out his gun.

"I knew it. You're a rapist," Molly said—getting up. "He's all yours – throw him in jail."

Brad took advantage of Charlie's inattention to grab his gun. But Nancy stepped in and punched the husky man in the stomach. Brad lurched forward – gasping for breath and dropping the gun he had just seized. As he reached for it, Nancy stomped on his hand – causing Brad to squeal like a pig.

"Stand still and put your hands behind your back," Nancy ordered, as Charlie slapped the cuffs on the culprit.

"I wish you had worked with me years ago when I was a private eye. You would have made my job a lot easier," Charlie said – grasping both of Brad's hands in one strong hand and cuffing them with the other.

"Watching his eyes, I saw he was gonna make a move," the slender woman said – keeping her eyes on Brad

A stranger came up to them. "Why are you taking him into custody?"

Charlie flashed his detective badge and Nancy pointed to Molly.

"He touched me inappropriately and wouldn't take no for an answer," the woman replied.

"He's wanted for a sexual assault on Staten Island. We're bringing him back to answer the charges," Nancy said firmly.

"So, your enacting vigilante justice on this guy. Ever hear of habeas corpus? A person accused of a crime has a right to know the charges against him and his accuser. And he's entitled to a lawyer."

"Are you a lawyer?" Nancy asked.

"Yes, I am."

"What's your name?" Charlie asked – holding on to Brad Owen firmly.

"Robert Cane."

"Then, come with us, Mister Cane. There's room in Mickey's old Chevy and in my big Dodge too."

Cane agreed to accompany them back to Staten Island. And the four of them walked to the staircase and descended it the litter-strewn Brooklyn streets – heading for Mickey's beat-up Chevy sedan. Approaching the car, they saw Mickey get out of the car and wave them over.

"What happened? Did you knab two perverts?"

"No. Brad's got a self-appointed lawyer," Charlie called out.

166

CHAPTER 26

THE TRIAL OF BRAD OWEN

Upon arriving on Staten Island, Nancy and Charlie carefully took the handcuffed Brad out of her big Dodge with Robert Cane scrutinizing the handling of his client. Over the lawyer's objections, Owen was placed in the six-foot wide five-foot high cage that Freddy had used for Pussyfoot, his male bobcat. The young bobcat was now tame enough to stay with Freddy in his apartment on Hooker Place. Though Freddy's roommate, Hank, wasn't totally convinced of the bobcat's domesticity. So, he kept his distance from the animal. Though Freddy kept Pussyfoot on a lease, the terse-talking telegraph operator was definitely leery of the big cat. After a quick supper in which Freddy fed the bobcat scraps from the table, Hank retreated to his room and locked his door. Thus, Pussyfoot's cage was made available for Brad Owen's incarceration – pending the trial which would start first thing in the morning.

Wasting no time, Nancy introduced Owen's self-appointed lawyer to Mildred Ainsley who related her unhappy story concerning the defendant that occurred when she worked as a bookkeeper in Manhattan.

"He talked me into showing him my apartment. First, he massaged my feet, which was O K. then he kissed them. Which made me feel uncomfortable. Then, he proceeded to assault me sexually," Mildred related.

"Did you say no? Did you tell him to stop?" Cane asked.

"I said please don't do this to me. I'm a virgin."

"Did you scream and resist him?"

"No, I lost consciousness."

"What year did this occur?"

I'll never forget the date – August second, two thousand two."

Robert Cane jotted down some notes

"Thanks for your time, ma'am. I'll see you tomorrow," Cane replied.

Mildred nodded and returned to her second-floor apartment next door.

The lawyer turned to Nancy. Who was soon joined by Freddy. "Technically, the statute of limitations has been exceeded. In the state of New York it's twenty years. The sexual assault occurred in the year two thousand two. We're in the year two thousand twenty-six. We're talking about a crime committed twenty-four years. So, the woman waited too long to take legal action."

"That's bullshit. The rapist is going on trial. If you don't want to defend him, then take a walk," Freddy replied vehemently.

"Fine. I'm just telling you the law regarding the statute of limitations. I'll defend Owen."

Nancy walked the lawyer back to her front porch, where she introduced him to Norton. It was clear Norton was not fond of the attorney.

"You can sleep in the sunporch." Turning to Norton, "Norton get him a fresh sheet and pillow case. And bring him something to eat."

Norton complied – bringing Brad fresh linen, along with a bowl of soup and some bread. The soup was chicken soup with vegetables made by Norton himself in a big pot. Brad finished off the soup and bread quickly. Adapting to the small cell, Brad was soon asleep under the blanket given to him. Nancy, Charlie, Cane, Freddy, and Norton also had the tasty vegetable-chicken soup in the kitchen. Nancy, calmer than her companions, kept the conversation going—telling Robert Cane about the tight-knit Elm Park community.

"We look out for each other. It's the only way to survive in this day and age," she remarked.

"Absolutely. Which is why I volunteered to defend Mister Owen. In this country everyone is entitled to know the charges against him, to have counsel, and to be judged by his peers."

Bright and early the next morning, the trial was held in Nancy's large front room, from which the bed had been moved out and several folding chairs moved in. Robert Cane had Brad Owen speak at length to open the trial. Brad related his version of the events on August 2nd, 2002. He said Mildred and himself went out to dinner at a diner on Stuyvesant Place. Then, they walked around St. George – passing Curtis High School and she invited him to her studio apartment.

"Mildred said she wanted advice on how to decorate and furnish the apartment. I walked around the place – giving her pointers. Then, she got me a drink – scotch on the rocks. And had some herself."

"I object! I've never drank liquor in my life and never kept any in my apartment."

"You'll get your turn to testify ma'am," Cane interrupted.

"After a while, she went to the bathroom and came out wearing a nightie. On thing led to another and soon we were having sex on her couch. This stuff about her being a virgin is bullshit. This gal knew her way around the male body from A to Z."

"That's total fabrication. Would that you tell the truth for once in your life," Mildred called out.

"Come on, Mildred. Don't you have any sentimental feelings about me?" Owen pleaded half-seriously.

"Sentimental? You're as sentimental as a sewer rat!" she replied heatedly.

This caused a few chuckles in the jury, which angered the defendant, who grew red in the face.

"Would that you weren't such a needy bitch. She craved my prick – putting it in her mouth!"

At this point, Mildred screamed and fainted. Freddy and the Rev carried the middle-aged woman to the middle room, set her down on the couch, and gave her a glass of water.

Then, Nancy stood up and went over to Brad – standing within a foot of him to counter his version of the story. Intimidated, Brad leaned backward in his chair. "So, you're saying the Midred was a willing and active participant in the sex taking place back in two thousand two."

"You betcha. She was hungry for it. She licked it like it was a peppermint candy cane. Couldn't get enough of it," he replied with a sneer and a forced laugh.

Revived by the water, Mildred sprang up and ran up to Owen, who fearfully leaned away from the angry woman. "Would that your tongue burst into flames from the lies that spew out of your evil lips. You forced yourself on me! You tore my blouse, tossed my skirt on the floor, threw me onto my couch, and raped me – hurting me. I was bleeding. And then you stormed out of my apartment."

Though looking away from Mildred, Brad continued his venom, "You wanted it. You craved it. Then, you pretended that it was forced on you. All you bitches are the same – playing the blame game after you got your jollies."

Even Robert Cane was disgusted by his client. He refused to expend more effort in Brad Owen's behalf. Shaking his head, he said: "The defense rests its case."

Freddy, who acted as the judge, said: "Let the jury decide."

The jury consisted of Nancy, Charlie, Norton, Hank, Mrs. Banks, Greg, the dwarfs Quinn and Quentin. Quinn had argued that Bubba, the bear, understood language and should be allowed to sit on the jury. Despite the black bear's preternatural intelligence, Cane, Freddy, and Nancy vetoed the idea. Upon hearing he was rejected for jury duty, Bubba was visibly upset. Nancy consoled the bruin by petting and whispering to him, and giving the bear a box of raisins. The jury retreated to Nancy's backyard – sitting under the old mulberry tree and deliberated for over an hour. The case boiled down to a "he-said-she-said" scenario in which the credibility of the plaintiff vis-a-vis the defendant would determine the verdict.

With the exception of Hank, everyone believed that Brad Owen was guilty of the sexual assault. The terse-talking telegraph operator disagreed. "When woman invites man to her apartment after a date. It's to have sex – etcetera."

"Where are you from – planet Mars?" Charlie asked – scrutinizing the Hank like he was indeed – an extraterrestrial.

"What era are you from – the 1950s?" Mrs Banks asked –shaking her head.

"You can't be serious, Hank" Nancy chimed in – recalling she had once thought about him romantically – before meeting Hal.

The telegraph operator shrugged his shoulders and stayed quiet, while the others went over the facts of the case.

Speaking up in behalf of the jury, Charlie said: "So let's have another vote. All those in favor of a guilty verdict – raise your hands.'

This time everyone raised their hands – guilty.

"Now comes the penalty phase. Ten years, twenty years. What's the consensus?"

"Where we gonna keep him? I want that cage back for Pussyfoot. She doesn't know how to use a cat box. Besides, Hank is scared shit of her," Freddy related – grinning and rubbing his hands.

"You're right. And none of want to feed and take care of this creep," Nancy declared.

Then, Robert Cane spoke up. "I heard Freddy talking about the Pine Barrens in South Jersey. Send him there with supplies and equipment –so he can survive. Like most places in the post Covid-20 era, it's mostly empty of people. So, even if he wanted to harass a woman, I highly doubt he'd find anyone."

"That's not a bad idea. With the understanding that if he shows up here or anywhere to make trouble, we'll track him down and shoot him," Nancy declared somberly.

Everyone concurred with sending Brad Owen to the Pine Barrens. He would be provided with food and water, plus a tent, matches, a canteen, a hunting knife, a shovel, and a hatchet to survive in the woods. Consequently, Brad's fate was in his own hands. Brad asked for a gun in order to hunt, but the request was turned down.

"At least give me a bow and arrows to hunt with."

That request was also turned down. After some deliberation, it was decided to give him an animal trap, a fishing pole, a net for catching fish, and one of Freddy's hunting knives. There were many streams which were ran throughout that the Pine Barrens. With the Covid-20 pandemic, populations in most areas of the country had plummeted and uninhabited wilderness areas had grown. Mother Nature had filled the void of declining human population with a surge in all forms of animal wildlife.

"Very good. A wise decision – worthy of King Solomon," Charlie commented.

"Wasn't he the guy who ordered a kid to be chopped in two – giving a piece to each woman arguing over him?" Freddy asked.

"That sounds cruel to me," Hank said.

"Hank, a lot of the stuff in the Bible isn't true. It's an allegory," Nancy responded.

"If you can't believe in the Bible, what can you believe in?" Hank said.

"Believe in the goodness of your neighbors and people in general – with a few exceptions," Nancy answered.

"I believe in goodness and right over wrong – etcetera," Hank replied.

"Well, I don't always believe in etcetera," Nancy snapped.

Early the next day, Nancy and Charlie borrowed Gregg's panel truck. The truck was filled with the all the equipment agreed upon, plus a few days supply of food and water. Freddy joined Brad in the back of the truck, the latter was cuffed — pending arrival in the Pine Barrens. The trip along mostly empty roads and highways would take about three hours. Brad seemed resigned to his fate – a solitary hunter-and-fisherman in the vast Pine Barrens. It certainly appeared to be better than spending years in a small cell. Whether Brad Osen saw it that way was a matter of conjecture.

At some point, Brad persuaded Freddy to remove his cuffs – to which the easy-going octogenarian agreed. He had a gun trained on the culprit. The ne'er-do-well looked at a magazine which featured scantily-clad women displaying their feet. Then, he asked Freddy if he could go through the stuff given to him. Again, Freddy assented. Taking advantage of the latter's inattention, Brad grabbed the hunting knife and slashed Freddy in the arm – causing a gash of several inches. Freddy dropped the gun on the floor and Brad grabbed it.

As he raised his gun to aim it at her, Nancy quickly drew her gun from her shoulder bag and shot Brad before he could pull the trigger. The bullet pierced his chest and entered his heart – killing him instantly. Charlie pulled off the highway and stopped on a shoulder. Working quickly, Nancy patched up Freddy with the iodine and bandages that had been donated to Brad.

"I think you'll live Mister von Voglio. I used most of the gauze," the slender woman said – admiring her handiwork.

"You're like a cat with nine lives," Charley chimed in.

"I'll need them to take care of Pussyfoot, It worked out fine – I got the hunting knife back," Freddy replied with a quick grin.

Things settled down after the trial. Brad Owen no longer walked the Earth. Mildred did her best to forget the unpleasantness of the trial – along with the bad memories it had engendered. With the court case over, attorney Robert Cane asked if he could remain in the area.

"I like Staten Island and I like you folks. Would it be possible for me to find a place in Elm Park?

"It's a free country and there's plenty of empty houses around. In fact, the apartment downstairs from Mildred and the Rev is empty," Nancy replied.

"The more, the merrier," Freddy added – smiling and rubbing his hands energetically.

The slender woman consulted with prim woman and her mate, who had no problems living upstairs from the lawyer. "There's already a lawyer living in Elm Park – Stan Mislicki, who moonlights as a baker. His girlfriend is Lora Langley, coppersmith and crystal-ball reader."

"It's fine, I realize there's not much legal work on the Island. I can commute to Brooklyn if I'm needed. And I do other things – like hothouse gardening. It's the biggest craze in Brooklyn. Every apartment has a greenhouse on the roof and I've become pretty good at it."

"Now that sound's promising. The flats have a long flat roof that might make a good garden," Nancy replied.

"I'll give you a hand. In the dead of winter, we don't want to run short of veggies," Norton said.

"I never go hungry. There's plenty of game around – deer, rabbits, wild turkeys, raccoons, snakes, frogs – even gators. It's all good," Freddy added.

Though she didn't talk about it, Nancy was disturbed about shooting Brad – though he was a sexual offender with the conscience of a viper. She decided to visit Lora and talk with her. Though busy working on copper bracelets, Lora was happy to talk with the slender woman. They weren't far part in age and had both grown up on the North Shore.

"I heard about the incident with that Owen creep. How are you feeling?" Lora inquired.

"I'm O K. It was a reflex shooting. I didn't mean to kill him."

"Nancy, you did the right thing. Owen would have killed Freddy and you," the pretty long-haired woman responded.

CHAPTER 27

A BAD STORM BREWING

"I JUST WISH YOUR CRYSTAL BALL COULD WARN US ABOUT BAD PEOPLE COMING to Elm Park

"You mean like a weather forecast – a bad people forecast, But, people can change for the better," Lora replied.

Lora put the copper aside and moved her crystal ball from a shelf to her work bench. She wiped the large crystal ball with a silk cloth and pulled down the shades. The crystal ball sparked with static electricity.

Addressing the crystal ball directly, she whispered, "Help us with those bent on wrongdoing and other impending dangers."

The crystal ball became cloudy, then there was an image of the merry-go-round rotating slowly. Magnets were distributed along the outer circumference of the whirligig. And a person faced he white-painted wooden wall and wall as before. But there was something different: two large opposite-facing mirrors had been attached at the ends of the white wall. In addition, two flashlights were mounted just above the mirrors – emitting beams which reflecting back and forth – bathing the viewer in high-intensity light. Then, there was a loud roaring and a dark cloud hovering above Morningstar Road.

"It looks like a rain storm with strong wind," Lora related.

"Actually, we could use some rain. We didn't have any snow this past winter and the streams around here are drying up," Nancy replied.

Peering into the crystal ball, "This looks like a tornado."

"This is New York – not Texas. We don't get tornados around here," Nancy responded.

"Maybe. Anyway, try that flashlight thing with the mirrors. You got nothing to lose," the pretty long-haired woman replied.

Early the next morning, Nancy decided to stand in front of the white wall herself. Freddy thought she was crazy, but he set up the flashlights with the opposing mirrors as Lora suggested.

"Run it slow," she called out to the octogenarian, who nodded.

The same high-pitched sound of an animal whining emanated from the whirligig – similar to a coyote pup. Freddy theorized that maybe coyotes had nested in the floor of the merry-go-round in the distant past.

"Maybe the its working like a magical tape recorder," Freddy said with a wry smile.

"Are you getting mystical on me?" Nancy said – trying not to smile.

Mildred and Reverend Staller, who had been watching the proceeding from their front steps, crossed the street.

"Would that the world was more mystical and less humdrum," the prim woman called out.

"Indeed, many everyday events cannot be explained by the laws of science," the Rev asserted.

"I'm no scientist, but I know anything that happens has a cause," Freddy remarked.

"Where does love come from?" Mildred asked.

"Why does man kill his fellow man?" the Rev added.

"And why is there something instead of nothing?" Freddy chimed in.

"There you go again Freddy! I think you're a philosopher," Nancy exclaimed.

Freddy rubbed his hands and smiled widely.

Turning back to the white screen, Nancy saw something disturbing. A loud raring sound, trees bending in the wind, branches blowing about and people running for cover. And a huge dark cloud hovering over the Kill van Kull. As the roaring increased, the cloud moved along Morningstar Road – carrying rain and hail.

Nancy rushed home and told Norton what she had seen on the screen. "We've got to tell everyone to get ready for a tornado. Board up windows and have extra food and water on hand."

Norton walked towards the flats to warn them and Nancy went south on Pulaski Avenue – stopping at each house and ending up at Charley's house to inform her neighbors of the impending storm threatening the area. Within a few hours, came the predicted rain – starting as light rainfall, becoming steady rain, and finally coming down in torrents with the passing hours. In addition, the wind kicked up as the storm approached, with wind gusts exceeding 40 miles per hour – amounting to gale force. Happily, the house along Pulaski Avenue were of sturdy construction – built decades ago when foundations were made of concrete, walls lined with sturdy wooden studs, while floors and ceilings supported by thick joists, and roofs fashioned out of real wood – topped with thick shingles nailed to the wood. And the outside walls were covered with wood clapboards, aluminum siding, or cement stucco.

Making her rounds, Nancy remembered that Dr. Emil and Alfred worked in the cottage in the grassy field under the Bayonne Bridge. With the rain and hail and wind increasing moment by moment, she ran to her big blue Dodge, turned onto Morningstar Road and headed for Richmond Terrace. Turning on the Terrace, she traversed the winding gravel road that lead to her doorstep. Anticipating the storm, the teenager convinced the middle-aged physician to store the medical supplies – including drugs, medicines, bandages, and equipment in a big steel box for safe storage.

Seeing her car, Alfred ran outside and greeted Nancy, "We're getting ready to hunker down during the storm."

"No. You'ill be flooded. Come with me. That little house won't withstand the winds that are coming."

Alfred ran inside to speak to Dr. Emil. It must have taken a lot of convincing, because the latter didn't emerge for fifteen minutes. At last, he came from the cottage with his doctor's bag smiling vaguely at Nancy. The slender woman ran into the house and with Alfred's help, carried the steel box of supplies and meds to the car – placing ir into her trunk. The physician got into the car next to Nancy and Alfred piled into the back. Then, the teenaged boy dashed into the house and emerged with a small cage, with a light-brown rat inside.

"I can't leave Ratty alone in the storm. If the house gets flooded, he'll drown."

"If Ratty gets out of his cage, I'll shoot him," Nancy warned.

"Ratty's nice. Want to pet him?"

"No thanks."

They drove back to Pulaski Avenue. Alfred and Dr. Emil went upstairs to stay with the boy's mom – Mrs. Banks. Nancy wondered how the woman would tolerate Ratty, but she was a patient woman who had survived tough times and managed to raise a hard-working boy – eager to learn and curious about the world. Nancy and Norton watched through the kitchen window as the mini-tornado made its noisy transit through the neighborhood. The storm arrived with roaring wind and torrential rain, but it passed through the North Shore within half an hour. Though fierce, the storm did not realize the worst fears of those in its path. With the exception of a weeping willow tree on Walker Street, there were no downed trees – though lots of branches were scattered in backyards, and on sidewalks and streets. Within an hour, folks were outside raking the fallen branches and strewn refuse blown around by the storm.

The next day, bright and sunny, was devoted to more sweeping and raking after the highly anticipated, but somewhat overrated storm. Nancy did some raking in the backyard, but then handed the rake to Norton. Crossing the street, she walked over to the merry-go-round to take a turn for the first time. The slender woman turned on the flashlights above the opposite-facing mirrors and picked up a horseshoe magnet. She called Freddy from his garden patch to start the merry-go-round. Smiling widely and rubbing his hands, Freddy turned on the motor and the whirligig began turning slowly. As the ride began to rotate, the machine seemed to come to life – with an amber glow and a whining sound similar to that of a coyote pup.

CHAPTER 28

NANCY TAKES A TIME TRIP

"Tell me about my family," Nancy said in a low voice.

The screen came to life and images took form. She was watching the story of her ancestors, who were Carib-American Indian people – living on islands now referred to as the Lesser Antilles. The Caribbean Sea took its name from the Carib people, who were skilled fishermen, but also expert farmers – growing maize, beans, peanuts, squash, tomatoes. and yuca or cassava. Subgroups of the Carib were Arawak and the Taino, who also lived on the South American continent. These were the native peoples encountered by Columbus, who were subsequently oppressed, treated brutally, and enslaved There were no chiefs or hierarchical governing structure among the Carib people. The men were mostly warriors, while the women did the farming and caregiving. Tribal wars resulted in the captive women becoming slave-wives, while the captured men were usually killed. The Caribs were excellent navigators – traveling to the many Caribbean Islands on dugout canoes. Carib metallurgy focused on copper ores – cuprite, chalcopyrite, chalcocite, and covellite – used for plates, bowls, knives, spears, and arrow heads.

As the screen faded, Nancy felt as sense of pride that came from knowing her roots – information that she had never been privy to directly or from her family. In school she had learned about immigrants from Europe, but there wasn't much information about people immigrating from Asia, Africa, Central and South America, or the Caribbean. The fact that immigrants from third-world countries flee violence, misery, and poverty to come to America was overlooked. The drug cartel's control over the lives of everyday people of these areas was not discussed. And the awful plight of Native Americans, plus centuries of oppression and discrimination against Black people were given short shrift by her teachers.

There was an incident that occurred when she was in junior high and a bunch of girls were picking on her.

Observant and perspicacious, Nancy understood that people of color were not given the same chance as the white majority. There was the feeling that she and her kind were second-class citizens. At Northshore Bank, where she worked as a bookkeeper, Nancy was dismissed by her fellow workers as unimportant. Soon, she was being sexually harassed by her supervisor, David Gloom. The bank manager, Lance Landum, gawked at Nancy from time to time, but did not go beyond that. When, Gloom went so far as to slap her on the backside, Nancy turned around and raised a fist – causing the burly accountant to flinch.

"Do that again and I'll beat the shit out of you!" she yelled – causing everyone to look in her direction.

The lack of respect for female office workers could be attributed to the absence of unions for such workers. Unlike factory workers, office workers had never been organized by labor unions. Though the 40-hour work week, the minimum wage, the prohibition of child labor, paid vacations and holidays, and the very notion of weekends benefitted all workers. All of these benefits could be placed at the doorstep of labor unions. The right to organize workers and the right to strike were crucial to organized labor in any free country.

Notwithstanding the absence of a union, Gloom's boss, Lance Landum, was aware that a charge of sexual harassment would raise questions about his competence in running the bank. So, he finally intervened. Landum took Gloom aside and told him to backoff or he'd be looking for another job. From that point on, Gloom kept his hands to himself, but he still eyeballed the slender woman up and down – wearing a smirk in so doing. With the Covid-20 pandemic, millions of people died, banks, businesses, and local governments shutdown, Along with Gloom and Landum, Nancy lost her job as businesses, large and small, collapsed everywhere. With the absence of local police, Nancy learned how to handle a gun – becoming a vigilante peacekeeper for Elm Park. She was quick on the draw and deadly accurate shooter.

Around this time, a self-styled billionaire, Darren Trupp emerged from the borough of Queens to run for President. Outspoken, impudent and rude, Trupp had the chutzpah of a man born with a silver spoon in his mouth. He also had the loyalty of thousands of men wearing brown uniforms and calling themselves "Brownshirts." With much fanfare, Darren Trupp entered politics. The Truppers were unaware that the Nazis had shock troops with the same uniform. In Germany during the1930s, the Brownshirts terrorized political opponents and looted Jewish-owned businesses – preparing the way for Hitler's takeover of the government.

Trupp made it clear he'd hold on to power regardless of the outcome of the election. Nancy had been recruited by Gerald Hopkins, to harass Trupp at a big rally of his supporters in St. George. Flying in a small Cessna airplane piloted by Chester Worthington. Freddy tossed leaflets on the Trupp supporters, while Nancy zapped David Gloom, Lance Landrum, and Darren Trupp himself with nonlethal lasers – singing their hair. Trupp's toupee was set on fire – revealing his bald pate. Throwing caution to the wind, the three leaders jumped off the speaker's platform and fled the rally. Nevertheless, the self-styled politician's support among certain people remained strong – although his populist image as a bold man of the people was tarnished.

But demagogues of varying political beliefs are hard to keep down – they tend to bounce back like a Spalding thrown again front porch steps. Nancy got a note from Gerald Hopkins to meet with him in his office rented from the owner of the recently opened Wolstein's Fish Factory, where fish from the Kill van Kull and New York Bay were brought in every day to be cleaned, deboned, processed, canned, and sold throughout the New York-New Jersey metropolitan area. It had become a thriving business – employing forty islanders, plus several fishermen working on five fishing boats – plowing the sea surrounding Staten Island and extending to Manhattan. With little industry and reduced sewage, the Kill van Kull and New York Bay had taken on their pristine blue-green color of the preindustrial days of the republic.

CHAPTER 29

A NEW PLAN FOR TRUPP AND COMPANY

AS NANCY AND FREDDY ENTERED GERALD HOPKINS' SMALL OFFICE, THEY were greeted by Mason, who's calm manner and nondescript appearance were unchanged. "It's been awhile Nancy. And for you too Freddy. But, who you Elm Park folks always look the same – cool, calm, and collected," the office assistant said – shaking their hands.

Freddy smiled widely while Nancy stepped forward and hugged Mason. Then Gerald Hopkins got up from his desk and took Freddy's hand in both of his hands and then hugged Nancy in a fatherly fashion. Unlike Mason, Hopkins had aged visibly. There was little of his red hair left, his brow was creased with permanent lines, and he had lost a significant amount of weight.

"Indeed, you never change Nancy. Pretty and self-assured. And Freddy, you're one of those ageless wonders who have defied father time. Without further ado – I regret that we are in need of your services. Our intelligence tells us that Darren Trupp is back in the city. He's holed up with his a small contingent of Brown Shirts and hangers-on in Manhattan at Trupp Square Hotel, which has become pretty rundown in recent years."

"Hangers-on, you mean David Gloom and Lance Landum?"

"Who else. They've been with him through thick and thin," Hopkins replied.

"I hate those guys! Trupp Square Hotel is kind of posh – isn't it?" Nancy commented.

"Not anymore. It definitely has seen better days," Mason interjected.

"I guess nothing ain't what it used to be," Freddy said with a rub of his hands.

"That's true Freddy. Trupp is no longer a billionaire. His net worth is probably below sea level," Hopkins replied.

181

"Which is why he's back. Becoming President is a good way to get your hands on lots of dough," Nancy commented.

"Why don't we send them to the Pine Barrens?" Freddy offered – rubbing his hands and smiling.

"The last time we tried that, it didn't turn out very well remember?" Nancy said – looking at the octogenarian with a half-smile.

To which Freddy shrugged his shoulders, "Stuff happens."

"Remember the story about a man who said he hated America, so they put him on a ship and never let him return?" Nancy asked.

"Yes. It was called The Man without a Country by Edward Hale," Gerald responded.

"So, exile Trupp out of the country. If returns – shoot him."

"I have an idea. You know those fishing boats which bring fish to Wolstein's Fish Factory? Maybe we can rent a boat to transport Trupp and his two buddies to an island in the Caribbean?" Mason suggested.

"From what I hear, they fish off the northern coast Puerto Rico. Las Croabas is a town where a lot of fishing goes on. We'll pay the fishermen to bring Trupp and his two sidekicks there. Pay the good folks there a fee to put them to work – helping the local fishermen and farmers."

"What if Trupp and his friends don't cooperate?" Nancy asked.

"Shoot 'em!" Freddy yelled – answering for Hopkins and Mason.

"Exactly. Mason will personally deliver a letter from me stipulating the conditions of their banishment to Puerto Rico, and the measures to be taken if Trupp, Gloom, and Landum step out of line."

"Sounds good, but first we have to wrest them from the Brown Shirts," Nancy replied.

"My intelligence tells me the Truppers are planning a big rally in lower Manhattan next week. Rather than abduct them from a crowd of thousands of Trupp supporters, it would be better to nab them when they're isolated. An old ferry boat has been commandeered from the ferry dock. Trupp, Gloom, and Landum can be placed on it and ferried across New York Bay to the Kill van Kull. The ferry will stop at the refurbished docks used by the fishing boats, where the three gentlemen will be placed on one of the bigger fishing boats for a leisurely trip to Puerto Rico."

"Fine, but how do we get the three musketeers on the ferry boat?"

"There's a nightclub, called the Hi-Top, Trupp and his buddies go to regularly. It's in midtown – the east forties. You, Blanche, and Mildred are going to dress up as go-go girls and with the assistance of Freddy, Norton,

Billy, and Hank –hustle them into Glenn's panel truck and drive them to the ferry terminal. A second car will be needed – your Dodge, which I trust is reliable?"

"It is. Thanks to Glenn, who is the best mechanic on the North Shore."

"So, you, Blanche, Mildred, and Billy drive your Dodge on to the ferry boat. And Glenn will drive Freddy, Hank, and Norton in his panel truck on to the boat. You'll cross New York Bay to lower Manhattan and then drive to East 44th Street and Second Avenue, where the Hi-Top is located. After a few drinks, do your go-go girl dance routine, wait 'til Mister Trupp is relaxed. Then, pull your guns on Trupp, Gloom, and Landum and their guards."

"I don't know about Norton. His foot still isn't one hundred percent."

"He can help with the handcuffing."

"How many guards does Trupp have with him?"

"There's usually four or five Brown Shirts. And they're armed."

"What if they pull their guns?" Nancy asked.

"You have the element of surprise. And no one is quicker and more accurate than you, Annie Oakley. And by the time you pull your guns on them, Trupp and company will be soused with liquor."

"You make it sound so easy. I doubt Trupp's guards will be drinking."

"You tell the bartenders and other customers to scram and handcuff Trupp, Gloom, and Landum, along with his guards. As I said surprise is key. As is good planning," Hopkins responded in a matter-of-fact tone.

"And so is luck. When bullets start flying, you never know where the bullets are gonna wind up," Nancy replied.

Gerald Hopkins reminded her of a five-star general planning an attack far from the heat of the battle. But wisely, she said nothing.

"I have hired a ferry pilot and crew to drive the seized ferry boat to its destination about a mile from here."

"We're going to need flashlights, cuffs, guns, and ammo," Nancy added.

"Of course. Everything you need will be provided – including the go-go costumes," Mason interjected.

"I want pictures taken of you in your costumes."

Freddy rubbed his hands and Nancy reacted with surprise. "Don't be offended, but you, Blanche, and even church lady are nice-looking gals. But why don't you let me shoot Trupp? It would save everybody a lot of trouble."

Nancy shook her head – turning her attention to Hopkins.

"Just kidding, about the costumes," the usually serious Hopkins said – stifling a smile.

Nancy didn't respond. She was aware that Hopkins had a thing for Blanche, but it was a hopeless cause. For the hot-blooded redhead, who was no kid herself, was loyal to the eccentric Billy and his invisible partner.

"The sooner we do this, the better. I want Charlie Krepinski in on it," Nancy said.

"He's no kid," Mason replied.

"Neither am I. But Charlie's cool under fire," Freddy commented.

"Fine, bring him in place of Norton," Hopkins responded.

"So, let's do it. The sooner, the better."

She understood that Trupp and his henchmen were apt to find other places to spend time – which might not be as advantageous.

"You're on for tomorrow night. It's time we put Darren Trupp in a place where he can't do any harm."

Early the next morning the go-go costumes were delivered to Nancy's house. Blanche was sent for and she arrived – eager to try on the outfit. It consisted of a a tight low-cut red blouse, a short black skirt, and fishnet stockings and red high heels, and a black domino mask covering the eyes. In her younger days, Blanche was a popular go-go girl in a notorious South Shore bar called the Pigsty. Historically, the domino mask was used during Carnival and over the year at masquerade balls all over the world. Unlike the audacious redhead, Nancy had mixed feelings about the go-go girl scheme, but she realized it was a clever way to catch Darren Tropp with his metaphorical pants down.

Like Napoleon Bonaparte, Ulysses Grant, Abraham Lincoln, Grover Cleveland, Winston Churchill, and Richard Nixon – Darren Trupp had made a career of comebacks against big odds. And no one enjoyed celebrating his triumphs more than the former real estate magnate. At the start of the Covid-20 pandemic, bars and nightclubs lost business, but the urge of folks to eat, drink, and be merry led to a resurgence in such establishments. Historically, alcohol consumption had been banned during the Prohibition Era in 1919 – with the passage of the 18th Amendment. But, Americans have an unquenchable thirst for alcohol – legal or otherwise. Hence, folks resorted to making bootleg liquor and drinking at speakeasies. Given the perversity of human nature, people are going to have fun – even if it involves breaking the law and harming themselves. By 1933, alcohol was brought back to its rightful place in American culture with the passage of the 21st Amendment.

Gerald Hopkins pulled some strings – convincing the owner of the Hi-Top to allow go-go girls to entertain the customers. The D J was notified of the ruse and given a hundred-dollar tip to cooperate. Fortunately, it was a slow weekday night with only a handful of customers at the nightclub – in addition to Trupp, Gloom, Landum and four Brown Shirts sitting at two tables near the stage. The waiters were also informed of the plan and bribed to ply Trupp and his cohorts with lots of liquor. Before going on, Nancy noticed Norton and Billy sitting with at a table in a dark corner of the nightclub – not far from where Freddy and Charley sat.

Noticing the slender woman's distress, Blanche whispered to her. "I didn't want to tell you – Billy's been working on his old Beetle. He contacted Norton who agreed to go in to the city with him. They both have guns."

At a signal from the DJ, Nancy, Blanche, and Mildred ran onto the small stage and began dancing to the music. Blanche, the ex-go-go girl, was the best of the three – flaunting her assets and swaying in time with the music. Mildred was more inhibited and Nancy kept her eye on Trupp and his buddies ready to pull her gun from her bodice at the slightest provocation.

The DJ went through a bunch of disco songs – put kept going back to a catchy song.

Rock the Boat
"So I'd like to know where you got the notion
Said I'd like to know where you got the notion
To rock the boat,
Don't rock the boat baby"

Gloom peered at Nancy intently. "I've seen that gal before. But I can't quite place her."

Scrutinizing the slender woman, Landum nodded. "Yup, there's something familiar about her."

Then, Trupp himself got up and went over to the dancing women and proceeded to dance with them –grabbing Nancy by the waist and plodding around her. This actually made it easy for Nancy to pull her gun and shout to the DJ — "Stop the music!"

Reacting quickly, the Brown Shirts pulled their guns, but Norton and Billy were quicker. Several shots ran out with Nancy and Charlie shooting the guns out of two of Trupp's guards, while Freddy persuaded Gloom and Landum to drop their weapons and hold their hands up. In the midst of the commotion, Trupp ran for an exit near Norton and Billy's table but the latter stuck out his foot – causing the obese real estate magnate to trip and fall heavily to the floor.

185

Within five minutes, Trupp, Gloom, Landum, and the four Brown Shirts were handcuffed. The latter were warned to remain in place. Gloom, and Landum were packed into Glenn's panel truck with Freddy, While Trupp was placed in the backseat of Nancy's roomy Dodge with Charlie pointing a gun at him. The Hi-Top staff was instructed to hold the Brownshirts through the night and release them with stern warnings to stay clear of the midtown nightclub.

As with Staten Island and Brooklyn, the streets of Manhattan had little traffic – especially late at night. Hence, Nancy's big Dodge, Gregg's panel truck, and Billy's old V W Beetle headed west to Broadway and then headed downtown.

Sitting next to Charlie in the worn backseat of Nancy's Dodge, Trupp began talking in an undertone to the ex-detective. "Let me go and I'll make it worthwhile beyond your widest dreams. How'd you like to have your own place in the Caribbean? No more rainy days, no snow or cold weather to put up with. Lots of willing native women at your beck and call. Your own house – surrounded by palm trees and coconuts."

"At my age, what am I gonna do with a twenty-five-year-old? If you had made that offer thirty years ago – I might have considered it."

"What are you doing with that goddamn vigilante chick? She'll windup getting you killed. The Brown Shirts will track you down. I guarantee it. There are no cops to protect you."

Mildred turned around. "Would that you refrain from idle threats, Mister Trupp."

"You looked pretty good in your costume – church lady," Trupp snapped.

"Oh, hush!"

"And Senorita Nancy didn't look too shabby either," Trupp added with a sneer.

"Why do politicians continually break the ninth commandment?"

"Which one is that –thinking obscene thoughts?"

Charley put his gun in Trupp's face. "Shut up!"

Trupp shook his head and smiled his crooked-lip smile.

Arriving at South Ferry on the lower tip of Manhattan, the three-vehicle caravan waited in the dark. With the recent rains and clogged sewers, some of the streets were flooded. The city no longer cleared the sewers of garbage. After Nancy beeped her horn, the lights came on and a man emerged from the ferry slip –directing them towards the ferry boat. The ferry ride across New York Bay and Kill van Kull was uneventful. As with the streets, there was almost no boat traffic- except for a fishing boat and a tugboat pushing a barge filled with garbage towards the Atlantic Ocean where its contents would be unceremoniously dumped. Since the start of the Covid-20 pandemic and the precipitous drop in world population, environmental regulations were ignored worldwide. The captain of a merchant ship bound for the Caribbean was paid (funds provided by Gerald Hopkins) to transport Darren Trupp, David Gloom, and Lance Landum to Puerto Rico.

Happy with Trump's removal from the city to the fishing village of Las Croabas, Puerto Rico. Nancy decided to pay a visit to Lora to get a peak of her future. On a sunny day, she made the short walk to Mislicki's Bakery on Morningstar Road. Lora seemed to anticipate Nancy's visit, as she was dusting off her crystal ball with the silk cloth the very moment she walked into the long-haired woman's workroom. As the long-haired woman stared at her crystal ball, she was taken aback. The large ball lit up and darkened with a series of brief images appearing and then fading. First of all, warn Norton to keep away from Eggert's Field –there appears to be more alligators living there. It's as if the Florida Everglades has moved to Elm Park.

"The good news is that Darren Trupp and his henchmen are nowhere in sight," Lora declared.

The crystal ball darkened and then glowed with a reddish light. There's an image of a rocket landing on the barren, rock-and-boulder strewn surface of Mars. Several American and astronauts are walking near the space probe – unloading materials, supplies, and equipment. An announcement blares from a loudspeaker mounted on the probe. "Chuck Perez-Krepinski is leading efforts to build a permanent base on the Red Planet."

"What? Who is that young man?"

"It seems that you and Charlie will get together at some point and have a son," Lora says – stifling a smile.

"That's crazy!"

"Why? Don't sell older men short. Being with the right woman is like a fountain of youth for these gents. Look at Stan – he's like a kid again."

"You're giving me more info than I want. It's like a self-fulfilling prophesy," Nancy replied.

"It's just a crystal ball. Nothing's set in stone."

"Yeah sure. After you tell me my son will walk on Mars."

CHAPTER 30

NORTON IS TAKEN

But the prophesy about Norton bothered Nancy. A few days later, they were sitting on the front porch. Norton wanted to walk in Eggert Field to look for duck eggs. "I saw a duck nesting by the stream near Walker Street. Duck eggs are supposed to be better for you than chicken eggs."

"Listen, Lora warned me that there were more alligators back there. She specifically told me you should stay out of there."

"Lora's a nice woman, but do you really believe the predictions of a crystal-ball gazer?"

"Even Freddy talked about gators popping up in that field with all the rain we've been having lately."

"The worst that can happen is I'll lose some toes from my left foot."

"That's not funny."

As if tempting fate itself, Norton ventured into Eggert's Field later that afternoon. Though, he carried his gun with him in a holster – fashioned from a belt and an old baseball glove. He wandered around the far edge of the field, close to Granite Avenue, where there no streams. Nancy observed him from her front porch. Suddenly, Norton appeared to trip and fall in an area of tall grasses. He got right up – smiling and waving at her – as if to ridicule her concern.

Annoyed, the slender woman went into the house to make herself a cup of instant coffee. She poked around the kitchen and found a stale jelly donut, which she chewed on while looking at the roofed wire cage where the hens were clucking abut. Walking to the cage, she opened the door, grabbed two freshly-laid eggs and carried them to the house. Returning to the front porch, there was no sign of Norton. Annoyed and worried, Nancy took out her gun and hurried onto Eggert's Field. She broke into a run and then stopped abruptly at the sight of Norton lying in the tall grass. A big kingsnake had wrapped itself around Norton's neck. His face had a bluish tinge and he had ceased breathing. The snake was poised above Norton's face readying to bite the deceased young man. Nancy fired once – putting a bullet through the reptile's head and killing it instantly. She kicked the dead snake away and gave mouth-to-mouth resuscitation to Norton. But it was to no avail, the South Jersey farm boy had passed on to the next realm. Nancy screamed out to an indifferent world, "Oh you foolish man. Now you're with your half-brother Hal and I'm all alone in this terrible world."

The awful news seemed to travel magically through the whole neighborhood. Soon, the slender woman was joined by Freddy, Mildred, Reverend Staller, Hank, Billy, and Blanche – shedding tears and mourning the loss of the quiet, inquisitive young man who probably should have remained in the rural community of Bloomington, Norton was remembered for his kindness and his keen interest in science – especially the time-traveling effects effect of magnets while riding the merry-go-round. A telegram was sent down to his mom, Connie Mullin, explaining the circumstance of her son's untimely death.

Mrs. Mullin arrived the very next day and a funeral quickly arranged. The middle-aged woman was overwrought with grief, but she did not blame the folks of Elm Park for her son's untimely death. "Unlike his brother, Bobby, Norton had little interest in farming. He was into science and was drawn to New York from the start."

A wooden casket was obtained from Dubinski's closed funeral home on Morningstar Road. The strangulation marks on his neck had been masked with heavy powder. Hence, Norton appeared to be asleep. Ironically, the singed rabbit's tail he had always carried for good luck did not help when he encountered the big snake. Nancy was startled because at one point his eyelids seem to flutter, but it was just the breeze. Nancy, grief stricken, said a few remarks. "Norton was so modest and laidback that we never realized how smart he was. And he was very nice." Mildred rushed across the street and returned with a glass of water. She had once read that staying hydrated ameliorates grief. Sipping the water and crying quietly, the slender woman sat down.

Then, Freddy stepped forward. "Norton knew stuff about magnets. He was the first to realize that the merry-go-round was a time machine." Shaking his head, smiling wryly, and rubbing his hands briefly, Freddy sat down.

The Reverend Staller mounted a wooden soapbox and read the 23rd Psalm, said the Lord's Prayer and then sat down. Mildred Aimsley had recently painted the soapbox with varnish which she bought from a hardware store in Port Richmond. The Rev had often referred to himself as a simple soapbox preacher. A grave had been dug in Eggert's Field not far from Granite Avenue and amongst the tall grasses where Norton had been strangled by the big kingsnake. A large granite boulder was inscribed with Norton's name and dates of his birth and death. Along with the words was the saying: "Curiosity is Life." Charlie Krepinski's neighbor, Kenny Worthington had done the inscription with a chisel. After his retirement as a T A bus driver, Kenny had taken up stone cutting as an avocation.

A few days later, another tragedy shocked the good folks of Elm Park. Actually, it was two deaths – bringing the death total to three and fulfilling the old adage that deaths occur in threes. Quentin, Quinn's fraternal twin, was walking with Foxy in Eggert's Field just beyond the garden patch cultivated by Freddy. Suddenly, a kingsnake attacked the dwarf – wrapping itself around the red-haired dwarf. Foxy snapped at the big reptile, but to no avail. The brown-haired dwarf was dead was strangled within a few minutes. Not satisfied with killing the dwarf, the snake wrapped itself around the hapless fox and quickly strangled it also.

Again, a funeral was quickly arranged with Nancy and the Rev Staller were called upon to preside over another sober ceremony. Honoring the dwarf's preference, Kenny obtained a small wooden box in which both Quentin and Foxy were placed, A big bonfire was built not far from Freddy's garden and the wooden box was placed in the fire. Usually grumpy and cantankerous, Quinn wept openly at his brother's funeral. Even Bubba, the meek black bear, bellowed in sorrow over the loss of the red fox and his owner. In a matter of minutes, Quentin and Foxy had been transformed to carbon dioxide and ashes – dust to dust. Thus, Reverend Stan Staller solemnly intoned "For out of it was thou taken, for dust thou art. And unto dust shall thou return."

A few days later, the good folks decided to flush out the snakes from Eggert's field, which was roughly three acres in area. The weapons utilized varied: Freddy wielded his big hunting knife, the Rev who carried a sickle, Hank swung a stickball bat, while Nancy and Mildred had their 22-caliber pistols, and last but not least, Charlie brought his 9-millimeter gun. Walking ten feet apart across the small field from the northern end to Walker Street on the southern end, only three small snakes wee encountered and dispatched. Reversing direction, the only critter found was a three-foot long baby alligator, which Freddy stabbed and bagged.

"It'll make a nice stew – simmered with a couple of frogs, a squirrel, a rat, plus some onions, garlic, and a carrot thrown in. Real good eatin," Freddy exclaimed – smiling widely and rubbing his hands forcefully.

"You're disgusting," Nancy responded.

Just then, Granny Schmidt came out of her house – looking sober. "Hey, you wnna get rid of snakes? Just springle garlic powder around. Snakes don't like garlic. I betcha you didn't know that – Baldy" she said – winking at Nancy.

"I oughta sprinkle garlic on you and feed you to the gators," Freddy replied.

"Give me a couple of bucks for a bottle of whiskey – you old skin flint," the unkempt dowager yelled back.

To everyone's surprise, Fredy handed Granny four dollars, along with some change. She flashed a toothless smile and headed for Kaffman's to buy a pint of cheap whiskey.

Amused by the kidding, Nancy stuck around – chatting and sharing a beer with Charlie, Mildred, and the Rev. The latter talked about the legend of St. Patrick, who lived in Ireland during the 5th century. "Supposedly, he drove snakes out of Ireland after a snake bit him while he was fasting on a mountain. Actually, there was a Little Ice Age in Europe from the 1300s to the 1800s throughout Europe. The cold weather was one of the factors that led England, France, Holland, Spain, and Portugal to establish colonies in North and South America. But, there is no fossil evidence of snakes or reptiles existing in Ireland – unless you go back to the Age of Dinosaurs."

"How long ago was that?" Nancy asked.

"Between sixty and a hundred million years ago – when most of the earth had a tropical climate.".

"Hal said that the dinosaurs were either killed off by a giant meteor crashing into the Earth or by the Ice Age."

"Indeed, those are the two most credible theories regarding the extinction of the dinosaurs," Rev Staller replied.

"I'd rather die from a giant meteor. It's quick and painless," Freddy replied with a grimace.

The others concurred. Despite global warming, winters were especially difficult with unreliable electric power and broken gas pipelines. In the post Covid-20 era, most people resorted to coal stoves found in junkyards for cooking and heating. Mankind had taken a giant step backward – with respect to technology. But there were signs that some of this worldwide techno-decline was slowly being reversed. In many cities, electric lines were being repaired to carry electricity once more.

The Con Ed generator in Travis had been converted so it could burn coal. Nancy recalled that Hal mentioning that in the 1960s, the power plant burned coal – with sulfur fumes permeating the North Shore. His dad, Tom

Haley, had worked thee as Bradford guard while going to C C N Y. Then, the power plant was converted so it burned natural gas – a cleaner fossil fuel. During the Covid-20 pandemic, infrastructure deteriorated and gas pipelines weren't maintained. Consequently, Con Ed reverted to burning coal to generate electricity – as it had done a half-century ago. In fact, use of coal had been increasing in recent years – powering factories, generating electricity, and even heating buildings. Across the country, coal mines were opening up to meet the demand for this highly polluting fossil fuel. With the sharp decline in population, air and water pollution were nowhere close to pre-pandemic levels. Fewer people meant cleaner air and less wastes spewing forth onto the land and into rivers and oceans.

Nancy decided to pay a visit to crystal ball reader, Lora Langley, to get a look what might be facing her in the near future. As usual, the pretty long-haired woman was working on some copper jewelry in her workroom above Mislicki's Bakery. Upon seeing Nancy, Lora stopped what she was doing and gave Nancy a hug. Then, she took her large crystal ball down from its shelf and dusted it off with her silk cloth.

"I'm terribly sorry about what happened to Norton. He was star-crossed from the moment he set foot in Elm Park."

"Norton had a morbid fascination with Eggert's Field – like a kid determined to play with matches until he set himself on fire," Nancy replied.

"Some folks seem to enjoy tempting fate. And we can't stop them," the pretty soothsayer replied – peering into her crystal ball.

"So, what do I have to watch at for? Are we done with Darren Trupp? Or will he escape his captors in Puerto Rico and enact revenge on us?"

Checking the crystal ball, Lora replied. "Actually, we may be done with Mister Trupp. He's actually enjoying his new life as a fisherman. But I see some bad guys in a truck aiming to sell drugs in the North Shore."

"Charley said he heard that the drug cartel was moving into the city. Trying to take advantage of the absence of police. Freddy concurred. There was talk about drug gangs when he was in Brooklyn."

"Speaking of Freddy, there's an image from the past of his great-great-great grandfather – I don't know how many greats – Frederick von Voglio blowing up some soldiers. It looks like a battalion of Red Coats marching along Richmond Terrace.—five or six hundred British soldiers. He used homemade explosives made out of saltpeter, charcoal, sulfur, and gunpowder."

The crystal ball shifts to the present – brightening with an image of two men driving along Richmond Terrace in an old van with a Texas license plate.

The man in the passenger seat carries a rifle. They're wearing cowboy hats and have the angry look of men who mean business The big truck slows to avoid a fallen tree blocking the road. There's a loud bang, a big puff of smoke and fire engulfing the truck. A bunch of men are running away the scene."

"Any other questions?" Lora asks – getting ready to put the crystal ball away.

"Let me write down the components Freddy's ancestor used: saltpeter, charcoal, sulfur, and gunpowder. Now what about Charlie Krepinski?"

The fire in the crystal ball dissipates and is replaced with clouds – a positive sign. "Hmm, an image of a force field. You are aware that love is a force field – not dissimilar to gravitational fields. Maybe a budding romance."

"I don't know. First Hal, then Sam, and now Norton – all of them dead. I don't bring good luck to the men in my life. From now on I'll remain celibate," the slender woman replied – hugging Lora and leaving the workroom.

"There's something to be said for May-December romances. Look at me and Stan," Lora called out.

Stan Mislicki, the local lawyer, baker, and supplier of guns and bullets, had a few decades on Lora.

CHAPTER 31

TWO IMMIGRANTS ARRIVE IN ELM PARK

LOST IN THOUGHT, NANCY TURNED THE CORNER ON MORNINGSTAR ROAD and turned down Hooker Place. She came upon a short middle-aged man emerging from a car, wearing a sombrero, and carrying a tattered suitcase. He was accompanied by another man in a Phillies cap, who was a bit younger a bit younger – carrying an old canvas bag They wore sweat shirts and jeans that were in need of washing. The two men looked tired, dazed, and lost.

"Madame, would you know a place where we could stay for the night?" the younger man inquired.

"You can stay in my sunporch. There's a twin bed you can share. Are you hungry?"

The two men took off their hats – first the sombrero and then the baseball cap – bowed, murmured a thank you, and nodded.

"Here guys, sit on my porch. I'll get you something in a jiffy."

She returned with a platter containing a bowl of tomato soap, some bread and butter, and a pitcher of lemon aide. The men thanked Nancy and ate heartily. In fairly good English, the younger man introduced himself as Angelo and his friend as Pedro. farm worker from Mexico. They had fled his native country – where conditions were bad due to the drug cartel. Doing farm work in Texas, they managed to send money to their families in Mexico. But, there was less and less work as a result of severe drought throughout the southwest. Their presence in Elm Park, as with all local news, spread quickly through the neighborhood. The next day, Joey Caprino knocked on Nancy's door to complain about the newcomers.

The slender woman came out and sat down next to the former semipro pitcher. "With all due respect, we can't be housing and feeding every migrant that walks into the neighborhood."

"We need people. The men are working with Freddy in his veggie patch as we speak," she replied – pointing across the street.

Pedro was weeding Freddy's veggie patch, while Angelo was watering the plants with a pitcher—both men nodded and followed the octogenarian's directions. Then, Freddy took Pussyfoot, his pet bobcat, out of its red-roofed cage. The cat growled at Angelo, but after Pedro talked softly to it, rubbed against him and allowed itself to be petted by the middle-aged farm worker.

Shrugging his shoulders, Joey seemed to relent. Then, he asked, "Do they play baseball?"

"Go over and ask them yourself."

Joey crossed Pulaski Avenue and began talking with the Fredddy and the immigrants. Soon they were laughing and Joey grabbed a rake and helped out. Later, Joey took out a baseball and three old baseball gloves. Freddy ran to his apartment and returned with his catcher's mitt. Before long, Joey, Angelo, Pedro, and Freddy had a four-way catch in the middle of Pulaski Avenue. Thee's nothing like baseball to bridge the language barrier.

"Do you guys play stickball?" Joey asked.

Though, they were aware of the game played with a broomstick handle and a Spalding, neither Angelo nor Pedro had ever played it. A game was arranged for Saturday morning at P S 21. Nancy demurred, "The guys been through a lot. They need to rest."

"Nothing's more relaxing than a friendly game of stickball," Freddy replied. And the immigrants concurred.

"Fine, it will help everyone get to know Angelo and Pedro. Hal used to call stickball a bonding ritual – a rite of passage to adulthood."

The men, along with Nancy trekked up Walker Avenue to P S 21 on a mild Saturday afternoon to play stickball. The two opposing teams were the oldsters, Freddy, Charlie, and Pedro, versus the youngsters Joey, Angelo, and Nancy. The game was low scoring as Freddy threw mostly fastballs that whizzed by the broomstick bats and pounded the big concrete wall with a loud noise. Joey managed only a groundball single for the youngsters, while Freddy slammed a double that struck the chain-link fence on one bounce off Joey. The latter mixed fastballs and knuckle curves – baffling the opposing hitters. The score remained zero-to-zero. But by the 7th inning, both pitchers began to tire and the Spalding wasn't banging against the concrete wall so loudly. Freddy threw a knuckle curve that Angelo deposited beyond into the little cemetery across beyond Walker Street for the game's only run at that point.

The very next inning, Freddy sent one of Joey's fastballs into the same place – the cemetery marked with graves nearly a century old. The score was now tied one-to-one. There was a couple of nice catches. Charley jumped and caught a flyball right in front of the fence hit by Joey –saving a run. Nancy caught a pop flyball after a short dash. In the bottom of the 9th inning, Joey walked and Angelo hit a groundball single. It was all up to Nancy as she faced Freddy, who whose arm was hurting. He got two quick strikes on fast balls. Thinking he'd fool the slender woman, he threw a slow blooper pitch. Nancy's eyes lit up, but she waited a split second and then smacked a line drive. The Spalding struck the chain-link fence for a double –driving in the winning run. There was jumping, shouting, and smiling by everyone – winners and losers. They decided to go to Kaffman's at the corner of Morningstar Road and Walker Street for some drinks.

In the poorly-lit bar, Angelo and Pedro were nervous at first – looking around in wonder. This was their first time in a drinking establishment. Going to bars and restaurants was considered a frivolous waste of money.

"This is barra," Pedro announced.

"Do you like beer?" Nancy asked.

The men hesitated until she pointed to a glass of beer a customer was drinking. Then, Angelo indicated they'd like a glass of beer. "We call it cerveza."

"How about hamburgers and fries?" Freddy suggested.

This time, both men assented. And soon everyone was enjoying the simple fare provided by Kaffman's elderly cook – Frankie.

After much haggling, Charley and Joey split the tab. "Next time Nancy and Freddy will dip into their pockets and treat everybody."

Nancy simply smiled, while Freddy rubbed his hands with a wry smile.

"So what do you think of Estados Unidos?" Charlie asked.

"Bien," Pedro replied.

"Estupendo," Angelo added.

The pleasures people derive from eating and drinking and gabbing – despite language barriers – cannot be overstated. Needless to say, a good time was had by all.

The very next day was Sunday. And so, Stan Staller mounted his soapbox to give his usual sermon – urging love, generosity, forgiveness, and kindness to all who enter our lives. "After so many died from Covid-20, the Lord commanded us to look after one another. And the good people of Elm Park have done so with open arms, generosity and love." Then, he opened his Bible and read from Matthew 25:

"I was hungry and you gave me food. I was thirsty and you gave me drink. I was a stranger and you welcomed me. I was naked and you clothed me. I was in prison and you came to visit me."

Later that day, Nancy got a surprise visit from Mason, who worked with Gerald Hopkins. He had a big wooden box filled with "materials that have to be handled carefully– along with typed instructions to assemble them into an explosive device."

"You're talking about saltpeter, charcoal, sulfur, and gunpowder – the ingredients of a homemade bomb," Nancy said – interrupting the low-keyed intermediary.

"Exactly."

"What if it goes off before its supposed to? I don't want to be blown to kingdom come. Especially now that my house is fixed up."

"The constituents will be shipped in separate boxes, along with a special fuse. They'll be assembled on the site of the interdiction – in the field at the bottom of Morningstar Road. You, Freddy, Charlie, Hank, and anyone else you deem reliable will assemble fifteen minutes before the drug cartel guys make that turn onto Morningstar Road."

"So, we'll know exactly when the bad guys are heading our way," Nancy

"Reports indicate they're coming on Tuesday – around six A M. Hopkins will have spies posted Richmond Terrace. Police Sirens will go off as their truck approaches that corner –beneath the Bayonne Bridge," Mason responded – trying to sound confident.

"It's risky business."

"We're living in a risky – might I say – dangerous world," he replied.

"Tell me about it. Three men I cared about—no, I loved – are gone." she replied in a near whisper.

Mason stepped forward and hugged the slender woman awkwardly. "You've given and lost more than anyone on the Island."

At that moment, Mildred walked up her front steps and Nancy shrugged.

Mason nodded towards the prim woman and then looked at Nancy.

"Of course, you should tell Mildred. I'd trust her with my life."

Mason quickly briefed Mildred on the welcome they were planning for the drug cartel guys. "They're coming to retrieve Angelo and Pedro and teach you Elm Park folks a lesson. Our intelligence says it will be Monday morning around eight o'clock. They're taking a ferry boat from Brooklyn they've seized from the city."

"We'll be ready and waiting at seven A M. It is we who will be doing the teaching. Would that they learn their lesson well," the prim woman replied firmly.

"Mildred knows how to handle a gun," Nancy commented.

"I had a great teacher."

"We all know how to defend ourselves," Nancy continued.

"Of that I'm sure. There's a box I have for you. It's extra guns and ammunition." Mason replied – hustling to his car and returning with a wooden box with the aforementioned supplies.

As soon as Mason left, Nancy rushed to Lora's office above Mislicki's Bakery. She briefed the pretty soothsayer on the planned ambush of the cartel gang Monday morning.

Getting her crystal ball down from the shelf, Lora asked. "What time did Mason say they'll be turning onto Morningstar Road?"

"He said to be in the bushes by the side of the road at seven o'clock."

The long-haired woman rubbed the crystal ball with her silk cloth and peered into it for a minute or so. The large crystal ball brightened and darkened repeatedly. Then, an image formed of a battered red truck carrying a dozen heavily armed men moving along the Terrace and turning onto Morningstar Road. It was pitch dark and a clock came into focus – showing the minute hand on the twelve and hour hand on the four.

"I'd have your guys posted and ready to go at three-thirty – no later – on Tuesday morning," Lora said bluntly.

And then glancing at her crystal ball, there's a stranger who's helping you -dressed as a clown with clown makeup."

"That must be Roy. Billy said he was back on the Island after working in a circus in the city."

"But you've got to be there on Morningstar Road at three-thirty sharp," Lora repeated.

"And that's what we'll do. I've heard the cartel guys tell their underlings one thing, but then change their plans at the last minute. They use the element of surprise. Plus, their brutality – they don't take prisoners."

"Be careful. One of your men is gonna be shot."

"Can you see who it is?"

Lora peered into her crystal ball. "No, the image is not clear. Predictions are that way."

"I'll remind them to shoot and then duck under cover. But in the heat of battle, adrenalin flows and everybody gets reckless," Nancy replied – shaking her head.

The word saturnine comes to mind for men like Freddy and Charlie and even Billy in the heat of battle – hot-tempered men. Whereas, the cartel guys were cold-blooded killers.

I'll pray for you," Lora said – hugging the slender woman as she got ready to leave the young woman's workshop.

CHAPTER 32

AMBUSH ON MORNINGSTAR ROAD

On Tuesday morning at three A M, Charley, Freddy, Billy, Hank, Glenn, Mildred, and Nancy were posted in the grassy area on both sides of Morningstar Road – near its junction with Richmond Terrace. As Lora predicted, Roy showed up – wearing an old army helmet and offering to help and Nancy told Mason to hand him a gun. The constituents of the bomb – saltpeter, charcoal, sulfur, and gunpowder – were carefully assembled in a small wooden box by Charley, Freddy, and Glenn in the middle of the street – with Nancy, Billy, Hank, and Mildred standing guard with their guns drawn. The box was covered with branches, bushes, and weeds. A 15-foot rope dipped in kerosene served as the fuse to the homemade bomb. Mason posted on Richmond Terrace, along with two aides, would signal the approach of the cartel truck along the Terrace with flashes of three powerful flashlights. Looking up at the sky, Nancy saw five planets lined up – Uranus, Neptune, Jupiter, Saturn, and Venus – which she saw as a sign of good luck. The same five-planet array was on display the night she first met Hal at a high school dance so many years ago. In addition, there was a bright half-moon in the clear nighttime sky.

Hank and Roy volunteered to stand on the corner – waiting for Mason's signal. There was an eerie silence and no traffic of any kind along the Terrace. Just the twinkling stars, the five planets, and the lonely moon poised above – as if waiting for something to happen. An owl flew circled above – looking for something to eat. It saw a brown rat nibbling on a discarded apple core amongst some weeds and dived down – grabbing the rat by its sharp talons and flying away. Just then a light beam flashed in their direction and Hank ran back to them.

"Get ready. They're coming," Hank called out, as Roy whistled. Everyone took their positions on each side with their guns pointed towards the street.

Freddy, calm as a summer breeze, had his matches ready to light the fuse for the homemade bomb. He waited until the battered red truck barreling along the Terrace turned onto Morningstar Road with its tires squealing. The octogenarian dashed out to the middle of the road and lit the fuse. Observing the glow of the fast-moving fuse, the driver yelled "Oh shit!" and jammed on his brakes. But Newton's law of inertia held sway and the truck barely slowed down. There were at least a eight heavily-armed men in the truck – wearing masks and holding handguns and shotguns ready to fire.

The dynamite went off with a resounding boom and the truck was engulfed in flames as the men were thrown out of the truck. Nancy, Charlie, Roy, and Hank moved forward firing their guns at the men – most of whom were unable to shoot back. On the opposite side of the street, Freddy, Glenn, Billy, and Mildred did likewise – mowing down the drug cartel guys – like shooting ducks at a carnival booth. It wasn't a pleasant sight, but the Elm Park folks had no remorse – they were eliminating a mortal threat to their neighborhood.

Quick and deadly, Nancy had shot three of the drug gangsters in the head within two minutes. Roy took a bullet which bounced off his old iron helmet – to everyone's amazement. Then, one of the drug cartel guys took aim at the slender woman. Reacting instinctively, Charlie grabbed her and took a bullet in his hand –nearly severing the pinky and ring fingers on his left hand. Nancy and Mildred wrapped their hankies around Charlie's hand to stop the bleeding. The two surviving drug guys were released. They were teenagers who seemed to be genuinely remorseful. They identified one of the dead men, who wore a sombrero, as the ringleader.

Charlie agreed that the two youngsters should be released. "Sometimes good people do bad things because they keep bad company." Addressing them directly: "Go forth and do good in the world. Live on the sunny side of life – not the dark side."

The two teenagers, whose knowledge of English was not as limited as it appeared – nodded in turn to Charlie, Nancy, and Mildred. They walked away – nodding and bowing with looks of contrition.

Nancy tossed her car keys to Hank, who ran back to Pulaski Avenue and soon returned with her big Dodge. Nancy and Roy helped Charlie into the backseat. Then with Mildred's help, she drove him to Dr. Emil's office under the Bayonne Bridge. As expected, Charlie bore his pain like a true stoic— remaining quiet and wincing when no one was looking. Nancy carefully steered her car onto the grassy field along the winding gravel path. Dr. Emil and Alfred had heard the explosion from their location and had their instruments and medications ready for the arrival of people in need of their care.

"What happened?"

Under Dr. Emil's direction. Alfred gave Charlie three injections of pain killer in his left hand. The former private eye's pinky was hanging by some skin and the ring finger had a long gash from which the blood was oozing

"I don't think we can save the pinky, but the ring finger can be stitched up," Dr. Emil said quietly – looking at Charlie for his reaction.

"Take the pinky off. Only thing I use it for is picking my nose and sticking it out when I drink a cup of coffee."

Nancy made like she was about to punch him, but shook her head and smiled at the hard-nosed detective.

"What that you take this procedure seriously" Mildred responded.

"Lady, its only a pinky. If it was my dicky, I'd be wailing and moaning."

Dr. Emil signaled the two women to leave his office. Nancy was reluctant, but Mildred left the office gladly.

"So, let's do it then. Do you want to do the amputation?" the physician said to his young assistant.

Nodding and shrugging his shoulders, Alfred carefully scrubbed his hands. Dr. Emil got the instruments ready and brought out the needle, scalpels, bandages, and medicines. He himself injected Charlie's left hand and in several places – including the two damaged fingers. Under the physician's guidance. The young assistant severed the pinky at the base – struggling a bit with the pinky's bone. Understanding that Alfred needed to master the technique, Dr. Emil did not intervene. His health was declining and before long, Alfred would be performing all the duties of a family doctor by himself.

Charlie was transported back to Nancy's house and made comfortable. Then, Nancy checked on the whereabouts of Roy – learning that Quinn had volunteered to let the ex-circus clown stay with him until a place was found for him. Roy was not afraid of the big black bear and in fact, the two of them bonded right away. This was good news. Quinn was in failing health and like his brother, Quentin, was not long for the world. He had worried about what would become of his beloved Bubba when he left this veil of tears. In fact, Quinn worked with Roy and Bubba – teaching them to do his singing-and-dancing bear routine – with an eye to his impending death

A few weeks later, an elderly man from the flats had fallen down the stairs and broken his arm. Quinn, Roy, and Bubba heard the man screaming in pain. Quinn and Roy placed the victim, whose name was Sandford, in a kid's wagon and pulled him two blocks to Nancy's house, with Bubba trailing along. Nancy and Charlie were sitting on the front porch – talking about the recent battle with the drug guys.

"Our neighbor fell down the stairs. I think he broke his arm," Quinn related, as Roy concurred and Bubba moaned sympathetically

Charlie was recovering from the removal of his left pinky and the deep gash on his left ring finger. Despite lingering pain, Charlie was in good spirits and ready to help out.

"You stay put. Roy and Quinn will get him into my car," Nancy barked to Charlie, who sat on the steps glumly and watched the proceedings.

With Roy's help, Quinn lifted Sandford into the backseat of Nancy's big Dodge. Mildred jumped into the front seat next to Nancy. Bidding goodbye to the black bear and the two men, Nancy zoomed down Pulaski Avenue and turned onto Morningstar Road – heading for Dr. Emil's office off Richmond Terrace. Arriving at the small house, which served as the elderly doctor's residence and his place of practice, Nancy and Mildred jumped out of her car and began helping the injured man from the backseat.

Instantly reading the situation, Alfred ran out of the office and assisted Nancy in carefully getting Sandford out of the car.

"I fell down the stairs and broke my arm," Sandford explained –grimacing in pain

"It looks like the ulna, the lower bone of the forearm," Alfred said – turning to the Dr. Emil, who nodded his head in agreement.

Sandford was clearly in pain, so the physician instructed Alfred. "Give him a needle to numb the pain. And then we'll set the bone and apply the cast."

"Don't you have to take X-rays?" Nancy asked.

"We don't have an X-ray machine nor reliable electricity. You may have noticed, there's no power today," Dr. Emil replied grimly.

Working carefully, Dr Emil aligned the bone. Then, Alfred mixed the plaster of Paris with water, wrapped Sandford's forearm in gauze. With the physician's guidance, the black teenager slowly applied the plaster around the elderly man's arm. Nancy helped by holding the patient's arm in a steady horizontal position. After twenty minutes, they sat Sandford's down at a desk –keeping his arm horizontal on the desk top. He remained seated while Dr. Emil talked about his practice.

"It varies. Some days we see more than a dozen people, other days just a few folks – for injections, bad colds and coughs, and minor cuts. Other days, you have broken bones, high fevers, heart attacks and strokes. For the latter, we give what meds we have and prescribe bed rest."

"What if you run out of medicines and supplies?" Nancy asked.

"Mason keeps tabs on us. He's able to pull strings and get most of what we need."

"So, is this guy a good intern?" the slender woman asked – pointing to the black teenager.

"He's a natural. Got a mind like a sponge – never forgets anything."

"What about medical school?" Mildred asked

"There's only Columbia – on a limited basis. The last I heard they were training about twenty-five interns. There's no money and a meager faculty."

"I study Dr. Emil's medical textbooks every day. I want to learn as much as I can about the body and diseases," Alfred replied proudly.

"Would that there were more young men like you," the prim woman exclaimed.

"It looks like the cast is dry. Come back into two weeks for an assessment. But, the cast will have to stay on for five or six weeks," Dr. Emil said – patting Sandford on the back.

Nancy and Mildred drove the patient back to the flats, where Quinn and Roy awaited the elderly man. They walked Sandford up the steps of the front porch.

"When Sandford needs to come downstairs, one of you walk with him and make sure he doesn't trip," the slender woman declared.

"Your word is our command Annie," the red-haired dwarf replied, as Bubba moaned in agreement and Roy snickered.

"Would that you spare us your circus humor," the prim woman responded.

At a signal from Quinn, Bubba bowed to Mildred, who curtsied in response. Walking back down Pulaski Avenue, Nancy suggested to Mildred that they pay Lora a visit.

"I'd like an alert of the next crisis of heading our way."

"Good idea. An ounce of forecast is worth a pound of postcast," the prim woman responded with a rare display of humor.

"I'm not sure postcast is a word? It's times like this that I miss Hal."

Mildred stopped and gave Nancy a hug. The latter was gripped by emotion but snapped out of it. There was so much riding on her shoulders. Mourning seemed to be an emotion she could ill afford to indulge in – except in the middle of the night. They walked up Hooker Place and turned onto Morningstar Road – reaching the bakery and mounting the stairs to Lora's workshop.

Wiping her crystal ball off with a silk cloth, Lora seemed to be expecting them. The pretty long-haired woman hugged Nancy and Mildred.

"You were right on target about the narco gang. They arrived earlier than Mason had expected."

"So I heard. How's Charlie doing?"

"Well, he lost his left pinky and got some stitches on his left ring finger. But otherwise, the guy's in good spirits."

"We're lucky to have Dr. Emil and his young assistant working nearby," Lora replied.

"Alfred has the makings of a great doctor."

"Would that we could send him to medical school," Mildred commented.

"That's out of the question. He's reading Dr. Emil's medical books and learning by doing," Nancy replied'

"Think of Alfred as an intern – who'll get better and better with experience," Lora said – scrutinizing her crystal ball which grew darker and brighter. "How about Charlie doing the time machine thing?"

"You're talking about the merry-go-round?"

"Yes. And he has to hold a magnet in his good hand and a four-leaf clover in his bandaged hand. We'll do it the day after tomorrow at six A M," the long-haired soothsayer responded.

"Aren't four-leaf clovers rare?": Mildred asked.

"Hal said, there's a probability of one in ten thousand finding one in a three-by-four foot area. And the probability is increased in a highly trafficked backyard," Nancy replied.

"Maybe there's a chance of romance between you two," the prim woman commented.

"I need another man in my life like a hole in the head," Nancy replied – hugging Lora and starting to leave her workroom.

"Wait a minute," Lora said as she was setting the crystal ball on the shelf.

"I see an image of that red-haired dwarf. He's fallen in the street and Bubba is pawing at him and moaning."

"That's Quinn. Maybe you're mistaken," Nancy replied.

"Maybe I am," Lora said putting her crystal ball away.

"Would that you are, but Quinn's the only red-haired dwarf around," Mildred said quietly.

Forgetting Lora's grim prophesy, the two women returned to Nancy's house and walked down her alleyway to the backyard. Within minutes, they found several four-leaf clovers.

But Charlie Krepinski's time travel trip was put on hold by Quinn's sudden death as he walked with Bubba down Pulaski Avenue. Quinn keeled over and was dead before he hit the pavement. It was a heart attack. Bubba was inconsolable and no one could coax the black bear away from his master.

With Roy's help, Bubba carried Quinn to Eggert's field. Fredie, Hank, and Charlie began digging a grave. Then, appearing to understand the burial process, Bubba used his paws to scoop away the dirt. A small casket was obtained from the undertaker, Ray Dubinski. And Stan Staller was called upon to give the funeral oration as the women cried for the hot-tempered, but devoted, caretaker of the gentle circus bear. But the saddest sound of all was the plaintive moaning of Bubba over the death of his beloved trainer and companion in life. With time, Bubba accepted Roy, the ex-circus clown as his new caregiver and trainer. Wisely, Roy took his time about resuming Bubba's show business career. A thirty-minute song-and dance routine was prepared:

> "Every morning about this time
> She throws the want ads right my way
> And never fails to say, get a job
> Get a job, sha na na, na, sha na na na"

A few days later, Nancy mentioned to the ex-private eye that Lora wants him take his turn on the merry-go-round. "Lora said you should take a ride on the time machine. She wants you to bring a magnet and a four-leaf clover."

"A trip through time, you say? O K – it'll get me out of the house for a bit."

Nancy grabbed one of Hal's horseshoe magnets from his box of teaching materials and a bunch of four-leaf clovers. She set them on the kitchen table while she figured out Charlie's outfit.

"I don't mind going back into the past. It's been a roller-coaster ride. But the future – who wants to know what's around the corner?"

"I'd like to see what you look like in a suit," Nancy commented – searching through his clothes for a suit, a collar shirt, and a tie.

"A suit? What am I going to a dance?" Charlie asked – trying to act annoyed.

"No, but you should look nice when you time travel," Nancy replied with the hint of a smile.

"Freddy didn't wear a suit when he went on the merry-go-round."

"Freddy hasn't worn a suit since his First Holy Communion. Besides, it would be nice to see how you look in a suit," Nancy responded.

The slim woman found a dark blue suit, a white shirt, and red-striped tie for the ex-detective. "Here, try this on, while I pick out sone shoes for you. When you time travel, you shouldn't look like a slob."

Charlie put on the suit and a white collared shirt, and then posed in front of the mirror in the small bedroom, which had a large mirror mounted on its clothes closet.

"I look like Ray Dubinski, the undertaker."

"Would that you were more appreciative. It's not every day we get a chance to time travel," Mildred offered.

"Going back in time is one thing, but the future is a different ballgame," Charlie replied.

"Would that you not be a wuss. This is an adventure," the prim woman admonished.

After much fussing and fuming, Nancy tied his tie in a Windsor knot. At last, Charlie emerged looking from the room looking dapper and even a few years younger.

"Not too shabby!" Nancy exclaimed.

"Would that Stanley looked so good," Midred remarked.

Nancy ran into the kitchen and returned with the horseshoe magnet and two four-leaf clovers. "Can't forget these, Charlie. It's almost six o'clock. You'd better hustle over to the merry-go-round for some time travel."

CHAPTER 33

CHARLIE TAKES A TIME TRIP

SHE GAVE HIM A PECK ON THE CHEEK AND THE TALL RETIRED DETECTIVE crossed the street and climbed onto the merry-go-round. Freddy set it in motion for a few revolutions and then stopped it in front of the white wall. Charlie saw images of his youth when he pitched for his little league, high school, and semipro teams. He was a hard-throwing lefthanded pitcher – hampered by control issues. Then one day, he threw a fastball by free-swinging longball hitter and something snapped in his elbow. Even after six weeks of rest, the twinge remained and his pitching career was over. He continued to play baseball as a hard-hitting first baseman, but whenever he swung and missed, the same twinge could be felt. So, he gave baseball for stickball – throwing a Spalding against concrete walls and swinging a broom handle bat.

Next, the images shifted to Charlie's life as a NYC street cop – working in lower Manhattan. He rose through the ranks – thanks to his fearlessness, sense of fair play, intelligence, and compassion for people – good and bad. He patrolled the streets, giving an occasional ticket for parking violations, and even stopping some muggings. Once he walked into his bank during an attempted heist and nabbed the two robbers without firing a shot. Charlie's good work led to a promotion as a plainclothes detective, where he worked hard and solved some cold-case homicides. There was a particular case involving a battered wife, in which there the police had responded several times over the course of three years. Finally, the man, Bob Smith, was found dead from stab wounds in the stomach. in the stomach. The prime suspect, the wife fled the apartment and left the area. Interviews with friends and family led nowhere. After a while, Charlie was given the case and told to track the woman. Meticulous and persevering, he learned from the woman's classmate that she a second cousin who lived in Bloomington, South Jersey. On his own time, Charlie drove down to the town, which was divided up into small farms – ranging from ten to twenty acres – growing a wide variety of crops – corn, tomatoes, carrots, lettuce, potatoes, onions, strawberries, blueberries, melons, and pumpkins. In addition, there were farms that had fruit trees – apple, pear, and peach trees. Plus, farms that grew trees for the Christmas holidays – Douglas fir, white pine, Scots pine, fir, cypress, spruce, red cedar, juniper, and holly trees.

Charlie knocked on the cousin's door, and the woman, herself, appeared before him. The detective recognized her at once from a photo he carried in his wallet. Her name was Molly Smith and she carried scars on her face and arms from her husband's beatings. "Are you going to arrest me?" she asked timidly.

For the first time in his investigation, Charlie realized he didn't want to do that. If the concept of justifiable homicide existed – this definitely was an example.

"You're not at fault. The blame is with the laws that allowed your husband to commit assault and battery with just a slap on the wrist."

"Come in.as just having some coffee. This is Maribel."

A little girl in curls, who faintly resembled her mom, smiled shyly.

"How are you, Maribel?" Charlie said to the youngster. Then turning to Molly, "Teach her to stick up for herself and take no guff from anyone – man or woman."

"My husband was very controlling from the get-go. I ignored the warning signs."

"Love is blind, but if there are bad vibes – end it fast. By the way, this is great coffee."

Smiling, she gave the tall detective a piece of apple pie.

Taking a bite, "Wow, this is the best pie I've ever had – bar none."

"I've always like to bake." The woman responded.

"Here's the problem. I found you by talking to your classmate, Mabel Browning, who mentioned your cousin and where she lived."

"I'm going to another town. My family just wants me to be safe. And they've lined up a job working off the books – cleaning houses."

"O K. But, you have keep your eyes open. Hopefully with time, this will all go away," Charlie replied.

"As long as I'm alive, those memories will stay with me."

"Here's something to help you with the move. Do it soon," the tall detective said – giving the woman seven hundred fifty dollars in cash."

"I cannot accept it."

"Take it. Please. Here's my phone number if you need anything."

As Charlie started to leave, he noticed a man about a block away. He was looking at them through binoculars.

"I'll be right back," Charlie said, hopping two fences and arriving at the observer's backyard within a minute

The man was so surprised, he still had the binoculars in his hand.

"Why are you spying on that woman?"

"I don't know. She has scars on her face and marks on her arms."

"Has anyone put you up to it?" Charlie asked – crowding the neighbor.

"No, it's nothing like that. We look out for each other in this neighborhood," the man replied, clearly intimidated.

"Good. I want you to look out for that woman and every other woman on this block. See that no harm comes to them. Can you do that?"

"Well, sure. Woman folk should be protected,"

"Good. You swear to look after them?"

Gulping, the man responded. "I do – so help me God."

"My name is Charlie Krepinski. Your now my deputy," Charlie responded – shaking the man's hand.

"I'm Joe Finley."

They shook hands again and Charlie dashed back to Molly Smith, who gave him a questioning look.

"I deputized your neighbor, Joe Finley to look after you and the other women of the neighborhood."

"O K. But I'm moving."

"Yeah. Don't lose my phone number. Any problems, give me a call."

Patting Maribel on the head and nodding to the woman, he left the house. Though raised Catholic, Charlie was not a religious man. Nonetheless, he mumbled a quick prayer that the Bob Smith murder case would remain a cold case forever. He understood that sometimes you had to break the rules for the sake of justice.

Then, the merry-go-round began whirling again – gradually slowing down and stopping in front of the white wall. An image of another world – a small city being built within a giant dome on the planet Mars. A tall young man is working with a group of men constructing buildings with cement blocks and steel rooves – designed to be meteorite-proof. Though built of thick plastic designed to bend on impact, a very large meteor traveling at 11,200 miles per hour (Martian escape velocity) could conceivably pierce the plastic dome – despite its thickness, strength, and elasticity. The Martian town is being built near the equator – the warmest region of Mars. On the Martian equator, temperatures range from minus one hundred degrees below zero to a balmy seventy degrees. Depending on their planetary paths around the sun, Mars is roughly 140 million miles from the Earth. And it takes radio signals from Mars between 12 and15 minutes to reach the Earth.

Thus, the workers were insulated space suits with portable oxygen masks in case of a catastrophic puncture in the dome. Eventually, nuclear generators would provide electric power for heat, cooling, and oxygen ventilation. Thus, a life-friendly environment will ultimately be maintained on the red planet. Big vacuum cleaners were sucking up the iron oxide dust covering the Martian surface – leaving a gravel-like surface. Over time, dirt, clay, bacteria, and fungus from Earth will be added to the Martian soil, along with water, to make it sufficiently fertile to grow a wide range of vegetables, plus apple, peach, and pear trees. Also, a wide range of deciduous and evergreen trees would be planted in the domed region to supply oxygen and create an earthlike environment. Nancy and Charlie, proud parents of Chuck Perez-Krepinski, observe him on a monitor million miles away. Chuck, in his space suit, is oblivious of their oohs and aahs. Space travel had been an obsession of the smart young man from his elementary school days through college. As with all Chuck's endeavors, his diligence and focus were evident as he works on the concrete building – one of the first being erected on the Red Planet.

From the get-go, Nancy and Charlie knew that Chuck was an exceptional kid. As a toddler he'd spend hours constructing towers and bridges out of blocks, playing cards, tin cans, and shoe boxes. He had Nancy's light-brown skin and straight black hair, and Charlie's above-average height, and physical strength. A natural athlete, he excelled at baseball, basketball, and stickball. Like both his parents, Chuck was brave and cool under fire. And, he was a gifted student with an insatiable curiosity about the world. In addition, he had one blue and one brown eye – inherited from his dad and mom respectively.

On a pleasant morning in late May, Nancy walks over to Lora's office above the bakery to find the next candidate for time travel. As usual, Lora was busy working on copper jewelry – a large circular pendant which had two stick figures throwing a ball against an outlined stoop.

"It's an awesome medallion. It looks like two kids playing stoop ball," Nancy commented.

"It represents Billy and his twin brother, Haney, throwing a Spalding against porch steps and catching the rebound. Rumor has it that Haney was struck by a car playing stoop ball with Billy."

"Yeah. Hal told me about it years ago. But Billy never talks about it," Nancy replied.

"I ran into Blanche the other day. She said Billy has been having nightmares. Yells Haney – watch out! Maybe that's why he talks to his invisible sidekick," Lora responded.

"So, what do you want to do about it.?"

"Blanche said that she'd try to get Billy to ride on the merry-go-round for a trip back in time According to Blanche, an old woman who had seen the accident, recently told her about it. The woman said Billy actually lifted the car off his brother. Maybe Blanche could use the pendant as a reward if he agrees to do it. And as with the others, Billy has to hold the horseshoe magnet when the merry-go-round starts to rotate.

CHAPTER 34

BILLY TAKES A TIME TRIP

NANCY DOUBTED THAT BLANCHE WOULD GET THE ECCENTRIC MAN, WHO was nearly Freddy's age, to go for a ride back in time. But the attractive redhead, used her ample charms to talk Billy into going for a ride on the merry-go-round. And a few days later, Billy Bumps mounted the merry-go-round and Freddy started the gasoline engine. The whirligig moved slowly at first and then faster, and the lights began to glow weakly and then brighter. Billy held onto the magnet — seeming to enjoy the ride. But when the high-pitched moaning sound, similar to a baby animal crying, Billy looked around nervously.

"Keep going Billy. It's O K. Hang in their Billy!" Blanche called out from the sideline – a few feet from the whirling merry-go-round.

Billly nodded his head and studied the white wall – upon which images began to form. On the screen his twin brother, Haney, appeared – looking as he did before he was struck by the car.

"Wow, Haney! You haven't aged a minute," Billy exclaimed.

"That what happens when you die. Your spirit represents the best version of yourself."

"I guess people shouldn't be so scared of dying," Billy replied.

"Well, I wouldn't go that far. Depends on the kind of person you were in life."

"I'm not a bad egg, Haney. I lifted that car off your chest," Billy said, starting to cry.

"You did your best, Billy. And you're a good egg, though sometimes you're a tightwad.":

"Yeah. Blanche says the same thing. I wish that car hadn't come along and hit you."

"It's fate. We can move back and forth in time, but only God can change fate," Haney commented.

"I guess that would be called a miracle."

"Yup. And miracles don't happen too often But, talking to you right now is a miracle."

"Do you get pissed when I talk to you?" Billy asked.

"Not at all. I'm with you all the time."

"People think I'm weird because I talk to you."

"Don't matter what other people think. Keep talking to me. But I feel myself fading. Good bye and hang in there, brother."

Then, the white wall went dark, the merry-go-round stopped rotating by itself, Billy stepped off the whirligig, and gave Blanche a big hug.

"I have something that Lora made for you," the red-haired woman said – handing Billy the pendant depicting Billy and his brother playing stoop ball in the street.

Freddy, who had watched the proceedings with Nancy from her front porch, crossed the street, turned off the gasoline engine that powered the merry-go-round and ran its lights. Billy and Blanche walked over to Nancy. Ask your friend Lora if I can take a whirl on the merry-go-round.

The next day, Nancy walked to Mislicki's Bakery on Morningstar Road and mounted the stairs to Lora's workshop.

"I know what you're gonna ask before you say her name," Lora said – taking her crystal ball from the shelf of her workshop.

"It's Billy's girlfriend or as Hal use to say – paramour."

Dusting the large crystal ball with her silk cloth and setting it her bench, Lora peered into it. "I see Blanche Boulette in her younger days. She's a go-go girl at a notorious South Shore bar called the Pigsty during the late 1960s. Wears a skimpy costume – red blouse, short tight skirt, and a black eye mask."

"I'll get her – I'm sure she's game for a trip into her illustrious past," Nancy replied – leaving the workshop.

The next day, Blanche, looking years younger than her mid-sixties, showed up at Lora's workshop – dressed conservatively in a nice mauve blouse and a blue skirt. Lora greeted the woman, who was an Elm Park legend with a hug.

"I'm ready to take a trip to memory lane," Blanche said – sitting down next to Lora.

Lora set the crystal ball on her workbench and wiped it with the silk cloth. Immediately, the large crystal ball began glowing – showing images of Blanche Boulette at various points in her life, plus images of her forbears.

"Show up at the merry-go-round tomorrow morning around seven A M. It's gonna be a long session."

"I know. I've lived a longtime," the striking redhead replied.

"It's not that. The crystal ball has images of your forbears in France – going back a couple of hundred years."

"I get up early and make a big breakfast for Billy and myself."

"Is Billy a big eater?"

"He's a skinny guy, but he can pack it away. He says he eats for two – himself and his invisible sidekick."

CHAPTER 35

BLANCHE TAKES A TIME TRIP

Bright and early, Blanche took her place on the merry-go-round and stood before the white wall with a nervous smile. The attractive red-haired woman was wearing a blue dress with yellow polka dots – appropriate for a balmy mid-May morning. Freddy started the merry-go-round on a slow rotation. As soon as Blanche grabbed the horseshoe magnet, the high-pitched animal sound emanated from the whirligig.

Immediately, the white wall showed Blanche dancing on a raised platform in a red blouse, a short black skirt, with fishnet stockings, and red high heels. The smoke-filled Pigpen was packed with people dancing to the blaring music, drinking beer, wine, and whisky. People talking without listening, Some, looking for a new heartthrob. Others, just looking for a good time. A few desirous of drinking themselves into a stupor. Plus, a wolf or two on the make—looking for a pickup and a none-nightstand. Then, there were those who checked their watches – mindful of the weekday drudgery facing them in the factories of Staten Island and the offices of lower Manhattan.

Blanche did her go-go routine with Maxine – half-hour on and half-hour off from nine until closing at one A M weekdays and two A M weekends. It amounted to a 30-hour work week for which Blanche was paid $250 – enough to pay her rent and buy groceries. She also gave her mom, who cleaned houses, extra money for her younger brother, Robbie, who was going to New Dorp School – when he wasn't a truant. Like her hard-working mom, Blanche was a stoic – happy despite "the slings and arrows of outrageous fortune."

On a slow weekday night, Blanche was sipping ginger ale and smoking a cigarette at the bar between her go-go stint. A well-dressed, nice-looking man, named Bart, sat down next to her and introduced himself. He offered to buy her a drink, but Blanche said she didn't drink while working. Bart talked about his job on Wall Street where stocks—particularly for companies supplying weapons for the military – continued to surge. As President Johnson sent more and more troops to Vietnam, that war jeopardized LBJ's War on Poverty and antagonized young people unwilling to fight in a third-world country. Johnson's big blunder was his failure to understand that young people were unmotivated by Cold War propaganda. They were interested in tunning out turning on, and making love,

However, Bart was part of the so called "Silent Majority" who supported the Vietnam War. He was making an outrageous six-figured salary on Wall Street. Thus, he was a hawk whose wealthy family pulled strings to get him into the Army reserves – an escape from combat almost as good as being a conscientious objector.

"If we don't fight those Commies in Vietnam, we'll be fighting them on on Hylan Boulevard," he remarked with a grimace

"So, what's your name?"

"Blanche Boulette."

"A Frenchie, hah?" he replied – putting his hand on her thigh and squeezing it.

"Please, don't do that."

Bart shrugged his shoulders and took a sip of his whiskey.

"TAs long as we don't have to fight them on Morningstar Road – my neck of the wood."

"I don't like the North Shore too many –"

"Don't ay it, Bart. It's not funny," Blanche replied.

In response, Bart reached over again –putting his hand on her thigh, ands squeezed.

Becoming uncomfortable, Blanche said quietly, "Don't do that, Bart," she said a bit louder than before.

"When do you get off?"

"It's a slow night. Probably around one," she replied.

Her gut told Blanche that Bart was bad news. Bit he looked so good in his fancy suit and his Old Spice aftershave lotion smelled so damned good. What the hell. That's what go-go dancers do. They're not choir singers after all – they live on a knife edge and sometimes take dumb chances.

Her three-room apartment was really two and half rooms – a tiny kitchen, a dinette not much bigger, and a small bedroom. It was sweltering in the summer and chilly in the winter. She had spruced it up by painting the kitchen yellow, the dining area eggshell white, and the bedroom pale blue. Blanche had prints of Versailles, the palace of the king and queen of France, and the Chateau de Brissac, a baroque castle on a rolling plain, in her dining room. She also had a print of the Chateau de Fayrac on the Dordogne River in her bedroom. Even after five hours of go-go dancing alternated with bar talk, she usually could not fall asleep until three A M. After waking up midmorning, Blanche often walked to South Beach, which was just a few blocks from her apartment. The salty sea breeze, the rhythmic pounding of the waves, and the plaintive cries of the sea gulls relaxed the pretty red-haired woman. With the demands of the hectic workaday world, mother nature was serene, comforting, and timeless.

It was a slow night and the owner of the Pigpen told Blanche to go home at twelve-thirty. She went over to Bart and smiled. "I'm done for the night."

Paying his tab and leaving nice tip, Bart followed Blanche to the parking lot. "I live near South Beach – 369 Sand Lane. Just follow my car – a red Chevy Corvair."

"Red hah? O K, Frenchie."

"The paint's chipping. It's in need of a paint job," she called out – getting into the car, which despite its scratches and dents, ran well.

Blanche hated the nickname Frenchie, which had been hurled at her in her schoolgirl days. But she said nothing. Arriving at her apartment, Bart went from room to room like room to room like a prospective apartment hunter.

"You're really into French culture. Do you speak French?"

"I took two years of French in high school. I did OK, but I had to help out my family. So, got an after-school job switched to a general diploma."

"That's why you're a go-go dancer?"

"Now that's not nice," she replied – ready to toss him out.

"Let me make it up to you," he responded – kissing and hugging her with a fervor that caught her off balance.

She went along with his advances – realizing she shouldn't have invited him to her place – his fancy suit didn't look so good in bright light and the Old Spice – alcohol mix wasn't so appealing. Bart's lovemaking was frenetic and rough – something to be endured without fanfare. Fortunately, Bart was soon asleep, while Blanche tossed and turned for hours before falling asleep. When she woke up around nine o'clock, Bart was gone. On her dresser was $60 in cash. Though she worked another six months at the Pigsty, the unhappy episode motivated Blanche to go back to school. She took typing, steno, and bookkeeping and then got a secretarial job in lower Manhattan. Her go-go dancing days were just a bitter-sweet memory. The images on the wall began to fade, the merry-go round slowed to a stop and Blanche stepped off. Lora and Nancy were there to greet the mature, but good-looking woman, whose reputation as a femme fatale was more myth than legend.

"How was it?" Nancy asked.

"Actually, it was great to relive my past. When you're my age, you've had a lot of memories. And most of them were good."

"Tomorrow, the time machine will explore your French ancestors," Lora explained.

That's cool. My grandmother said our family goes back to the French Revolution."

"See you tomorrow at eight A M," Nancy called out as Blanche walked up Pulaski Avenue—heading for Walker Street, where Billy awaited her.

"How was it?" Billy asked.

Turning to his unseen sidekick, Billy said, "She looks like she just ran a marathon."

"Like most things, it was good and bad," she replied – kissing Billy and holding his hand as they walked up Walker Street.

"Tomorrow, I'm going to go way back to the French Revolution."

"Maybe she's a cousin of the French queen and there's money coming to her," Billy whispered to his silent companion.

"Yeah, sure. And you're a long-lost Rockefeller cousin who has a million dollars in a secret bank account.

"She's kidding us. Ain't she?" Billy said – turning to his ever-present sidekick.

Around eight o'clock the next morning, Blanche walked down Pulaski Avenue. Freddy had the merry-go-round rotating slowly. He had moved the white wall a bit closer to the ride and dusted off the horseshoe magnet – placing near the its perimeter. Wearing a short white dress decorated with red roses, Blanche stepped onto the merry-go-round and grabbed the horseshoe magnet. Immediately, a soft moaning sound like that of a child crying issued from the merry-go-round and the lights fluttered on and off. After a several rotations, the whirligig came to a stop, the moaning sound ceased, and the lights faded. Images and sound began to emanate from the white wall. Freddy crossed the street and sat next to Lora and Nancy on the latter's front porch.

The pages of an old calendar flipped backwards in rapid succession – stopping at July 14, 1789, There was an image of an angry mob of French peasants storming the Bastille, a prison housing the political opponents of the Bourbon monarchy. This was the start of the long and bloody French Revolution, which ended the Bourbon monarchy and made France a republic. Many members of the French nobility were beheaded after show trials, their heads placed on a pike, and marched through the streets in a grim display of gruesome revolutionary justice.

Blanche's distant ancestor, Eloise, was a pretty red-haired peasant girl, who could have passed for a cousin of Blanche. Like Blanche, she was hard-working, steadfast, and savvy. She was Marie Antoinette's favorite servant because of these traits, plus her honesty, the French queen asked Eloise about the world outside the Tuileries Palace.

"Madame la Reine, may I be honest?"

"Of course, my dear Eloise."

"There is trouble brewing. The peasants need bread. Please, do not tell them to eat cake."

"I never said those word. Princess de Lamballe put those words in my mouth. She is a malicious gossip."

"Perhaps you can speak to your husband, the King. He has the authority to request brad to be shipped to Paris from the countryside."

"There was a very poor harvest this summer."

"Maybe, have the King request bread be sent to France from our allies in Holland, Austria, and Sweden?"

"I will ask my husband, but he is a fool," Marie Antoinette said bluntly.

Eloise was stunned, but said nothing.

"Let me rephrase what I just said. My husband has a lot on his plate and he seldom thinks about what's on the plates of the peasants," the queen said – trying to keep a straight face.

"Greed is one of the seven deadly sins."

"Greed, gluttony, lust, sloth, wrath, envy, and pride – Louis the Sixteenth has them all."

"But, Madame la Reine, I've heard talk on the streets. Trouble is brewing. I beseech you to speak with the King," Eloise said – going on her knees.

"I'm ready to meet my fate. I have no fear of the guillotine."

"There's talk that Madame Defarge wants to see you mount the steps to the guillotine," Eloise replied in a near whisper.

"Of that I'm sure. I'll wink at her as I climb the steps. Only a monster can watch something so barbaric while knitting a sweater," Marie Antoinette replied.

The next day, the Bastille was stormed and all prisoners inside were set free. Realizing the end was in sight, Marie Antoinette told Eloise to pack her clothes, leave the palace, and return to her family on the outskirts of Paris.

"Here's a purse of gold coins. You're a smart girl. Take up sewing to support yourself and your family."

Eloise gave Marie Antoinette a hug. She noticed that in the past few weeks, the queen's blonde hair had become white and her pretty face was marked with wrinkles. When that awful day came, the queen was calm and matter-of-fact. Eloise couldn't bear to see Marie Antoinette beheaded. That night Eloise prayed that the French queen would be saved at the last minute by Robespierre, the architect of the Reign of Terror. But Madame Defarge opposed granting her amnesty – citing the hardships her family suffered at the hands of "Madame Deficit" and the royal family.

On a mild October morning, Marie Antoinette calmly mounted the steeps to the guillotine platform – often called the "French Razor." Walking towards the wood-framed guillotine, the queen inadvertently stepped on the executioner's foot.

"Pardon me sir. I didn't mean to."

After the awful deed was done, the executioner held up the queen's head to the crowd.

"Viva la Republique," he exclaimed.

Marie Antoinette's head and torso wee tossed on a wagon and transported to Madeleine Cemetery, where others who had been guillotined were taken. Eloise followed it at a safe distance and watched gravediggers bury her remains without ceremony. She waited quietly, hidden by the tombstones and trees, until everyone had left. Then, she placed wildflowers she had picked at the gravesite and recited a prayer. The tombstone was unmarked except the name "Marie Antoinette" crudely etched on it. Each day for six months, Eloise returned with flowers. Then, a scruffy gravedigger approached Eloise – warning her to cease visiting the grave.

"If the Jacobins discover you visiting the grave, you will join the queen in the ground. And you're far too pretty to have your head removed from your body. Now go and do not return."

Eloise reluctantly complied – keeping her distance from Madeleine Cemetery. But, she always returned each October 16th – the anniversary of Marie Antoinette's untimely death.

Ironically, the blood-letting of Robespierre and the Jacobins provoked a reaction by another group of French revolutionaries, the Thermidors, who brought charges against Robespierre and his henchmen. Soon, the bloodthirsty leader found himself kneeling under the guillotine – waiting for the blade to fall on his neck. And one day, Madame Defarge, the gruesome sweater knitter, was found in her apartment with her chubby neck slit from ear to ear. The Paris gendarmes conducted a cursory investigation and then stopped – realizing the notorious yarn knitter had as many enemies as Robespierre himself. With regard to the latter, there's a Metro station in Paris named for Robespierre and a few like-named roads in France, but his place in history is not one of high regard.

With Blanche's journey into her own past and her family's history, the merry-go-round had time traveled into just about everyone's past. Nancy and Freddy were thinking of removing the white wooden board and giving away the horseshoe magnet to one of the neighborhood kids. Then, a day or so later, Mildred and the Reverend walked over to the front stoop, where Nancy, Freddy, and Charley sat – sipping coffee. Mildred Aimsley came over to them.

"Well if it isn't Mildred – the Prim Woman."

"Freddy, would that you refrain from using that appellation."

"Yeah Freddy. Knock it off," Nancy said quietly.

"Sorry, Mildred. Old habits are hard to break," Freddy replied with a wry smile

"Apology accepted. I have a request. The Reverend would like to stand on the merry-go-round and journey into his past."

"Sure. No better time than the present," Nancy responded.

"Actually, tomorrow's a good time. Folks around here want us to knock down the wooden wall and give the magnet to one of the kids," Charlie added.

"O K, we'll fetch the Rev for a shot at the time machine," Nancy reiterated

"Last time I heard fetch was in – Jack and Jill went up the hill to fetch a pail of water," Freddy recited – smiling at Nancy.

Nancy punched the octogenarian in the shoulder.

"Ow! I never should have taught you to box," Freddy said – rubbing his shoulder in mock pain.

CHAPTER 36

THE REV TAKES A TIME TRIP

EARLY THE NEXT MORNING, REV STAN STALLER HELD THE HORSESHOE magnet as the merry-go-round rotated slowly. After three rotations, Freddy stopped the whirligig so the Reverend faced the white wall. The wall came to life with vivid images of Stanley Staller as a young man – walking the streets of Jersey City with a big suitcase. Stan was a born salesman – bragging he could sell a New Yorker the Brooklyn Bridge. Yet, he lived in flophouse in gritty neighborhood of Jersey City. Despite his selling ability, Stan had a drinking problem. He had been a high-functioning alcoholic since his early twenties. Because he never drank before early evening, Stan told himself he was not an alcoholic. Most of the time he believed it.

Stan Staller stopped at a five- story apartment house and climbed the steps – entering the hallway. He rang the bell and a woman opened the door. Immediately, Stan launched his sales pitch. "Mame, I'm here to sell you a college education at a fraction of the cost."

A woman in a house dress, accompanied by a little girl, was mildly interested in Stan's sales pitch. Pointing to the child, "Sally is in the first grade. She's just learning to read."

"It's the perfect time to have The Globe Book in your house. You can read it to her every day. It has lots of pictures—all in color. There are twenty-four volumes – encompassing more than eight thousand articles. You buy one volume a month for twelve dollars each over a period of two years. Plus, you free supplements every year for ten years."

"Sir, I can't afford it. We're just about making ends meet."

"Call me Stan. I can give you a discount – eight bucks a volume. When you buy Globe Book, you're actually buying a college education for Sally at a fraction of the cost."

"A college education? I never thought of it that way. My name is also Sally – Sally Smathers."

"I tell you what. I'll give you the first volume free – no obligations. And I'll come back in a month."

"Alright, my husband and I will look it over and decide."

"Here's my card if you want to contact me prior. Remember, you're giving your kid an education right at home."

Moving on, Stan Staller knocked on some more doors in the apartment with less success. All of them cut his sales pitch short and refused to take the first volume. Stan decided to try a street with two-family houses. Again, they refused to listen to his sale pitch – quickly sending on his way. At the end of the block, there was a deli where Stan bought a cup of plastic cup of coffee and a jelly donut. The store owner, an immigrant from Ethiopia, was mulling over whether to buy the encyclopedia from Stan – for his kids.

Stan noticed a stack of bibles behind the counter. "Were you in the book-selling business also?"

"Yes. I sold the Bible and read it from cover to cover. Have you read it?"

"To be honest with you no."

The store owner, whose name was Sal, gave him a Bible. "Read the good book. It's the greatest story ever told."

"I read all twenty-four volumes of The Globe Book. The Bible shouldn't be too hard to tackle," Stan replied –taking the book and flipping through its pages.

That night Stan picked up the Bible and began reading – starting with Genesis. He read for about an hour and then he went into the kitchen and grabbed the whiskey bottle stored in a cabinet. Hearing the rumble of thunder, Stan went to the kitchen window with the bottle and looked out the open window. Suddenly a flash of lightening illuminated his apartment and a lightning bolt shot through the window – exploding the bottle with its contents. After being unconscious for an indeterminate length of time, Stan picked himself off the floor. Glass shards from the bottle and whiskey were strewn on the kitchen floor and his right hand had been singed. This was an intervention from the almighty. God had spoken: "No more drinking." From that point on, despite a thirst for alcohol that never subsided and many temptations over the years – Stan Staller never took another drop.

Stan continued to sell The Globe Book door to door, but he added the Bible to his inventory. On weekends, instead of hanging out in neighborhood bars, he began preaching in parks, squares, and sidewalks of Jersey City. Then, Stan had a vivid dream of himself preaching on a soapbox in Times Square – "the crossroad of the world." The so-called Big Apple – New York City – was where he really wanted to preach the gospel. He worked hard selling The Globe Book and saved his pennies for six months. Finally, he had enough money to move and rent a dingy one-room apartment on the West Side – within walking distance of Times Square. Stan still spent most of the day hawking his Globe Book encyclopedias, but after sun down, he returned to his tiny apartment.

Putting away his Globe Book suitcase, Stan took out his Bible and sturdy soapbox and headed for Times Square. He preached to New Yorkers of every stripe – rich and poor, black and white, believers and nonbelievers, liberal and conservative, curious and indifferent – for more than a decade. One day, a group of teenagers started to hassle Stan. "You're no preacher. You're dressed like a bum." One of them pushed Stan off his wooden soapbox and another grabbed it and started to run away. Until a husky black man ripped the soapbox from him and sent the kid flying off in the opposite direction.

Though he was outnumbered four to one – the man shouted "You want a piece of me? Come on!" As Stan watched the teenagers hurry away – the expression dogs fleeing with tails between their legs – came to mind.

"Thank you for coming to my aid. Indeed, you are the Good Samaritan," Stan said to the black man, who introduced himself as Sam Worthington.

"This is not a good place for a preacher," Sam replied.

"As Jesus said, a Prophet is without honor in his own country."

"There's a new mayor who wants hawkers and preachers out of Times Square. I'm from Elm Park, Staten Island. It might be a safer place for a soapbox preacher," Sam related.

"You mean Major Kootch – Mister How Am I doing?"

"Absolutely! That's the bloke. He promised to cleanup Times Square get rid of prostitutes, peepshows, pickpockets, petty criminals, and soapbox preachers."

Stan thanked Sam again and gathered his stuff. He decided to heed the Good Samaritan's advice and head for Staten Island. Believing that there were no coincidences in life, Stan felt he was destined to preach in a place he had never set foot upon. He went back to his dingy apartment, packed his clothes, his Globe Books, his Bible, and his soapbox. Some of the people who listened to his soapbox sermons were from Staten Island. They also said it was a good place to live. Stan was tired of living in cockroach infested flophouses. So, he took a downtown bus for South Ferry and spent five cents on a ferry ride across New York Bay.

It was first ferry boat ride and he wondered why he had not availed himself of this inexpensive pleasure sooner. As the ferry approached Staten Island,

Stan felt the need to go to the toilet – leaving his suitcase just outside the stall. In the few minutes he answered nature's call, his suitcase packed with clothes and the unsold Globe Books was stolen. All he had left was the clothes he wore, his Bible, and his soapbox. Not one to cry over spilt milk, Stan got directions and began a five-mile trek on Richmond Terrace – heading for Elm Park. He was told to walk towards the Bayonne Bridge –visible from St. George and upon reaching Morningstar Road, Elm Park would be beyond the crest of the gently sloping hill. Walking in a southward direction, he noticed the abandoned tracks of the defunct Staten Island railroad. It had begun to rain, so the soapbox preacher took refuge under the Morningstar Road underpass. The peanut butter and jelly sandwich, along with a can of apple juice, made a satisfactory repast. Despite the theft of his suitcase, Stan was content. He said a brief prayer—falling asleep to the rhythmical rat-tat-tat of the raindrops pelting the rusty rails next to him.

Early the next morning, Stan Staller walked along Pulaski Avenue and sat down on the corner of Hooker Place – near the apartment building where Freddy and Hank resided. Closing his eyes briefly, the soapbox preacher was astonished to see Sam walking towards him – carrying his suitcase and his canvas bag of Globe Books.

"I took off the sleezy crook who stole it from you. As soon as I opened it up, I knew it was yours," the husky black man said.

"This is a sign from God. How did you know I'd be here?" Stan asked – getting up and shaking Sam's hand.

"I figured that you would take my advice and settle in Elm Park," Sam replied with a shrug.

"Sam, you're more than a good Samaritan. You're an angel sent by God!"

"The opposite has sometimes been said about me. So, I'll take it as a complement" Sam replied with a smile that lit up his face.

"Jesus's message is not only one of love, but also one of redemption."

Sam Worthington had been a fixture in Elm Park for many years, though he had gone through some tough times. As a teenager, Sam got mixed up in drugs and was sent to live with his grandmother in the South. Returning to the Island ten years later, Sam worked in Wolstein's factory when they made Bosco, Yoo-Hoo, and Mars Bars. When Wolstein's shuttered, Sam worked in construction, as a Bradford guard in various locations on Staten Island – including the Con Ed power plant in Travis. Hal had worked there while attending C C N Y. Sam had never crossed paths with Hal because there was a four-year difference in age and the latter had been killed by the time Sam returned to the Island.

"Check the houses along Pulaski and the flats too, You're bound to find something. – of that I'm sure."

"Thank you again," Stan replied. He carried the suitcase in one hand and his soapbox and Bible in the other.

Fortunately, Mildred Aimsley happened to be sitting on her front porch. Noticing the Globe Book salesman struggling with the burden of his suitcase, the canvas bag of encyclopedias, and his wooden soapbox, she called out to him.

"Sir, it concerns me to see you struggle under such a great burden. Kindly sit on my front steps while I fetch you a glass of lemon aide."

"Fetch, convey, conduct, bring, deliver, or transport– whatever verb you use to place a cold refreshing libation before me will be greatly appreciated ma'am. My name is Reverend Stanley Staller," he replied with a sweeping bow.

"I am Mildred Aimsley, former bookkeeper of Northshore Bank."

"It sounds like a very demanding job, Miss Aimsley," the Rev replied.

"It was quite demanding. But when the pandemic hit, it went out of business – like most banks."

"Boom or bust – that seems to be the pattern for banks and businesses in this money-driven world of ours," Stan said – bowing again. A habit that appealed to the

Within a few minutes, Mildred returned with a big glass of lemon aide and some oatmeal cookies on a tray. Stan started quaff the lemon aide in one big gulp, but stopped out of politeness. Though famished, he had just two cookies – stopping and offering the remainder to his hostess.

"Would that I partake in them, but if I regulate my caloric intake with great care. Once, I ingest a single cookie, my resistance to such snacks disappears and I will consume every last one on the platter," the prim woman remarked.

"Miss Aimsley . . ."

"Call me Mildred," she responded – blushing a bit.

"And kindly address me as Stan. But may I be so bold as to ask if you have a spare room to rent?"

"Indeed I do, Reverend Stan."

"To quote Bejamin Franklin – Beware of little expenses. A small leak will sink a great ship. Pray tell me, what is the cost?"

Pausing for a several second, Mildred said, "Forty per month for the room, plus an additional sixty dollars for food – three meals per day.

The reverend paused a moment. "So, it's one hundred dollars for bed and board – Miss Aimsley?"

The latter term made the prim woman blush.

"Very fair. In fact, it's a bargain. I'll take it."

"Would, that I prepare a lease for you?"

"Such formalities are not necessary. I am a man of my word."

"Kindly sit on the porch and enjoy the sun. I'll have the room ready in a jiffy," the prim woman went upstairs to her apartment to clean up the spare room.

An unused bedroom, the small room had served as a storage place for out-of-season clothes, books, records, photo albums, report cards, college transcripts, plus seashells and rocks like fool's gold and quartz collected on past trips to the seashore and the mountains. Mopping the floor and dusting the end tables and a tiny closet, Mildred dusted the blinds and hung clean yellow curtains on the window. She made the narrow single bed – covering it with clean sheets, a blanket and quilt. Then, Mildred placed a vase with wild flowers on one end table, and a dish of hard candy and a hand bell on the other. There was also a carboard box of softcover books in one corner of the room.

Running downstairs to the front porch, the prim woman guided the weary soapbox preacher to his room – even carrying the canvas bag of Globe Books upstairs – despite Stan's protests. Upon reaching the small, but neat room, Stan was ecstatic: "Without a doubt, this is the nicest room I've ever had!"

Studying Stan's weather-beaten face, she realized the soapbox preacher was telling the truth. "If you need anything, would that you ring the bell. I'll bring you a simple repast shortly."

Within twenty minutes, Mildred brought Stan a peanut butter and jelly sandwich, a cup of hot tea, and some more oatmeal cookies. "Good night, Reverend Stan."

"Stan is preferable. And thank you for your kindness. I noticed the books – quite a collection."

"Yes, I've read them over the years. Help yourself."

"Quoting Mister Franklin again – Reading makes a full man, meditation a profound man, and discourse a clear man."

"My goodness, Reverend Stan. You're an expert on Benjamin Franklin."

The next few days passed pleasantly, as Stan and Mildred spent time on her front stoop – watching the doings on Pulaski Avenue. There was more foot traffic than little street traffic. The kids of Elm Park did what kids have done for ages: jump rope, tag, hide and seek, stoopball, stickball, and games of catch. A basket was attached to a telephone pole near the apartment house became the source of noisy games of twenty-one and HORSE. Nancy and Freddy invited them to join in, but only Mildred responded. Eventually, the Rev was coaxed to join in the street games. Surprisingly, he enjoyed himself and wasn't bad at basketball, though his nearsightedness hampered his ability to hit the bouncing Spalding.

Nancy ran inside and returned with an old cigar box of eyeglasses. After much trial and error, a suitable pair of glasses was found. Upon putting them on, Reverend Staller exclaimed, "Lord of Mercy! The world has never looked so beautiful."

"I wondered why you were always squinting and scrunching your eyebrows, Rev," Nancy remarked.

"I figured you didn't like what you were looking at," Freddy said – smiling and rubbing his hands.

The Reverend tried to earn his keep by going door to door selling the remainder of his supply of Globe Books. Unfortunately, he had few offers. Becoming desperate, he offered the encyclopedias at a discount – with a bit more success. Then, Nancy learned that Dr. Emil had retired – leaving the Island for parts south. Alfred, well-trained by the physician, continued his family practice, but he needed an assistant. When no one stepped up, Reverend Staller offered his services and the youngster gladly accepted the ex-soapbox preacher. A quick study, the Rev was adept at giving injections, stitching up wounds, setting broken bones, and even diagnosing garden variety illnesses. Of course, Sundays, were reserved for the Rev's soapbox sermons and as word got around, he attracted a sizeable following from the entire North Shore.

A few weeks later, on a sunny Saturday morning, Mildred and Stan were sitting on her front porch watching the world walk by, when two young men came along – holding hands. Stan shook his head in disgust, but Mildred bid them good morning with a warm smile.

"Miss Aimsley, you see nothing amiss about those two men?"

"Love between any two persons is a blessing and wonder to behold," she replied – scrutinizing the ex-soapbox preacher

"Have you not read the story of Sodom and Gomorrah from the Bible? God destroyed those two cities with sulfur and fire because of their wickedness."

"Much of the Bible is allegory. It's not literally true. After all, the Earth was not made in seven days. It's over four billion years old."

"I never thought I'd wind up with a Christian modernist," Stan said – shaking his head.

"Modernism versus traditionalism, literal versus figurative. I'm not a biblical scholar. Would that we not argue about such abstruse matters," the prim woman responded.

"Agreed. We might as well argue about the number of atoms on the head of a pin."

"So, how are things going at with Alfred's practice in his cottage?"

"Not bad. He's a good teacher. That reminds me, I promised Alfred I'd peruse his textbook on diseases," Stan said.

He entered the house and returned with the book in question.

"I' tell you what. After you finish a chapter, I'll quiz you on it," Mildred suggested.

"Good idea. Two heads are better than one."

"Just as two interpretations of the Bible are better than one," she replied with a quick smile.

"Miss Aimsley, you should have been a lawyer."

"And with awareness of the sin of sodomy, we'll have to limit the ways we express affection for each other," Mildred added in a quiet voice.

"Apparently, the appellation prim woman is evidently a misnomer," the ex-soapbox preacher replied – trying not to smile.

Overall, Mildred influenced Stan in subtle ways – humanizing him and softening his ministerial rigidity. He was born in humble circumstances that were aggravated by an alcoholic dad and a spare-the-rod-spoil-the-child mom. An older sister consoled Stan when his parents fought – upon the return of his dad from a long night of drinking. Stan found solace in a local Baptist church. The preacher took the boy under his wing –spending time with him and reading the Bible to him. The Bible providing answers to Stan's questions and pointed the way to an orderly realm away from the chaos of his difunctional family. When his older sister got married, Stan was left to fend for himself. Though a good reader, he was an indifferent student.

After graduating high school, Stan left his factory town outside of Philadelphia and headed for the Big Apple. He found a job in a book-binding company in lower Manhattan – working there for twenty-five years. When the company left the city for the South, Stan found another way to support himself – selling Globe Book encyclopedia door-to-door. Possessing a gift for gab, Stan was a persuasive salesman. He sold enough of the encyclopedia, to support his spartan lifestyle – living in a one-room apartment in a rundown tenement in midtown. More importantly, Stan found his raison d'etre – soapbox preacher at "the crossroad of the world" – Times Square. Clearly, Stan would have passed the remainder of his existence selling the Globe Book by day and preaching to the folks by night –until Mayor Kootch drove the prostitutes and peepshows, the hawkers and soapbox preachers out of Times Square.

CHAPTER 37

AN ORDINARY MERRY-GO-ROUND

NANCY COMPOSED A LIST OF ALL THE LOCALS WHO HAD STOOD ON THE merry-go-round time machine – reliving the happy and unhappy events of their lives – Alfred, Norton, Freddy, Billy Blanche, Mildred, Rev Staller, Charlie Krepinski, and Nancy herself. No one else from the neighborhood wanted to time travel. Like Bubba, there was a reluctance and even a fear of the of the whirligig. But there were also folks from the area who wanted to get a peek at the future. Looking into the past was one thing, but discerning what was ahead – disturbed her.

She consulted Rev Stan Staller about that issue. His response was simple: "You don't want to play God." Hence, Nancy decided to disassemble the time machine – to return the merry-go-round to just being an amusement park ride. But before doing so, the slender woman walked over to Lora for advice.

The pretty long-haired woman took her crystal ball down from the shelf, rubbed with a silk cloth, and peered into it. "No problem. Get rid of the white-painted wall and remove the magnets from its perimeter. Keep the big horseshoe magnet for your son Chuck, who will make his appearance next year."

"What are you talking about?"

Peering into her crystal ball, Lora declared in a matter-of-fact manner: "After a whirlwind romance, you and Charlie Krepinski will get married. Within a year, you'll be the proud mother of Chuck – a smart, adventurous boy with a strong interest in astronomy. He'll be trained as a pilot by Chester Worthington in his Cessna Skyhawk flying out of the mini airport in New Dorp. Chuck will grab the attention of NASA in their rocket-pilot program You've already seen that image of Chuck building the enclosed settlement on Mars under a big plastic meteor-proof dome. As a result of climate change, the federal government is planning to invest billions on space travel – with the ultimate goal of building a permanent settlement on Mars."

"Are you playing God?"

Looking around to make sure no one was listening. "Only for those I trust. You and my husband are the only two in that category."

With that, she started to place the crystal ball on the shelf. However, the ball slipped out of her grip, fell to the floor and broke into pieces. Lora stared at the scattered pieces and shrugged her shoulders.

"I guess your crystal-ball gazing days are over," Nancy said with the hint of a smile.

"Which is good thing. It was becoming a burden," the long-haired woman said.

"Where did you get it?"

"I found it in the woods behind the flats, It was near the stream that runs through that area. Half-buried and covered with leaves, in the middle of a clump of gingko trees. It might have been sitting there for a hundred years."

"Well, it served its purpose," Nancy replied – hugging Lora and leaving Lora's workshop.

The flowing day, Nancy with help from Charlie, Freddy, and Mildred removed the magnets from the merry-go-round. The white wooden board was broken up into boards by Freddy and used for firewood. At first, children were reluctant to go on the merry-go-round, but when Nancy, Freddy, and Mildred went on the whirligig – Bubba and Roy jumped on it with them. Soon, big kids jumped on it and eventually little kids joined in – riding happily. Best of all, the eerie high-pitched animal sound was no longer heard as the merry-go-round spun round and round. It was just an ordinary amusement ride.

THE END

ABOUT THE AUTHOR

The author grew up on Staten Island – attending CCNY, Johns Hopkins University, and NYU earning BS, MAT, and PhD degrees respectively. He taught physics and mathematics many years in the high school and junior college levels. As a teacher, he tried to make abstract principles concrete by connecting them to everyday life. Ideally, the student should come away with essential information and the ability to solve problems, think rationally, and act ethically. The author has written the following nonfiction books: Apples and Oranges, Mathematical Concepts , and A Brief Guide to Philosophy. His novels include: 1950s-1960s Fable, 1960s-1970s Fable, The Mariners Harbor Messiah, Blue Collar Folks, The Pulaski Prowler, Love in the Days of Covid-20, The Maiden Maverick, and The Elm Park Time Travelers.